N(

Queen of Oblivion

By Giles Carwyn and Todd Fahnestock

The Heartstone Trilogy

Heir of Autumn
Mistress of Winter
Queen of Oblivion

Queen of Oblivion

Giles Carwyn &
Todd Fahnestock

EOS

An Imprint of HarperCollinsPublishers

GILES'S DEDICATION

To my mother and father.
Because of you, I have never doubted for a single moment that I was loved.

TODD'S DEDICATION

For Amy and Tiana, who showed me what family should be.

HarperCollins books may be purchased for educational, business, or sales promotional use. For information please write: Special Markets Department, HarperCollins Publishers, 10 East 53rd Street, New York, NY 10022.

FIRST EDITION

Eos is a federally registered trademark of HarperCollins Publishers.

Designed by Ashley Halsey

Maps and drawings by Langdon Foss; langdonfoss.com

Library of Congress Cataloging-in-Publication Data has been applied for.

ISBN 978-0-06-082979-7

08 09 10 11 12 OV/RRD 10 9 8 7 6 5 4 3 2 1

Pronunciation Guide

Arefaine—ÄR-e-fān

Astor—AS-tôr

Baedellin—bā-DEL-in

Baelandra—bā-LÄN-drä

Brezelle—bruh-ZELL

Brophy—BRŌ-fē

Brydeon—BRĪ-dē-un

Celtigar—SEL-ti-gär

Darius—DÄ-rē-us

Dewland—DOO-lund

Efflum—EF-lum

Efften—EF-ten

Emmeria—e-ME-rē-uh

Faedellin—fā-DEL-in

Faradan—FE-ruh-dan

Fessa—FE-suh

Floani—flō-A-nē

Galliana—ga-lē-Ä-nuh

Heidvell—HĒD-vel

Issefyn—IS-e-fin

Jesheks—JE-sheks

Kherif—KER-if

Lawdon—LÄ-dun

Lewlem—LOO-lum

Lowani—lō-ä-nē

Mikal—mi-KÄL

Morgeon—MÔR-jē-un

Necani—ne-KÄ-nē

Ohndarien—on-DÄ-rē-en

Ohohhim—ō-HÄ-him

Ohohhom—ō-HÄ-hum

Ossamyr—OS-uh-mur

Physendria—fī-SEN-drē-uh

Reignholtz—RĪN-holts

Shara—SHÄ-ruh

Speevor—SPĒ-vōr

Vallia—VÄ-lē-uh

Victeris—vik-TER-is

Vinghelt—VING-helt

Vizar—vi-ZÄR

Zelani—ze-LÄ-nē

WHERE WE LEFT OFF . . .

Brophy and Arefaine are still on the Cinder. They were just attacked by a group of Lightning Swords trying to recover the Heartstone that Arefaine stole from Ohndarien. The Opal Emperor died in the attack, leaving Arefaine regent of the Opal Empire.

Following the instructions of her father, Darius Morgeon, Arefaine plans to combine the might of the Opal Empire and the Summer Fleet to destroy the Silver Islanders and return to Efften. But her ambitions to re-create her homeland are undermined by her growing feelings for Brophy and the dead emperor's schemes to force her down another path.

Shara departs for Ohndarien with Lawdon and Mikal. After her personal transformation at the hands of the Necani mage, Jesheks, she is determined to reunite with Brophy at all costs.

Jesheks disappeared following the burning of the Floating Palace. Lord Vinghelt has seized complete control of the Summer Fleet and prepares to attack Ohndarien.

After drinking the Siren's Blood, Ossamyr joined Reef and the Silver Islanders in their fanatical quest to prevent anyone from reaching the shores of Efften. She has just arrived in the Opal Empire determined to assassinate Arefaine before she unlocks the secrets of the cursed isle.

Hopelessly addicted to the black emmeria, Issefyn is locked in a constant power struggle with the manipulative voice within the vile magic. She just used the emmeria to corrupt Baelandra's daughter, Baedellin, and send her to annihilate Ohndarien's council.

PART I

Slaves of Wrath and Tears

Ohndarien

Fortress
of Light

Prologue

"Darius Morgeon!"

Darius winced at the sound of his mother's voice. The golden parrot he'd been trying to feed shrieked and flapped back to its owner. It settled onto the woman's shoulder and perched there, staring at him with unblinking eyes.

"Leave that creature alone," his mother said, snapping her fingers twice. She always did that when she was angry with him and didn't want anyone else to know.

With a sigh, Darius put the acorn back in his pocket. Mother was scared. He could tell by the way she kept her lips pressed together when no one was looking. She didn't want to be at this party. Neither did he.

Darius had never been in Efften's Great Tower before. The Illuminated had all gathered in the silver spire's great room. They were dressed in their shimmering sarongs with little silver chains wrapped around their arms. Mother had told him they were there for him, that this was his party. But there were no other kids there. No one talked to him. The adults wouldn't even look at him. All they did was stand around sipping wine and talking through their smiles.

Darius checked a sigh and looked up at his mother, hoping this wouldn't drag on for hours. She was listening to Aunt Rellana. Darius didn't like her. She was tall and thin, and reminded him of a wicked bug. She always looked half asleep, but she was a faker. She saw everything, and every time she looked at Darius, she made him feel like one of the black-eyed servants.

His stomach started to hurt, and he looked away. The round walls of the great room rose so tall above that they disappeared into darkness. The walls were filled with row after row of little alcoves, like a silver honeycomb. Every niche was filled with a dark crystal in a silver holder. The angry stones looked down at Darius and told him what a bad person he was.

He kicked the floor a few times with the toe of his sandal, knowing he should stand up straight the way his mother liked, but the stones were up there. Better to look at the ground.

I hate it here, he thought, glancing back at his mother. He didn't want to start his training. He didn't want to be a great sorcerer someday. Why couldn't he wait until he was nine or ten like all the others?

Darius took a long, slow breath, trying to calm himself the way his mother had taught him. His scalp prickled as he glanced toward the far side of the room. He'd felt something over there since the moment he'd entered the tower, glowing without light, calling to him without a voice. Moving closer, he peered through the crowd at a large black box resting on a raised platform in the center of the room. There were people all around, but no one stood too close to its tarnished silver lid. As he stared, he suddenly realized what it was. It was a coffin, The Coffin.

Swallowing hard, he started toward it. Adults frowned at him as he slipped past their silky sarongs, avoiding their eyes. Reaching out, he touched the lid. It vibrated under his fingers, and he jerked them back. The lid didn't fit right. He could see a little gap on the right side where it looked like someone had pried it open.

He pulled the acorn from his pocket and knelt. Careful not to touch the silver, he stuffed the acorn through the gap—

"Do you know what this is, child?" a man said behind him.

Darius jumped to his feet and stumbled. He reached out to steady himself, then recoiled from touching the coffin and almost fell over.

"Yes, Father," he said quickly, finally finding his feet. The man towered over him, his robes as black as the night between the stars. His narrow eyes made him look angry, though he spoke with that fake calm that adults sometimes used.

"Great Father," Father Efflum corrected, a little bit of his anger leaking into his voice.

Darius nodded, but he didn't say anything. A slight downward curve appeared at the corner of the archmage's mouth, but he forced his lips into a smile and said, "This box contains the dust and haze of my first teacher."

Darius nodded again.

"And now I'm going to be your first teacher."

Darius nodded. *Why can't my mother just teach me?* he thought.

Father Efflum rapped a knuckle smartly on the lid, and Darius winced. "He killed my wife, you know," Father Efflum said.

Darius looked sideways at the archmage's wife. She stood alone in the shadows near the spiral stairs, chewing on her lower lip while she stared into her drink. Her curly black hair flowed down the sides of her face. It was supposed to make her look beautiful, but it didn't. It made her look like she was peeking out from between curtains because she was too afraid to come outside.

Darius turned his gaze away. He knew that Father Efflum didn't mean that wife.

"She was dying in my arms," he continued. "Pierced by an arrow, and the man lying in there refused to help her. Refused to bless her with the sacred fire."

"Why?"

Father Efflum didn't seem to hear him. "We fought a war to bring this to our island." He rapped on the lid again. "And several more to keep it here. We placed it here in the center of our city to remind us of what happens to cowards and fools."

Darius nodded.

"You're not a coward or a fool," the archmage said, bending over and bringing his face closer. "Are you, Darius Morgeon?"

"No, Great Father."

Father Efflum leaned down even farther, and Darius could feel the man's breath. It was cool, as though he had been sucking on ice. "Then why were you stuffing something into the crack like a brainless little monkey?"

Darius stepped back and bumped into his mother.

"Answer his question, Darius," she said, squeezing his shoulder so hard it hurt.

"He told me to do it," he said, too loudly.

"What?" Father Efflum asked, turning his head as if to hear better.

Darius pointed. "He did. The man in the box."

The talking in the big room stopped. Everyone was either looking at him, or pretending not to look at him.

"Child," Father Efflum said in a voice as cool as his breath. He straightened to his full height. Meanness curled inside him like smoke. "The man in this tomb has been dead for a very long time."

"I know he's dead. Dead people can still talk."

Mother squeezed his shoulder again, tight.

"But dead people can still talk," Darius insisted. "Everyone knows that. Everyone."

She pulled him to her side. "My apologies, Great Father," she said quickly. "My son is obviously not ready to begin his studies. Perhaps next year."

Father Efflum raised one of his thin eyebrows. "Perhaps."

"We had better go," she said.

"I think you should."

She scooped Darius up in her arms and strode away from the coffin. Darius peered over her shoulder.

"Not another word," she whispered fiercely.

Darius felt tears coming to his eyes.

"I'm not afraid of you!" he shouted at Father Efflum. "I'm not!"

But his heart raced as he locked eyes with the Father of Efften, and Darius knew it was a lie.

Chapter 1

Baedellin crouched in the shadows, hiding from the moon. Bony knees pushed against her shoulders as she wrapped her arms around her mud-caked shins. Her breath came in ragged gasps, drying the inside of her mouth, cracking her tongue. She had to get away, get out of here. The dark queen was looking for her.

She crept forward, hiding behind the dried up ferns of a roof garden, watching the street below. Her filthy dress fluttered in the breeze and her heart pounded so hard her chest ached. Tears streamed down her face, burning her skin. She couldn't stop crying. After all this time, the tears kept coming. She was all alone in the empty city. They were all gone. Everyone gone. Or dead. Or running, like her.

She had to find Astor. No. Her brother had thrown her away. And her father had sent her to the queen. Baedellin was never going back there. Not to the filthy tower and foul darkness of that voice.

She would find her mother. Mother would wrap her up in her arms and it would all stop. It would all go away. Mother was strong, not lying on cold stone covered in flowers. Mother was happy and smiling, in a clean white dress. Waiting for her. Waiting in the north.

Baedellin reached the edge of the roof and paused, listening carefully to the streets below. She had to be careful, so careful, or she would never get away.

Someone had to find her. Help her. Before it was too late.

Shadows shifted, shortened and lengthened again as the moon traveled across the sky. Wind tried to lift her greasy hair as she stared at the empty streets, the darkened city, the boarded-up buildings.

Then she heard whispers in the distance. The clink of metal. It was them.

She swung her legs over the edge of the roof and dropped to the street below. Her bare feet slapped across cobblestones as she hurried into an abandoned café at the end of the block. She crept along one wall, hiding below a window filled with dead flowers.

She heard them turn the corner outside the window. Nine or ten of them. They had to help her. She had to get away.

"Go slow. Go careful. Listen for their breathing," someone said. "Check every cellar, every cupboard."

Baedellin peered outside, her grimy face hidden among the dying leaves that had shriveled long ago. Fear and joy rushed through her as she saw the golden slashes on the tunics of the Lightning Swords. Maybe her father was with them. He could take her home, back to Astor and the Sisters. They would bring her north to find her mother. Clean white dress. Smiling. Red hair shining in the sunlight. She tried to cry out, tried to scream, "I'm here. I'm here. Help me!" But nothing came from her mouth except the huffs of ragged breath.

The Lightning Swords split up and she heard footsteps approaching the café. She clung to the shadows, drifting behind the thick red curtains. Two of the Lightning Swords paused just outside the doorway, lifting lanterns high in the air. "Help me!" Baedellin shouted, but again she made no sound but the tortured breathing. She pressed her hand to her mouth to muffle the sound.

"I'll check the kitchen," the first one said, crossing the threshold. His sword glimmered in the torchlight.

"Look sharp," said the other, a woman with a gaunt face and ill-fitting armor.

Baedellin wanted to run to them, cling to their knees and beg for help. They had to help her, but she shrank farther into the shadows as they weaved through the overturned tables and disappeared into the kitchen. She followed them, perfectly quiet on bare feet, and peered around the doorway behind them.

"There's a soup pot in the fireplace," the man said. He crept to the far side of the room and peered into the pot. His head jerked away in disgust as a rancid smell hit him.

"By the Seasons!" he hissed. "Why do we even try?"

He moved to the cupboard and checked inside. "Nothing but rat droppings!"

"Look everywhere," the woman told him. "Check the oven." She strained to look into the shadows all around them.

Baedellin held deathly still in the darkness. She clutched the doorjamb, feeling her fingernails sink into the soft wood. "Help me!" she cried silently.

The man knelt before the oven built into the fireplace and looked inside. He started laughing. "Bread! Two loaves!" He held them up to show her. "They're a little burnt and very stale." The soldier tried to bite one and could barely break off a chunk. "But soften them up in a little water and—"

The dark queen's voice slid into Baedellin's mind. *Now, my child*, she whispered. *Now.*

Baedellin leapt, clinging to the woman soldier's back. She shouted as Baedellin slipped her knife under her chin and slashed. Hot liquid flooded down her arm.

"No!" Baedellin screamed, but it only came out as ragged breathing, quick and rhythmic.

"Maelin!" the man screamed, dropping the loaves of bread. He rushed forward and swung his sword, knocking Baedellin into the wall. It didn't hurt. Nothing hurt anymore.

"They're here! They're here!" the soldier screamed, fleeing from the room.

Hunt them down, my child. The horrible voice filled her head. *Hunt them down and kill whenever you can.*

Baedellin rolled to her feet and gave chase. She tried to stop herself, tried to curl into a ball and make it go away, but the queen's voice was so close and she was so far away.

She chased the man across the room and jumped on his back, knocking him to the ground. "Help me!" Baedellin whispered, slashing at his face with the knife. He screamed, trying to turn over, trying to grab her, but Baedellin surged forward and buried the blade in his neck. Dark blood splattered the tile beneath her and the man's head rolled backward, his mouth opening and closing wordlessly.

Baedellin yanked the knife out and scrambled away. "Make it stop. Make it stop."

Other voices shouted from outside the cafe. Heavy feet stomped across the street.

"It got Keln!" a soldier yelled, the jeweled pommel of his sword glowing in the dark as they rushed through the door.

"Kill it!" the man behind him shouted. He threw his spear.

Baedellin spun around as the spear slammed into her shoulder. It knocked her backward, but didn't hurt her. Nothing hurt on the outside, nothing except the glowing swords.

She stumbled to her feet and ran, leaping over the broken tables and into the kitchen. She rushed through the back door and into the alley, tripping over something in the darkness. Why wouldn't they help her? Why wouldn't anyone help?

Leaping to her feet, she kept running, racing along the alley. The buildings blurred on either side of her, whipping past as she swerved into the street—

—and ran headlong into someone. Strong hands grasped for her wrists, twisting. The knife clattered to the cobblestones.

She struggled, clawing frantically at her captor. Dark hair blew around her.

"It's all right," the woman said, her hands faster than Baedellin's, catching every strike and turning it aside. "Hush, little one."

Baedellin tried to lash out at her captor, but couldn't free her hands. She kicked mightily, but the woman pinched Baedellin's legs between her thighs.

Mother?

"Hush. Hush. It's Shara. Everything is going to be all right."

Chapter 2

Issefyn lounged on her immense silver throne. Leaves encrusted with glittering jewels were carved on the high back and thick armrests. Baskets of lush flowers surrounded her, accenting the gentle breeze with the heady perfume of spring. Her beautiful servants, naked beneath their feather robes, knelt at attention throughout the room, awaiting her orders. Pillows of lion fur and silk held her gently as she stared at the ceiling with a smile.

The black containment stone lay cradled in the crook of her arm, and she stroked it gently with her fingertips. Her son took another candied berry from an iced dish and dropped it into her mouth. She let out a long, contented breath. Swirls of honey ribbons raced across her tongue, down her limbs, filling her. Success was certainly sweet.

"So," Victeris said, settling himself on one arm of her huge throne. "Will you be getting dressed today, Mother?"

Issefyn stretched, draping her naked legs across his lap. She took a deep breath of the scented air, and glanced lazily at the moonlit gardens outside her palatial chambers.

"Not yet," she said, turning and looking down the length of her body at the sardonic smile of her long-dead son. "Perhaps I shall take a lover first."

"Will you?"

"Perhaps three," she said, waving her hand at her blissful attendants. "If they please me, I shall train them to be Zelani."

"Will you start a school for them? Send them out into the world to shine the light of love upon tyrants and madmen?"

Issefyn sniffed. "Mockery is the sign of a feeble mind, Victeris."

"And hubris?" He dropped another berry into her mouth. "What is that a sign of?"

She leaned her head against the soft fur pillow as the sensation spread through her again. "I hope you realize that I still plan on killing you," she murmured, twirling her finger across her stone.

"A magnificent plan, Mother. But I'm already dead. I have been for quite some time."

"No, 'Teris is dead. You are still very much alive," Issefyn said, eyeing the creature that mimicked her dead son so well. "I believe I have deduced who you actually are."

"Really?" He placed a glistening berry in his mouth and closed his eyes as he chewed it. "Do tell, Mother."

"I believe you are a relative of mine."

"But not your son?"

She gave him a withering stare. "I believe you are one of my great-, great-, great-. . . ." She waved her hand to indicate more. "Grandfathers."

"An interesting theory."

"Anyone who has studied at all could piece it together." She gave him a sly glance. "You, a betrayer of gods, a father of nations, and former master of abominations. Am I right?"

Victeris smiled. "A *former* master? You seem to have forgotten who taught you how to yoke your little pets."

He indicated the line of exquisite servants waiting patiently on their knees. "You would still be controlling mindless beasts one at a time if not for me."

"True, but I command them. Not you."

"For now, Mother. Everything in its time," he said, reaching for another berry.

Issefyn kicked the bowl from his hands. It clattered on the marble and Victeris raised an eyebrow at her.

"We certainly make a lovely couple," he said. He snapped his fingers, and a young woman with jet-black eyes and dark streaks of subservience down her face stepped forward to place a fresh bowl of fruit in his hand.

He dropped another berry into Issefyn's mouth. She closed her eyes, lost for a moment. It was so sweet, so delicious, like the smell of plum blossoms after a light rain. Victeris prattled on about something, and she let her mind wander, feeling the power within her stone hum beneath her fingertips.

"Magistrates," she said suddenly.

He paused. "Absolutely, magistrates, how clever of you."

"I will need attendants in my regime. Magistrates, ministers, soldiers, artisans. And Zelanis, of course. To do my bidding. To spread my majesty throughout the world."

"They shall sing the praises of the Naked Queen. I think you shall be quite popular with the commoners."

"Shut up, 'Teris," she mumbled. "You had your chance at greatness and you lost it centuries ago."

Victeris chuckled. "As you say, my queen."

"Empress."

"Are we Ohohhim now?"

"I shall make them mine as well. The whole world will be my empire."

"How can they follow the sleeve of a naked queen?" His fingers stroked the inside of her knee. "Is there some other place you would like them to pinch?"

"Feeble, feeble little mind. No wonder Morgeon imprisoned you."

"He merely sent me to a place where I could better assist you."

"I'll be sure to thank him."

Victeris hopped off the throne and tossed the remaining berries into the fire. "It is almost morning, Mother. Will today be the day you pluck the remaining thorns from your side?"

Issefyn sighed. "You are so wearisome. The city has been mine for weeks. The pathetic bands of survivors aren't enough to stop the Summer Fleet from entering the city."

"I see. And the ani blades they carry, they are no longer a threat to you?"

Issefyn waved him away. "This city is a whore with her broken legs spread wide. Her council is dead. Her citizens fled. Those few who remain wander aimlessly, swinging at shadows while my pets feast on them one by one. The Summermen will be here any day. I intend to enjoy the spoils of my victory."

Victeris smiled thinly, but didn't say anything.

Issefyn was no fool. She knew when action was required and when it was not. When the Summermen arrived, they would take her to Arefaine. Issefyn would rejoin the little bitch with smiles and hugs. And then, when they had engaged the Silver Islanders, when those drunken pirates were spilling their entrails into the ocean, Issefyn would show the upstart how much she had learned since they'd last met. She would unleash all the power of her new toy and watch Arefaine's flesh melt from her bones.

Then Issefyn would continue on with the rest of the fleet, land on Efften, and unlock her towers. All of the ancient secrets would belong to her, and she would give birth to empire beyond the wildest imaginings of the great Emperor Oh. Where he had failed and run from power, she would embrace it and succeed.

Victeris turned his head, looking out the window at the moonlit gardens. "Your victory celebration might be cut a bit short, Mother."

She blinked, then frowned. "Really, 'Teris. Must you be such a constant annoyance?"

"Annoyance? I am your greatest ally, especially now that your mistress has returned."

Issefyn looked at him sharply. His visage swam for a moment, then solidified. "What did you say?"

He smiled innocently. "Your mistress has returned."

The bitter taste of bile stripped away the sweetness of the berries. The beautiful garden outside the window rippled like a mirage. Her silver throne, the pillows, the magnificent marble pillars of her throne room all lost their luster, and the lights dimmed.

She sat up, sending out her awareness into the growing darkness. "Arefaine?" she murmured. "Arefaine is here?"

Victeris chuckled.

Issefyn shook her head, snapping out of her fantasy. The rose-marble walls of Shara's room closed around her, barely illuminated by a dying lamp in the corner. The windows and the garden beyond disappeared, becoming the open view of Ohndarien from the height of Shara's tower. Issefyn sat on the floor atop a pile of muddy blankets that stank of mold and sweat. The hollowed-out Ohndariens she had enslaved knelt unblinkingly along one wall, black tears trickling constantly from empty eyes. Their strained breathing seemed suddenly loud in the little room.

Issefyn struggled to her feet, fighting her torn and filthy nightgown. Her head swam and she nearly fell. Holding the containment stone close to her chest, she gathered her power, cleared her senses.

"I am not amused by your little joke, 'Teris. There is no reason for Morgeon's daughter to return."

He smiled, speaking directly into her mind. *Not Arefaine. The other one.*

"Shara!" She gripped the containment stone tighter. "Where?"

"She's found your favorite pet."

Issefyn sent her attention into the city, searching for Baelandra's brat. The ugly little cur had been her first transformation. The reins that controlled her mind were always close at hand. She followed the tendrils of emmeria, finding the child, seeing through her eyes.

She hissed and turned a blazing gaze on Victeris. "Why didn't you tell me earlier?"

"Why didn't you know yourself?"

Issefyn pressed her palms against her containment stone and sucked the black emmeria from it, a long heady draft. She grinned as she swelled with power, feeling the blinding light burning within her.

She would send ten. No, *twenty*. Let the righteous bitch deal with that.

Seven indentured jerked as she pushed the black emmeria into them, filling their hollow bodies with life. Issefyn clenched her teeth, fighting to extend her reach. It was like pushing her fist into cold mud. Controlling three or four was simple, but each one beyond that seemed to double the difficulty.

An eighth shuddered, its dead eyes turning to look at her. Sweat broke out on her forehead. She clenched her fist and pushed into a ninth.

"Having trouble, Mother?" Victeris asked.

She let out a little grunt and lost her hold on the last. Her body shook, and she ignored the shade's smug grin as she took control of it again.

That is enough, she thought. *Plenty to squash the cowardly little slut.*

Panting like one of the indentured, she gave the slaves their orders.

They rose from their knees as one and raced to the broken door. With inhuman speed they hurled it aside and rushed down the spiral stairs.

"So few, Mother? Why not send fifty?"

"Shut up, 'Teris." By the gods, she would destroy that shade very soon. His voice sent needles into her neck. She needed to concentrate. The strain increased as the indentured rushed down the stairs and out of the tower.

"If nine is all you can manage, then let me send more for you. I will send a hundred."

"And let you out of Morgeon's box?" she whispered through her teeth. "Do you think I'm an idiot?"

He chuckled.

She left the shade to his posturing and let her attention run with her ani slaves. Dark buildings blurred past them. She could hear their breathing in her ears and the thud of their feet on the cobblestones as they ran toward the alley where Shara held the struggling Baedellin. Issefyn smiled. And when they reached her, they—

Her arms jerked as her stone was ripped from her grip.

"No!" she shouted, her consciousness snapping back into her body. One of the indentured bobbled her containment stone as she clawed it out of his grasp.

It clattered to the ground, spinning awkwardly. The black-eyed man shoved her aside, his big, sluggish hands fumbling with the crystal. Issefyn dove, spearing her arm past the big man's shoulder and tackling the stone. She clutched it to her chest and sucked the black emmeria into herself.

"Get back!" she screamed, using her will like a whip. The indentured toppled sideways and convulsed on the ground.

Shoving aside all resistance, she grabbed the creature's mind. He scuttled over the wall, his panting breath hissing through his teeth like a cornered cat's.

Pushing her lank hair out of her eyes, she turned back to the mockery of her son, who sat innocently on the arm of the throne, his eyes twinkling.

"A feeble attempt," she breathed, determined not to let him see how scared she was, how close she had come to losing everything. "You seem to have forgotten who is the master here and who is the servant."

He shrugged. "Forgive me if I grow impatient, Mother. That stone is the key to my salvation." .

"You have no salvation," she said. "The stone is mine, and it will always be mine."

"But, Mother, surely—"

"Be gone!" she snapped. Victeris disappeared like a popped soap bubble. "I am master here," she affirmed quietly to herself. Closing her eyes, she breathed long and carefully, calming her racing heart, forging her rage into power.

Now, she thought. *I have business elsewhere.*

She turned her attention back to her slaves, reaching out for their minds in the distance. She found them standing in the middle of a street along the canal. Forcing her hand back into the cold mud, she made their limbs her own, and they leapt to action once more.

"This time they will kill her," Issefyn muttered to herself. "They will bring me her head."

Of course they will, Mother, Victeris whispered in her mind. *Of course they will.*

Chapter 3

hara fought the filthy girl thrashing in her arms. She couldn't believe the child's strength and had to keep the Floani energy coursing through her body just to keep her restrained. Her vicious little nails tore into her skin as those impossibly skinny arms reached for Shara's neck. She sent a flood of calming energy into the frantic child, but it had no effect. The girl's heart pounded beneath her fragile ribs.

"Enough!" Shara shouted, shaking the girl.

And then she saw her face. Her eyes were jet black. Stripes of black tears stained her cheeks, continually leaking from her obsidian eyes. "By the Seasons," Shara breathed as she recognized the little filth-crusted face. "Oh no, Baedellin!" Shara whispered, sinking to the ground. "No, not you."

Shara sent her awareness deep into the girl, looking for the foul magic that possessed her. But there was nothing. No life force, no ani, nothing. Her spirit was simply . . . gone, leaving behind an empty shell, a dead lifeless thing that wouldn't hold still.

Shara adjusted her grip on Baedellin, pinning the flailing, blood-slicked arms to her sides. The girl stank of black emmeria, but she wasn't corrupted. At least not in any way Shara had known. There had been no transformation, no altering of the girl's body except for the constant stream of black emmeria from her eyes. The foul magic wasn't in her; it was all around her, flowing into her from the very air itself, like ani that flowed through Shara when she used her magic.

"What did they do to you?" Shara whispered, delving deeper, looking as closely as she could. "What have you become?"

Pounding footsteps drew closer, and a handful of Lightning Swords rushed into the alley, weapons raised.

"Wait!" Shara shouted, and they did, stunned by the power she wove into her voice. Baedellin nearly slipped from her grasp, and Shara had to roll on top of her to keep her still. "Hold your swords, I'm not corrupted," Shara said, trying to ease their fear.

"Shara! Is that you?" A small solder pushed to the front of the crowd and pulled off her helmet, revealing a bandaged forehead and clumsily cropped blond hair. Her Zelani silks had been traded for soft leather breeches and hard leather plates. Bits of steel protected her shoulders, her forearms.

"Galliana!" Shara shouted, flooding with relief at the sight of her niece. Shara jerked as Baedellin thrashed against her implacable grip, but kept her in hand.

"Where have you been?" the girl whispered. "Do you have any idea what happened? Any idea what we've been through?"

Shara winced at the pain written on her niece's face.

"Set it down, Shara-lani," said one of the Lightning Swords. Shara recognized the man's craggy face, but couldn't recall his name. She also recognized the sword in the man's hand. It was one of the ani blades she and Ossamyr had created so long ago. "We need to kill the weeper and then get out of here."

The soldiers drew nearer, raising their weapons. Shara pulled Baedellin's trembling body closer to her.

"Just set it down. We'll do the rest," the grim-eyed leader of the Lightning Swords said.

Shara rose to her feet. "No." She shook her head. "They'll be no more killing."

"That thing killed Maelen and—"

The veteran held up a hand for silence. Shara looked at the Lightning

Swords with their slumped shoulders and red-rimmed eyes, white knuckles tight against their weapons, spearheads pointed at her face.

"Back away, Shara-lani. It's not a request."

"I'm sorry," Shara said. "But I will not give up this child."

"We can't linger here, Shara," Galliana said. "There will be more soon. There is no point in trying to save it. It's not even really alive anymore. It's a thing."

"No," Shara said. "Look. Don't you recognize her?"

Galliana leaned closer as Shara forced Baedellin's face upward. Recognition lit in Galliana's face, and then she closed her eyes, shook her head. "It's Faedellin's daughter," she murmured.

The grizzled leader hissed through clenched teeth. "Then it's better we kill it now. The commander doesn't need to see this."

Shara was about to protest when a cry went up from the long-limbed Lightning Sword watching the street behind them. "They're coming! In numbers!"

"Run!" the commander shouted, his weary face suddenly transformed by fear. "Back to the tunnel!"

The soldiers rushed past Shara and down the alley. Galliana's magic flared, suffusing the soldiers with energy.

"No! No! It's a dead end," Shara shouted.

The commander skidded to a stop on the dusty cobblestones. "Form a circle!" he shouted. With the speed of long practice, the Lightning Swords reversed direction and formed ranks around Shara and Baedellin. It was barely quick enough.

The creatures rushed into the alley. The men and women ran together in a feral pack, each of their faces stained black. The weeping ones leapt upon them. Two had short swords. The others were armed with knives, cleavers, clubs, and hatchets. Two of the Lightning Swords were knocked to the ground, fighting blades poised at their throats. The Ohndariens fought back, forming a wall with their shields, but their weapons simply bounced off the attackers.

Shara sent her magic to bolster the defenders, but it would never be enough. There were almost a dozen of the creatures and fewer than half that many 'Swords. Shara pushed her attention into the nearest attacker and found the same thing she had with Baedellin, a hollow shell drawing endless black emmeria from some outside source. She tried grabbing hold of the weeping one's mind, tried to bend it to her will, but there was nothing there. No personality. No mind to grasp.

One of the defenders stumbled to his knees, and the entire formation collapsed. The attackers broke through. One of them leapt on Galliana, slashing at her neck.

"No!" Shara shouted, throwing raw magic into the blank-eyed old woman clutching a kitchen knife in each hand. The old woman's strikes wobbled, barely missing Galliana, who threw herself to the side. The attacker stood there for a moment, mouth hanging open, as if she'd forgotten why she was there. Shara had pushed the emmeria out of her body, forced it away like pouring sand into a full cup of water.

The effect only lasted for a moment before the old woman reanimated, scrambling back to her feet. Shara drew a deep breath and shouted again, knocking her back to the ground. She shouted again and again, throwing raw magic into one attacker after the other, stunning them.

The Lightning Swords attacked them where they fell, but their weapons seemed to have no effect. They could knock them down, but they could not hurt them. Only the commander's ani sword struck true. He swung the blade with deadly efficiency, decapitating the creatures the others had knocked down, spattering the cobblestones with their dark red blood.

It was over in less than a minute. Three wounded Lightning Swords and their attackers lay side by side, filling the alley with dead bodies.

"Shara, are you all right?" Galliana said breathlessly as she made her way over the corpses. "How did you do that? How did you stop them?"

Shara shook her head to clear it. She was weak, dizzy, and sick to her stomach from her exertions. Baedellin still struggled desperately in her arms. "I stunned them." She paused, groping for a term that made sense. "I tangled their puppet strings."

"Puppet stings?" Galliana asked.

"Someone's controlling them," Shara answered. She felt the tendrils of the black emmeria flowing through Baedellin's pounding heart. She had to find the source, find the mage that had created this abomination.

"Who?"

"I don't know, but I'm going to find out," she said, looking into the blackened eyes of the old woman she'd helped kill.

Chapter 4

A refaine dipped the cloth into the washbasin. Pink tendrils of blood stained the steaming water. She turned back to the emperor's corpse, gently washing the dried blood from his pale skin. In the half-light of the imperial bedchamber, His Eternal Wisdom looked more like a boy than a man. His long slender limbs and smooth, hairless skin looked like a child's. His body retained some heat even though he'd been dead more than an hour.

Arefaine stared at his unmoving face. Her brow furrowed, and she pressed her lips together to keep them from quivering. She had never felt like this. It was like a great stone was crushing her from the inside out. How could she feel so much numbness and so much pain at the same time?

She soaked the rag again and dabbed at the gaping wound in the emperor's side. The sword thrust had broken ribs and cut deep into his internal organs. The wound would have to be sewn up before the body could be wrapped for burial. Looking through her supplies, she found a needle and thread. Taking a shuddering breath, she pinched the sides of his wound together and forced the needle through the lifeless flesh.

The emperor's words from a few days ago kept running through her mind. *How far would you go to fulfill your dream? Would you really have killed me to do so?* Would she really have done this? Could she have swung the blade, could she have cut him so deep?

Arefaine finished sewing up the wound and picked up a roll of silk bandages. As news of the emperor's death spread, a crowd of women had come to dress his body. Arefaine had sent them away, insisting upon completing the task herself. Preparing the body for burial had always been a sacred duty for Ohohhim women and the tradition had continued in Efften. She didn't know why it had always been a woman's task, but it made her feel better to do it.

The emperor had been killed by a stray sword knocked from one of the Ohndariens' hands. It was a simple accident, a whim of chance. But it was not fate that had killed the emperor.

Oh has shown me the time and place of my demise. It is nearly upon me.

The emperor had chosen this death. He knew it was coming and stood patiently as it descended upon him. He did it for her.

I admit that death is a very difficult thing to face with faith and decorum. But my passing is a critical turning point in Oh's struggle against the darkness.

Arefaine had fought with the man, insulted him when he told her what would soon happen. She told herself it was all a lie, a manipulation, and put it out of her mind.

Oh has shown me all possible futures. The only path that leads out of the darkness begins with my death and ends with your decision.

Was he a fool? A madman? Was he truly the incarnation of god on earth?

If you choose unwisely, you will start down a road from which you would never return.

Arefaine put the emperor's feet together and gently began to wrap them in silk. He would be brought back to Ohohhom and placed in the Cave of Oh beside all of the emperors that came before him. He would rot and disappear, wiped away forever . . . For what? To make a point? To give her yet another vague and manipulative lesson in morality?

There is no victory against the darkness. All we can do is follow Oh's example, by turning our backs to temptation and giving our lives in service of the light.

There was no way to serve the light in death. People had to live and learn, fight and strive, create and love if they wanted to do good in this world. Fearing the darkness was not the same as loving the light. Why couldn't he see that?

Arefaine wiped away her tears and continued wrapping the man who should have been her friend, encasing him in yet another flawless white Ohohhim mask.

When I die, she decided, *I want to be burned. I want the flames to soar into the sky and the smoke to carry me up to the heavens.*

Arefaine woke with a gentle hand on her shoulder. She turned and saw Brophy kneeling beside the bed. His face was battered, cut and swollen from his fight with his cousin, but he managed to give her a gentle smile.

Arefaine blinked at the morning sun. "It's too bright," she said, looking at the silk cocoon around the emperor's body. She had fallen asleep at his side.

Brophy nodded and crossed to the windows at the back of the room. He pulled the heavy curtains closed, creating a little peace for the dead. He came back and sat down next to her. The Sword of Autumn hung by his side. Its dusky red pommel looked right on him. She reached out and took his hand.

"I can't stop crying," she murmured, squeezing his hand so hard it hurt. "It feels like it's all my fault."

He looked at her, and his stern features softened a little. "That's the way everybody feels. I felt that way when my aunt died. I still feel that way. It never goes away, not completely."

"I hated him," she said, looking at the emperor's body. "I thought I hated him." She tried to swallow. "I would have killed him to reach Efften."

He put a hand on her shoulder, and she looked back at his bruised face. His brows were slightly furrowed. "I don't believe you would have done that."

"Then you don't know me very well."

Brophy reached up and touched the wet corner of her eye. "Your tears tell a different story."

Arefaine turned away. "I don't know what to do now. Are they waiting for me out there? Waiting for an empress with a face of perfect white?"

"Yes, they are. But they can wait a little longer."

"Then what? I don't know how to run an empire. Will they even accept me as regent? A woman? A foreigner? A—"

Brophy took her into his arms, pressed her head against his chest. "You don't have to do anything. Not right now."

His arms were warm and solid, and she could hear the steady beating of his heart in his chest. He smelled good, like salt and stone dust from the quarry. She looked up into his green eyes, one of them half hidden by the swelling of his battered face.

She leaned forward and kissed him. His gentle lips pressed softly against hers for a moment and then they were gone. Again he pulled her close, pressing her cheek against his heart.

"Don't worry," he whispered. "You're not alone. We'll decide together what to do next. But not yet, not right now."

Arefaine closed her eyes and let him hold her. Her mind fogged over, and she felt nothing but his closeness for a long, long time.

A knock sounded at the door. Arefaine felt a surge of fear and rose from Brophy's arms. She straightened her dress and looked to the door.

"Yes?" she called, her voice even and steady. The door opened and one of her handmaids entered the room. The girl descended to her knees and pressed her head to the floor.

"Rise, Delilah," Arefaine said.

"Mother Regent," the young woman said, raising, but still keeping her gaze respectfully on Arefaine's feet. She had never before said a word to Arefaine.

"Speak freely."

"The Ohndarien assassins are being lined up to be executed."

"What?" Brophy said, leaping to his feet. "When?"

The girl flinched away from him. "Right now," she whispered, staring at the floor. "The Carriers have lined them up on the quay."

Brophy charged to the door, dodging around the cowering handmaiden. Arefaine sprinted after him. "You will be rewarded," she murmured to Delilah as she passed.

Arefaine followed Brophy down the corridor, up the stairs, and onto the deck. He crossed the ship and vaulted over the side, landing on the dock at a full run. Breathing into the Floani form, Arefaine charged her legs and followed him. She leapt overboard onto the stone wharf, spinning gracefully into a sprint.

They raced along the dock. Through the shifting mists, she could see the gathering. One of the Carriers of the Opal Fire forced a struggling Ohndarien to his knees at the edge of the quay. An entire line of the Lightning Swords was hunched on their knees, their wrists bound tightly behind their backs and tied to their ankles so that they couldn't stand. Astor, the boy she'd kissed in the Hall of Windows so long ago, was the first in the line. He looked at her, his eyes filled with dread. Five Carriers stood guard behind them with drawn swords. A crowd of courtiers, sailors, and pilgrims had gathered around the Carriers and their victims. None of them moved to stop this treason.

"Stop!" Arefaine called, adding a little ani to her voice so that half the crowd flinched.

Brophy skidded to a stop in front of the would-be executioners. Two of the Carriers moved closer, hands on their weapons. Brophy clenched his fists, but didn't draw the Sword of Autumn.

Arefaine slowed to a walk and strode forward to stand next to Brophy. She felt naked without her makeup, exposed by the tracks of her tears down her face. "Who ordered this!" she demanded, in a cold voice.

The Carrier directly in front of Brophy removed his helmet. The soldier's curly black hair was cropped short, but his face had been powdered like any other high-ranking Ohohhim. "Oh ordered this," he said without a trace of irony. "Those who resist Oh's wisdom shall be watched. Those who defy Oh's example shall be punished. Those who attack Oh's chosen shall be slain," he said, quoting the ancient scrolls.

"You claim to speak for Oh?" she hissed. "I did not realize that the priests recognized you as his latest incarnation."

The man winced from the look she gave him. He was a young man, still in his thirties, with a stern face and powerful build, but he was still an Ohohhim, pushed from the womb with someone else's sleeve in his hand. Arefaine thought he would back down immediately, but his jaw clenched and he held his ground.

"Oh's will on this issue is clear. I am the senior member of the sacred Carriers of the Opal Fire. I was third in the divine queue behind His Eternal

Wisdom and the Opal Advisor, who have both passed into the darkness of Oh's cave. The burden of justice now falls upon me."

Arefaine felt her temper twist inside her. So he meant to defy her directly, ignore the emperor's wishes, and cut her out of the divine queue. The emperor had disregarded tradition and named her regent before his death. Customarily, the Opal Advisor stood as regent until the next emperor was found and had come of age, but the advisor had been slain alongside the emperor. This man would have been third in line if the emperor hadn't given express orders to the contrary.

"You seem to have forgotten that His Eternal Wisdom named me regent upon his death." A quiet shifting rippled through the crowd. "Who are you to deny the Voice of Oh?"

The First Carrier's lip curled into a snarl. "It is you who deny His voice. You deny his very existence. You cannot hide your nature, your *ambitions.*" He said the word as if it were the most vile thing imaginable. "The Opal Empire will not follow your sleeve, daughter of traitors. You will not corrupt us with your lust for power, your contempt for Oh's example."

Arefaine fought down her temper. She could kill this man in an instant, but his death would mean nothing. She must find a way to kill the words he'd spoken, the superstitions he lived by. Every member of the crowd hung their heads, embarrassed by the unseemly confrontation. How could she reclaim Oh's authority in their eyes? The First Carrier gave her the barest flicker of a smile as she hesitated to respond. He raised his sword over Astor's head.

"Swing that sword and you will die," Brophy said. His injured face held the same feral look he'd had back in the boulder field above Ohndarien. Arefaine could feel the emmeria surging within him. The First Carrier's sword quivered, but he did not lower it.

"I know why the emperor chose her as regent," Brophy continued, barely contained. "He told me himself before he died. You are the one consumed by *asris.* You are the one lost in the dark, chasing your own sleeve."

Arefaine felt a surge of pride to have Brophy standing at her side. Oh's Chosen should not have to defend herself. Brophy understood that better than anybody.

"I do not fear you," the First Carrier replied. "I do not fear the filth of Efften that flows through your veins."

"You should fear me," Brophy said, seeming to grow larger.

The Carrier had trouble speaking, but he got the words out. "You may kill me. You may kill everyone here and run to hide behind Ohndarien's walls, but there is a queue of millions behind me who will remember this day. Nothing you can do will turn them from Oh's path. The emperor's murder will be avenged."

Arefaine's heart lurched as she saw what was about to happen. The Carrier's blade flashed as he moved, but Brophy was faster. He hammered a fist into the Carrier's jaw and the man's sword fell from nerveless fingers. The blade clattered across the stones as the would-be executioner crashed to the ground.

The other Carriers drew their weapons.

Brophy whirled and drew his sword, crouching low. A single line of blood trickled down his forearm.

Arefaine seized the moment and turned to the crowd. "Enough!" she shouted, her voice echoed off the distant cliffs. "His Eternal Wisdom chose our path. Oh showed him what our future holds, and I am humbled that he chose me to lead us through that darkness."

Arefaine paused, sensing the crowd's reaction. Their emotions were mixed, but fear predominated. That was fine. Fear was an acceptable place to start. The four remaining Carriers were paralyzed in indecision, unsure where their duty lay.

"My sleeve is here for those who wish to follow it," she continued. "Those who doubt me may seek Oh's voice on their own."

Arefaine scanned the faces in the crowd. Brophy stood beside her like a volcano waiting to erupt, his hands quivering with rage. The Carrier farthest from her slowly lowered his weapon and knelt before her. The crowd of sailors, courtiers, and pilgrims quickly did the same. The three other Carriers were the last to bow, planting their foreheads upon the dock in front of them.

Arefaine felt a surge of triumph, but kept it from her face. She turned to Brophy and nodded. He gave her a slight bow, still struggling with the rage boiling inside him.

"Arrest that man and strip him of his uniform," the first Carrier to kneel said, pointing at his companion who had defied her.

Two Carriers walked over and turned the man onto his back. Brophy gasped and rushed to the man, felt for a pulse on his limp neck. The side of his head was caved in. His jawbone fell away from the rest of his face, hanging by a few tendons. Swallowing, Brophy looked down at the blood on his fist.

Arefaine narrowed her eyes, hesitating only a moment before she turned to face the assemblage. "Such a fate awaits all those who defy Oh's will," she said. They bowed again, keeping their foreheads firmly on the ground.

Chapter 5

Brophy knelt next to the man he had killed and forced himself to stare at the bloody mess. Howls of black emmeria roared through his head, and he hated it, loathed what it had made him do, but his venom only added to its strength. He could still feel the sensation of impact lingering on his fist. It had felt so good to strike him, a rush of pure joy, and he ached at the loss of it. He wanted more.

Arefaine began giving orders, telling the onlookers to prepare the ships for departure. The four Carriers took the body away, and Brophy couldn't look them in the face.

He closed his eyes and concentrated on the warmth of his father's spirit light in his fist. Brophy was stronger than the black emmeria. He knew he was, and he had to resist it. Slowly, the roaring faded to the background, leaving nothing but an acid pit of regret in his chest.

Arefaine's light fingers touched his shoulder, and a gentle warmth seeped into him, soothing his bitter emotions until he felt empty and raw. Brophy reached up and squeezed her hand.

"Thank you," he whispered.

"No," she said. "Thank you. What you did was of the utmost importance."

"But at what price? That man is dead, and I still can't control myself."

"That man's death was unfortunate, but necessary. And you will learn that control. In time. You're already so much stronger."

Brophy rose, looking once more at the blood on his knuckles. He and Arefaine were alone on the dock with the Ohndarien prisoners. "We need to get them out of here," he said.

Arefaine appraised him carefully. The young woman who had been crying over the emperor's body a few minutes before was nowhere to be found now. "Are you sure that is wise? A few deaths might prevent a war between our peoples."

Brophy glanced over at Astor. His cousin met that gaze, tense and unsure. "There won't be a war," Brophy said, rising to his feet. "We won't allow it."

Arefaine paused. She was scared. He could see it in the slight tension around her eyes. But her doubts and fears seemed to make her more regal, more determined. Once again, he wondered if he could accomplish the task the emperor demanded of him. Could he make this woman fall in love with him?

"I am afraid you are overestimating our ability to countermand a thousand years of tradition," she said, choosing each word carefully. "The divine queue does not change direction quickly. Imperial blood has been spilled; millions of Ohohhim will want him to be avenged."

Before Brophy could protest, she held up a hand. "But I will leave their fate up to you. I see no justice to be found in their deaths. The emperor was killed by his own superstitions. Not an Ohndarien sword."

Brophy glanced at Astor and the rest of the Lightning Swords. "I'll send them back to Ohndarien. The emperor said there would be trouble there soon."

Arefaine looked over at the prisoners, and Brophy feared for a moment that she would disagree with him, but she nodded. "Do it quickly. The very sight of them breeds bad blood."

Brophy nodded and she left him on the dock with the prisoners. Brophy watched her ascend back to the ship, her every step infused with grace and dignity. He knew where she was going, back to her chambers to bathe and reapply her impeccable makeup. *You must teach a lost child how to love,* the emperor had told him. Anger surged through Brophy at the memory of his conversation with the Ohohhim ruler. Someone should have taught the emperor how to love. The man had sacrificed his own life on the altar of Oh's wisdom and expected Brophy to manipulate Arefaine into doing the same. Just as Scythe manipulated Brophy into a Nine Squares champion, Brophy was supposed to twist Arefaine into a mindless, white-faced martyr.

But Brophy hadn't played Nine Squares the way Scythe wanted, and he didn't intend to play the emperor's game either. Love couldn't be taught. It could only be shared.

"Brophy," Astor whispered, breaking him out of his thoughts.

Brophy turned, pulled his dagger from his belt, and cut Astor's bonds. He helped his cousin to his feet. Wincing, Astor rubbed his wrists.

"Thank you," he said quietly.

"Thank Arefaine," Brophy said.

"She couldn't have stopped that swordsman in time."

Brophy gave him a grim smile. "Don't be too sure of that."

Astor gave him a skeptical look, but didn't push the issue. "What are you going to do with us?"

Brophy looked down the line of Ohndarien soldiers. They looked back at him, grim and determined. "I'll take you back to your ship and send you back to Ohndarien."

Astor nodded. "May I speak to you alone for a moment?" he asked.

Brophy led him down the dock until they were out of earshot.

"It won't be that simple," Astor started. "I came here for . . ." He paused. "For selfish reasons. But they came here for the Heartstone. Those men are determined to reclaim what should never have been stolen. They'll never walk away empty-handed. They'll keep coming back until they reclaim Her or until they are dead."

Brophy took a deep breath as he felt the anger rise within him. He glanced at his father's soul light resting on his palm and squeezed it.

"They want the Heartstone?"

"Yes."

"Very well, I'll give it to them." He handed Astor his dagger. "Cut them loose, I'll be right back."

Astor eyed the blade suspiciously, but he took it and returned to the prisoners.

Brophy walked back to the emperor's flagship. He went belowdecks and headed for the emperor's bedchamber. A pair of Carriers guarded the door. Brophy walked right past them into the room. The imperial guards followed him, with their hands on the pommels of their swords, but they didn't stop him. He walked to the silver cabinet at the far side of the room. He could feel the emmeria swirling within. With a grunt he picked up the heavy container and balanced it on his shoulder.

The Carriers stepped into his path, ready to draw their blades.

"You'd better come with me," Brophy said. "You'll want to see this as well."

He headed back to the quay, enjoying the hard work of carrying the silver cabinet. The Carriers followed him silently.

When Brophy reached Astor and the Ohndariens, they were already untied and busy rubbing the stiffness out of their limbs. Brophy looked down the line of dirty, battered, and exhausted Ohndarien soldiers. He watched their faces. Each of them held that Ohndarien fire behind their eyes. They'd lost, but weren't defeated. It gave Brophy a sense of fierce pride, and he wondered if he'd lost his own fire, his own indestructible love for Ohndarien.

He set the cabinet on the dock, and it thumped loudly. "If you want the Heartstone, there She is. Take Her." He flung the doors open. The Lightning Swords flinched away. Astor's eyes narrowed and his lip curled into a snarl. They all felt the weight of the black emmeria swirling within the Heartstone and the other containment stones in the cabinet.

"This is what you came for," Brophy said. "Come take it." Nobody stepped forward.

"That's—" Astor started.

"That's the black emmeria. You can feel it in your bellies. You can feel it in your hearts, in your very skin."

Astor nodded, and Brophy looked down the line of Ohndarien soldiers. He could see the disgust etched into every face. Even the two Carriers held themselves differently. Their eyes were hidden by their helmets, but their bodes were tense, repulsed by foul magic. "This is our enemy. Not each other, not the Silver Islanders. This is what we are fighting. This is what caused the Nightmare Battle. This is what drew the corrupted to our walls. This is what I held in my dreams for so many years."

Brophy closed the cabinet doors with a clang and felt a palpable sense of relief sweep through the crowd.

"I understand why you came here. I appreciate what you risked to do so. But the Heartstone does not belong in Ohndarien. She was not created to make our city great. She was created to imprison and eventually destroy the black emmeria. There is only one place that can happen: the isle of Efften. And there is only one person who can do it: Arefaine Morgeon. We're going there to fight this evil. To destroy it." He looked to the Carriers. "That is what the emperor gave his life for. That is why he named Arefaine regent."

He looked back to the Ohndariens. "Is there anyone here who wants to stop me from doing that? Is there anyone here who knows better what must be done?"

The frightened soldiers shook their heads.

"Let us help you," Astor said suddenly. "Let us fight by your side."

A chorus of agreement rose from the assembled Lightning Swords.

"Yes!" one said. "This is what the Lightning Swords were assembled for!"

Many more joined that sentiment, calling out that they would sail to Efften to put down the threat forever.

Brophy felt a surge of pride at the strength of their conviction, their immediate understanding of what must be done.

"Please, please, listen to me," he said in a low voice.

The Lightning Swords fell silent, and Brophy looked at all of them.

"I am honored by your offer, but the emperor's blood is on your hands. I know you did not want that to happen, but it did. His death has made a very difficult task even harder. And your presence makes it harder still. I need you to go back to Ohndarien. Protect her as you can. Arefaine and I will see this through."

No one said anything.

"Go on." He pointed up the shore where the Carriers had found their ship hidden. "Tell the council what is happening here. Let them know what is at stake."

A flurry of murmurs ran through the Ohndariens.

"There must be something we can do," one of them said.

"There will be," Brophy assured them. "This fight is far from over. But right now I need your swords on top of Ohndarien's walls."

Slowly, they nodded and left, their footsteps heavy and sullen. A dull pain lodged in Brophy's chest as he watched them march up the dock. He longed to go with them. Back home. Back to Shara. But he couldn't return to her like this. Not yet. He looked at the bloodstains on the dock from the man he'd killed. The black emmeria still had him. The Fiend was still out there, laughing, and Brophy would have to force a reckoning with that man before he returned to Shara's arms.

Brophy glanced at Astor, who lingered behind the others. As though reading Brophy's mind, he said, "Are you sure you can do this?"

Brophy shot a glance at the backs of the Lightning Swords as they walked into the mists that swirled past the ship's rail. The two Carriers were only a few feet away and Brophy leaned close to Astor so they couldn't overhear. "No. I'm not sure I can do this."

"Wouldn't it be safer to return the stone to Ohndarien until things have calmed down?"

Brophy winced, remembering the emperor's words. *Ohndarien will soon fall to treachery from within. There is nothing that either one of us can do about that now.* "That's no longer an option, Astor."

"Why? These Ohohhim are practically in open revolt. Ohndarien is the safest place for Her." Brophy smiled. Looking at Astor was like looking into a mirror. The simple earnestness in his eyes was Brophy all over again, before the years of nightmare, before his soul had been stained. His cousin was overflowing with belief, hope, things Brophy could barely remember. There was nothing but anger left inside him, rage and fierce determination.

"It's not about keeping Her safe anymore. We've run out of time for that."

"Then let me help you. Dress me as a Carrier. I don't care. Just let me help."

Brophy smiled. "A few hours ago, you were going to kill me."

"I know," Astor said, glancing at the ground. "I'm sorry."

"So am I, Astor. So am I."

Astor waited a long moment, perhaps trying to find the words to convince Brophy to let him come along. Brophy waited. Astor nodded.

"If I can't stay, what else can I do?"

Brophy glanced around. The Carriers stood at a distance on either side of the silver cabinet. Arefaine was still belowdecks. There was no one else around. "Actually, there is something very important I need you to do." Astor nodded. "Before he died, the emperor told me Ohndarien was in danger of being betrayed."

Astor stood up straighter. "By who?"

Brophy took a deep breath. He remembered Arefaine crying in his arms. He remembered the emperor's cryptic warnings about the girl. "I don't know who the traitor is, but I do know that a fleet from the Summer Cities is headed toward Ohndarien."

Astor frowned. "That doesn't sound very likely. Uniting the Summer Princes under one banner is like herding a school of fish. I don't think that—"

"It's already done," Brophy said. "Arefaine set this in motion years ago. They could be at Clifftown before you return to Ohndarien."

"But they could never get past our walls. . . ." Astor trailed off. "Unless we are betrayed."

Brophy nodded.

"But I thought Arefaine was helping you," Astor said. "I thought you were working together."

"We are, but she fights the same demons that I do."

"I don't understand."

"Arefaine needs to return to Efften. I believe that very strongly. But I don't want her to start a war to do it. If the Summer Fleet gets into the Great Ocean it will be a bloodbath. I need you to prevent that."

"But she's a sorceress. She'll know you're going behind her back."

"I plan to tell her, just not right now. But if I limit her options, she will be forced to find a better one. The Summer Fleet must not be allowed into the Great Ocean."

Astor looked away south. "I'll do what I can."

"Thank you."

"Are you sure you will be all right?"

"I'll do what I can."

Astor gave him a smile, and it reminded Brophy of the way he used to smile at Trent when his cousin was talking him into yet another glorious bit of mischief. His mind flashed back to a distant memory of laughing with

Trent as they drunkenly pulled each other through the boulder field atop Southridge. Trent had swiped a bottle of his father's wine, and they drank the whole thing, wasting the night scrambling over rocks and talking about girls. Trent never tired of talking about girls. And Brophy never tired of listening to him. They only fought when Trent mentioned Shara's legs and the way her breasts were getting bigger. But even their fights were more of a game; at least they seemed that way to him now.

Brophy clung to the memory. It hovered at a distance like a familiar painting. He knew what the details were, but he couldn't feel them, couldn't touch them.

"Are you all right?" Astor asked.

Brophy didn't answer. He simply unbuckled his sword belt and passed the Sword of Autumn to Astor. "Take this with you."

Astor backed up. "No—"

Brophy shook his head and pressed the sheath into his hand. "Nothing is more precious to me than Ohndarien and the people within her walls. There is joy within that city. There is life and love and hope that this will all be worth it some day. I need you to protect that. I need you to keep that safe."

Astor nodded, holding the sword to his chest. "I will. I promise I will."

Brophy pulled him into a strong hug.

The two of them clung to each other until Brophy couldn't take it anymore and pushed his cousin back. Clearing his throat, he said, "Promise me one more thing."

"Anything," Astor said.

"When I get back, let's steal a bottle of wine. We'll climb to the top of Southridge, sit, and drink it."

Astor smiled a little, confused. "Sure, anything."

"And we'll talk about girls."

Astor laughed.

"Not sorceresses or Sisters of the Council or queens. Just normal girls."

"It's a deal."

"I'll see you there, cousin," Brophy said. He looked at Astor for one more long moment, then turned and walked back up the dock. He strode down the length of the stone quay to the silver cabinet. It seemed to shine in the gloomy light, and Brophy could feel the black emmeria inside, throbbing like an open wound.

The two Carriers stood on either side of the container, but they parted for Brophy as he threw open the doors and stared at the blackened stones resting within. Light whispers slithered through his mind. Black tendrils of evil twisted like smoke inside the battered crystal.

Brophy's lip curled. Taking a deep breath, he reached out and grabbed the top of the Heartstone. The whispers became howls, and the swirling blackness inside leapt up at his fingers.

He clenched his teeth.

Hello, little brother. Have you missed our chats? whispered the familiar voice within the emmeria.

Muscles corded in Brophy's forearm. His fears screamed at him to yank his hand away before it was too late. Somewhere in the distance, he heard the Carriers draw their swords.

Have you grown weary of fighting? Have you come to embrace me and return home?

Brophy's fingertips turned black, and the ichor crept up his fingers. The back of his hand darkened. Wiry hairs sprouted upward. Scales puckered across his skin.

He growled, and a fierce joy leapt inside him, wanting to connect with that limitless ocean of power, to let it wash him away.

He gazed at his hand, narrowed his eyes. The black stopped spreading.

"I'm coming for you," Brophy said. He held the memory of Shara in his mind. He imagined standing with her atop the Hall of Windows, and he threw his will against the Fiend's. The bristling hairs shortened. His skin smoothed and lightened. The swirls of black inside the Heartstone spun faster, agitated, as he pushed the corruption back into the crystal.

"I will find you," Brophy whispered. "I will take the child of Morgeon to the hole where you hide, and together we will dig you out of the shadows and rip you apart."

Those are strong words from such a frightened and angry little boy.

"I'm not frightened anymore," Brophy said. "You've never beaten me. And you never will."

The howls grew weaker. The last of the black left his fingers, flowing back down into the Heartstone. "I'll see you soon," Brophy promised the fading voice. "Very soon."

I'm looking forward to it. The voice faded into the distance. *I'm looking forward to it.*

Brophy slammed the doors.

Chapter 6

ait here," Commander Geldis said, twisting his torch into a wall sconce. "We've almost reached the Citadel, but I want to scout ahead before we head back above ground."

Shara nodded, grateful for the rest. She shifted her grip on Baedellin's wrists. The girl hadn't stopped struggling for a single moment on their long trip through the tunnels. She fought like a cornered cat, constantly panting and wheezing from her exertions. Restraining the child all this time had been incredibly draining. Shara hated to see Baelandra's daughter this way, blackened eyes staring at nothing, tiny ribs straining through her filthy skin with every labored breath. The child was obviously suffering, as if every moment were agony. Shara almost thought it would be a mercy to end the girl's suffering, but she promised herself that she would not give up. Shara had abandoned Ohndarien when the city needed her most, but she would not abandon this child.

After the initial attack, their little group had fled underground. They had crossed the city using the network of tunnels that radiated outward from the Heart. The Lightning Swords had traveled in wary silence. Shara had never seen a group of Ohndariens so grim, so beaten down. The Lightning Swords had fought the corrupted for years, without ever losing faith or courage. But facing this new threat, seeing friends and neighbors turned against them, seemed to have drained the life out of them.

Geldis and his men filed past her and up the narrow stone steps and Shara sank to the floor of the dimly lit tunnel. A single soldier stayed behind. To protect her or guard her, she wasn't sure which. He was a young man, probably seventeen or eighteen, but his baby face made him look even younger. He eyed the child thrashing in her arms.

"Shara-lani," the young man said, keeping his distance. "How did you stop them? Before? What did you do to those weeping ones?"

"Yes, I'd like to know as well," a voice said out of the darkness. Shara turned to see Galliana emerging from the shadows into the flickering torchlight. Shara's niece had kept her distance during their long walk under the city. She was upset and made no attempt to hide it. Shara didn't blame her. The young Zelani had every right to be angry after the way Shara had abandoned her.

"Do you actually think these creatures can be saved?" Galliana asked, tapping Baedellin with her toe.

Shara looked down at the little girl. Even with the added strength from her magic, Shara's hands ached from the effort of restraining the child. "They're not creatures, Galliana, they're still people. They're still Ohndariens."

Galliana obviously didn't agree. "Go on ahead, Rathus," she said to the Lightning Sword. "I'll keep an eye on Shara-lani."

The boy hesitated for a moment before doing as he was told. He headed up the narrow stairs and disappeared from sight.

Shara stared at her niece. The Lightning Sword armor looked wrong on her. Galliana should be dressed in enticing silks, not hard leather and steel. The girl had changed much in the last few weeks. It wasn't just her head wound and her beautiful blond hair, cruelly shorn. She looked like a girl who had been married too young to an ungentle husband. She resembled the terrified orphan who had fled to Ohndarien from Faradan. The serene and confident Zelani student was long gone.

"It's good to see you again," Shara said. She offered her niece a smile. "But I do miss your hair. I was always so jealous of your hair."

"You can go get it. It's in a gutter somewhere near Donovan's Bridge. One of them caught my braid, yanked me off my feet, and nearly killed me. That's how I got this." She pointed to the head wound. It was wrapped in a thin bandage that looked like it hadn't been changed in days. "I cut my hair right after I woke up."

Shara took a deep breath. "I owe you an apology," she said.

Galliana said nothing.

"I feel," Shara started, having a hard time speaking. "I should have been here."

"Why did you go? Where did you go?" Galliana said, biting every word as if it hurt her.

"I ran away and tried to stop caring. I failed."

"Well," Galliana said with more sorrow than anger. "While you were busy failing, we were busy dying. They're all gone. The council, Caleb, nearly all the Lightning Swords, the entire Zelani school except for Bashtin and me . . ." Her voice trailed off into silence.

"Galliana—"

"Those things came after us first, Shara. They broke into the school, killed us in our beds. Even the children."

Shara closed her eyes tight, unable to speak. Everyone. Caleb. Even the little ones. She saw them all in her mind's eye, and each face was a knife in her heart. She felt hollowed out, helpless. How much had her one moment of pain cost this city? She swallowed. "What about Gedge and Reela? And Issefyn? What about the rest of Baedellin's family. Her father? Astor?"

"Gedge and Reela were ambushed at the Quarry Gate a week ago. They were trying to protect a group of civilians fleeing the city."

Shara breathed through the image of it.

"Nobody has seen Issefyn," Galliana continued. "If she's lucky, she's dead and not one of them."

"What about Faedellin?"

"The captain is still with us." Galliana shook her head. "You'll see him soon." Shara heard the odd tone in Galliana's voice, but didn't push the issue.

"Astor?"

Galliana gave another snort. "The Heir of Autumn betrayed us. He sailed east before the weeping ones arrived and took half the Lightning Swords with him. The emperor stole the Heartstone, and he went to get it back."

She nodded, though she doubted the emperor had anything to do with the Heartstone's theft. With every step Shara took, she realized how encompassing young Arefaine's plans were. No doubt she had somehow manipulated or tricked the emperor into taking the Heartstone.

Shara was still angry at herself for not seeing the depths of Arefaine's ambitions earlier. Jesheks had said a queen was behind the gathering of the Summer Fleet, but the scope of the Morgeon's daughter's plans was astonishing. After meeting Arefaine, Shara knew in an instant how smart and eager the sorceress was. But even at that, she could not have guessed that Arefaine's reach extended far enough to orchestrate a joining of the Imperial and Summer Fleets in the Great Ocean.

Looking back, she cursed herself for the number of warning signs she had ignored. Shara had felt the girl's reckless hate that night when the Silver Islanders had tried to steal Brophy's sleeping body. She should have known that Arefaine would stop at nothing to get what she wanted. Shara had been so focused on releasing Brophy that she'd blinded herself to all else. And then she'd run off and left a limitless supply of black emmeria in the girl's possession. If the emmeria gained full freedom, it would consume the world.

Shara didn't yet know what Arefaine's final goal was, but she knew that she didn't want Brophy anywhere near her. She longed to leave all this behind and rush after him, but she couldn't leave Ohndarien now, not like this.

"I am sorry I left," she said. "Had I any idea what would happen, I never would have gone. But I'm here now."

Galliana turned away from her apology, struggling to contain her emotions. "Why did you come back? Why now?"

Shara considered telling her about the approaching Summer Fleet, but now was not the time. She would talk to Faedellin about that. "I returned from the Summer Seas as quickly as I could. Some friends dropped me off on the Petal Islands. The refugees there told me what had happened, and I snuck into the city as soon as I found a way in."

Shara remembered her painful return to the island, where she had built a cottage for Brophy. The herd of goats had been slaughtered and eaten; her and Brophy's cabin was full of frightened orphans and the few women who were trying to watch them all. Lawdon and Mikal hadn't wanted to leave Shara, but she insisted that they continue on to Port Royal and find where Lord Reignholtz's children had gone into hiding. As much as Shara wanted the two of them by her side, she was glad for their sakes that they hadn't seen this.

Galliana looked at Shara intently. "You said you knew what happened to them, how they became like this?"

Shara nodded as Baedellin thrashed in her arms, her thin muscles straining against Shara's implacable hold. Shara kept her breathing even and steady, cycling the Floani power into herself. "I'm sure you have heard how ancient Efften was built by magically enhanced slaves. The sorcerers called them the indentured. I believe Baedellin and the others were enslaved in the same way."

"How?"

"I don't know exactly. Before the fall of Efften, the use of ani slaves was forbidden and all written references to their creation were destroyed. The new laws nearly caused a civil war. Perhaps they would have, but it didn't matter because the Silver Islanders attacked them just a little while later." Shara looked down at the black stains on Baedellin's face. "My understanding is that the victim's soul is ripped from their body. Their minds are left intact, but their ani, their life essence, is removed, leaving them no will to act on their own. They are essentially intelligent puppets. Any mage can grab their strings and force them to act as they wish."

"Can you control them like you've controlled the corrupted?" Galliana asked.

"I haven't tried."

"Why not? If we could control them, we could fight back."

"True, but at what price? What you call the weeping ones aren't like the corrupted. The mindless beasts that attacked Ohndarien for so long were physically transformed by the black emmeria. The vile magic invaded their bodies like a disease. But that disease could be cured. The invader could be cast out. The weeping ones are something much different. They draw power from the emmeria like a plant draws power from the sun. I cannot pull the emmeria out of them any more than I could pull the sunlight out of a tree."

"But you could block the sunlight? Shade the tree?"

"Yes. But if you shade the tree, it will die."

"Good, I want them to die."

"Do you really? Or is that the easier path?"

"Don't talk to me of easier paths. While you were dancing on pleasure barges in the Summer Seas, we were here fighting those things."

"You are right," Shara said, looking into her niece's tortured eyes. "I left, but I am back now. And I am going to help you defeat whoever is controlling these people. We're going to win Ohndarien back."

Galliana was unconvinced. "If you want to help us, tell me how to fight them," she pleaded. "What did you do back there to stop them?"

"I stunned them, nothing more. I flooded them with my own ani and disrupted their connection to the black emmeria."

"Why can't we control them like the mages of Efften did?" Galliana asked.

"Because we would have to use black emmeria to do it."

Galliana paused at that. She ran her hands through her ragged hair. "But it's possible," she said, looking guilty as she said it.

"Yes, it's possible."

Galliana held Shara's gaze for a long moment. Shara knew her niece was tempted to use the black emmeria against their enemies. Her sister's daughter had always had a quick temper, but she knew right from wrong. She knew there were lines never to be crossed. Thankfully, she let the subject drop. Galliana stood up and paced back and forth in the narrow confines of the tunnel. "I've heard this is the tunnel the Sleeping Warden and Mother Medew used to sneak into the city during the Nightmare Battle."

"Really?" Shara said. "I wasn't sure where we were."

"Yes. It's one of the closest tunnels to the Citadel. None of them extend into the fortress itself. The city's founders must have thought that would have been too big of a risk."

"Makes sense. Have you all withdrawn to the Citadel, then? Is there no one else in the city?"

Galliana shook her head. "There are only a few of us left. Maybe fifty Lightning Swords, most of them recruited after the crisis began. We're doing our best to protect the few hundred citizens that haven't been corrupted or fled the city. Our food stores ran out a couple of days ago, and we only leave the Citadel to forage for more. There's not much to be found."

"Sounds desperate."

Galliana sighed. "We're long past desperate, Shara. Long past."

"Come," Shara said. "Sit by me. Rest your feet for a moment."

Galliana did. She slumped against the tunnel wall right next to her aunt. After a long sigh, she leaned over and placed her head on Shara's shoulder.

"Geldis isn't scouting ahead," Galliana said. "He's gone to discuss with the others whether they should kill Baedellin before allowing you to enter the Citadel."

"I know," Shara replied. "But they'll make the right choice. All of them must have friends and family who have been twisted into weeping ones. If there is any hope of saving them, they'll take the risk."

"Is there really any hope of saving them?"

"We saved Brophy," Shara said. "We'll save them, too." As she said it, Shara tried not to think about the fact that it was Arefaine who saved Brophy.

Galliana pulled back from Shara and looked at her carefully. "You've changed," she said. "I used to feel sorry for you, how sad you were. But you're not sad anymore."

"No," Shara said softly. "Not anymore."

"What happened to you in the Summer Seas?"

"I met . . . someone. A man who taught me something about myself that I really needed to know." Shara had a sudden image of that night with Jesheks when she finally broke down and admitted what she really wanted.

"What was that?"

Shara smiled, remembering a story that Brophy told her long ago about a stupid game he used to play with Trent. "He taught me how to stand still and get hit in the face with a rock."

"What?"

She shook her head. "It's a long story. I'll tell you sometime, when all this is over."

Galliana was about to reply when they heard the creak of a distant door and hurried footsteps rushing down the stairs.

"Shara, do you have her? Is she there?" a frantic man nearly shouted above them.

Shara instantly recognized Faedellin's voice, but had never heard the leader of the Lightning Swords sound so distraught. "She's here," she said, rising to her feet. "She's alive."

Baedellin's father jumped the last few steps and ran over to Shara, trying to take his daughter from her arms. "Little Dell, it's me, it's Daddy," he cried, trying to grab hold of the wriggling child. "What's wrong with her? What's wrong! Give her to me!" Faedellin fought with Shara, and the child's wrist slipped from her grasp. Baedellin lashed out, raking her nails across her father's face.

Faedellin leapt back, stumbling in the narrow passageway. He landed on the ground, his hand going to a pair of scratches running down his cheek. He stared at Shara, dumbfounded. Her heart went out to the man she'd always thought of as the best father she'd ever met. He looked twenty years older. His face was sallow and sunken, his bloodshot eyes looked dazed, unfocused.

Geldis and a few more Lightning Swords reached the bottom of the stairs and started at the sight of their commander sitting in a crumpled heap.

"Is she gone," Faedellin whispered. "Is she already dead?"

"No," Shara assured him. "She's not gone. She's still in there somewhere and I'll find a way to bring her back."

Chapter 7

Faedellin insisted on keeping a hand on his daughter all the way to the Citadel. Shara hated to see him like this. Baelandra's husband had always carried himself with grace and dignity, but the loss of his family and his home had taken a severe toll on the man. Somehow he seemed frantic and resigned at the same time. He tried holding Baedellin once, but she was obviously too strong for him. And he reluctantly allowed Shara to carry his daughter for him.

A squad of ten Lightning Swords had arrived to escort them from the tunnel beneath the warehouse to the fortress on the hill. They kept staring at Baedellin until Commander Geldis reminded them to stay sharp.

Shara had entered the city at night and hadn't realized how much it had changed. The lush roof gardens of the south shore mansions were withered and brown. Blackened bones of the dockside warehouses thrust at the sky, casualties of fire. Shop windows were boarded up. Broken carts and discarded belongings littered the streets. Waterlogged chunks of wood and garbage lapped against the stone quays. A single ship leaned against the docks of Stoneside, wounded and abandoned. Its ragged sails fluttered futilely in the light breeze. Even the birds seemed to have fled, and silence pervaded the once bustling city.

Several of the windmills atop the Windmill Wall had stopped turning, which meant the locks were closed down as well. The city that had always been so full of life felt like a desiccated corpse, as empty and lifeless as the weeping ones.

Geldis led them to the gates of the Citadel. The crude fortress was the first structure Donovan Morgeon had built after founding Ohndarien. It was the only major building in the city made from dark gray Physendrian sandstone rather then blue-white marble. The stronghold had withstood many attacks before Ohndarien's famous walls were completed. The Citadel stood as a stark reminder that the garden city had been built atop a battlefield. Now it was a battlefield once again.

The outer doors of the fortress opened as they approached, and their little group walked into a narrow tunnel beneath the fortress walls. There were holes in the ceiling and Shara could smell the open barrels of whale oil above them. If invaders entered this room, they would be doused in oil and burned alive. As soon as they were all inside, an overhead winch creaked and the massive double doors closed behind them, plunging the tunnel into darkness. The only sounds in the darkness were the clink of metal and Baedellin's ghastly panting. Shara had never felt frightened entering the Citadel before, but with Baedellin struggling in her arms, she had a momentary fear that they wouldn't let a weeping one into their safe haven. But her fears were unfounded. The inner doors creaked open, and they crossed into the fortress's main courtyard unchallenged.

The place was packed with people, many of them children, huddled under makeshift shelters. Geldis quickly removed his tunic and draped it over Baedellin. "They don't need to see this," he whispered.

Shara and the others hurried across the open space, but a crowd quickly converged on them. The sea of gaunt faces hit Shara harder than she expected. There were so many of them.

"Did you find any food?" asked a young woman nursing a baby. Shara could see desperation in her eyes. A gaunt little boy clung to the woman's thigh. No one answered her.

Shara found it hard to keep her legs moving. Even if they found this puppet master, even if they somehow held the walls against Vinghelt's fleet, how would she feed these people? How would she keep them safe?

Keeping her fears from her face, Shara pressed onward through the crowd. She spotted an elderly man who used to deliver fresh flowers to the Zelani school. She didn't know his name, had only chatted with him a few times, but it was nice to see a face she recognized. He noticed her immediately.

"Shara-lani," he breathed, his wrinkled lips curling into a smile. "You're back. Shara-lani is back."

The mood of the crowd suddenly changed as they drew closer to her. A few of them reached out to touch her on the arm. "Thank the Seasons," the nursing mother said.

As they pressed closer, someone stepped on Geldis's cloak. Baedellin jerked and the cloth fell from her head.

Everyone gasped and drew back. A rumble of dismay swept through the crowd. "She's got one of them," someone cried. "One of them!"

"Quickly now," Geldis said, urging the Lightning Swords forward.

"It's all right," Faedellin shouted to the crowd. "It's my daughter. Shara-lani can cure her."

The courtyard exploded into a sea of screaming voices. Shara was mobbed by grasping hands. "My husband!" a middle-aged woman with a freshly broken nose screamed in Shara's ear. "Can you help him? Can you help him? I know he doesn't want to hurt anyone."

Shara fought the crowd as the Lightning Swords formed a wedge around her with their shields. Faedellin did his best to protect his daughter with his own body as they forced their way through the desperate crowd to a set of double doors on the far side of the courtyard. Shara tumbled inside as the Lightning Swords pushed back the frantic mob and shut the doors.

"I'm sorry," Faedellin panted. "That was probably unwise."

Geldis gave his captain a withering look, but Faedellin didn't notice.

"You can help her, can't you?" Faedellin asked, practically begging as desperate fists pounded on the door behind them.

Shara took a deep breath, staring into the utterly black and empty eyes of the little girl writhing in her arms. "I'll need hot water and fresh bandages," she said. "And someone get me the strongest rope you've got and two sets of manacles small enough to fit her wrists."

Faedellin stared at her in horror as Geldis snapped his fingers and two soldiers ran off to do her bidding.

Shara had never seen the Citadel so muted, so dead. Its tall arched hallways had always been alive with activity, Lightning Swords coming and going. But in every room she passed, the soldiers eyed her warily. Their courage was rimed with fear, and their hope hung by a thread.

But they'd kept the fires going. Soldiers still stood at their posts. Thin thread or not, they hung on.

Shara followed Faedellin to his personal chambers. They were a mess. The room smelled of stale sweat and vomit, and broken furniture lay scattered about the room as if destroyed in a fit of rage. Faedellin rushed to the rumpled bed and threw the blankets in a corner. "Put her here," he said as he gathered fresh bedding from a chest and began to spread it across the mattress.

Galliana gave Shara a wary look and then inclined her head toward Faedellin. Shara nodded, knowing her thoughts. Faedellin was a broken man, lost and overwhelmed. Shara could only imagine what it must have been like serving under him for the past few weeks, desperately needing a leader and not finding one.

Shara leaned in close to her niece and whispered, "Gather the Lightning Swords, all those still able to fight. I'd like to talk to them as soon as I am done here."

Galliana nodded and left the room as Faedellin finished preparing the bed.

"Set her down. Please, set her down," he said, trying to stroke his daughter's hair, but pulling back as she thrashed in Shara's arms. "I've called for hot water. We'll clean her up and—"

"Faedellin, we need to talk."

He tentatively touched Baedellin again. "Why is she breathing so loud? Why can't she catch her breath?"

"Faedellin."

"She's so small, so thin. Can you—"

"Faedellin!" Shara shouted, snapping the man back to his senses.

"I'm sorry, Shara. I'm sorry. I've lost my grip, haven't I? I never realized how much I relied on my wife. Baelandra was my strength. Everything I did—"

"Faedellin!"

The commander shut up.

"I'm going to try and help her," Shara said, returning to her normal tone of voice. The effort of restraining Baedellin was starting to wear on her temper. "It may not work—"

"Try. Anything, just try."

Shara held up her hand for silence and continued. "If it doesn't work—" He began to speak and she stopped him. "If it doesn't work, I still need you. There is much to discuss. Plans must be made. We must bring the fight to whoever is controlling these people."

Faedellin took a deep breath and looked at his daughter. "Bring her back to me," he whispered. "Make her stop breathing like that. I can't stand it."

"I'll do what I can."

She sat on the edge of the bed and gathered her power. Faedellin knelt beside her. The Sword of Winter at his hip made kneeling difficult, so he unbuckled his scabbard and tossed it aside.

Shara concentrated on her breath, cycling through the five gates. She gathered her ani until it swirled through her like a storm. When she was ready, she turned her magical sight on Baedellin. Currents of ani swirled all around the girl, connecting her to all living things. Shara had been trained to see and connect with the fiercely glowing balls of ani that composed the mental and emotional body of all living things. But there was no such glowing ball in the center of Baedellin. She was still connected to everything around her, ani still flowed into and out of her, but those connections were very hard to see. Finding them was like looking for wisps of light in the dark places between blazing stars. Slowly, Shara began to see faint black tendrils flowing into Baedellin from all different directions. With great effort of will, she wrapped her own ani around the girl, cocooning her in a golden light. The emmeria fought Shara like a river fights being dammed, insensate and inexorable. She breathed slow and steady, forcing the black emmeria back with every exhalation.

Slowly the child's flailing limbs relaxed. She hung limp in Shara's arms like a dead fish. Her frantically beating heart began to slow.

Faedellin reached out and took the girl into his arms. "Thank the Seasons," he whispered, kissing her on the forehead. "Thank you. Thank you so much."

Shara squinted with the effort of maintaining the spell. The black emmeria fought her, struggling to regain its prize. She kept the mindless force at bay, but it was far more difficult than she had hoped, and Baedellin still wasn't there. Her body was an empty shell, nothing more. Shara had cut the puppet strings, but Baedellin was still limp and lifeless.

"When will she wake?" Faedellin asked, rocking back and forth with his child in his arms.

Shara was about to tell him things were not that simple when a surge of magic flooded the room. Shara's golden cocoon shattered, and Baedellin bolted upright. Her little hands latched onto Faedellin's throat, thumbs digging into his windpipe.

"No!" Shara yelled, and grabbed Baedellin's hands.

Shara fought the surge of energy, diving into the ani, trying to regain control of the child. This time someone fought her with a powerful will.

"You won't take my pet that easily," Baedellin said with an inhuman voice. Faedellin gasped for breath.

Shara pushed back with all her strength. Images rushed through her mind: swimming through the tunnels into the wet cells, Jesheks piercing her flesh with a red-hot steel rod, flying hand in hand with Brophy. She drew strength from her past, spinning the raw emotions into her power.

"I've waited a long time for this, pig butcher's daughter," Baedellin intoned. Her little thumbs pushed deep into her father's windpipe. "You're no longer mistress here."

Shara gathered her power into one massive burst and threw it at the mind that was resisting her. The opposition shattered, and whoever was fighting her fled, disappeared down the currents of the black emmeria.

Baedellin went limp again, and Shara yanked her back. Faedellin fell to the floor, sucking in a desperate breath, his hand going to his bruised throat.

"What happened?" he gasped, struggling to speak.

Shara pulled Baedellin closer, restraining her again just to be sure. She sent her awareness outward, looking for whoever had attacked her. But that was useless. He could be anywhere.

"What did you do to her?" He rose to his knees and placed a tentative hand on his unconscious daughter's chest.

"That was another mage," Shara replied. "The one who is controlling them, probably the one who created them in the first place."

"What mage?"

"I don't know." Shara kept breathing deeply, trying to regain her composure.

Shara knew of only two mages powerful enough to fight her like that: Jesheks and Arefaine. Shara doubted Jesheks was still alive. He'd never emerged from the sea after the burning of the Floating Palace. But even if he was alive, this did not feel like him. Jesheks would never stoop to petty insults like "pig butcher's daughter."

Could Arefaine have returned to Ohndarien in secret? Had she come back to make sure the Summermen reached the Great Ocean unopposed? Shara doubted it. As much as she feared Arefaine's intentions, as much as she hated the idea of Brophy alone with the girl, the person she had fought did not feel or sound like Arefaine. It sounded like the black emmeria, the voice she heard whenever she worked with the vile stuff. That haunted voice that flattered and threatened by turns. Whoever was behind that voice was so insanely power-hungry that it kept offering Shara bargains that weren't the slightest bit tempting. It seemed to know everything and understand nothing.

Was that voice the emmeria itself, as she had originally thought? Or was it someone using the emmeria as a tool? Whoever it was, it went wherever the emmeria went, which now meant it was whispering in Arefaine's ear.

Shara pushed the thoughts from her head, concentrating on the task at hand. Baedellin hung limp in her arms. She was no longer thrashing, but her heart still beat out of control.

"Is that it?" Faedellin said. "Is she all right?"

"No," Shara admitted. "She's not all right. She's just quiet for now."

"What do you mean?"

"Faedellin, your daughter is still a slave of whoever did this to her. The puppet master has simply stopped pulling her strings for now."

Baedellin's father turned to her, his face a mask of anguish. "You said you could help her."

"No, I said I would try. Your daughter is not dead. She's still in there somewhere. But I don't know how to reach her. Not yet."

Faedellin stroked the girl's hair, carefully avoiding the steaks of black emmeria on her cheeks. "You have to bring her back. I can't stand her like this."

Shara wasn't sure what was more heart wrenching, watching Baedellin or her father. Baelandra's husband had been so kind to her over the years, an overflowing well of quiet support that she hadn't used nearly often enough. She wanted to reach out and give him a hug, but she didn't dare take her hands off Baedellin in case the girl attacked again.

"We need to find whoever is controlling these weeping ones," Shara said. "That's the key. He, or she, is somewhere in the city. We have to find the puppet master before it's too late."

Shara stayed with Faedellin as he tenderly washed the grime from his daughter's tiny body. A basin of warm water sat next to him, and he methodically dunked the soft cloth in it and wrung it out, continuing his task. Her pale skin was covered with scrapes and open sores. "She's so skinny," he said, his voice raw with pain.

Shara put both of her hands on his shoulders and suffused him with a mist of calming energy. "She'll come back to you," she assured him. "She just needs time." She wished she believed those words. But if she couldn't find what had been taken from the girl and put it back, Baedellin might remain this way forever.

The commander's daughter hadn't moved since Shara's skirmish with the other mage, but Shara insisted that they not take any chances. Someone had brought two sets of manacles to restrain her. A long chain rose from the shackles to the bolt in the ceiling that once held the chandelier. It brought back unpleasant memories of seeing the corrupted emperor restrained in his flagship so many years ago.

Galliana slipped into the room and walked over to Shara. Faedellin didn't even notice. "How can I help her?" he said hoarsely. "What can I do? She needs to eat. She'll die if she doesn't eat."

Galliana pulled Shara away from the man and urged her to sit down on a stool. She moved behind her aunt and began massaging her aching shoulders. Shara sighed and tried to relax. She needed a rest. She knew she wouldn't be getting one.

"The Lightning Swords have assembled in the armory," Galliana whispered in Shara's ear. "They're waiting for you."

Shara nodded. She hated to make them wait, but she wanted to talk to Faedellin first, and he wasn't ready yet.

"What happened?" Galliana asked, giving up on the massage and kneeling down next to Shara. "Do you control her now?"

Shara shook her head, staring at the little girl. Her pitch-black eyes stared unblinkingly up at the ceiling and her mouth hung open as she continued to pant like a woman dying in childbirth.

"I could control her. You could probably control her now."

"Is it that easy?" Galliana asked.

"Yes and no." Shara fought the emotions boiling in her stomach. "Unless someone opposes you, it is very easy to control the weeping ones. All you have to do is grab hold of the black emmeria swirling around them."

Galliana hissed through her teeth.

"That's the thing about power," Shara continued. "It's very easy to come by if you are willing to sell your soul."

Galliana nodded. She took Shara's hand and squeezed it.

"Promise me you'll never do that," Shara said. "It's better to die. Believe me, I've been there. I know."

"I promise."

Shara looked in to her niece's eyes and knew she was telling the truth.

Shara took a calming breath and turned to Faedellin. His face was contorted as he tended to his daughter, but he didn't cry. He continued to wash her gently, though she was scrubbed as clean as she could be.

"Faedellin, we need to talk about what to do next."

The commander of the Lightning Swords closed his eyes and nodded.

"I will find out who created all the weeping ones and what they are trying to accomplish," Shara said.

Faedellin took a thick wool blanket and drew it over Baedellin's tiny body, awkwardly tucking it around her chains.

"But there are other dangers to this city, close at hand. The Summer Fleet approaches. I need your help, Faedellin."

He said nothing, continued staring at his daughter, brushing a stray lock of hair out of her face.

"Faedellin, I need you to fight for your daughter. We need to get the refugees out of the city. I've already sent two of my friends to the King of Faradan, begging for supplies. I know the man. He will help us if the request comes from me. Once the people are safe, I want to abandon the Citadel and move the Lightning Swords to Clifftown. We must guard the Sunrise Gate against the approaching Summermen. We have to keep them out of the Great Ocean."

"She has her mother's hair," Faedellin said. "Her mother's beautiful red hair."

"Yes, she does," Shara whispered. "And she has her mother's fiery spirit as well. She will be fine. I will take care of her. I need you to take care of everybody else."

"I sent her away," he said. "Sent her away because there was work to be done. And this is what happened to her. I won't leave her again. She's all I have left." He lay down and wrapped his arms around his daughter.

Shara started to speak again, but Galliana's hand on her shoulder stopped her. She watched Faedellin as he stroked his daughter's arm. Slowly, Shara bowed her head, holding back the sorrow that welled up within her.

Galliana walked across the room, picked up the Sword of Winter, and handed it to Shara. "The Lightning Swords are waiting, Captain."

Shara sighed and stood up, taking the sword belt from her niece's hands. The smooth leather of the scabbard felt strange in her hands. The oversized diamond in its pommel seemed to glow with a life of its own. The gem had come from the Heartstone herself. It was the city's last connection to the Brothers and Sisters of the past.

Shara turned to face Faedellin. He hadn't noticed that she had his sword. "Stay here," she told him. "Keep holding her hand. Keep telling her you love her, and she'll find her way back to you."

Shara buckled the sword around her waist and followed Galliana out of the room.

Chapter 8

"W e'll send what help we can, when we can.'" Lawdon mimicked the King of Faradan in a low voice. "What the hell does that mean?"

"It means No."

Lawdon and Mikal tromped through the muddy streets of Port Royal. They weaved around the haphazard throng of street vendors who assaulted anyone exiting the shabby wooden stockade that Farads called a palace. "That smug bastard showered Shara with jewels a month ago," Lawdon said to Mikal, not caring anymore who might overhear her. "But now he can't afford a few boatloads of grain to keep her people from starving?"

Mikal dodged around a mud puddle with a look of extreme distaste. "You can't blame the man. A letter from a friend in need is hardly the same as a visit from the great Shara-lani . . ." He paused dramatically. "In the flesh."

"If flesh is all the man wants, I'd be happy to drop my pants, squat on his face, and smother the bastard in mine."

"A delightful image, I assure you. Murder by maidenhood would certainly inspire a cad like me, but kings are made of sterner stuff."

Lawdon laughed in spite of herself. "It's about fifteen years too late to fear my maidenhood."

Mikal stopped in his tracks, aghast. "Say it isn't so, my lady. I can't bear the thought of you with another man."

"It was a boy, not a man, and a clumsy one at that."

"I weep for your indignity."

"You should weep for his indignity; I practically had to hold the poor boy down."

"I will not weep for him. I cannot abide that he has tasted of your most precious fruit, and yet I have not."

"That's your choice, my fickle prince, not mine. I've got a whole bowl of fruit waiting for you whenever you're ready."

"Patience, patience, my royal assassin of love. Our murder weapons will cross soon enough."

Lawdon gave Mikal a shove, and he let himself be pushed into an ankle-deep mud puddle, reveling in the indignity of it all. She was actually really enjoying that she and Mikal had not taken that final step. At first it was just a little game they played. Her verbal pursuit of him was an amusing jest, considering the way he'd thrown himself at her every waking moment when they'd first met. But beneath the levity, there was something more, something unspoken between them, that Lawdon was saving for a better time and place. Right now they both had larger issues on their minds.

Lawdon still wasn't sure they had done the right thing by leaving Shara in Ohndarien. The stories told by the refugees they had met on the Petal Islands were rather hard to believe. They claimed that most of the city had been taken over by some new kind of corrupted. She was actually not very surprised that the Farad king didn't take her warning very seriously. Lawdon had never seen one of these "new" corrupted. Between Reignholtz's death, the end of the Eternal Summer, and the madness of Vinghelt's invasion of Physendria, a magical plague in Ohndarien was just one more tragedy too large to comprehend. Lawdon and Mikal's playful banter was the only way they kept from drowning in it all.

And on top of all of it, Lawdon and Mikal were still looking for her brothers and sisters. Lord Reignholtz's natural-born children had been sent to King Celtigar for safekeeping right after their father and oldest sister were murdered. Lawdon hadn't even had a chance to say good-bye to them. But the Farad king insisted that they had never arrived. Lawdon didn't want to panic at the first sign of trouble. Hastily arranged rendezvous were notorious for running afoul. Still, the children should have been here four or five days ahead of them. And Lawdon had heard that Vinghelt had put a modest price on the children's heads.

"Do you think the king was lying about the children not arriving?" Lawdon asked Mikal as he made a great show of shaking mud off his boots.

"The man is such a liar that his stern smells better than his prow, but . . ." Mikal paused, grew serious for a moment. "I don't think he was lying about that. He seemed as mystified as we were. How well do you know the men sailing with them?"

"Very well. Any one of them would have died to protect those kids."

"Let's hope they didn't have to."

Lawdon nodded, fighting back her growing sense of dread. Mikal gave her a quick embrace. It was such a simple thing, but it made a huge difference. It frightened Lawdon a little how easily Mikal could make her feel better.

He gave her a little kiss on top of her head and danced away with a flourish. "It is better this way. I'd hate to see the noble progeny of the great Lord Reignholtz succumb to the indignity of setting foot on land. They are undoubtedly off somewhere, sailing the Summer Seas, stylishly slipping through the claws of danger at every turn."

"I'm sure you are right," she returned. "We did say we would meet in Ohndarien if something went wrong."

"Ohndarien it is, then," Mikal said, offering his arm. "They are probably sitting at Shara-lani's feet at this very moment, hearing wondrous tales of how she caught all those newly corrupted in a giant silver net and cast them into the sun."

"And she probably looked really good doing it."

"Undoubtedly she did."

The two of them shared a smile for a moment, but the mirth faded as quickly as it had come. Lawdon's thoughts turned to plans for the voyage back to Ohndarien.

They were nearly back to the docks when a very hungover-looking sailor, scrawny and well past his prime, spotted them through the window of an alehouse. He hopped though the open window with more dexterity than Lawdon would have expected. He was wearing a coarse Farad tunic, but he was undoubtedly a dust-born Summerman.

"Good Captain," he called, hurrying across the street, his gait lopsided because of a sideways curve to his spine. "It's a joy to see a summer smile on these dusty streets." Lawdon looked around for trouble, but didn't see anyone else. She was glad to have Mikal at her back. His hands were conspicuously far from the handle of his blade, but she knew he was ready for anything.

"Any chance you be needing a little floating crew on your next haul?" the old sailor asked. "Me and some of my mates are all good hands and we'd work for meals and a wee bit of jingle if we could get a hop back home."

"You looking to join the fleet?" Mikal asked.

The twisted man laughed. "No chance of that. I'd rather be a whore for hogs than a soldier. That's Fessa's own truth. But with all those fools heading off to drink sand, there'll be a lot of good work they'll be leaving behind. I'd hate to miss that."

Lawdon looked the man up and down and decided she didn't like him. They were short on crew, but she didn't like the idea of this man on her boat. "Sorry, friend," she replied. "We're not headed south."

"We don't mind going roundabout. We've been stuck here for a few weeks. With all this war nonsense, it'll be tough to find another hop."

"My boat's full," Lawdon told him, and continued on her way.

The crooked sailor hurried after her. Lawdon was about to draw her dagger when the man leaned in and whispered, "I hear you lost some cargo. Six little packages that belong to a fallen summer prince."

A rush of heat filled Lawdon's chest, and she stopped in the middle of the street, hope and suspicion warring for control of her thoughts.

"I'll be in there," the sailor said, pointing to the alehouse he'd come from. "If you want to discuss it."

Lawdon let the man walk away and then turned to Mikal. "I don't trust him," she said.

"Neither do I. He's one of my countrymen after all. But we still need to talk to him."

"You're right," Lawdon agreed, flexing her ankle to make sure her spare knife was still in her boot. "You ever fought a hunchback before?"

"Only when she wouldn't let me out of her bed."

Lawdon smiled and followed the sailor into the alehouse.

The place was small, crowded, and dirty like most taverns near Port Royal's docks. It smelled like a cross between a brewery and a latrine. Lawdon spotted the hunchback on the far side of the room. He caught her eye for a moment and then slipped through a narrow door. Lawdon and Mikal followed. The door led into a blind alley behind the kitchen. It was filled with broken barrels and a rotting scrap heap below the kitchen window. The rest of the alley was empty. Lawdon checked that the door wouldn't lock and closed it behind her.

"You Reignholtz's captain?" the sailor asked her.

Lawdon nodded. "And his daughter."

"You know there's a fair price on your head?"

"That's what I've heard."

"I hear there's a price on all of the lord's brood. That's why they never made it to the dusteater's palace. They were snapped up the moment they arrived in Port Royal. Never even got off the docks."

Lawdon felt the heat of anger rise through her neck and into her face. "Who took them?"

"I did, of course," the sailor said with a crooked grin.

Lawdon drew her dagger.

"Looks like a party back here," Mikal interjected.

Lawdon turned and saw four more men step into the mouth of the alley, blocking their escape.

"I'd like you to meet my mates," the crooked man said, drawing a blade from inside his sleeve. "Now I suggest you stay nice and calm before someone gets hurt. Lord Vinghelt don't want you dead, but he'll take you that way if he has to."

Fighting back her fear, Lawdon forced herself to smile. "You really don't know who I'm with, do you?"

The sailor glanced at Mikal. "Looks like a little fishlicker too yellow to join the war." He turned to Mikal. "Don't worry, precious, we don't need you, just her. Now get your rich little ass outta here."

Lawdon started laughing. "You've been in Farad too long, my friend. Allow me to introduce Mikal Heidvelt."

The sailor's jaw dropped. His friends stopped in their tracks.

Lawdon raised her eyebrows at them. "I see you've heard of the duelist who humiliated the great Avon Leftblade right before he took young Nat-shea's life."

The sailor's friends looked at him, not sure what to do.

"Take him in a rush, lads," the crooked man said. "This is an alley fight, not a duel."

Mikal drew his blade with a flourish and spun it about lazily.

This certainly is your lucky day,
Brawling in alleys is not my forté.
A rush of blades would surely do the trick,
And this rich little ass is yours to prick.

"Enough," the crooked sailor shouted. "He can't kill a man with words. Don't you want a little noble blood on your blade?"

Lawdon's heart was pounding like mad, but Mikal smiled as if he didn't have a care in the world. He stood there waiting for the five men to attack him. None of them made a move.

Come now, my friends, don't be shy.
My words make women sigh, not men not die.
And there's nothing better than a sack full of gold
When waveborn blood spills so easily for the bold.

"Now, lads!" the crooked sailor yelled. "Now! That little whore is worth ten thousand in Physendria."

Nobody moved.

Lawdon hissed and walked up to the man. He retreated, taking feeble swipes at her until his back was pressed against the far side of the alley and her knife was at his throat.

"What are you, little girls?" the leader yelled. "We've got them five on one and—"

"Actually," she said, right to his face. "I think it's two on one, because those men are free to go. We're only interested in you."

With a spinning lunge, Mikal leapt toward the four swordsmen. They turned and fled from the alley. He shrugged and sheathed his sword before turning back to the crooked sailor. "I suggest you drop your dagger, my friend. She's been known to geld men for the joy of it."

The sailor dropped his dagger.

Mikal walked up and leaned on the hunchback's shoulder. "Silly of them to run, really," he told Lawdon. "I've never fought more than one person at a time in my entire life. I wouldn't have the slightest idea how to go about it."

The old sailor hissed and glanced at his blade on the ground, but Lawdon pressed her dagger into his chin and brought his gaze back up to meet her own.

"Now, I believe you were about to tell us where the Reignholtz children are."

Chapter 9

"Y" ou're in my spot," Brophy said, walking up behind Arefaine and leaning on the rail next to her.

She stood at the back of the ship, watching the moonlit tip of the Cinder disappear beneath the horizon. The steady tailwind blew her dark hair away from her powdered face, which seemed to glow in the scant light.

"Have I stolen your job as the gloomiest person on board?" she asked him.

She didn't turn to face him, and Brophy found his gaze traveling down the length of her body. Her dress hugged her sides down to her narrow waist and sloped out along her slender hips before falling straight to her ankles. A heat grew in his chest, and he instantly thought of Shara. It had happened every time he and Arefaine shared a quiet moment together. In the past he had fought that feeling, locked it away with his anger and rage, but this time he let the feeling grow and fade within him like the drawing and releasing of a breath.

"You can't be as gloomy as I was," Brophy replied. "I wouldn't even hold your hand."

Arefaine turned to him and smiled. "That was very sweet of you, protecting the poor Ohohhim from such an unseemly show of affection." She put her hand over his. "I, however, as the new regent, feel it is my duty to make my new subjects as uncomfortable as possible. Shall we disrobe and incite a rebellion?"

Brophy chuckled and turned his palm upward, entwining his fingers with hers. "It might be worth it," he said.

You must teach a lost child how to love, Brophy heard the emperor saying, but he put the words out of his mind and concentrated on Arefaine. Despite his disdain for the task the emperor had charged him with, Brophy found himself drawn to her. He admired her courage and the way she seemed to draw strength from solitude. She had endured far more than he at the hands of the dark emmeria and emerged unbroken on the far side. What would it be like to be on the inside of all that passion? What would it be like to be her trusted confidant, to be a friend to this woman whom everyone else seemed to fear?

Arefaine looked up at him. Her face was freshly powdered, but it no longer seemed like a mask. For once, she made no attempt to hide the emotions swirling behind her eyes.

"Come," Brophy said, leading her away from the rail. "Let's go to your chambers. We should talk."

Arefaine looked at him strangely, but didn't release his hand. If anything, her grip tightened. She nodded and allowed herself to be led away from the rail. Her hand was warm and a little sweaty, squeezing his harder than she needed to. Brophy glanced once at the ship's crow's nest, thinking of another ship in another time, then turned away and took her belowdecks.

Arefaine had kept her old chambers, leaving the huge aft stateroom to the emperor's body. He led her into the little room with black lacquered walls and brought her to the bunk. She stared at him for a long moment before sitting down on the glossy black bedcover. Brophy took the chair from her changing table and sat down opposite her.

"Arefaine, we—"

She leaned over and kissed him, cutting off his words. Startled, he moved back slightly, but she followed him, wrapping her trembling arms around his neck. Her lips pressed against his a bit too hard, not quite sure what to do. He only hesitated a moment, then he responded, his chest expanding as he leaned closer to her.

He was struck by how strange Arefaine felt when it was Shara's body he remembered. Touching Shara was like having your skin kissed by the sun. She flowed into you, inhabited every inch your body. But touching the Ohohhim sorceress was like cradling a fragile egg, waiting for it to hatch.

Arefaine pulled back before he did, biting her lip. Her breath was faster than normal, and he could see the curve of her breasts pushing against the silks she wore. They were smaller than Shara's, firmer when she pressed up against him.

She swallowed, not taking her eyes off of him. "I want to wash my face," she said.

"I'd like that," Brophy said, trying to calm his own breathing. Standing up, she walked to a washbasin on the far side of the room. She poured fresh water into the bowl and began to wipe the white powder from her face with a wet cloth.

Brophy struggled with the black emmeria still swirling within him. The distant cries of anguish seemed to diminish as he watched her move.

You have strength, Brophy. The emperor's words lingered in his thoughts. *That is why you are so desperately needed.*

Brophy reached into his pocket and pressed his father's soul light against his chest. The stone's reddish glow seemed to expand into his body, and Brophy felt a stab of guilt in his heart. Annoyed, he took his hand away from the stone and rubbed his face, wondering what he was doing here and why he was doing it.

He looked back at Arefaine and forced himself to speak. "I have a confession to make."

She stopped washing and turned to face him. She was so much prettier without all that powder on her face. "What?" she asked, bracing herself for the answer.

"I sent Astor and the Lightning Swords back to Ohndarien."

"I know."

"And I told him to make sure the Summer Fleet never gets past the Sunrise Gate."

Arefaine paused, and he suddenly had no idea what she was thinking. Lewlem's soul light shot out of her sleeve and began to circle her head.

"I know what you told them. I listened."

Brophy nodded, suspecting that much.

"But why tell me now?" she asked. "Why right now, right before we're about to . . ." She turned back to the basin and washed the last of the powder from her face. Her mind was working again, always working. Piecing together bits of information, sorting, cataloging.

And coming to conclusions.

Brophy stood up and walked to her, but she stepped aside the moment before he reached her.

"Arefaine—" he said.

"Go. If you don't want to be here, just go."

He shook his head. "It's not that."

Her lips pressed together. "You're only here because of him, aren't you? The emperor made you my keeper before he died."

Brophy could feel her sudden anger, caged though it was. His own rage swelled in response, but he held it back and focused on her. "That's not why I'm here."

"All right," she said, crossing her arms in front of her chest. "Then why are you here?"

Brophy squeezed his father's heartstone. He could feel the spirit light within, calming him, making him feel better. "I believe the emperor intended for me to seduce you."

She showed no reaction, merely that narrow-eyed scrutiny. She'd already worked it out in her head.

Brophy continued. "He wanted you to fall in love with me. He wanted me to manipulate you into following Oh's plan."

"And what made him think I would fall in love with you?" She lifted her chin, a girlish gesture.

Brophy sighed. "You know the answer to that. You know what we've both been through."

Lewlem's golden light landed on Arefaine's hand, and she pressed him to her lips. "Why are you telling me this?" she whispered from behind her fingers.

"Because I think the emperor was a madman. I think the Ohohhim are all insane, following each other around in little lines like ants. People can be so much more than that. People *should* be much more than that."

Her voice softened. "But if you believe that, why would you listen to him? Why did you send your cousin to stop the fleet?"

"To give me time."

"Time for what?"

"To change your mind."

Her momentary softness disappeared behind her implacable Ohohhim facade. "I'm going to Efften. With or without you," she said.

"I know. I want you to go. I want to go with you. But I don't want you to bring the fleet. We don't need to start a war."

"I don't need to start a war. I *want* to start one!" she said, raising her voice.

"You actually want to build a bridge to Efften out of the corpses of your enemies?"

"If that's what it takes, yes!"

"And then what? Are you going to skip merrily across that bridge and then rebuild the world as a more beautiful place?"

Arefaine paused, her eyes growing wider. For a moment Brophy thought she would turn and run from the room, but her lips curled back into a snarl and she took two quick steps toward him.

"You have no idea what those vermin did to us!" she shouted in his face, backing him against the wall.

"Yes, I do know!" he shouted back. His hands itched to shove her through the wall. "I know exactly what horrible things people can do to each other. I've done those things. I've reveled in that madness, and I'm still paying the price!"

"Don't lie to yourself, Brophy! Do you have any plans to forgive the corrupted for what they did to your father, your aunt, your city?"

"That's not the same," Brophy shouted. "The Silver Islanders are not the corrupted."

"And why not? How is your family, your home, different than mine?"

"Because your family deserved to die!"

She lashed out to slap him across the face. He blocked her hand, but the force of the blow knocked him a step sideways. Brophy grabbed her. She fought him, but he spun her around and slammed her against the wall.

"Efften created the black emmeria!" he screamed at her. "They brought this vileness into the world! All this hatred we feel, all this rage. That's not us. That's the black emmeria. That's what they've done to us! What *your* ancestors have done to us!"

Power swelled around her. Arefaine took a deep breath and shoved him halfway across the room.

Brophy stumbled to a stop against the dressing table and stood there, panting heavily. "I'm drowning in the filth of Efften," he hissed. "And so are you. It's seeped into our bones. I'm not going to Efften to re create the City of Dreams. I'm going there to bury it so deep it will never harm anybody ever again!"

Arefaine stared at him, struggling to control her breath. Her eyes narrowed and the rage slowly faded from her face, seeping into her like water into a sponge. When her breathing was back to normal, she plucked Lewlem out of the air and tucked him back in her sleeve.

"We seem to have a little disagreement here," she said with forced formality.

"Yes, we do," Brophy agreed, wary at her sudden coolness. "What are we going to do about it?"

"Right now I want to kill you."

Brophy nodded. "I know. Believe me, I know." He took a deep breath. "Have you ever killed someone, Arefaine?"

She swallowed. "Yes," she admitted. "Yes, I have."

"And you liked it so much you wanted more."

She shook her head, not able to look him in the eye.

"Then why are you doing this? What do you expect to find when you get to Efften?"

Arefaine closed her eyes and turned her face away from him. Her throat quivered, and she said something Brophy couldn't hear.

"What was that?" he asked, walking closer.

"I expect to find my father," she said.

"What?"

"He's still alive, Brophy. He's there, trapped in the ruins, imprisoned by the Silver Islanders."

Brophy was silent for a long moment. "Your father?"

She nodded, looking back at him. "He wove the spell that put the emmeria in my dreams, but he stayed with me, through every minute, every year, every long century. He talked to me, whispering that he loved me, that it would all be over soon. That voice was all I had in that world of darkness. He's the only reason I survived, the only reason I made it through."

Brophy felt a glimmer of understanding, followed by a swift chill. "You heard a voice? When you were in the darkness? In the black emmeria?"

"Not only then; he has spoken to me since then. He's stayed with me the entire time I've grown up. He told me what books to read, who to talk to, how to set events in motion. But he's still trapped. And I have to rescue him."

"A voice?"

"My father's voice."

"In the black emmeria?"

"The emmeria, yes."

"Arefaine—" he started, but stopped himself. Everything suddenly made perfect sense. It was the Fiend. Talking to her. Guiding her actions. Twisting her love for a long-dead father.

He looked at her, struggling with the rage that threatened to overwhelm him. The Fiend was lying to her, as he'd lied to Brophy all those years. She needed to hear the truth, needed to know whom she was dealing with. But as Brophy stared in her eyes, he saw her fierce protectiveness. She'd lost her family before she even knew what family was, and she wanted it back more than anything, more than the emperor's approval, more than Brophy's love. If that voice had been the only thing that had ever loved her, she'd die before she let it go. He wanted to blurt out the truth and face the storm that followed, but he had to be careful. He couldn't save her by ripping her heart out.

"Are you certain about this?" he asked her.

She nodded. "I know how you feel about the emmeria. You have every reason to feel that way. But Efften and the emmeria are not the same thing. My mother and father were part of a renaissance in the City of Sorcerers. They were putting an end to the worst types of magic. They outlawed slavery; they defied the elders and were starting to undo the damage that had been done. The emmeria can be cleansed, purified, and used for the benefit of others. You've seen that for yourself, with Shara, in the Wet Cells."

Brophy kept his silence, wondering how she knew about such things.

She stepped forward, her liquid gaze searching his. Searching for weakness or searching for acceptance? He watched her, trying to keep his ironclad heart open. Swallowing, she held her arms out to him, and Brophy wrapped her in an embrace. It felt better than he thought it would. Much better.

"I say we make a pact," Arefaine whispered to him. "If I can find a way to reach Efften without bloodshed, I will do so."

"And what do you want from me?"

"I want you to do the same."

"What do you mean?"

"You want to destroy the emmeria." Brophy nodded and Arefaine continued. "But I want you to consider the possibility that my father is right and all that power can be used to free people instead of enslave them."

"Arefaine, it doesn't work that—"

"A sword can be used to defend as well as destroy. Why should magic be any different?"

Brophy felt his stomach clench as he bit back everything he wanted to say.

"Will you make that pact?" Arefaine asked.

"I'll promise you this," Brophy said. "I'll go with you to Efften. Together we will see what is actually hidden there and together we will decide what to do about it."

Arefaine looked up at him. Once again, Brophy was struck by the color of her eyes. "I can promise that," she whispered. "Whatever we do, we'll do it together."

Brophy leaned down and kissed her. Their lips met gently, and he felt something wrench in his chest and then release. A sob bubbled up in his throat, and he grabbed the sides of her face, pressing her forehead against his. He wanted to climb inside her and disappear.

Arefaine gasped and stepped back from the kiss. She brought her hands to her waist and untied her robes. He reached out and pushed the silk off her shoulders. Arefaine let the robe drop to the floor.

Brophy bit his lip as she stood before him, looking like she was about to run away. "You're so beautiful," he breathed, almost afraid to touch her.

"Am I?" she asked, so unsure of herself that he couldn't help reaching out and pulling her to him. "I don't ever want to fight again," she said.

"All right," he said, pressing his cheek against her long, dark hair. "No more fighting."

He picked her up and carried her to the bed, lying on top of her as he set her down. They kissed again, and her hands dug into his hair.

"You're trembling," he said.

"I can't stop. I don't know why."

Brophy pulled back and looked down at her. She looked so young, like a lost child. He rolled off her, grabbed the bedcovers, and pulled them over both of them.

"What are you doing?" she asked.

"I'm going slow." He kissed her again. "Arefaine, I want to be your lover. I want to do everything with you. Twice. Three times."

She smiled.

"But it doesn't have to be right now. It doesn't have to be tonight. Or the next or the next."

Arefaine nodded.

"Right now all I want to do is kiss you, kiss you until the sun comes up. The rest will take care of itself."

"Then kiss me," she said.

And he did.

Chapter 10

Shara hurried down the hill, fighting the urge to run ahead of the six Lightning Swords escorting her. She hated to waste the time if someone might be dying, but she was the one who'd decreed that no one travel in the city in groups of fewer than six. And she could hardly justify undermining her own authority.

"Are they close?" Galliana asked.

"Yes," Shara said, pointing. "Just a block down on the other side of the street."

Shara's niece had become indispensable over the past eight days. Shara had spent most of her time in a trance, scouring the city with her magic, looking for some sign of the mage who had created the weeping ones. She had found little pockets of survivors here and there, hiding in attics and cellars, but so far there had been no sign of the true threat. While Shara was spending every waking moment looking for their enemy, Galliana had taken over the role of second-in-command, making sure Shara's instructions were carried out.

"Can you sense them yet?" Shara asked, and felt her niece gather her ani and send her awareness down the street, looking for the pocket of possible survivors Shara had detected.

Galliana shook her head. "I can sense some rats, but that is all."

"It is very subtle," Shara assured her. "I went over this neighborhood at least a dozen times before I noticed anything. There are several of them, definitely human, but their life forces are so faint that I'm afraid they must be dying."

"We've found many others alive," Galliana reminded her. "I'm sure they'll be fine."

Shara wished she shared her niece's optimism. Even though she had failed in her primary objective, Shara had to admit that what the Ohndariens had accomplished in the last few days was amazing. They had already moved the survivors from the Citadel to Clifftown. The little stronghold below the eastern ridge had been built as a way station where ships could be inspected and pay their tolls before passing through the locks. But it was also the city's primary defense against an attack from the Summer Seas. It would be nearly as easy to defend as the Citadel. Shara had encountered a great deal of fear and doubt when she first suggested abandoning the Citadel and marching everyone to the far side of the city along the top of the Water Wall's aqueduct. People were especially reluctant to walk through the dark tunnel where the dried-up waterway cut through the side of the mountain, but Shara needed every possible sword defending the Sunrise Gate when the Summermen arrived. There had been almost no wind in the past couple of days, which had certainly slowed the Summer Fleet, but they would be arriving at any moment.

Despite people's fears, changing locations seemed to change the mood as well. In the Citadel, the Ohndariens had been locked in despair, almost waiting to die. Getting them moving again seemed to bring them back to life. Some had built rafts and started going on short fishing trips beyond the wall. Other small groups had started foraging for shellfish and harvesting wild vegetables on the Petal Islands. Not one of them had decided to leave the city when Shara gave them the opportunity. Those who wanted to flee had done so at the first sign of trouble. Those who wanted to stay were determined to see this through.

It certainly didn't hurt that there had been no attacks from the weeping ones after Shara fought their master over control of Baedellin. The ani slaves had gone inert. Their master was either hiding or had fled the city. Shara had found evidence that the sorcerer had previously taken up housing in her tower. She had visited the Zelani school a few days ago, looking for books that might have more information on the mindless slaves and had found her workroom ransacked. It reeked of blood and feces, bringing back hated memories of her time with Victeris. The pall of black emmeria lingered like a shadow, but her enemy was no longer there.

It was frustrating. Shara had never had to find a sorcerer before. It was proving harder than she could have guessed, and time was running out. With a few more days of good food in them, the citizens and Lightning Swords should be able to defend Clifftown, but they didn't have much hope against a simultaneous attack from weeping ones from within the city.

"This one right here," Shara said, pointing to a shop whose sign sported a dancing goat holding a wedge of cheese. The once-cheery establishment looked dark and dead, like every other shop and café in the city. Not a whisper of sound came from inside.

"Allow us, Shara-lani," said a Lightning Sword with a black ponytail. His name was Speevor, and he seemed to have taken it upon himself to be her personal bodyguard. He gave her one of his mirthless smiles, the barest widening of his mouth.

Shara paused, nodded. She wouldn't do the Lightning Swords the disservice of rejecting their help. Speevor and two others stepped into the shop. After a few minutes they called out that all was clear.

She and Galliana stepped inside, and both covered their noses against the overpowering smell of rotting cheese. Everyone in the room looked like they wanted to gag. The shop had been demolished. Shredded cheesecloth and furniture were scattered all around the room. Shara could hear the frantic scurry of rats' feet, but couldn't see them.

"They're down below," Shara said, pointing to an open cellar door. The stench of foul cheese flowed upward from the trapdoor.

Shara sent her awareness down the dark hole. She could feel the hollow nothingness of weeping ones below, dozens of them. But there were people there, too, somewhere beyond the weeping ones.

"Whatever I'm feeling, it's coming from down there."

Shara started toward the ladder leading into the darkness, but Speevor waved her aside. "I'll go first," he said, not waiting for her answer.

"Be careful. There are weeping ones down there."

He nodded, grim, but apparently unworried. One of his men handed him a torch and he headed below. The Lightning Swords followed him. Shara and Galliana trailed last, descending into the cellar. Rats scurried into the shadows as they reached the bottom.

The tiny room was packed with a crowd of weeping ones, the rasping of their frantic breath filling the room. They stood slack-jawed and motionless, staring at nothing with their pitch-black eyes. Tears made black streaks down their cheeks, over their jaws, and down their necks. Many of them had large black stains on their clothing or bare chests. The Lightning Swords fanned out, shields first, and began herding them into one corner. When bumped with a shield, the weeping ones would move away with shuffling steps like brainless sheep. "Keep alert," Speevor warned his men. "This time could be different."

But Shara knew it wouldn't be different. The soulless ani slaves had all been like this ever since that first time she was attacked. Not a single weeping one had fought back. Every group they'd found had been like this one, standing, waiting for orders. The only reason they looked alive was their constant gasping for breath. Their faces showed no emotion, but Shara couldn't help feeling like they were in constant agony.

It was entirely possible that the mage Shara sought had fled the city. Every indication pointed to it. But why bother to enslave an entire city and then simply walk away? Was that the original plan? Simply to soften Ohndarien's defenses for a future attack?

For a moment she considered again that it was Arefaine. Could the girl be powerful enough to be controlling these slaves all the way from Ohohhom? Was that why Shara had been able to overpower her when they clashed over Baedellin?

She shook her head. It couldn't possibly be that. Sending one's ani across great distances was very difficult. No one was powerful enough to exert their will across an entire ocean.

Were they?

There were too many questions, and not enough time to answer them.

"I think I feel them," Galliana said, her eyebrows furrowing as she concentrated. "They're right there." She pointed. "Very faint, beyond that wall."

"Very good," Shara said, impressed by her niece's sensitivity. "That's exactly what I feel."

At a nod from Speevor, the Lightning Swords nudged the weeping ones away from the spot where Galliana was pointing. Shara hated seeing human beings move like that, shuffling aside out of pure instinct like beaten dogs slinking away from a cruel master. However, the lack of resistance from the ani slaves had made it relatively easy to herd them into the courtyard of the abandoned Citadel for safekeeping. Shara had no delusions that the makeshift prison would hold the wretched creatures if they came back to life, but for now it made everyone feel safer to know where they were.

Speevor looked closely at the wall and pushed aside a huge stack of cheese wheels, revealing a little hole where the bricks had been removed. Shara heard a little gasp from within. It sounded like a child.

"Is there anyone in there?" she called, kneeling at the opening.

"Shara?" A weak, cracked voice spoke from the blackness within.

Shara nearly stumbled. "Issefyn!" she shouted, crawling through the hole.

The faint glow of three separate life forces blazed to life in her magical vision.

"Issefyn, is that you?"

Speevor handed her the torch and Shara peered into the narrow, hand-carved passageway. Shara's once beautiful and stately friend was huddled at the end of the tiny niche. She held a sickly-looking boy on her lap and a pair of frightened eyes peered at Shara from around Issefyn's shoulder.

"By the Seasons!" Shara winced, wanting to cover her face at the wretched sight.

"It's me," Issefyn said, barely able to speak. "Thank the Seasons you've come."

Shara crawled in farther to help them. With a wince, Issefyn handed the child to her. Shara took the boy and began crawling backward to pull him out. He hung limp in her arms, barely conscious. The boy was so skinny that Shara wanted to weep. It took her a few moments to realize that he was Pimmor, one of the newest students at the Zelani school. That meant that the little girl behind Issefyn had to be his older sister, Fleuren.

Shara crawled out of the tiny opening and handed the boy to Galliana. Then she turned and helped Issefyn out of the hole. The Zelani teacher felt like a skeleton in her arms. Shara could feel each individual rib as she helped

Issefyn to her feet. Issefyn hung on Shara, barely able to stand.

"Have you been in there the whole time?" Shara said. "Since the school was attacked?"

Issefyn nodded. "I tried," she said, nearly crying. "I tried, but I could only save two."

Shara fought back her own tears. She'd never seen Issefyn like this, so utterly defeated. Despite her lack of magical talent, Issefyn had always carried herself like a queen, commanding respect from even the most advanced Zelani students.

Shara held her for a long time, giving her a chance to collect herself. Galliana glanced at her with a horrified expression. One of the Lightning Swords was offering the little boy a drink of water, but he was too lethargic to swallow it. The liquid just ran down the side of his face.

They hadn't found anyone this bad off, not even close.

Speevor kept trying to coax the little girl out of the tunnel, but she wouldn't come to him. "They're still out there," the child whispered. "I can hear them breathing. They're still there."

"It's all right," Speevor said. "They can't hurt you, not anymore."

Shara sent the girl a steady stream of calming energy as Speevor gently coaxed her out of the tunnel. She was glad to see that he wrapped his hand around the girl's head, covering her eyes so she couldn't see the crowd of weeping ones in the corner.

"How long has it been?" Issefyn asked. "It was so dark in there, we couldn't tell day from night . . ." She paused to catch her breath. Her dress was stained white with dried sweat. One of the Lightning Swords offered her his water pouch and helped her drink. She only got a few sips down before pushing him away. "The man came looking for us once, brought those things to find us. But he didn't see us. I . . . I hid our life lights."

"Man? What man?" Shara asked, feeling a surge of hope.

Issefyn nodded at the weeping ones. "Their master," she murmured, then swayed on her feet. Shara caught her, held her upright.

"I'm sorry," Shara said. "I'm so sorry, my friend." She motioned to the other Lightning Swords. "Quick, let's get them back to Clifftown. They need food and rest. We can go back for the weeping ones later." Shara breathed the power of the Floani form into her body and lifted Issefyn in her arms.

"It's all right, my friend. We'll get you cleaned up. You'll feel like yourself in no time."

The Lightning Swords picked up the children and followed her out of the rat-infested cheese shop.

Shara stood in the little gatehouse next to the Sunset Gate. She had given up trying to count the number of sails in the distance. The Summer Fleet had arrived, but they had anchored themselves a few miles offshore, waiting to consolidate their forces before moving forward.

Shara tapped her knuckles on the blue-white marble battlements. Ohndarien's walls would hold. The Summermen had ridiculous numbers, but she remembered how fickle they had been during poet duels. They were hardly a disciplined fighting force, and she couldn't imagine them maintaining a protracted assault with heavy losses.

She heard the sound of heavy boots on the stairs behind her and knew immediately that it was Speevor. No one else stomped like him, as if every step sent roots deep into the ground.

He walked up to her and grunted at the ships in the distance. "You were right. They seem to have brought everybody."

"It won't matter. Summermen change their minds faster than they change clothes."

Speevor grunted. The man seemed immune to hope. And despair. He planted his big feet on the ground and dared the world to move him.

"Issefyn-lani is asking for you."

"Isn't she sleeping?" Shara asked, ignoring his mistake about Issefyn's title. She was descended from the mages of Efften and knew almost as much about the ten paths as Shara did, but she had never come close to mastering any of them. She simply didn't have the talent.

"No, Shara-lani," Speevor said. "She insisted on waiting up for you."

Beloved Issefyn. Of course she would realize how important her information would be to Shara.

"Did you bring her food?" Shara asked.

"She was bathed and is eating now."

"Good," Shara said, leaving the battlements and heading for the spiral staircase that led down from the wall.

Clifftown was little more than a cluster of buildings surrounding a bay nestled at the base of a cliff. Ohndarien was built on a narrow ridge that separated the two halves of the world. The west side of the ridge had a very gentle slope, but the east side was nearly vertical. Being here always made Shara feel like she was trapped at the bottom of a well.

It only took a few minutes to get from the Sunrise Gate to the port master's residence that she and the Lightning Swords had taken over. The blue stone mansion was a bustle of activity. Shara made her way through the front room with a few quick nods and smiles before heading upstairs to her own chambers.

Issefyn sat at the little table in the corner of the room. She looked worlds better than she had when Shara had found her. Her curly black hair had been washed and combed. The cotton robe hung from painfully thin shoulders, but she sat with the stately grace that Shara remembered. A steaming bowl of fish stew and a half bowl of porridge sat before her, and she had just put a spoonful into her mouth. She smiled wearily around the bite and nodded, indicating that Shara should sit.

"My friend," Shara said, taking her hands and squeezing them. "It makes me sick to think of what you have endured."

Issefyn swallowed her mouthful and gave a weak smile. "It could always be worse, child. I could be one of them."

"You should be sleeping."

"No, there was nothing to do in that little hole except sleep. What I want to do now is fight back."

"Good," Shara said with a sigh of relief. "I could use any help you can give me."

"Then let's not waste any time. Do you think the man who created the indentured is still in the city?"

"I don't know," Shara admitted. "But we have to assume he is."

"I agree. He's undoubtedly waiting for the right moment to attack. We have to find him before he does."

"Thank you," Shara breathed. "It is so good not to face this alone. I thought you had been slain."

"There were times I wish I had been. For the first few days I was able to leave the children and go search for food, but I must have been spotted because those indentured followed me into the cheese shop."

"Is that when you saw him?"

"Yes, he followed them into the cellar, searching for me with his ani."

"But he never found you?"

Issefyn shook her head. "I don't believe I have ever put that much emotion into a simple glamour before."

"You even fooled me for a while."

"Fear is a powerful tool."

Shara nodded. "And it is easy for powerful mages to rely so much on their magical sight that they forget to use their own eyes. That's a painful lesson I had to learn for myself."

"So we agree that this mage must be very powerful."

"Yes, but also arrogant enough to miss things. We might be able to use that against him."

Issefyn frowned. "I wouldn't count on that."

"Neither will I. What did the man look like?"

"He was short, and dark-skinned. Probably of Kherish descent, but I must admit that I didn't get as good a look as I would have wanted. He had a dark beard and mustache and black hair. He wore leather."

"It is a tremendous help. I've been afraid that he was hiding in plain sight, right among us."

"That is the best place to hide, if you can manage it," Issefyn agreed.

"I was also worried that perhaps Arefaine had done all of this from a distance."

"Arefaine?" Issefyn said, raising an eyebrow. "Do you think she is involved in this somehow?"

"I know she is. If she wants to return to Efften, she'll have to go through the Silver Islanders to get there. That's why she needs the Summer Fleet. I met another sorcerer on the Floating Palace who was helping her. He mentioned that Arefaine had an agent in Ohndarien, but I didn't know who. Now we have something to go on, at least."

"Could this sorcerer from the Summer Seas be the one controlling the weeping ones here in Ohndarien?"

"Based on your description, definitely not."

Issefyn waited for more, but Shara decided not to offer any details. It still bothered her that Jesheks's body had never been found. She didn't want him to be dead, but she didn't necessarily want him skulking in shadows either.

"And you think Arefaine sent the man I saw?"

"I am almost certain, and I feel the idiot that I didn't see through her lies when I had the chance."

"It's hard to see a lie you aren't looking for," Issefyn said, giving Shara's hand a squeeze. "How do you plan to treat with the fleet once it arrives?"

"I'm not sure what you mean."

"What makes you think that Arefaine has complete control of this fleet? Why would that many Summermen join a pitched battle that gains them nothing?"

That was something Shara had not thought of before. "I had assumed that they were in league together. Their leader, Lord Vinghelt, is a dangerous fool, easily deceived. He plans on using the fleet to invade Physendria."

Issefyn shook her head. "Then he must be a fool."

"Believe me, he is."

Issefyn took another bite of her stew, chewed and swallowed. "But not everyone around him is a fool. How do you think the other princes will react if he orders them to sail to Efften instead of Physen?"

"I'm not sure."

"I don't know either, but Arefaine certainly does."

Shara paused, trying to see what Issefyn was getting at.

Issefyn continued. "If Arefaine sent a sorcerer to enslave all of Ohndarien, how difficult would it be for him to do the same to the Summer Fleet?"

Shara gasped. "We have to warn them."

Issefyn nodded. "But would they listen?"

"If we showed them proof, they might." Shara waved her hand. "It's our best chance, unless I can find this mage. He has been devilishly clever at hiding."

"And powerful, too, to have done this." She took a bit of the bread and chewed thoughtfully.

"But luckily not too powerful," Shara said. "I already fought him once.

I beat him. It wasn't even that difficult. I think that's why the coward is hiding."

Issefyn smiled thinly. "Be careful of your own overconfidence now. You've landed one blow, but the fight isn't over yet."

Shara took a deep breath, rallying her energy. "You're right, of course, but first things first. We have to keep the fleet away from Ohndarien. I have met Vinghelt before. I know how his mind works. I think I could play upon the man's fears and ambitions better than any. If he won't listen, I'll find someone who will. I'll go at once."

Issefyn put a hand on Shara's. "No, you must not."

"What?"

"Someone needs to go, but Ohndarien needs you right here. How many weeping ones are in the city waiting for their next orders? If you leave, what is to stop this mage from resurfacing?"

Shara struggled with Issefyn's words. As usual, the older woman was right. "But who can I send in my place? I can't send Faedellin. He hasn't left his daughter's side in the past eight days. And Galliana is too young, too hot-tempered. Perhaps—"

"I will go," Issefyn said.

Shara looked up. "No," she said. "I cannot ask that of you. You have been through too much."

"My dear, we have all been through too much. Who here is more quali- fied to parley? Only you. And you must stay. I'll take one of the weeping ones with me and let the Summer Princes see firsthand what awaits them in Ohndarien."

Shara looked deep into Issefyn's eyes. So much pain. She'd seen the Zelani students slaughtered in front of her. She'd huddled in that hole with no hope of rescue. "I can't let you," Shara said. "I will go. The Lightning Swords survived the weeping ones for weeks. They can do it for a few more hours while I am gone."

Issefyn's eyes flashed, and the kind matron was replaced by the severe teacher who had all but run the Zelani school for years. "Shara," she said. "You can't do everything yourself. You tried to save Brophy that way. How well did that work out?"

Shara looked at her friend, shocked by the harshness of her words. But

Issefyn had never been one to dance around the truth. That was why Shara had always trusted her.

"These people's lives are in your hands," Issefyn said. "Are you actually willing to leave them undefended so I can take a nap?"

Shara hung her head, then slowly nodded.

"You're right, of course. I simply didn't want . . ." She paused, then looked into Issefyn's eyes again. Shara nodded. "All right. But take heed. Don't be fooled by Vinghelt's smile. The man is stupid and righteous, a very dangerous combination. He would drown his own children to get ahead."

Issefyn patted Shara's hand. "I think I can handle an upstart Summer Prince with delusions of grandeur."

Shara smiled. It was so good to have someone she could talk to, someone who knew and saw things that she didn't. "You're right," she said. "Go to the Summermen. Make them understand. If anyone can do it, it's you."

"I'll be very careful." Issefyn patted her hand again. "I promise."

"It's so good to have you back," Shara said. "I didn't realize how much I missed you until now."

"Thank you, dear. It is so very good to be back."

Chapter 11

Arefaine stared at the Heartstone, feeling the emmeria swirl inside. The power within called to her: angry, frightened, longing to be free. Standing near it made her stomach turn. Vague memories of distant screams and tumbling through darkness hovered at the edge of her thoughts. Those thoughts had always been there, never quite touching her, never quite going away.

Taking a slow breath, she pushed away her feelings and concentrated on this moment, on what she could see and feel. The gemstone was nothing like she'd imagined it as a child. She'd pictured a glittering jewel, flawless in every way, but the Heartstone was uncut, unpolished. It was misshapen and scarred where diamond shards had broken off as generation after generation of Ohndariens took the Test of the Stone. Each of those shards held a piece of her sister's life force. Jazryth had given her life to create the stone and she continued to give that life, piece by piece, like a mother spider that cocooned herself to feed her hungry babies when they hatched.

She turned from the stone and looked at the emperor's body, still lying on his bed encased in white bandages. Was he her mother spider? When was she supposed to hatch?

The servants had kept the incense burners smoldering in the corners to mask the smell of death. But Arefaine couldn't smell anything yet. Death wouldn't touch that man. It wouldn't dare.

Turning away from the emperor, she looked back at the Heartstone. She'd come here after spending hours lying awake in the dark. They were nearing the tip of Vizar, more than halfway home, and she and Brophy still hadn't made love yet. Something was wrong, but she didn't know what, didn't know what was supposed to happen.

Unable to sleep, she had come here looking for answers. She had never once come back to look at the Heartstone since giving it to the emperor in Ohndarien. She didn't like to be in its presence. She couldn't help thinking of her sister locked in there, alone in the dark.

Arefaine longed to talk to her father again. She wanted to tell him about Brophy, about their possible change in plans. Was there a way to reach Efften without a war? Would she take it if there was?

The things he'd screamed at her during their fight kept tumbling through her head. She felt her chest constrict as she remembered his angry words, the way he looked when he'd said them. But was that her anger she was feeling, or was it the emmeria he claimed she was tainted with?

Arefaine reached out and picked up the stone. It felt heavier than it should be and warmer than the rest of the room. Her skin recoiled from contact with the crystal, tasting the malice within. Her ancestors had created this. They inspired the hatred she could feel on the other side of the rough surface. Could she really undo what so many had done?

"What are you doing?"

She whirled around to see Brophy standing in the door to the emperor's chambers. His father's soul light spun frenetically around his head. Why hadn't she heard him?

"What are you doing?" he said again. He reached for a sword at his hip, but it wasn't there.

"I was wondering if you were right."

"About what?" he asked, taking a step closer.

"About the emmeria, that it's still in me. That it never left."

As she put the stone back, he walked behind her and put his hands on her shoulders.

"Were you spying on me?" she asked.

"No." He rested his chin on top of her head. "My father led me here. He's spying on you."

She laughed. "Nobody seems to trust me around these stones."

"They're dangerous."

"Do you really believe they must be destroyed?"

"Yes. I do."

"Do you know how?"

"No, but the emperor believed you are the only one who can do it. He said all would be made clear to me when we reached Ohohhom."

She turned around in his arms, looked up at him. "What exactly did he tell you? What does he want me to do?"

"I honestly don't know. The Ohohhim seem to delight in half-spoken riddles."

Arefaine let out a little huff that was not quite a laugh. "Wait until we get into the belly of the beast. You won't believe how loud the silence is in the Opal Palace."

Brophy reached over her shoulder and closed the doors of the silver cabinet. Arefaine felt better the moment he did it.

"Come," Brophy said. "Let's go back to bed."

He tried to lead her away, but Arefaine wouldn't let him. "Do you really think I am tainted by the black emmeria?"

"Yes."

"How? I don't have any of your symptoms. There are no voices in my head. I am not overwhelmed by sudden rages or lingering despair. My eyes have never gone . . . dark. Like yours did before you struck that Carrier."

"My eyes turned dark?"

"Yes."

He sighed. "Do you really believe that all those decades you held the black emmeria have left you unaffected?"

"No, no, of course not. But I've grown beyond that. I'm no longer a child. I've learned to use the ani, control it."

"I can control it, too. Sometimes. When things are easy. But that day on the dock, I didn't control it. It controlled me."

"Give it time, Brophy. You'll get beyond this."

"Arefaine—" He paused.

"What? Tell me."

He shook his head.

"What?"

"Don't you see that you aren't thinking rationally, that your goals don't make any sense?"

"What do you mean?"

"How you plan to rebuild an entire city by yourself? That's ludicrous? It's like—"

"Like a child's dream?"

"Yes." He nodded, flinching at the words she put in his mouth.

"Maybe it is a child's fantasy to dream that you can go home, find the place where you belong. But I'm not dreaming it alone. There are hundreds more of us scattered across the oceans. My father has been watching over them from afar just as he had watched over me. And you."

He opened his mouth to speak, but she cut him off.

"Not everyone died in the massacre. A few of us survived by fleeing to the far corners of the world, and some of us were overseas when the attack occurred. And their descendants are still alive. Many of them have already been contacted by my father. They are waiting to join us."

"Who is waiting to join you?"

"The children of Efften. Some of them are living as nomadic herders in Upper Kherif. They still cling to the old ways, longing to go home. The descendants of Hestorn the Blind still live hidden in the Southwyldes. And there are a few others scattered across the other kingdoms. A handful of Ohndarien Zelanis remain. You, Astor, the other Children of the Seasons all carry the illuminated blood in your veins."

"Illuminated blood?"

"Don't pretend that you aren't different, that you can't do things that others only dream of."

Brophy sighed. "What I want to know is if you meant what you said before? Will you find a way to get to Efften without attacking the Silver Islanders?"

Arefaine paused. Childhood images flashed through her head. The flames. The screaming. She saw her mother's face, staring at nothing as a line of blood ran across her open eye.

Lewlem flew out of her sleeve, calming her thoughts. Arefaine took a deep breath. "I will not let those cowards stop me from restoring the City of Dreams. I will not let them win."

He opened his mouth to speak, but again she cut him off.

"But I will make you this promise. If we can find a way, we will go there first, just the two of us. We will find my father, and decide together what must be done."

Brophy considered her words carefully. His father's soul light spun around his head, and she could feel the disapproval flowing from it.

"You will know your father when you see him?"

Arefaine nodded.

"Then we will go meet the man, look him in the eye, and decide what must be done."

She felt a little thrill at his words, but not as much of one as she hoped. There was something he wasn't telling her. Something he didn't trust her with.

"Let's go back to bed," he said. And she let him lead her out of the room.

Arefaine lay next to Brophy for an hour, pretending to be asleep. When his breathing was finally steady, she carefully sat up to look at him. They had left a single candle burning in the room. The rocking of the ship threw strange shadows across his sleeping face.

She was ready to make love to him that night. They had kissed for a little while, but it didn't go any further. It never went any further. She couldn't tell what he was thinking, and it was killing her. She ached to reach into his brain and pluck out his thoughts. But she couldn't, not with his heartstone, not without his noticing.

She had removed her clothes many times in their last few nights together, but Brophy had never even taken off his shirt. She'd never seen him naked, though she had felt every part of him beneath the cloth.

She stared at him for a long time, watching his chest rise and fall, longing for more. Careful not to wake him, she touched the heartstone buried in his chest. A slight jolt went through her, and he stirred in his sleep. It was so strange to think that stone was a part of her own sister. Jazryth had gotten past the surface, but Arefaine could not.

Setting aside her disappointment, she concentrated on the moment, the eternal now. Her fingers traveled over his chest until they came across the feather hidden under his shirt. Arefaine had asked him about it once. All he told her was that it reminded him of someone very special. He may as well have named her. She knew who it was, of course. She'd seen a similar leather thong around Shara's neck, bearing a golden feather. Was that why he wouldn't take his shirt off? Was that why he wouldn't do anything more than kiss her?

Shara. The woman he'd struck back in Ohndarien? The one who'd failed to rescue him for all those years?

She longed to rip the feather from his neck, throw it into the fire. Her fingers curled into fists as she imagined grabbing him by the hair, pulling his face to hers, forcing him to look at her. Really look at her.

Brydeon's spirit light flew out of Brophy's pocket and spun around her, radiating disapproval. Arefaine snatched the light out of the air. It fluttered in her fist and Brophy squinched his eyes, groaning in his sleep. Wincing, she carefully pressed the fluttering light against the diamond shard in Brophy's pocket. Lewlem flew around her like an annoying insect. She ignored him and swirled her ani into a little spell, trapping Brophy's father within the crystal shard.

Brophy rolled over, slowly waking up. He patted the heartstone in his pocket and then reached for her, wrapping his arms around her back, pulling her close.

"What are you doing?" he rumbled sleepily.

"Just . . ."

"Just what?"

She forced herself to say the words. "Just loving you."

Brophy smiled and breathed out, half a grumble, half a purr. "Good," he whispered. "You keep doing that. That's a good thing to do."

He kissed her once and fell back asleep.

Chapter 12

Issefyn smiled in the depths of her cowl as the Sunrise Gate closed behind her little sailboat. She felt suddenly free, as if an overly tight corset had been ripped from her by powerful hands. It had been years since she left the confines of that wretched city's sanctimonious blue walls. She'd forgotten how much she hated the place and once again savored the thought of her army tearing the city down block by block and throwing it into the ocean.

It was a warm summer morning with little breeze. The thick cloak she wore would soon become uncomfortably warm, but it easily hid the containment stone she held clutched to her chest. The few hours she'd spent away from it while slipping back into Shara's confidence had been torturous. Issefyn promised herself that she would never be parted from it again.

Shara's latest little puppy strained against the oars over and over again. Issefyn watched the way his broad shoulders pulled the cloth tight across his chest with every stroke. Speevor hadn't even tried raising the sail on the calm morning. He seemed content to row them all the way to the Summer Fleet, if need be. The Lightning Sword was certainly handsome, though a bit past the age that Issefyn preferred. Shara had insisted that he accompany Issefyn on her trip to visit the Summer Fleet. She was probably tired of the fool sniffing around her skirts all day, dreaming of sampling the well-used treasures hidden within. Men were such idiots. By now it almost bored Issefyn to continue yanking them around by those little handles they were so proud of.

Shara's puppy hadn't met Issefyn's gaze since the moment she was introduced to him. His eyes had strayed to her breasts. She'd seen that, but he wouldn't look her in the face. The man probably hadn't gotten his cock damp in years. He was too busy being the perfect little soldier, with a straight back, sharp sword, and empty head. She knew the type. They amused her briefly, nothing more.

The puppy glanced backward at the indentured woman sitting stiffly in the bow of the boat. Her black eyes stared at nothing, and her ragged breath drowned out the rhythmic lapping of the oars.

"Is something wrong?" Issefyn asked.

Speevor turned back around and grunted. "I don't like that thing behind me."

"It is perfectly safe. It is well tied."

He sneered. "It's not that. It's bad for the balance of the boat. That's all."

Issefyn suppressed a grin at the man's petty lies. If there was anything she despised, it was someone pathetic enough to lie to themselves.

"I can bring it back here, if you prefer," she offered.

Speevor glanced back at the recently enslaved peasant girl with the black streaks on her precious little chubby cheeks. He grunted. "The boat would glide better if you did." Issefyn knew what he was thinking. She knew what he wanted to do between the milky thighs of the girl who couldn't resist him. He would probably close his eyes and pretend she was still a virgin.

"Of course," she said, stepping over the oars and moving to the bow of the boat.

Shara was convinced that sending an ani slave as an example would help convince the Summerfools to stay out of Ohndarien. Seeing a desirable young woman bathed in black tears would be more than the prancing half-wits could bear. Just as with everything else, the Zelani mistress agreed to everything Issefyn suggested. The baseborn whore was becoming easier and easier to manipulate. Issefyn regretted that she wouldn't have more time to play with the little bitch before ordering her pets to strip her naked and give her the death she so truly deserved. Time was short, but Shara would crawl before the end. There was no doubt of that.

As Issefyn sat down next to the slave, she drew a tiny dagger from her sleeve and quickly cut the ropes around its wrists. Before she could cut the bonds around its ankles, Speevor spun around, staring at the knife. He was on his feet in an instant, sword in hand.

"Hold him," Issefyn whispered into the slave's ear, projecting her desires through the threads of emmeria that connected them.

The girl leapt forward, stumbling over her still-bound feet. She fell face-forward onto the bench where Speevor had been rowing. The oaf beat on her with his sword like a man chopping wood, but the blade bounced off.

He gave up on the slave and lunged toward Issefyn. The peasant girl tackled him as he leapt. They fell in a tangled heap, grappling with each other in the bottom of the boat. The contest was fierce, but short-lived. Within a few moments her pet had the much larger man wrapped up in an unbreakable grip.

"Are you mad?" Shara's puppy shouted, blood spraying from his spilt lip.

She drew the containment stone from her cloak and knelt next to him. He thrashed wildly, but couldn't break free.

"What do you think you're doing?" he screamed, his voice cracking at the end.

"Putting you in your place," she whispered, pressing her lips to his.

Emmeria surged through Issefyn's body as she reached into the screaming man's life force and wrapped her dark fingers around the blazing light at the center of his chest. He fought her. Weakly. Pathetically. And in a moment she felt his soul give way. His entire body spasmed and Issefyn heard the scrape of wood on wood. She looked up in time to see the oar he'd kicked come swinging around straight at her face.

There was a loud crack and everything went black for a moment. The boat lurched and she was suddenly in the water.

Her hands went to her face, unable to stop the pain racing through her skull. Where was her stone? She'd lost her stone. Issefyn searched for it, kicking desperately, but her limbs were slow to respond. She knew she was sinking, her heavy cloak was pulling her down, but couldn't tell which way was up. She flailed about, unable to open her eyes, fighting to find her magic, to connect to her power.

She finally managed to open her eyes and spun around looking for the surface. She found it, but it was so far away and her arms were so heavy. She saw the little boat, a dark blotch against the distant sunlight. Something leapt from the boat, knifing through the water. It was coming toward her, dark and unknowable. Where was her stone? Who had her stone?

Issefyn woke to the pain of retching and the sting of seawater pouring through her nose. Someone pounded on her back and she retched some more. Salt burned from her lips to the depths of her lungs.

"Come, Mother, where's your dignity."

Issefyn's hands clenched into fists and she looked up from the bottom of the boat. Victeris leaned casually against the mast. The bovine ani slave sat on the bench next to him, effortlessly pulling the oars.

"It's just a little bump on the head," Victeris said with a half grin.

She felt her forehead, wincing as her finger slid into the gash that had split her skin down to the bone. Her palm came away covered with blood.

Issefyn tried to take a deep breath, but ended up in another uncontrollable coughing spasm.

"Where's my stone?" she finally managed to get out.

"Right behind you."

Issefyn turned to see Speevor behind her. His hair and clothes were soaked with seawater and the black stains had started to form on his cheeks. He held her containment stone cradled in one of his weathered hands.

Desperately, she reached out with her magic, following the tendrils of emmeria into the empty shell of a man. "Give it to me," she demanded.

Speevor did nothing, staring blankly forward as if he'd never heard her.

Victeris laughed. "That's not going to work anymore."

Issefyn tried again with all her strength. Again, Speevor did nothing.

"Mother, that's *me* he's holding in his hand. That stone is as much a part of me as your hand is a part of you. You can't possibly imagine that I would put myself back into your control?"

Issefyn leapt upon the stone, tried to tear it from the indentured's grasp. She yanked on it with all of her might, but the stone wouldn't budge. Speevor ignored her as if he were a mountain she was trying to pull down with her bare hands.

"Dignity, Mother. Dignity."

"Shut up!" Issefyn whirled on the shade as he calmly contemplated his fingernails. "You're not my son! You're nothing like my son! You have what you want, now go ahead. Crack the stone and let the black emmeria sweep over the world. Bask in the smoking ruin of your legacy!"

Victeris chucked. He started to speak, but she cut him off.

"Enough of your games. You're not Victeris. You're the first of the Twelve, father of Efften, betrayer of Oh, and wretched prisoner in your own tower. I know you, shade. You're Efflum the Black and your folly destroyed our people."

Victeris sketched a slight bow. "Efflum the Black? I must admit I've been called that before, but not by my friends."

The image of her son faded in the bright sunlight, slowly evolving into a different image of a severe man with narrow eyes and long black curly hair that cascaded down his shoulders over a floor-length black robe.

"It appears the nature of our relationship must change," the new image said. He spoke slowly in exquisitely polished words. The very tone of them made Issefyn feel smaller, like a child on the edge of tears.

"I hate you," she whispered.

He raised one thin eyebrow. "What parent hasn't heard that from a child?"

"I'm not your child, any more than I am your mother."

"Perhaps not directly, but you are of the illuminated line of Efften. You may not be my granddaughter's granddaughter, but we are kin nonetheless."

"What are you waiting for? Destroy the stone. Release your venom upon the world as you tried to get me to do so many times."

Efflum nodded, his face returning to a perfect Ohohhim mask. "That is no longer my intention."

Issefyn snorted, hating the lingering taste of salt down the back of her throat. "What? Have you suddenly evolved somehow?"

"I suppose I have."

Issefyn glanced at the stone in the ani slave's hand. She needed it back, needed it more than anything.

"I was alone too long," the shade said with what sounded like regret. "I was desperate to escape and was ready to employ the crudest methods to attain my release. A horde of creatures overwhelmed by emmeria would probably have been enough to overcome the Islanders that guard my prison and tear down the walls that confine me. I admit that at one time such methods appealed to my sense of rage." Issefyn watched the shade's face. Despite the illusion he was hiding behind, he did a poor job of concealing the emotions behind his words. "But now," he continued, "I have much better options to choose from."

Issefyn knew the shade's words were lies, all lies, but she could not see what his goal was, what he was trying to manipulate her into. "You speak of Arefaine?"

"Yes. The child is bringing our legacy to me as we speak. She will liberate me. She will bring the Illuminated back to the City of Dreams."

There! Issefyn thought. That is the heart of his madness. He believes the same lies as the girl. He wants to bring the cursed city back from the dead. That was something she could use against him.

"Is that why you pulled me out of the water?" she asked.

"Yes. You carry the illuminated spark in your veins. We are family, you and I, and family is the only thing that matters."

Issefyn hid her contempt. She'd heard the stories about Efflum. Some of his own children had helped imprison him. And there were rumors that he'd strangled his eldest son in a fit of rage. He loved his family the way a rapist loved his cock.

Issefyn gathered her breath and stood in the little boat. "Why didn't you tell me this before?"

The shade chuckled. "You didn't need to know before, but there is a battle coming. A battle you cannot win on your own."

"Really?"

"Issefyn. Child. Your sister is a better sorceress than you. You could turn that entire fleet into your servants." He pointed at the Summer Fleet in the distance. "But if you led that army against Shara, she would simply take it from you."

Issefyn breathed through her teeth, biding her time, waiting as she did so well. "We'll see about that."

"No, we won't. The stone is in my power now. I will be the one to lead the Summermen against Ohndarien's walls. It has been my intention all along."

"Lucky for you that a stray oar swung so nicely into line with your plans."

"Luck had nothing to do with it."

Issefyn flexed her fingers, feeling the presence of the stone hovering just out of reach.

"Then why am I here? Why work though me if you are so powerful."

"I wanted to get to know you, wanted to see what kind of person you are. You certainly weren't shy about sharing your ambitions." He paused. "Which I must admit are less generous than mine."

Issefyn suppressed a sneer. What a fool. At least she didn't lie to herself about her ambitions, dress them up in some ridiculous sentimentality about lost family.

"Until I got that stone out of your hands," he continued, "I never had the power to redirect your aspirations."

"Redirect them?" Issefyn said, keeping her face an implacable mask.

"Yes. I would like you to join me on Efften. I would like you to set aside your personal objectives, your desire for revenge upon those who were merely defending themselves."

Issefyn scoffed. "Like the Silver Islanders were merely defending themselves?"

The shade showed his teeth. "Don't test me."

Issefyn swallowed as a spike of fear shot though her. She gritted her teeth until she forged the fear into hate, something she could use. "You truly can't see into the hearts of others, can you?"

"Every parent needs to turn a blind eye every now and then. I know who you are, Issefyn, daughter of cowards, wife of fools, mother of monsters. I hold little faith that you can ever heal the wound that drives you. But you are family. Blood calls to blood and I will give you one more chance."

"One more chance to what, kneel at your feet in adoration?"

"No. One more chance to stand by my side, to rejoin the family."

"Rejoin the family? Do you think I'm some kind of child?"

"You certainly act like a child, a particularly petulant and disobedient child."

Issefyn glared at the shade in front of her. She would find this man and kill him. She swore it. But she would have to tread lightly. "What do you want me to do?" she asked.

"Do what you always do. Hover in the shadows. Lie to me. Try to manipulate me. Plot against me."

Issefyn snorted. "And what will you do?"

"What any parent does. I will love you and hope your heart changes before it is too late."

Issefyn clenched her fists, aching to claw her nails across the fool's face.

"Very well," she finally managed to say. "We will wait and see whose heart changes."

The shade nodded once and then pointed at the Summer Fleet in the distance. "Come, we have family business to attend to."

Chapter 13

*L*awdon awoke at the sound of approaching boot steps. She shivered in the damp darkness of the leaky hold, wincing at the manacles that bit into her wrists. Only a thin shaft of dusty sunlight crept under the door overhead, and she could barely see the dim outline of the crates and barrels stacked around her. Rolling over, she placed a hand on Mikal's chest to make sure he was still breathing. He shivered in his sleep, but he was alive, thank the deep.

As the steps grew closer, she leaned over and kissed him on the forehead, feeling the dried blood that matted his hair against his scalp. Her stomach knotted at the memory of the blow that had felled him. She'd never felt so stupid. So helpless.

She had been so confident back in Port Royal when she and Mikal had forced the crook-backed sailor to spill his guts.

The man was working for Llysa Munkholtz, the second daughter of Lord Havect Munkholtz. The Lady Munkholtz was holding the children on her ship awaiting Lawdon and Mikal's capture so she could deliver the entire family to Lord Vinghelt on the Summer Fleet.

Stupidly, Lawdon thought she and Mikal could sneak aboard the ship and rescue the children. But Llysa and her men had been waiting for them.

It seemed such a foolish plan in retrospect. Lawdon had underestimated Vinghelt's hold on the Waveborn. She still thought of Llysa as the rebellious teenager she had gone to school with for a short time. Despite Llysa's higher station, the two of them had almost been friends. They had both been rebellious in their youth and Lawdon had liked the way Llysa downplayed her stunning beauty, completely undermining it with a vicious and filthy tongue that lacerated any starry-eyed would-be suitors. By the time she was seventeen there wasn't a single man on land or sea who could tell her what to do. She reminded Lawdon more than a little of Brezelle.

Lawdon couldn't believe such a headstrong girl would ever blindly follow a man like Vinghelt. But she was wrong. Very very wrong.

The boots stopped overhead, the latch creaked, and the hatch flew open. Lawdon squinted at the harsh light, momentarily blinded.

"Captain Reignholtz," Llysa Munkholtz said, her voice tinged with regret. Her silhouette was a dark blot in front of the sun. Behind her lurked her hulking redheaded first mate, who'd felled Mikal with two brutal punches.

"The Summer Fleet is within sight," Llysa said. "I've brought you some warm water if you want to wash up before your meeting with Lord Vinghelt."

Lawdon sat up, her manacles clinking.

Why was Llysa so terrified of Vinghelt? The woman had blithely endured countless punishments from her schoolmasters for her insubordination. Yet now she seemed to be crushed under Vinghelt's thumb like everyone else. Llysa had no need for the reward placed on Lawdon and Mikal's capture. But here she was, delivering an old friend into the hands of a madman.

Llysa moved down the steep steps into the hold. Lawdon squinted, drew a deep breath, and tried to put as much stern dignity into her voice as she could.

"You don't have to follow him," she said.

Llysa paused on the stairs. Lawdon could see the side of her face in the light now, though most of her remained in shadow. The line of her wide mouth was turned down slightly.

"I have a crew to take care of, Lawdon. Surely you can understand that." She descended the last two steps and placed a steaming bucket of water at the base of the stairs. She laid a clean, thick rag next to the bucket.

"Llysa—"

"I'll come back for you within the hour," she said, turning and thumping up the steps.

"We can still fight him. We can stop this madness."

Llysa paused in the hatchway and turned. Her features were hidden by the bright light. "Summer's over, Captain. Why are you the only one who can't see that?"

"Can you at least tell me where my brothers and sisters are?" Lawdon pleaded. "Are they all right?"

Llysa paused for a moment before shaking her head and slamming the door back into its casing. The hold plunged into darkness once again.

"So . . ." Mikal grunted, shifting. "Is our little cruise over so soon?"

Lawdon gave a smile. "You're supposed to be dying," she said, groping for his hand in the darkness.

He twined his fingers in hers and coughed, his voice rough. "If that smell is me, I think I already am."

Lawdon let go of his hand and reached for the bucket of steaming water. Her chains clinked as they pulled tight. Her fingers fumbled with the edge of the bucket, tipping it toward herself until she could get a grip.

She dunked the cloth, wrung it out, and brought it to his face. She felt him tense, but he didn't say anything as she pressed it against the cut on his forehead.

"I hate men who wear rings," he said.

"You wear three rings," she said.

"And my self-loathing is legendary."

She wiped softly across his face, dunked the rag, and did the other side.

"You realize this is all your fault," he said.

"Mine?"

"Indeed. Llysa's men would never have captured us if you let me fight them."

"There were nine of them. Half of them had bows."

"You say that like arrows can't be dodged."

"If they were shooting blame or responsibility at us, I have no doubt you could dodge." She shrugged in the dark.

"I think I could have taken four of them," he said, "leaving only five for you."

"Well, obviously I could have handled five," she said, "but I thought you'd never fought more than one person at a time."

"I'm good at improvising."

"Then improvise a way out of this," she said.

"One that doesn't involve our deaths?"

She laughed. "Preferably."

"Give me a minute. I'll come up with something."

"I have no doubt."

Lawdon dipped the rag into the pail and washed her own face, letting Mikal dream about his escape plan, which no doubt included outfighting a dozen men, leaping from ship to ship, slicing hawsers, and catching a fierce wind that filled only their sails, dodging arrows the entire way.

She couldn't help hoping that her brothers and sisters were on the same ship, or one nearby. The Summer Fleet was poised to lay siege to Ohndarien in an insane quest to reach the Great Ocean. Had they forgotten everything they stood for, everything Salice Mick had taught them?

"How did it come this far?" she murmured. "Betrayed and bound by our own countrymen."

He didn't say anything for a time, and then: "How do lynch mobs form? How do gang rapes start? Why do big kids pick on little kids?" he said softly. "Sometimes people are . . ."

"What?" she asked softly. "What are we?"

"Stupid, sad, lost. We'll do anything to feel part of something important."

"Is that why men do it? Is that why they go to war, to feel important?"

"Pretty much."

"I'm so glad I don't have a penis," she said with a sigh.

"I'm glad you don't have one either; two of them in the same bed can be devilishly awkward."

"I'm sure I could manage if I needed to. I'm good at improvising." She thought she felt his smile in the darkness, but it didn't warm her as it might have yesterday. Her own helplessness made their prison suffocating, and she found her breath coming quicker and thought of Reignholtz.

You cannot fight the wind any more than you can fight the sea. When she blows against you, you take what she gives, and you use it to your advantage.

Lawdon sighed. She hated waiting. When she spoke, she tried to put a playful tone in her voice. "At least our jailer is pleasing to the eye."

"You think so?" he replied. "I prefer my redheads without the bristly beards and tobacco-stained teeth."

"Llysa," Lawdon said. "Not her first mate."

"Oh, yes, the slinky Lady Munkholtz. Were you planning to seduce her to secure our freedom? Just say the word, I won't get in your way." He paused. "I'll stand very *close* to your way, but not directly in your way."

"How noble of you."

"I live to serve, my lady."

She gave his shoulder a quick squeeze. A few weeks ago Mikal would have fallen over himself to sing Llysa's praises and prattle on for hours about her beauty, but he'd not yet said a word. It was an act, of course. Lawdon knew that Mikal noticed and appreciated other women, but he kept his thoughts to himself. It was a little gift to her, like his quiet smiles and brief touches, and she treasured them all.

"So how is that plan coming?" she asked.

"I'm already finished."

"Oh?"

"Yes. We break our chains and rush through that hatch as soon as they open it."

Lawdon waited for the rest, but he stayed silent.

"That's a genius plan," she said.

"First rule of dueling. Never think more than one verse ahead," he said. "It kills the poetry."

"I see. Well, there's nothing worse than dead poetry."

"True. You wouldn't believe the taste it leaves in your mouth on the way out."

"Or the scars it leaves in your ears on the way in."

Lawdon waited for another snappy reply, but for once Mikal didn't have one.

"So we wait?" she asked.

"We could nibble on each other."

Lawdon was jolted awake by Mikal's gentle touch on her shoulder. She'd fallen asleep against his chest.

"They return, my lady," he said.

She shook her head and sat up. It felt like she had been asleep for hours. The hold door creaked open and slammed against the deck. Moonlight streamed into the hold as Llysa's slender figure crept down the steps. Her movements were slow and stiff, and she was panting like someone who'd just been violently seasick.

"What's wrong with her?" Mikal whispered.

Lawdon fought a sudden surge of panic as Llysa stumbled off the last step and lurched toward them.

"No," Lawdon whispered, backing away as far as her chains would let her. Without saying a word, Llysa grabbed the chains connecting them to the floor of the hold and snapped them as if they were string.

Lawdon gasped as she and Mikal were yanked to their feet and dragged toward the steps.

Mikal leapt forward and wrapped his chain around Llysa's throat, putting his knee on her back and pulling with all his might. Lawdon was sure Llysa's neck was about to snap, but she simply kept walking forward, dragging the two of them up the stairs.

Lawdon punched her in the kidney and nearly screamed. Her body was like stone! Llysa ignored the blow and dragged the two of them up the last few steps onto the deck.

Mikal was on his feet first and turned to face their captor. "Fessa!" he cried, backing away from her, and then Lawdon saw. Inky tears streaked down Llysa's cheeks. Her face was utterly blank, and her eyes glittered pure black in the moonlight. The woman she had known was gone. Utterly gone.

Lawdon glanced around desperately. The rest of Llysa's crew stood inert on the deck of the ship. All of them had the same black tears.

"What's happened to them?" Mikal said, his eyes wide.

Lawdon felt her knees grow weak, and she grabbed Mikal's shirt to keep from falling.

"It's the infection," she whispered. "The one that ran through Ohndarien."

When they had dropped Shara off in the Petal Islands, the Ohndarien refugees had told wild stories of an infection of black emmeria that had run through their city. They had called the victims weeping ones, but she had hardly believed them at the time.

"But we're not in Ohndarien," Mikal said.

Llysa, or what remained of her, kept walking forward, dragging them to the rail, where her ship was lashed to one three times its size. The far deck was packed with Summermen standing like statues. Each of them had the same streaks down their faces, shining black in the moonlight.

"What is that leaking from their eyes?" Mikal murmured.

"The infection must have spread," she murmured, looking at the other ships around them. There were a hundred ships in the Summer Fleet. Were they all like this?

Beyond the fluttering banners of the Summer Fleet rose the cliffs of Ohndarien. Shara was in that city. She was supposed to have stopped this.

Llysa led them up the plank to the larger ship and through a crowd of her countrymen all staring blankly ahead. They panted like their hearts were about to burst, as if each pained breath would be their last. It made Lawdon want to kill them all, put them out of their misery and then run, run away and never stop.

Gritting her teeth, Lawdon dodged through the throng of weeping ones, trying to hold her breath and avoid touching any of them.

"What do we do?" Mikal whispered to her.

"I don't know," she replied. "I don't know."

Llysa dragged them toward the back of the ship. The windows of the aft stateroom were curtained, but she could see light coming from within. Llysa opened the door and ushered Lawdon inside. Mikal tried to follow, but Llysa barred his path with her arm, shoved Lawdon inside, and shut the door.

She stumbled into an enormous stateroom. It was opulent to a fault, dripping with gold and silks. A cut-crystal chandelier filled with candles lit the room bright as day. Six weeping ones stood at attention along the walls. A dark-haired man leaned over an oak desk covered with scattered charts and navigation equipment. He looked up the moment she entered.

Vinghelt.

He stared at her for a moment, his eyes narrowing, and Lawdon was surprised to see that his eyes were blue. He wasn't infected.

"Lady Reignholtz, we meet again," he said graciously. "Please come in." He walked around the desk and reached for her hand. She pulled back, not letting him touch her. He held his hand out for a moment, then let it slip to his side.

"What happened?" Lawdon asked through stiff lips. "What's wrong with them?"

"Wrong with them?" Vinghelt laughed and waved his hand about in a sweeping gesture. "These are the chosen of the goddess. They have all received her blessing."

"Blessing?!" Lawdon cried. "They're barely human!"

"No, they are more than human," Vinghelt corrected. Quick as a snake, he drew his dagger and dragged the edge along Llysa's cheek. The blade pushed her skin tight against the bone but left no scratch. "The goddess has made us invincible."

For a moment Lawdon was so stunned that she couldn't find anything to say. Vinghelt waited with that smug smile.

"You don't actually believe that, do you?" she finally spat. "You don't actually believe the goddess had anything to do with this?"

"Who else?" Vinghelt said, looking genuinely surprised. "Fessa set us upon this path. She choose me to lead us to victory against Ohndarien and then the Silver Islanders."

"Silver Islanders? What are you talking about?"

"We have allied with Ohohhom and the Lady Arefaine against a common foe."

"What common foe?"

"The Silver Islanders fear the goddess's growing influence in their waters. They have been supporting the Physendrian rebels against us. They were behind the burning of the Floating Palace."

"You were behind the burning of the Floating Palace!" Lawdon exploded.

He laughed again. "Where do you come up with these wild theories? The world is full of people seething with greed and jealousy of our Eternal Summer. The Silver Islanders started this war. They have attacked our very way of life. We are simply defending ourselves."

She gaped at him. "I can't tell whether you're the dumbest man in history, or the most wretched coward I've ever seen."

Vinghelt paused, his lips pulled back into a quick snarl. "I truly feel sorry for you," he finally said. "You have been poisoned from childhood with fear and lies. You can't see the face of the goddess when she is right in front of you."

"All I see in front of me . . ." Lawdon started, but her voice trailed off when she suddenly saw a shimmering green figure appear behind Vinghelt's left shoulder. She stared at the shimmering shape, suddenly feeling searing black worms slithering in her stomach. Slowly the figure solidified, and Lawdon started in amazement at the most beautiful woman she had ever seen. She was completely naked, and blue-green hair cascaded down her body, flowing and shimmering like a waterfall.

Lawdon felt an overwhelming urge to kneel, but stopped herself and stared harder at the creature. Within the majestic beauty she saw another figure, a tall, skinny woman in her late fifties who looked like she hadn't eaten in a week. Her body was frail, her cheeks sunken, her gray hair unkempt and brittle, but her gaze glittered with a malevolence that made Lawdon's flesh crawl. Next to her stood a man dressed like an Ohndarien Lightning Sword. His eyes also dripped black, and he held an ebony stone tightly under one arm.

"I tire of this game, Lord Vinghelt," the skinny woman to his left said. "It is time this one received her blessing."

Lawdon started backing toward the door.

"As you say." Vinghelt nodded sagely, staring adoringly at the crone who made herself look like a goddess.

Lawdon ran for the door. She flung it open and crashed into someone just outside. Hands like steel clamped on her arms. She fought back, but Llysa's first mate slammed her against the wall. Beyond him, another weeping one held Mikal's arms pinned against his sides.

"Lawdon!" Mikal shouted, but the weeping one clamped a hand over his mouth before he could say any more.

The skinny woman emerged from the stateroom, the Lightning Sword with the black stone right behind her. The image of the naked goddess she wore about herself like a cloak wavered as she walked. Her grin spread as she slipped past Lawdon.

"Him first, don't you think?" she asked Lawdon with a cold chuckle.

"No! Stay away from him!" Lawdon yanked against her captor, but she might as well have tried to break steel bars.

Mikal's feet scrabbled on the deck as he tried to shove himself backward. The witch reached out and touched him on the chest. He screamed, the sound muffled by the hand over his mouth, and his body convulsed as if she were pulling his heart out through his ribs.

"Mikal!" Lawdon shrieked, struggling against the red-bearded brute who was squeezing her so tight she couldn't draw another breath.

The skinny woman dug her fingernails into Mikal's skin, and he arched his back until his feet were lifted from the deck. The tendons and veins stood out on his neck as he flung his body back and forth against his captor's unbreakable grip. The hideous woman smiled at his pain, seeming to relish it.

"Stop it!" Lawdon shouted. "Stop it!" She screamed the words until Llysa's first mate reached up and muffled her with his callused hand.

The woman turned to Lawdon and smiled. "Would you like me to stop, dear?"

Lawdon nodded fiercely, and the witch suddenly yanked her hand away from Mikal. He spasmed once and then slumped forward, limp as a dead eel.

"Mikal!" Lawdon shrieked into her captor's palm.

The weeping one dropped Mikal, and he fell to the deck in a heap, staring blankly at the sky.

"Stand up," the skinny woman said. He rose to his feet and turned to face Lawdon. His breathing was ragged and quick, and his eyes were solid black. Obsidian tears welled in the corners, ready to spill over.

"And now, my dear," the woman said, turning to her. "Are you ready to join your little man here and those precious brothers and sisters of yours?" She laughed as she reached for Lawdon's chest. "Are you ready to be blessed?"

Lawdon tried to scream, but she couldn't even do that.

Chapter 14

ello!" Astor shouted so loudly his throat burned. "Is! Any! Body! There!" His voice echoed off the hundred foot walls, but there was no reply.

He clenched his teeth and squeezed the railing around the ship's tiny crow's nest. They had been stuck outside the Sunset Gate for more than an hour, and it was nearly dark. Astor thought he saw the face of a sentry in the guardhouse when they first called for the gate to be opened. But the boy had run away. How could the gate be undefended? Even the Windmill Wall was empty. Several of the mills weren't running. Something was terribly, terribly wrong with the city. But he couldn't see inside to find out what.

Astor had never been locked outside of Ohndarien's walls before. He'd never realized how frustrating it could be. His eyes kept scanning the fortifications for any crack or crevice he might use to climb inside. But there was nothing. The walls were perfect, unscalable. He had heard the stories of how Brophy had entered the city through one of the windmills' screws, but he wasn't ready to try anything that crazy, not yet.

"Anything?" Bendrick called from below.

Astor shook his head at his second-in-command. "I can't see a thing."

Their ship was small, her mast only thirty feet high. There could be a whole army atop Ohndarien's walls, and they wouldn't see them from here.

Bendrick frowned and started climbing up to the crow's nest. With a grunt he threw a leg over the railing and joined Astor on the tiny platform.

"Hello!" Astor called again. Again there was no answer.

"Enough yelling," Bendrick said. "You're starting to sound like a dying toad."

Astor sighed. "Where could they be?"

Bendrick shook his head. "I didn't expect a hero's welcome after we sailed off without permission, but I did expect some sort of reception."

"Yeah, I spent the whole trip back here imagining my father ripping the sash from my shoulder and sending me out the Physendrian Gate. Now it would almost be worth it to see him and know he's all right."

Astor couldn't get Brophy's warning out of his head. Had the city already been betrayed? Was the Summer Fleet within her walls?

"Hello!" Astor yelled again, wincing as he did.

There was no reply except the echo of his voice and the gentle lapping of the surf against the base of Ohndarien's walls.

"Shara, wait!"

Shara paused, turning back to look along the top of the Water Wall. Someone was running after her. Galliana, she realized after checking the girl's life force. Shara was tempted to keep on running, but she forced herself to wait for her niece.

Shara had run all the way from Clifftown when she first heard the news. The breathless boy had come from the Sunset Gate. Between gasps he said a ship had arrived from the west carrying a small group of Lightning Swords. A man on board looked like the Sleeping Warden.

Galliana caught up with her in a few moments. Her breathing was strong and steady as she slowed to a stop right next to Shara. The young woman's proficiency with the Floani form was growing stronger every day.

"I heard the news," Galliana said. "Do you think it's Brophy?"

Shara shook her head. "No. It's probably Astor returning from his quest for the Heartstone. The boy at the gate probably just confused the two of them."

Galliana nodded. "I'm sure he'd rather see a hero returning than a deserter."

Shara wouldn't have used the word "deserter" for what Astor and the others did, but they certainly wouldn't receive a warm welcome. Still, Shara couldn't shake the hope that Brophy had decided to return with Astor.

"Either way," Shara said, "I need to see them as soon as possible."

Galliana nodded and the two women began to run along the aqueduct side by side. Shara matched her breathing to Galliana's as their feet flew along the top of the Water Wall. She hated to leave Clifftown with the Summer Fleet within sight, but Summermen hadn't made a move for the entire day. It looked like Issefyn had convinced them to keep their distance, but Shara couldn't be sure until she met with Vinghelt face-to-face.

The two Zelani had reached the edge of the Citadel when Shara skidded to a stop. Her stomach lurched as if the ground were crumbling beneath her. "Where are they?" she gasped.

Galliana turned to look where Shara was pointing and stumbled, nearly falling on her face. "Oh no."

Shara stared at the empty courtyard within the Citadel, far below. The weeping ones were gone.

"Did you give orders to move them?" Galliana asked, grasping at straws.

Shara shook her head. Every last weeping one in the city had been herded into the Citadel's high-walled courtyard. There had been thousands of them in there, unmoving, unblinking. Desperately, she looked for a way they could have gotten out, but all the doors she could see were still locked. The gates were still closed.

Shara turned to Galliana, and she could see the fear in her niece's eyes. "How could anyone possibly . . ." the girl started, but couldn't finish.

"I have no idea," Shara whispered. "I got a report on them an hour ago. They were fine. Just standing there, doing nothing, like always."

Shara shook off her daze and steadied her breathing, gathering her magic as quickly as she could. She had to find who was controlling them. He couldn't use that kind of power without being noticed.

Galliana tugged on her sleeve. "Shara," she breathed.

Shara opened her eyes to see a weeping one ascending the last few steps of the spiral staircase that led up from the heart of the Citadel. He had been an older man with thin gray hair and stooped shoulders before he'd been turned. He had probably walked with a cane, but now he shuffled along like a withered hunchback.

The stooped ani slave was followed by another one. And another. And another.

The line of weeping ones marched slowly and silently onto the roof of the Citadel, blocking their path westward. She whirled around and saw another group emerge from a staircase farther along the battlements, cutting off their escape back along the Water Wall. They were trapped.

"Use your breath," Shara whispered to her niece, pushing her fear down. "Be calm. Be ready."

The weeping ones continued emerging from below until there were dozens of them on either side. They shuffled closer and closer. Shara glanced into the empty courtyard below. It was an eighty-foot drop. She might be able to make it. Galliana wouldn't.

The two groups of weeping ones stopped a few paces away on either side of them.

"Shara-lani," one of the female ani slaves said in a man's voice. "It is an honor to see you again." The soulless woman spoke without inflection or expression. Her black eyes stared forward, unfocused.

Shara tentatively reached out with her magic, testing her. Tainted emmeria swept around and through her body like an unseen wind. It swirled around all of them.

"You're the voice," Shara said as her magic swelled within her body. "The voice in the black emmeria."

"I am much more than that," the woman said. A black droplet fell from her chin onto her tattered shirt. "I apologize for the crudeness of my attempts at communication before, but my options have been limited."

"What do you want?"

"The same thing that you want, lovely Shara-lani."

"I doubt that."

"I want to be with the ones I love. I want to keep them safe."

Shara thought of Brophy, imagined him lying with his head on Arefaine's lap as she caressed the blackened Heartstone.

"Who do you love?"

"My children. My grandchildren. My great-great-grandchildren. I love those who shine the brightest. And you and your niece shine brighter than any others in the world."

"I disagree."

"Your humility is part of your charm. In fact, you remind me of someone I knew long, long ago. The two of you share the same heart." The voice sighed, but the weeping one it came from showed no expression whatsoever. "You are extraordinary, Shara. And you, Galliana, could be as powerful. You two are children of Efften, the illuminated blood flows like fire through your veins. Your days of exile among these wretched shepherds and merchants will soon be over. Once again we will be among our own kind in a place where we can thrive in complete peace and safety. I am building a garden, and I would like the two of you to come to live in it."

Shara shook her head slowly, trying to understand. It was the same voice that spoke to her every time she worked with the black emmeria, but that voice had been angry and desperate. Now he sounded quietly confident like a polite general treating with an enemy prisoner.

"I am no more tempted by these lies than any others you have offered."

"I have never lied to you, I assure you," the weeping woman continued. "Your inheritance awaits you, our garden has already begun to bloom."

"Sorry, I like the garden I already have."

"Shara-lani!" Shara flinched as every weeping one within sight spoke with the same voice at the same instant. She suddenly felt like a little girl again, waiting to be hit by her father.

"I am a patient man," dozens of weeping ones said in perfect chorus. "But do not test my good nature."

Shara glanced at Galliana. Her niece had lost control of her breath. She was starting to panic.

"The attack against this city has begun."

Shara glanced to the east. A line of black smoke rose from the far side of the ridge. Clifftown was under attack.

"Ohndarien will fall within the hour," the mob of black-eyed slaves continued. "Once the locks are repaired, we will be continuing on to Efften. The two of you will be joining me."

Shara reached out and grabbed Galliana's hand. She sent her niece a stream of ani.

"I don't expect you to agree," the chorus of weeping ones said. "Children rarely do what is best for them, but it is the parent's job to remain firm."

Shara squeezed Galliana's hand twice and started to run. Her niece was right behind her and Shara charged at weeping ones in front of them.

"No!" Shara shouted, throwing a flood of ani into the minds of those closest to her. She knocked them aside with her shoulder, charging through the crowd.

The weeping ones rushed at them from all sides. Hands wrapped around Shara's arms and hair. "No!" Shara shouted again, and more fell from her path.

"Back!" Galliana shouted as they surged forward, helping to clear a path.

Shara screamed over and over again, easily stunning those around her, but every time one of them fell limp, another arrived to take its place. She strained against the wall of bodies, but they would not budge.

Galliana's hand was ripped from Shara's grip. She fought to locate her niece in the crowd. Shara flung her ani against her attackers, desperate to get free. Each attempt was feebler than the last.

"No!" she screamed again, but there was no power to it beyond the sound of her own voice.

A chilly hand wrapped around her face. Cold fingers locked around her mouth and nose, cutting off her breath. Shara flung her head from side to side, but she could not escape the grip. Her chest spasmed, and she caught a glimpse of Galliana lying limp in the arms of the weeping ones.

"Hush, child," one of them whispered in her ear. "Everything will be all right. Everything will be all right."

Astor's lungs burned as he pushed himself faster, farther. He ran with the Sword of Autumn naked in his hand, praying he could find a way to the battle.

They had waited outside the Sunset Gate, until Bendrick noticed the column of black smoke. Astor and the other Lightning Swords gave up on getting into the city and decided to run around it instead. They put ashore, scrambled up the ragged cliffs to the north of the Sunset Gate, and started running overland.

Astor had outdistanced his companions by over a hundred yards by the time he reached the Quarry Gate. The blue-white marble wall was still cracked where the corrupted whale had thrown itself against the stone just a few weeks before.

Astor shouted to the gatekeepers, if there were any, but there was no response. Casting about, he found a stone the size of two fists and snatched it up. He ran to the metal doors of the gate and pounded the stone against them over and over again. The echoing boom from each strike hurt Astor's ears, but there was no reply. Where was everyone?

Cursing, Astor gave up on the gate and ran back to the quarry floor. Bendrick and the others were still well behind him. He knew it was dumb to rush into battle alone. It was the same dumb mistake he'd made fighting the corrupted sharks before Brophy awoke, but he had to at least see what they were facing. He had to know if they had a chance.

Turning from his friends, Astor ran along the quarry wall. It would be a grueling trek up the jagged steps of the quarry to the top of the ridge. Astor had run Ohndarien's wall many times. The run up the ridge was by far the hardest part, but at least the top of the wall was cut into perfect steps. Running over the rough ground at the base of the wall would be much, much harder. Astor's shoulder already ached from carrying the heavy sword, and his legs were starting to feel the strain. But he couldn't give up. He had promised Brophy. The Summer Fleet must not get through Ohndarien.

Astor scanned the route ahead as he ran across the quarry floor. Climbing out of the quarry would be like running through a maze, zigzagging back and forth on the narrow staircases that led from ledge to ledge up the steep sides. He reached the first stairway and looked back to check on the others. They had nearly reached the Quarry Gate when they skidded to a stop.

A small group of people emerged from the tunnel. It looked like there were fifteen or twenty of them. They were unarmed, but several of them seemed to be holding a pair of struggling prisoners in their arms. The two groups stopped and stared at each other for a few moments. Astor could see Bendrick creeping backward, sword in hand.

And then the newcomers attacked. One of them leaped on Bendrick, knocking him to the ground. The others rushed forward, and Astor heard a distant cry of pain. He ran back toward them at a dead sprint. His feet flew across the uneven ground, his aches and pains forgotten.

The fight was pure chaos, but somehow the unarmed newcomers seemed to be pushing the Lightning Swords back. Astor looked for Bendrick. He was on the ground, still fighting. He stabbed his attacker over and over with a dagger, but the unarmed man ignored the blows.

One of the prisoners, a woman with long dark hair, broke free from her captors. She only got a few steps before they overwhelmed her again.

Astor grew more bewildered as he drew closer. The attackers were not soldiers of any kind. Some were women, old people, even a child. They were dressed in rags and seemed to have some sort of black paint on their faces.

Two of them spotted him and broke from the group to intercept. Astor raised his sword to strike, but hesitated when he saw that one of them wore the sash of a Lightning Sword.

Unwilling to use his blade, Astor lowered his shoulder and crashed into his attacker. Something popped in his shoulder. White pain shot thought his body at the force of the impact. He bounced sideways and tumbled across the ground. Hitting the man was like running into a wall.

Astor rolled back onto his feet and struggled to get his bearings. Three people attacked him at once, and he spun sideways to take them one at a time. An old woman in her sixties charged at him, skeletal fingers outstretched.

Her eyes were black.

Black like the Heartstone.

Black like Brophy's eyes when he'd killed Astor's mother.

Astor swung with all his might. The Sword of Autumn cut the woman in half and he spun into another blow. A naked man with fresh blood dripping from his chin lost his head.

Fingernails raked at Astor's neck from behind, and he dropped to the ground, cutting through the third attacker's legs in one blow.

Frantic arms continued to grab at him, but Astor spun away and plunged his sword into the thing's chest. It was a heavyset woman with greasy hair and eyes as black as midnight. She panted uncontrollably for a few seconds and then went limp. Her black eyes never closed. The blank expression on her face never changed.

Astor yanked his sword free and turned to face the others.

Bendrick and the rest of his comrades were dead, their necks broken or throats torn out. There were at least ten of the creatures with black stains on their faces. Astor stood his ground as they all turned their blackened eyes toward him. A few were still struggling with the two women prisoners, but the rest fanned out and began to surround him. They had armed themselves with the fallen Lightning Swords' weapons and were panting uncontrollably as if they had been running for days.

"Astor," someone called out, nearly out of breath.

He risked a glance at one of the prisoners. She struggled against the hands trying to suffocate her. "Shara!"

He got a sudden mental picture of himself rushing to the right and cutting down an attacker that had collapsed to the ground. Before he could respond, the black-eyed creatures came at him in a rush.

Astor followed the image in his mind, flinging himself to the right. Someone shouted and the creature in front of him stumbled to its knees, and Astor took its head off.

Another image came to him, and he realized that Shara was sending them. He followed it implicitly, spinning around and cutting down a filthy fat man, who stumbled just at the right moment to die. And then they were all around him. Astor fought on instinct, spinning, twisting, and hacking about himself. Someone jumped on his back, knocking him to the ground. The attacker suddenly went limp and fell away. Astor rolled back to his feet. Hands grasped at him, and he cut them off. Feet kicked him, and he rolled away from the blows. Something grabbed his sword hand, and he yanked it free. Somewhere in the distance someone kept shouting, "No! No! No!"

"Astor?"

Shara stopped a few paces from where Brophy's cousin had collapsed on hands and knees, covered in gore. She couldn't tell which blood belonged to him and which to the weeping ones. His chin was slashed open and a flap of skin fluttered with his labored breathing.

He looked so much like Brophy. So much.

"Can I have the sword?" Shara asked. "There might be more."

Astor nodded, but didn't raise his head. He made a feeble attempt to push the sword toward her, but he didn't let go.

She pried the blood-soaked blade from his fingers. Taking it in one hand, she rose and walked over to where Galliana lay unconscious on the quarry floor. Her nose had been broken and bruises were already starting to form over her mouth where she'd fought the hands that strangled her. But she was breathing, at least there was that.

Dead weeping ones and Lightning Swords lay all around them. Shara closed her eyes against the sight, fighting through the throbbing pain in her head and aches throughout her body. She took a deep breath, resisting the tears that threatened to pull her under.

For a brief moment she had thought it was Brophy running toward them, Sword of Autumn blazing. But that one moment had been enough. That one moment of self-deception had filled her with a surge of hope, a sudden explosion of power, when all her other reserves had run out. Her mistaking Astor for Brophy had saved them all.

Shara turned back to Astor when she heard him rising to his feet. The boy still hadn't caught his breath, but his brown eyes were determined. He walked over to her on wooden legs, struggling for balance. Shara handed him the sword, and he took it.

"What happened?" he managed to say between breaths.

Shara looked at the bodies of the handful of weeping ones lying around them. There had been thousands in the Citadel. Thousands.

"Ohndarien just fell," she said, trying to hold back the sob.

Chapter 15

hara sat alone in the dying light and watched Ohndarien burn.

She had hidden herself amid the jagged boulders on one of the peaks overlooking Ohndarien. She could see the entire city from here, both sides of the ridge from Clifftown to the Windmill Wall. Smoke from dozens of fires still obscured most of the city. The worst was in the bay, where every ship had been put to the torch. Weeping ones ran through the streets like wraiths, looking for more victims to join their soulless horde.

The battle had taken less than an hour, just like the voice in the emmeria had said. Weeping ones from the Citadel attacked from the east as weeping ones from the Summer Fleet attacked from the west. Even at height of her power, Ohndarien would have struggled to stand against an organized attack by that many ani slaves.

Even from this distance, Shara could sense Issefyn's life force on the deck of one of the summer ships. She was the only human Shara could detect amid the thousands of soulless ani slaves. And Issefyn never strayed more than a few feet from the engorged containment stone that blazed in Shara's magical sight like a pitch-black sun. Shara felt her shame like a wound. Issefyn had played her for a fool. It had been Shara's old friend, not some mysterious Kherish mage, who had been controlling the weeping ones before. And Shara had sent her right into the midst of another army just waiting to be dominated.

In the first few hours after the battle, an endless line of Ohndarien prisoners was brought before Issefyn. One after the other, she ripped out their
souls, swelling the ranks of her weeping army. It took every ounce of willpower Shara had to watch the travesty from a distance rather than rushing
in to stop it and losing her life in a fight she could not win.

Shara and Astor had barely survived a fight with fifteen of the weeping
ones. And the city was filled with thousands of them, all of them controlled
and connected to that one containment stone and the voice locked within
it. What could possibly have possessed Issefyn to let loose the voice of the
black emmeria?

Had Arefaine recruited Issefyn during her time in Ohndarien? Or had
the two been allies all along? How long had Shara been played the fool?

The weeping ones were already swarming over the Windmill Wall, repairing the damage, prepping the locks for the Summer Fleet. By this time
tomorrow they would be in the Great Ocean.

Shara heard a sound behind her and turned. Astor hobbled over the
rocky terrain. He winced as he crouched next to her, massaging the shoulder
he'd hurt in the battle. His face was scratched and battered. His split chin
was painfully swollen, and he still looked like Brophy.

"Any more survivors?" Astor asked.

Shara shook her head. "I can't sense anyone who hasn't been enslaved,"
she admitted. "There's only Issefyn and a few in the Summer Fleet."

"All descendants of Efften?"

"Probably."

Astor's shoulders slumped. He had dark circles under his bloodshot eyes,
and his brown hair was bedraggled, still matted with blood.

"You looked for my father, my sister?"

"Yes. I'm sorry. I couldn't find them. The weeping ones all look alike to
my magical sight."

Astor nodded, the exhaustion etched deeply on his face.

She wanted to reach out to him, to enfold him in her arms and tell him
it would be all right, but she was spent. He was a man now, and he had to
find his own strength.

"You should be resting," Shara said. "There's nothing more to see here."

Astor grunted. "It doesn't matter. I couldn't sleep if I wanted to."

"What about Galliana?"

"She finally drifted off as I left."

Shara's niece could barely walk. She had nearly killed herself trying to use power she didn't have, all in an effort to fight the weeping ones.

Astor stared at Ohndarien. As much as the city's devastation hurt Shara, she knew it hurt him more.

"I never thought it would end this way," he murmured. "All those years that Brophy held vigil. I never thought it would end with us losing."

Shara took his hands and pulled him closer.

"It's not over," she said firmly. "We are still alive, and I'm not about to give up. Not yet."

"But how can we fight something like that? It's hopeless."

She squeezed his hands hard, clenching her teeth. "It was hopeless when King Phandir's army burst through the Sunset Gate. But Brophy found a way."

"I'm not Brophy!" Astor said, his voice breaking.

She looked at him wearily, and she gave him a sad smile. "No. You're Astor, Heir of Autumn. A Child of the Seasons. Maybe the last one. And Ohndarien still needs you."

His fist clenched, and he closed his eyes tight. He had no response to that. She could only hope that he would find it. He was lost, but he was angry, and that was something, at least. He could use anger. She wished she could work with him to mold that anger into resolve, but she couldn't shepherd the Ohndariens anymore, not if there was to be an end to this nightmare. Shara had run out of time.

"You have to stand strong, Astor," she said, wishing she weren't so exhausted. "If all that is left of Ohndarien is those few people in the woods, then you need to protect them. To the bitter end."

"What do you mean?"

"I have to go," she said quietly, suddenly. "I have to leave Ohndarien."

"What?" he cried.

She nodded. "Arefaine must be stopped. Issefyn was just the beginning. That woman has loosed something more powerful than I have ever encountered. All this misery came from a single stone full of black emmeria and Arefaine has fifty times that power. I need to go to Ohohhom, find those stones, and stop them from reaching their destination."

He nodded, a look of dread overcoming his exhaustion. "Do you want me to—"

"No," she assured him. "You stay here. You can't follow me where I'm going."

"How are you going to get there?"

"All the ships in Ohndarien are either burned or under the control of the Summer Fleet. I suppose I shall simply have to stow away."

"There are ships at Torbury. Or there ought to be," Astor suggested. "It's a Farad village up the coast in the Narrows. It wouldn't take you more than a day to get there, and you could buy a boat you could sail yourself."

Shara nodded. That would certainly give her more freedom, and she could spare her strength rather than using it on a constant glamour.

"Good idea," she said. "That's what I'll do."

"What should I do?"

She ached at the uncertainty in his voice, the supplication, but she hardened her heart. "That is up to you."

He paused, watching her, waiting for something more. Shara wished she could give it to him, but she had nothing left to say.

He nodded, slowly, and her heart gladdened. She saw the fire in his eyes when he looked back at her. It was surrounded on all sides by doubt and fear, but there was still a spark. "I'll do what I can," he said.

She smiled. "Good," she said. "That's all any of us can do." She kissed him on the cheek and wrapped him in a hug. "Perhaps we will meet again after this is all done."

"Yes," he murmured into her neck. "You and me and Brophy. And a stolen bottle of wine. We'll talk about girls."

She slowly let go of him, looking at him questioningly.

He shook his head, and managed a smile. "Something Brophy said, right before I left him."

Light and shadow passed over her heart quickly, one after the other. "Did he—" she paused "—say anything else?"

Astor searched her gaze. "You mean about you?"

Taking a deep breath, she said, "Do you know . . . Do you think . . ." Her voice died in her throat. She closed her eyes, opened them again. "Have

Brophy and Arefaine become lovers?" she asked in a monotone. She felt small as she said it, petty. She wanted to take it back, but the arrow had flown, and there was nothing she could do now. In painful silence, she waited.

"He still loves you, Shara," Astor said quietly, "He loves you desperately. He told me so."

The tension left her so suddenly that the tears did come to her eyes. She cleared her throat. "Thank you, Astor." She hugged him again, burying her face in his shoulder. "Thank you. That's all I needed to know."

Part II

Martyrs of Duty
and Rage

Prologue

"Darius Morgeon!"

Darius winced at the sound of Efflum's voice. The archmage shouted curses at him, thrashing in the delicate silver chains that held him fast. After all these years, after everything that had just happened, he was still terrified of that man.

Darius slammed the cell door, cutting off Efflum's screams of rage. *Let him howl for eternity*, he thought. *Let him rot.*

His hand, slick with blood, slipped on the door handle, and he stumbled. He sat down hard on the stone floor and breathed for a moment. He didn't want to turn and see the price of closing that door. He didn't want to count the cost of an entire nation betraying its own father.

With a sigh, Darius rose to his feet again and turned around.

A dozen bodies lay scattered across the gardens. A few lay contorted as if in agony, blood pouring from their eyes and ears. Others died like soldiers, stabbed by their friends at Efflum's brutal command. But most of them showed no sign of why they had died. They simply lay motionless on the grass like snuffed candles. Yet somehow the Great Tower's skygarden was as beautiful as ever. A cool wind blew through the flowers. Birds chased one another around the trees.

A few of those who fought beside him had survived. Friends, kinsmen, students. Most of them sat in the grass in a daze. Only Efflum's youngest son, Lyss, was still on his feet, checking the bodies to see if any might yet live.

Gathering himself, Darius crossed the grass to the stairs in the center of the garden. He reached for the railing, but held himself back. The cut on his forearm was still flowing. He didn't want to leave any more bloodstains. Cradling his arms to his chest, he headed down the stairs.

Step after step, he moved past the endless alcoves full of containment stones. Each one was a testament to the depths of their corruption. They held the legacy of Efflum's reign, exuding the wrath and loathing that Darius felt for them in return. "If such is the cost of security," Efflum had once told him, "it is a price I will gladly pay."

But Darius refused to protect his children's lives at the cost of their souls.

He reached the bottom of the stairs and slipped down the last step into the empty great room. A crowd of people gathered beyond the filigreed doors, shouting at him.

With a wave of his hand, he unlocked the doors, and they rushed into the tower.

"Is it over?" a young woman asked. "Is he dead?"

"Aristah?" someone else said. "Where is my sister?"

He turned away, too weak, too sad, to answer.

"Darius!" Another woman took his arm, and he winced as the pain fired into his shoulder. He couldn't remember her name. "My son. He went with you," the woman begged. "Please tell me—"

They crowded around him, but Darius pulled away without saying a word. He simply pointed upward. The crowd rushed toward the stairs. Their footsteps echoed in the hollow tower. Let them see for themselves.

Darius shuffled to the center of the room and placed his hands on Oh's tomb, smearing blood upon it. His fingernails curled against the dull silver.

"Father!" a voice called to him, and Darius breathed a sigh of relief.

He turned to see his willowy seventeen-year-old daughter pushing through the crowd. Jazryth's brown hair was bound back in a braid with a silver circlet shining on her forehead. She rushed to him and wrapped her arms around him.

"Is it over?" she breathed. "Is Efflum—"

"It's over."

"How . . . How bad was it?"

He drew a shuddering breath. "We lost seventeen. Aristah, Keestor—"

"What about—"

"Lyss is fine."

She let out a pent-up breath. Jazryth and Lyss had been inseparable since they were fifteen.

"But his brothers were not so lucky," Darius finished.

"He killed his own sons!" Jazryth said, her voice barely audible.

Darius nodded. "They were the first to fall."

Her face became stony. "We're going to kill him, aren't we?"

Darius sighed, remembering how they had tried, how they had failed. "I don't know about that. But I can promise you, that man will never again set foot out of this tower. Never."

"Darius," a voice shouted over the din of the crowd rushing into the tower.

Darius turned a weary smile upon his wife. Jahriah moved toward him with some difficulty, her arms protecting her swelling belly from the jostling of the crowd. He staggered forward and embraced her.

"Thank the stones," she breathed in his ear. "You're all right? You're safe?" Her honey hair tickled his nose as he nodded into her shoulder. "I should have been there," she said. "I should have been with you."

"Hush," he said, releasing her and pressing a hand to her belly. "Enough of that. It's done."

The three of them held one another tightly. Darius closed his eyes and let the mingled grief and joy wash over him. He could hardly believe this day had finally come. There was still a mountain of work to be done. They were beset upon all sides, rotting without and within, but the City of Dreams would finally have a chance to become what she was meant to be. After today, they might actually be able to bleed their own souls clean.

Darius opened his eyes and looked over his daughter's shoulder at Oh's coffin. He remembered that day as a child when he had first heard the voice within, the voice that had started it all. Darius's gaze hardened, and he set his jaw.

I've done what you asked me to do, he thought to the coffin. *I've cleaned up your mess. Now leave me and my family alone.*

The box remained silent. And for a few short months, it remained that way.

Chapter 1

J esheks put his hand on the rose marble wall and looked at the tower looming overhead. It was *her* tower. *She* had lived there.

He remembered seeing the school when he first came through Ohndarien on his way to the Summer Cities. At the time he had discounted it, scoffing at the Zelani and their cowardly form of magic. He considered it an idle amusement for the rich and timid. That was before he met Shara, before she showed him that he had been the coward all along.

Jesheks closed his eyes and breathed deeply until he found his center. *She isn't here,* he told himself. *She's not in the city.* She had almost certainly left with the Summer Fleet. Still, he hesitated, staring at the Zelani school's open gates.

He could still smell her if he tried. He could feel her skin moving against his, her thighs on either side of his waist, her breasts pressed against his belly, her hand over his heart. Jesheks clenched his jaw and breathed through his teeth. He remembered other things, too. He remembered the slight resistance of his blade against her skin. He remembered her screams, raw in her throat, before she stopped resisting, before she gave herself over to him.

His heart beat faster as he banished the thoughts from his mind. He didn't even know why he was here. What did he expect to find?

Opening his eyes, he crossed the dusty courtyard and entered the school. The foyer looked as though a herd of cattle had rushed through it.

The polished marble floors were filthy. The gardens within the inner courtyard lay withered and dead.

All of Ohndarien looked like this: broken, deserted, haunted by the black-eyed wraiths in their eternal pain. Jesheks had kept himself hidden from the indentured as he entered the city. There were thousands of them, standing listlessly, awaiting orders. It appeared that Issefyn and Arefaine had re-created the glories of Efften sooner than expected.

He started up the stairs. A brief set of claw marks raked the banister halfway up the first flight. There was a pool of dried blood under a broken statue on the first landing. He imagined Shara lying naked, facedown in the blood. Then he imagined himself lying next to her, side by side, their dead bodies not quite touching.

Clenching his fists, he continued on, climbing up another flight before starting up the tower's spiral stairs. Walking was no longer so painful. The trip through the desert had transformed his body. His skin hung from him in loose folds as the extra pounds had melted away. He was becoming someone else, losing what he once was. He hated the feeling. And he reveled in it. Just like Shara. He hated her. And he wanted her, wanted her more than he could endure.

He'd run away from her that night they both plunged into the Summer Seas, narrowly escaping an inferno of Jesheks's making. It was a benighted thing to do, the decision of a coward, of a broken and twisted man.

He'd swum ashore and watched the blaze from the shadows. He saw that fool, Vinghelt, playing the hero. He saw seven years of planning unfolding like a flower. The Summer Princes were screaming for blood, and Jesheks didn't care. His path to Efften was clear. The ancient mysteries were his to reclaim, but he no longer wanted them.

Jesheks wasn't the only one to flee the Floating Palace that night. One of the Physendrian saboteurs knew how to swim and had escaped to shore. Phanqui still thought Jesheks was a Kherish spy. The two of them returned to Physendria and joined with the rebels hiding in the mountains. The insurgents were emboldened by Phanqui's "victory," and talked excitedly of mounting an assault on their defeated oppressors. Jesheks had slipped away from the fools a day after they came down from the pass. They would soon die for their folly, just as the Ohndariens had.

The trip to Physen had been easier than expected. He had healed his broken toes along the way to improve his walking, and he fed on lizards and birds coaxed to him through magic. Water had been scarce, but there was some to be found in tiny springs between the cracks of the blasted badlands. He had to hide his fair skin from the sun under a heavy cloak, making the heat nearly unbearable, but he used his misery to spur him on. The long walk had given him time to think. The heat burned away his petty little dreams. By the time he reached Physen and hired his own ship and crew, all his plans for the future had been left behind like footprints. Only one thing shone bright in his mind: Shara.

He reached the top of the tower's stairs, where a swath of brown stains covered the pink marble. A lot of people had died here.

The broken door had been ripped from its hinges and cast aside. He stepped inside and stopped beyond the threshold. The room smelled of old feces and something else he could not place. Shara's bed sat at an angle, blocking his way. The mattress leaned against the frame, half covering a rug mottled with more dried blood. The instruments of Shara's craft lay scattered across the worktables as if they'd been torn through and cast aside.

Crouching down, he touched a black stain on the floor. It was still wet, and the moment he touched it, it soaked into his finger like water into sand. Jesheks felt the emmeria swirling in his belly and waited for the sensation to pass. A large number of indentured had been stored here. There was little doubt of that. Issefyn had been busy.

He stood and looked around the empty room, fighting a rising tide of despair. He knew she wouldn't be here. He knew it, yet he was still disappointed. Had Shara even visited this tower when she returned to Ohndarien? Had she succumbed to Issefyn's mass enslavement? Was she somewhere nearby, an empty shell panting for breath?

The weight of his disappointment slowly transformed into a crushing hatred. She hadn't even looked for him after the fire. Not once in the next few days had she cast out her magic, seeking to find him where he sat watching from a distance. All she cared for was that boy and the city he was born in. Her compassion for these Ohndariens was a black cloth pulled over her head. She could never stop the Summer Fleet. Arefaine's plan was too perfect. The hurricane was coming, no matter what Shara did. The Zelani had courage, no one could deny that. Her will could take her long past the point where others would fail, but she didn't belong here. This was not her fight.

It was not his fight either. His ship was waiting for him just beyond the Windmill Wall. So why did he linger?

Taking a deep breath, he walked over to a worktable. He fingered an old scroll then moved to her wardrobe. He opened the double doors and looked at her clothing. Dresses hung from a rod. Jewelry boxes and face powders were stacked neatly on a shelf. He slid open one of her drawers. From within, he pulled a sheer, silky piece of cloth. He pressed the white undergarment against his cheek, filling himself with the scent of her.

He closed his eyes, and his mind flew away to that moment when Shara had straddled him, her body pressed against his as she strove to take him. He'd glimpsed something in that moment, something beyond her straining muscles, her excited breathing. For one glorious moment, he neared it, but it had been snatched away. It had ripped a gaping hole in him, a hole that needed to be filled.

He'd tried to reach that place on his own, tried to follow where she'd led him. But he could barely find the path. He needed her. And she needed him. He licked his lips, remembering her hanging limp from his silk scarves, the heat of the fire caressing her body.

Jesheks took the undergarment away from his face, and it slid between his fingers.

He should have killed her, should have driven the rod through her heart and watched the dark blood run along the steel as she looked at him, wide-eyed, her light slowly fading as she died. She was a blade in his soul that needed to be yanked out and tossed aside.

Jesheks put the white silk back into the drawer and slowly closed it. His hands lingered on the wood, squeezing tighter and tighter.

Where was she? He couldn't go on like this. He had to find her. He had to be done with her. Had to burn her face from his mind's eye.

With a wrenching effort, he forced himself to let go. Backing up, he slammed the wardrobe doors. One of them swung back open. He slammed it again. Both of them swung open. Jesheks punched the door, shattering the thin wood and slicing open his fist. He grabbed the other one, and yanked it off its hinges. The entire wardrobe tipped over and crashed to the floor.

Jesheks hissed, reveling in the pain, drawing it into himself, burning himself clean.

In a few moments he was calm again, and he watched with fascination as a stream of blood ran across his knuckles. His heart pounded, and his chest rose and fell like the sea, but he was calm.

He would be free of her. One way or another, he would be free. He and Shara had been cheated of their reckoning, and he meant to have it back.

"Oceans cannot separate us any more than deserts, my lovely Zelani," he said. "We will finish what we started."

He turned to go, but paused when he saw a faint glow between the fallen wardrobe and the wall. Looking closer, he found a bottle of wine filled with lights. They swirled around the inside of the cut crystal, casting a shifting rainbow of colors upon the wall.

Jesheks reached down and plucked the bottle from its hiding place. He could instantly feel the power within, and a slow smile spread across his face.

"Well," he said to the empty room. "What have we here?"

Chapter 2

ssamyr pushed herself to the front of the rain-soaked crowd to get a better view. Lush green mountains loomed on either side of the narrow channel that led to the Opal City. The Ohohhim capital clung to the sides of those mountains like sea foam washed up on a mossy shore. A single black ship with triangular sails tacked slowly into a headwind through the narrow waterway. Arefaine Morgeon was on that ship, the girl Ossamyr had come to kill.

Ossamyr had never been squeamish about violence. She had grown up with bloodshed; it was an everyday part of Physendrian life. In a pit of scorpions, you stung any who came near. But that was long ago, in a different land and a different life. Before Brophy. Before Ohndarien. Before Reef. She was not that woman anymore, and the poisoned dagger strapped to her thigh stung like a badge of shame.

Thousands of black-robed Ohohhim had crowded the docks, waiting for the return of the emperor's body and their new regent. They were eerily silent as they waited for the ship to land. The constant drizzle seemed to reinforce the perpetual hush as if Ossamyr were lost in a fog of black robes and cowled faces. Every moment she spent in the Opal Empire made her feel like she was being punished, like she was a child forced to stand in a corner and think about what she'd done wrong.

Even though she was constantly in a crowd, she had never felt this isolated, this cut off from other people. It had been two weeks since Reef had dropped her off at the far edge of the city under the cloak of darkness. She longed to have the Islander's calm, reassuring presence next to her, but he was far too large to ever pass for an Ohohhim. Even Ossamyr was conspicuously tall in the Opal Empire. Fortunately, the constant rain gave her a good excuse to keep her cowl up and a subtle glamour did the rest.

She had been amazed by the city when she first arrived. The vibrancy of the vegetation still seemed unreal to her desert-born eyes. Waves of green flowed down the mountainsides like waterfalls, pouring around the buildings and flooding the city with life. Black wooden structures rose from the forest like obsidian giants, lacquered to a mirror finish, glistening in the constant rain. Many of them were five or six stories tall, but they did not come close to the height of the tallest May Dragon trees. The intricately carved buildings were all linked by arching causeways high above the ground that created long queues of structures running parallel to the shore. The city was shocking in its uniformity. Every building, every street, every shop, sign, and flower box had been built in the exact same style. The entire city seemed to be frozen in one perfect moment, unchanging and untouchable.

Even the people seemed frozen in time. The streets were constantly packed with the ebb and flow of humanity going about their daily business, but the city always seemed calm and tranquil. There was never a harsh word, never a shout. Neither were there any smiles or heartfelt meetings between friends. Even the children played deliberately and quietly in small groups. It was almost as if they were painted dolls instead of people.

Two days ago, though, all of that changed. Ossamyr was returning from scouting the palace for possible entrances. She was crossing the Dragon Bridge when a crying woman bumped into her, mumbled an apology and ran on. What would have been an everyday occurrence anywhere else felt like an earthquake in Ohohhom. Moments later she saw an old man huddled against the railing, hugging himself and rocking side to side like a child. The streets were soon filled with hordes of anguished Ohohhim, hoods pulled back as they stared up at the sky, crying into the rain as the white powder washed from their faces. A ship had arrived from the Cinder with news of the emperor's death. The shops were closed. All work halted as the black-haired, black-robed people gathered together in the street in silent sorrow.

Everywhere she walked, the once-emotionless Ohohhim were weeping, consoling one another.

Word quickly spread that the Opal Advisor had died alongside His Eternal Wisdom and the Awakened Child, Arefaine Morgeon, had been named regent. When the twelve official days of mourning were over, the priests of Oh would form a great queue and begin their trek across the empire looking for the next Incarnation of God on Earth. Until that child came of age, the Opal Empire would be in the hands of a tortured girl with the power of a god.

Ossamyr had eavesdropped on mumbled conversations about the new regent. "I will not bow to that girl," one old woman said. "His Eternal Wisdom would never choose a child of Efften to lead the divine queue. She suffered for the light. That is true, but she does not hear the voice of Oh. You can see it in her eyes."

For the past two days, Ossamyr had been trying to decide if this sudden turn of events made her task more or less difficult. It probably didn't matter. She still needed to get the girl alone in a confined space. The rest would be easy. She already had a few ideas of how it might happen.

She watched Arefaine's ship as it glided up to the docks and sailors jumped ashore to make it fast. The silence among the Ohohhim was so complete that she could hear her own heart throbbing in her temples. An unexpected fear twisted in her belly. Suddenly her task seemed painfully real. Simply imagining Arefaine's death had been easy. Now she had to actually do it.

A few soldiers in black robes and helmets that looked like shark fins appeared from belowdecks and marched down the gangplank. They spread out on the docks and waited, still as posts. Ossamyr had seen the Carriers of the Opal Fire before in Ohndarien. There should be twelve of them. There were only four.

Once the dock was secure, twelve women with black veils over their faces emerged from within the ship. Upon their linked arms they carried a body wrapped in white silks.

The thousands of people lining the shores of the Opal City bowed as one. Ossamyr joined them as they pressed their foreheads to the ground. There was no sound. No birds called out. Not a single baby cried.

Ossamyr intensified her glamour and looked up from the rain-soaked cobblestones where she knelt. The ten women in mourning veils walked across the deck. A young woman with straight black hair and a powdered face followed the corpse, holding a strand of silk trailing from his shoulder. Ossamyr gritted her teeth, staring at the cold beauty in the distance. She remembered her night on the island, the images she had been shown by the Siren's Blood. Once again she felt like someone was ripping her soul out of her chest. She closed her eyes against the hazy shared memories given to her by that magical liquid. The tears of the countless indentured flashed through her mind, so that she could almost feel the black tears streaming down her face.

She opened her eyes and stared at the young woman. The girl intended to unlock a cage that should never be opened. She would turn those black tears into a flood, setting loose the voices and sending them screaming across the face of the earth. It could not happen again. Ossamyr would not let it.

The procession turned to go down the gangplank and she was finally able to see who stood behind Arefaine. Ossamyr took a sharp breath, which almost turned to a whimper in her throat. His blond hair shone like a spot of sunlight in a black-and-white world. His face was unpowdered and unguarded. He took in the sight of the city, the ten thousand kneeling faithful with unabashed amazement. He looked just the same after all these years.

Ossamyr forced her head back to the ground. Her body ached to leap forward and run to him. She wanted to snatch him up, fly away with him back to his cell in Physendria with the round bed suspended from the ceiling.

She pressed her head against the wet ground, feeling like she was being torn to pieces. One part of her was still kneeling on the arena floor begging a young man for forgiveness. Another part was back on Reef's ship, cradled in his arms and rolling with the swells as she slept. The rest of her was lost in a howling darkness, feeling her heart being ripped from her chest.

She squeezed her legs together, pressing the sheath of the poisoned dagger painfully into her thighs.

First things first.

She could only hope Brophy would forgive her after it was done.

Chapter 3

rophy felt an uncomfortable knot in his stomach when he first laid eyes on the Opal City. He gripped Arefaine's sleeve tighter as he followed her and the emperor's body down the gangplank and onto the dock.

As far as he could see, robed and cowled Ohohhim filled the streets, their faces pressed firmly to the ground. The prostrate hordes extended along the shore until the haze of rain obscured them. It was more people than he'd ever seen in his life, far more than the Nine Squares arena at full capacity. And they were all eerily silent.

The only color in the city of gray skies and dark robes was the vibrant green of the trees that seemed to press on the buildings from all sides, trying to push them back into the ocean. There was no denying the beauty and grandeur of the glossy black city, but it was a cold beauty, as chilly and depressing as the constant rain.

Arefaine continued along the dock. The crowd had left a narrow passageway for the procession to follow. The people on either side could have reached out and touched Brophy's feet, but none of them moved. They didn't even look up as the body of their emperor passed.

The place set Brophy's teeth on edge. The oppressive clouds and unnatural silence reminded him of his nightmares. He kept expecting the kneeling figures to rise up with the glowing red eyes and ragged claws of the corrupted. The Fiend would emerge from their midst with the Sword of Autumn in his skeletal hands.

Brophy patted the pocket that held his father's heartstone, but Brydeon's soul light did not emerge.

It's worse than I feared.

He started, hearing Arefaine's voice from behind him and turned to look at the Ohohhim man following him, who kept his head bowed. "What—"

Don't speak, Arefaine's voice said, again from somewhere behind his head. *Keep your eyes forward.*

Her voice wasn't coming from behind him. It was within him, emerging inside his own mind. He groped for the ability to respond, but it was like trying to move a limb that didn't exist.

Whenever the emperor returned from Ohndarien, the city was filled with flowers. His feet never touched the ground for all the petals strewn before him, she spoke to him.

Brophy glanced at the ground. There was nothing but rain-slicked cobblestones, not a single petal to be seen.

They might as well be spitting in our faces.

Brophy took a deep breath to calm himself. He looked at the endless crowd of kneeling Ohohhim and was suddenly struck by the enormity of Arefaine's task. The emperor had left her in a terribly precarious position. Her own Carriers had defied her succession. This entire city could be on the verge of doing the same. She was vulnerable here, alone and hopelessly outnumbered. Brophy released her sleeve for a moment to give her shoulder a squeeze. He wished he could do more, but the entire city was dead silent. Any supportive words he spoke would be easily overheard.

I'm glad you're here, she thought to him as they continued forward, leaving the dock and turning onto a vast street that wound along the shore. *We walk a dangerous path. They do not trust me. Perhaps they never have. And they don't know what to think about you. They know who you are, but I think they'd prefer if you lived only in their stories. It frightens them to see a foreigner with an unpowdered face in the Opal Advisor's place in line. They fear change above all things. They fear it like other people fear death.*

During their journey, Arefaine's attendants had politely offered to powder Brophy's face and dress him in long, black velvet robes. He had declined, despite their repeated requests. Though Arefaine had never spoken of the issue, he suddenly realized that resisting their customs might have a far more profound effect than he intended. He was coming to learn that every nuance of behavior had meaning to the Ohohhim. He was going to have to pay more attention if he intended to get the two of them to Efften safely.

They proceeded forward, and Brophy noticed their line was getting longer. People from the crowd rose and attached themselves to the end of the queue, each knowing exactly where they belonged in the divine order.

The buildings seemed to mimic them. Arched balconies connected the upper levels, creating long lines that ran parallel to the shore. The meticulously crafted symmetry was impossible to ignore.

All will remain peaceful during the twelve days of mourning, Arefaine thought to him. *But after that, things may get difficult. I must move quickly to solidify my power as regent.*

Brophy thought back to the conflict over the Ohndarien prisoners on the docks of the Cinder. Could Arefaine have maintained control if he hadn't been there to kill that Carrier? Would she be forced to resort to violence again? Would he?

"Let's just leave," Brophy whispered.

No. We already discussed that.

Toward the end of their voyage, Brophy had argued many times that they didn't need the Ohohhim if they were going to Efften alone. But Arefaine had refused, and Brophy had come to realize that she wanted to be regent. People who had ignored her for years were suddenly hanging on her every word. She reveled in the acceptance and attention. She craved it like a starving child craves food.

"But—"

No words. We are being watched at all times.

Reluctantly, Brophy held his silence as the procession continued on. There would be time to talk later, but he doubted it would do any good. Despite her promises, despite the danger she faced, Arefaine was already rooted to her newfound throne. It was going to take something drastic to pry her free.

This street is called the Path to Oh, she continued after a few moments. Brophy wondered if the silence bothered her as much as it did him. *Roads from the far corners of the empire converge into this one. It leads across the bridge and through the palace up to the Cave of Oh. It is said that no single person has walked its entire length.*

Brophy looked ahead and saw where the path turned onto an immense bridge between the mainland and an island so tall and steep its summit was lost amid the gray clouds. The bridge was built to look like a giant black dragon spanning the narrow channel in a series of arches. The path started on its tail, wound up and down a series of hills along its sinuous back and emerged through its jaws on the far side. The surf rolled and crashed fifty feet below, pounding ceaselessly against the thick stone pillars that supported the arches. He counted them. Twelve, of course.

Brophy followed Arefaine and the emperor's body across the bridge to the island on the far side. Once they were on the bridge, the path changed from simple cobblestones to an elaborate mosaic depicting scenes from the ancient past.

The bridge represents the mythical dragon that Oh fought and learned his magic from. The beast was said to have swallowed him whole. Oh slew the dragon by absorbing the sacred fire within its belly and emerged as the world's first mage. I expect the legend is purely metaphorical, as is the bridge itself. The beast represents the barbarism of our ancient past and the sacred fire is the knowledge it took to tame it. The rising and falling of the bridge represents the difficult spiritual and physical paths Oh endured while in the belly of the beast.

Their way passed through the dragon's enormous carved head and entered a narrow valley alongside a short waterfall where a modest river plunged into the sea. The impressive May Dragon trees closed overhead like a canopy. Their trunks twisted toward the sky, sprouting thick clumps of star-shaped leaves.

The path grew steeper as it continued through the trees alongside the stream. Brophy spotted a stone building overgrown with ferns and vines hidden back among the trees. Risking a look back, he realized they had passed several others that he hadn't even noticed. The temples were obviously weathered and ancient, but still breathtaking in their size and majesty.

This is the Valley of the Temples, Arefaine sent to him. *I grew up here. Father Lewlem and I used to walk this path and I would play among the May Dragon trees.*

Some of the temples were huge, trying to reach for the tops of the trees. Others were tiny shrines tucked in between the larger buildings.

There is a temple for each and every emperor that ever lived. The most recent emperor's temple is only half finished. If you look to the left and deeper into the forest, you will see another half-finished temple. That one is dedicated to me.

Brophy looked ahead, trying to see more temples through the trees.

And beyond that bend is the Opal Palace.

Brophy looked up and spotted a single black stone tower peeking through the vegetation ahead of them. He gradually saw more and more of it as the path turned a corner and the valley opened into a huge clearing. The palace filled the entire valley from side to side, butting up against the sheer cliff faces. A dozen towers thrust like spears at the sky from the midst of the tightly packed architecture, rising above the sides of the valleys. Some of the spires were so tall that they were lost in the low-hanging clouds. Brophy stared at the sheer size of it.

Keep walking.

Brophy realized that he'd paused, and quickly started his feet moving.

If you think this is majestic, wait until you see Efften. Her silver towers can be seen from twenty miles away. But the wonders that we create together will be ten times as grand. We will light a beacon to call home all descendants of the great race.

Brophy's gaze fell from the towers, and he noticed that the Path of Oh ran straight through the center of the magnificent palace, neatly parting it like the narrow valley parted the mountain. Beyond the Opal Palace, the path became stairs that switchbacked farther up the mountain and finally disappeared into the rough mouth of a distant cave.

That was the cave the emperor told him he must visit. That was the cave where he must listen closely for the Voice of Oh.

Chapter 4

Baedellin!"

Astor ran through the crowd of weeping ones, knocking them aside. He grabbed the young girl and spun her around. The child's face was covered in grime, lank hair hung over her pitch-black eyes. Her mouth hung open like a panting dog's, showing the gap where her baby teeth had fallen out.

Astor sighed, letting go of the soulless child's arm. His heart raced, still aching in his chest from the sudden rush and crash of hope.

The girl wasn't Baedellin. The child couldn't have been more than five or six. She was a foot shorter than his sister. How could he have thought it was her?

He left the cluster of weeping ones where he had found them in a side street near Donovan's Bridge and headed down the hill. He had spent the last three days looking for his father and sister. He knew he was grasping at straws, but there was nothing else to do.

He had been cautious at first, afraid the weeping ones would attack again. But they had been dormant ever since the Summer Fleet passed through the locks, and sailed into the Great Ocean. Every last one of the Summermen had gone, leaving behind a horde of the soulless corrupted standing around like abandoned toy soldiers.

He didn't even know what he would do once he found his family. Would he be better off not seeing the black streaks down their cheeks? How could seeing that emptiness in their eyes make anything better? Shara assured him that the weeping ones were not lost, that they could be cured. But Astor could scarcely hope it was true. He needed to see Baedellin's face, needed to look into his father's black eyes and see for himself that they were truly gone before he could move on.

Is this what it's like to be defeated? he thought. Everything he cared about had been destroyed, but he couldn't help sifting through the ashes looking for scraps of what once was.

Galliana had come with him the first day he went searching. They spent the whole time fighting, and she had been kind enough to leave him alone ever since. She'd wanted to leave for Faradan days ago, but she stayed with him out of loyalty, waiting for him to find his family, or perhaps to simply accept the truth. After all those years, Ohndarien had finally been defeated. She was a dead city, as empty and lifeless as her citizens.

He sighed and retraced his steps in his mind. He had been to all the obvious places. Most of the weeping ones were still in Clifftown, where the battle had been fought. Others were scattered along the most direct path between the Citadel and the locks. Baedellin and his father weren't anywhere along the major route, so they had to be somewhere else, tucked aside in some room somewhere. It could take weeks for him to search the city alone, and he still might not find them.

Astor leaned against a wall and slid down into a crouch. He pressed his palms against his eyes and massaged his head. He was hungry, tired, and still sore from the battle. He and Galliana had found a little food in the woods, but not much. Tonight he would try to convince her to head north without him. He knew it in his heart; he wasn't going to leave Ohndarien. No matter what the future would bring, he would stay in Ohndarien and face it. He would rather die in his home than live anywhere else.

Astor pulled his hands away from his face. He looked down the street and saw someone walking toward him with slow, hesitant steps. He was on his feet in an instant, the Sword of Autumn in his hand. The figure was cowled in white, with a cloth wrapped around his face like a Physendrian. The stranger held up his hand in greeting.

"That's close enough," Astor shouted. "Who are you?"

The man reached up and unwound the cloth from his face. Astor winced at the sight of him. Pale lank hair framed his white face, and red eyes glimmered behind pudgy cheeks. His skin hung loose below his chin and neck, as if he'd recently lost a lot of weight.

Shara had mentioned something about meeting an albino in the Summer Seas, but he couldn't remember what she'd said.

"How did you get in here?" Astor demanded.

The pasty-white man continued walking forward and smiled. Astor blinked.

"Greetings, stranger. It is good to see another free man in this tomb of slavery." The albino's voice was high and light like a child's.

A slight chill scampered up Astor's spine, and he opened his mouth to speak, but forgot what he was going to say.

The stranger walked up and extended his hand. Astor took it, and they shook. The stranger's grip was feeble, his flesh clammy.

"You're a Kher, aren't you?" he asked the stranger.

"Yes, I am."

"What are you doing here?"

"That doesn't matter right now."

Astor nodded. Of course. He was right. That didn't matter at all.

"What matters is that I must find Shara-lani as soon as possible," he continued. "Do you know where she is?"

Astor started to shake his head, but it was very hard to complete the motion.

"I haven't seen her," he said, his tongue feeling thick.

The man nodded. "You have seen her. And you must help me."

Astor found himself nodding.

"Shara is about to die," the man said, his childlike voice seeming out of place coming from such a man. "I am the only person who can save her. Her and a great many others."

"She's gone to Ohohhom to stop Arefaine," Astor said. "She's getting a ship at Torbury, up the coast in the Narrows."

The albino let out a small, disappointed breath. "That is as I feared."

"I'm sure Shara can take care of herself," Astor said. He blinked, feeling like he should say something else. Or ask something. Hadn't he wanted to ask this man something?

The stranger nodded at the Sword of Autumn. "That is a fine blade."

"It is one of the Swords of the Seasons."

"Brother Brophy held this sword for a time, yes?"

Astor nodded.

"And they say the legendary Scythe wielded it through his final stand. Is it true?"

"Yes."

"It can slay the corrupted?"

"Yes. Very little else can."

"Amazing. May I see it?" The Kher held out his hand.

Astor hesitated, opening his mouth to speak. Again, he found no words. But he handed the blade over.

"It is truly extraordinary," the albino said, tucking the blade into his belt beneath the voluminous cloak.

Astor watched him, said nothing. He blinked.

"I'm looking for my sister," he finally said.

"I am sure you will find her, young Astor," the stranger said. "I must leave you now. I have urgent business elsewhere."

Astor nodded. The albino shook his hand again and headed back down the hill.

Astor turned and walked in the opposite direction. He would have to start a meticulous house-by-house search. That was the only way to find them.

Chapter 5

rophy reached the end of the cavernous hallway and placed his hands against the smooth black walls. They were slightly greasy to the touch, as if the masonry had been oiled to make it shiny. The walls glistened in the steady light of oil lamps muted with alabaster hoods so pale and thin that the cool light shone through. The glossy walls rose so high the ceilings were lost on the shadows. Hundreds of servants and attendants worked in the palace, constantly cleaning and polishing, but the opulent hallways were always empty.

The Opal Palace reminded Brophy of a story that he had loved as a child, about a castle of ice. In that story a young girl's tears had melted the castle and revived the wondrous garden hidden beneath it. What would a child's tears do in this place? Would they even be allowed to fall?

Brophy ran his fingers along the curved stone in front of him. It had to be the base of one of the towers Brophy had seen from outside, but he hadn't been able to find an entrance to any of them. He remembered back to his days as a captive in Physendria's Catacombs and imagined finding the hidden mechanism that would allow him to open a secret door into the towering spire that hid all of Ohohhom's secrets. Maybe there was a massive gem like the Heartstone hidden up there somewhere. If any city needed a heart, this was the one.

Giving up his search, he headed back down the hall and tried the first set of double doors he came to. They were unlocked. Inside was yet another empty banquet hall that could seat hundreds. A line of about ten young women were down on hands and knees, busy polishing the intricately carved legs of the banquet chairs. They all froze the moment Brophy walked in. He immediately felt guilty as they turned toward him and placed their foreheads on the ground.

Arefaine had left him alone in the Opal Palace for the better part of a day and he'd been treated the same everywhere. He was allowed free rein over the palace, city, and gardens. No one challenged him wherever he went, but they all stopped in his presence, prostrated themselves, and refused to rise until he'd continued on. Arefaine had warned him about the Ohohhim customs, but they bothered him much more than he thought they would. He felt as if he was being constantly watched, judged, and found wanting.

Arefaine had explained that those at a certain level in the divine queue could only be addressed by others of like station. Since Arefaine had set Brophy's place just behind her own, that meant that there were perhaps three people who were allowed to talk to him. At first he found the whole business rather silly, but the Ohohhim took it so seriously that it soon became chilling. Arefaine had urged him to simply nod politely and continue on his way, but he couldn't help trying to make eye contact, trying to find some connection with these strange little people.

Brophy approached the nearest servant girl and knelt down next to her. "I am sorry to interrupt," he said to the back of her hood as she lay with her face to the floor. "But could you tell me how to get into one of the towers. I'd like to see the view from up there."

"Please . . ." the young woman's voice caught in her throat, and she struggled to continue. "My humble apologies, but this is not done."

"Not done? I'm not allowed to go up there?"

"Please, Father. I am so sorry, but there is no way, no path into the towers."

"You can't get inside? There are no stairs, no passageways?"

"My apologies, but it is so."

Brophy laughed. "Then what are they for?"

The girl cringed lower, saying nothing.

Brophy gritted his teeth at the sight of her utter subservience. He nearly yanked her to her feet and threw back that black hood to make sure there was a face beneath it. He wanted to shake her until she cried out or fought back, anything to prove she was human.

Clenching his fists, he took a deep breath until the images faded from his mind's eye. The black emmeria boiled within him, turning the slightest annoyance into a mortal insult. There was never a respite from it, but he was getting better at letting it go. His sudden rages were fading, becoming easier to control. More and more, they felt like an old wound that had healed, but refused to stop hurting.

"Never mind," he told her. "You've done well." He wanted to touch her on the shoulder to reassure her, but he knew that would only make things worse. He kept his hands at his sides.

He rose to leave and the girl spoke again.

"They are there for grace."

"Excuse me?"

"I am sorry, Father. You asked a question. The towers are there for beauty, to honor the sacred Twelve. Decorum follows grace, grace follows dignity, and dignity follows inner peace—"

"And inner peace leads to the Voice of Oh." Brophy finished the adage that he had heard many times since he'd been here.

"Yes, Father."

"Thank you," Brophy said, nodding politely and leaving the room. He wished Shara were here. He would love to see her kidnap those poor girls and carry them off to Ohndarien to train them as Zelani. They deserved better than this.

He slipped through the double doors into the vast hallway. A heavyset man in rough-spun gray robes stood a few yards away examining one of the oil lamps. His features were covered with a hood, but his slender hands showed his age. Brophy wondered if he'd left a fingerprint somewhere, and they'd sent an expert to wipe it off.

Brophy approached the man, preparing to nod politely and move on his way.

"You would like to see the view?" the man asked. He pushed back his cowl to reveal a wide face and friendly eyes. His curly black hair was twisted into a long braid that draped over his shoulder before disappearing beneath his cloak. He had the soft, potbellied body of a man who spent more time studying than laboring.

Brophy stopped and stared at him, shocked that he had spoken. "I'm sorry, what did you say?"

"Would you like to see the view of the palace," the old man repeated. "From above?"

Brophy stared at the stranger, trying to gauge his intentions. "Yes," he finally said. "I would."

"Then follow me."

The old man paused as if waiting for Brophy to grab his sleeve. Brophy ignored the gesture, and the old man turned back and gave him an unreadable glance. After only a moment's hesitation, the old man started walking and Brophy joined him. They continued on, side by side.

"Where are we going?" Brophy asked.

"First the gardens. There is something I would like to show you." The old man's voice was very calm and serious, but somehow less formal, less stiff, than the other Ohohhim. It reminded Brophy of the tone Scythe took when they'd first met, back when the mysterious assassin was pretending to be a Vizai merchant.

"Are you a monk?" Brophy asked, noticing how crude his clothing was compared to everyone else.

"I am Dewland, high priest of Oh," the man said. "Monks are allowed to seek the Voice of Oh in solitude high in the mountains. Priests must walk a more complicated path."

"You were Arefaine's teacher. She told me about you."

He nodded. "I am surprised that she mentioned me."

"She said you taught her how to overcome her bad dreams."

"I did what I could," he said, turning from the main hallway and heading toward a pair of open double doors in the distance.

"I have heard you will begin the search for the next emperor soon."

"Yes. In a few days the priests of Oh will gather at his cave and begin a pilgrimage throughout the land looking for a newborn child whose heart has been touched by Oh's wisdom."

"How will you know this child when you see it?"

The old priest looked over at him and shrugged. "I have no idea. But I am certain that all will be made clear when the time is right."

"I used to think that way," Brophy said, suddenly feeling an intense dislike for this man. He breathed through his anger and touched the pocket that held the shard of his father's heartstone.

"Were you right to think that way?" the priest asked.

Brophy paused. They were a few steps inside a set of towering doors that led outside into the imperial gardens. A light rain fell on the myriad flowers beyond and Brophy could smell the wet earth.

"What do you mean?"

"Were you right to think that all would be made clear to you when the time was right?"

Brophy thought back to that moment when he took the Test. He remembered the blinding pain and flood of joy when he thrust the shard of the Heartstone into his chest and heard Her voice clearly for the first time.

"Do you regret the part you played in the struggle against the shadows?" the priest continued. "Do you resent the years you lost, the burden you still carry?"

Brophy reached into his pocket and squeezed Brydeon's heartstone in his fist. He had a sudden urge to yank it out and plunge it into the old man's eye. But the more he held it, the calmer he became.

"I don't know what I think anymore," he said tightly. "My mind is not my own. My heart betrays me."

"Yet here you are, searching for a better view."

Brophy paused. The priest was leading him somewhere, steering him with this conversation, but he couldn't see where. "I suppose I am."

"Remember, a lifetime of choices brought you to this spot. You chose over and over again the path that led you to this moment, standing next to me. You were not bought here like a babe in arms by Lady Arefaine or His Eternal Wisdom. You walked here as a man on your own two feet."

Brophy stared closely into Dewland's powdered face. He had fierce gray eyes under a deeply creased brow, etched with decades of concern. Brophy wasn't sure how much he should confide in this man. Was he a rival of Arefaine's or a potential ally? And where did Brophy's own loyalty lie? Was he following Arefaine's sleeve or the dead emperor's? Or was he trying to follow his own?

"Do you support Arefaine as regent?" he decided to ask.

"Absolutely. His Eternal Wisdom and I discussed the succession exten-
sively before he left for Ohndarien."

"Then you knew he would die?"

"I knew everything, Brophy. I helped His Eternal Wisdom choose the
exact words he spoke to you before his death. All of this has been planned
for years. Perhaps it has been planned since Oh went into his cave."

Brophy hissed. "Enough prophecy and mysticism!" His voice echoed in
the long hallway. "Speak your mind. What do you want from me?"

Dewland paused, taking a long breath before speaking. "A better question might be: What are you seeking from me?"

Brophy's lip curled. "I want answers. I want an end to these stupid, cryptic puzzles. I want it simple. What is this choice that Arefaine will have to
make on Efften? How do you expect me to help her make the right one?"

"I will answer all of your questions very soon, but there are two things I
would like to show you in the garden first."

Brophy glared at the priest.

"Please, I assure you. The vagueness, the delays, the incomplete information were all crafted to make your task easier, not more difficult."

"How does herding me like a sheep make anything easier?"

Dewland smiled at him and shrugged. "Will you come?" he asked with
that infuriatingly calm tone.

Brophy stalked outside into the steady rain. The old priest had to hurry
to keep up with him. The gardens were strangely comforting. The towering
May Dragon trees hid the gray skies behind a leafy green canopy. They
felt like loyal sentries protecting a sacred space. The gardens were carefully
arranged, but still felt natural and welcoming. He looked around with different eyes and slowly regained his composure. Despite the unnaturally thick
vegetation and constant rain, he realized this was the most comforting place
he had yet found in Ohohhom.

"The peace of Oh flows down from his cave into these gardens," Dewland said, as though sensing Brophy's emotions.

He glanced up the hill, spotting the winding path up the mountainside
through a gap in the leaves.

"I think the quiet rain and the trees have more to do with it," he said.

"Oh's reflection stares out from all things."

The priest's platitudes annoyed Brophy, but he kept his silence as they continued through the gardens for a few minutes. Brophy paused when he noticed a section of the mosaic path they were walking on. It showed a single eye, black as night. A tear fell from the corner of the blackened orb.

"What is this? What are we walking on?"

"This is the Path of Oh. The mosaics start on the Dragon Bridge and continue halfway up the mountain. The images tell the story of Oh's life."

"Arefaine told me much of his story. I know he corrupted himself and then sacrificed his life to lock the black emmeria away. Is that what this shows, his corruption?"

"Indeed it does. The images on this path tell the entire story from his humble birth to his transcendence and betrayal."

Brophy tapped the image with his toe. "So this god you revere so much was once a man like any other?"

"He was."

"And he discovered magic."

"The sacred flames have always existed, but Oh was the first to embrace them."

"I heard he got a little too close."

Dewland nodded. "Long ago, they called black emmeria the smoke from the sacred fire. Oh used those flames to unite the twelve tribes and defend them from their many enemies. But he did so at terrible personal cost. After wrestling so long with that dragon, he finally accepted that the allure of such great power was too much for any man to resist. He turned his back on the flames and gave his life to remove that temptation from the world."

"That certainly didn't stop the mages of Efften from perfecting the work he started."

Dewland paused. "Arefaine didn't tell you the rest, did she?"

"The rest of what?"

"The rest of the story."

He paused. "No. She didn't."

Dewland nodded and a bitter frown tightened his powdered lips. "Let me show you." He led Brophy farther along the path, telling the story that followed the images below their feet.

At first they traveled the story that Brophy already knew. It showed the emperor's unsuccessful struggle to resist the black emmeria and his eventual sacrifice to lock it away forever. His restraint and self-sacrifice was the cornerstone upon which the entire Ohohhim culture was built.

Father Dewland stopped over an image of a simple silver tomb standing alone in a cave. "This is where the story should have ended," he said. "This was to be the end of that abomination. But the call of power is hard to resist, and some could not see the wisdom in Oh's decision."

The next image showed a man standing next to Oh's coffin, his face turned in rage toward the heavens. Dewland walked slowly from image to image, narrating as he went. "After Oh's sacrifice, his disciples fought for control of the empire. The twelve kingdoms splintered and fell into a long and bloody civil war. The leader of the rebels was once Oh's most talented pupil, a man named Efflum, who had lost his wife in a war with the Vizai. He blamed the emperor for his wife's death and refused to follow Oh's example. He lost the war and was banished from the empire, but he and his followers returned to Ohohhom in disguise and fought their way into Oh's cave. The emperor's supporters tried to collapse the tunnel to seal Oh's tomb. Efflum survived, but many of his comrades were crushed by the falling rubble. In his rage, Efflum killed his rivals and stole Oh's silver coffin."

The images stopped at an elaborate wooden gate in the garden wall. Beyond it, the path continued up the valley toward the Cave of Oh.

"He stole it?" Brophy asked. "Why?"

"Power. All the tainted ani in the world was trapped within that coffin. Ever since his wife died, Efflum was cursed by an insatiable thirst for power."

"What did he do with it?"

"He fled to an island in the middle of the Great Ocean. Several hundred of his followers joined him, and together they released the foul magic from Oh's coffin and used it to found the nation of Efften."

"So the archmages of Efften were all renegades from the Opal Empire?"

"The first of them, yes. They turned their back on Oh and left their homes in treachery and disgrace. We tried three times to invade and punish Efflum's betrayal. We failed three times. They freely used magic that we refused to touch and tens of thousands lost their lives in the attempt."

"Does this path tell the rest of that story?"

"It does."

"I would like to see it."

"I would like you to see it also, but our Mother Regent has ordered this gate to be locked, something that has never before happened in my lifetime."

"Why?"

"Perhaps she does not want you to visit the Cave of Oh. Perhaps she is afraid of what you will hear there."

"You fear her, don't you?"

"Oh yes, very much," he said, though his tone was as calm as ever.

"Why?"

He smiled gently. "Let me show you."

Dewland led Brophy off the main path back into the gardens, past the dripping ferns and meticulously manicured shrubs to a place where the foliage was overgrown. Twisting vines stretched across the ground and wrapped around a particularly beautiful tree with wide branches and fat leaves. Red blossoms speckled the boughs.

"Is this what you wanted to show me?" Brophy asked.

"It is. I was Arefaine's teacher when she was growing up," Dewland said, stopping in front of the tree and turning to face Brophy. "I was her second teacher. A man named Father Lewlem was the first."

Brophy nodded, wondering again at the light that constantly accompanied her, at what she must have done to create such a thing.

Dewland looked up at the red-blossomed tree. "This tree was planted to mark the spot where that great man died. Arefaine killed him when she was still a child." He watched Brophy's reaction, but Brophy kept his emotions carefully hidden. "Or perhaps it is more accurate to say that the black emmeria killed him. It appeared to be a normal death. He was an old man, but the truth was never in doubt. Father Lewlem and I were very good friends. We spoke often of his struggles with the girl and his fears of what she was capable of."

"That was years ago. She was a child."

"In many ways she is still that child."

"So you don't believe that she can redeem herself?" Brophy fought with his emotions. "You don't believe she can escape what has been done to her?"

Dewland looked up at him. The old man's skin crinkled around gray eyes filled with emotion. "She *must* redeem herself. That is our only hope."

"Then tell me how. What does she need to do?"

"What did the emperor tell you?"

"He said I had to teach a lost child how to love."

"What do you think he meant?"

"I think he wanted me to seduce her, manipulate her in some way."

"Have you seduced her?"

"No," he said, his voice tight.

"Why not?"

"Because I care more about her than your emperor and his plans for her!"

"I see," Dewland said with a slight bow. "I don't blame you. I, too, have great affection for her. She is extraordinary in so many ways."

"Isn't that a crime here?" Brophy spat, wrestling with his temper.

The priest nodded. "I suppose it is." He walked up to the tree, touched some of the leaves. "I took Arefaine's education upon myself after Lewlem's death. I worked with her for years. When she was thirteen, I took her back to this place, told her what she had done. She has not spoken to me since that day."

Brophy said nothing.

"The young woman has an amazing capacity to avoid what she doesn't want to see."

"That's a very human trait."

"Yes, but some have it more than others."

Brophy took a deep, easy breath. He was quickly losing patience with this man. "You promised to speak plainly. I'm still waiting for you to keep your word."

"Very well. I wasn't sure if you truly understand how dangerous she is. Arefaine will not hesitate to kill anyone who thwarts her desires."

"I know that."

"And she still believes that she controls the black emmeria, when, in fact, it controls her."

"I know that as well. But I believe she can overcome it."

"That is very admirable. I hope you are right, but I question how well you know Arefaine."

"I know her well enough."

"Really? What does she desire more than anything else?"

Brophy closed his eyes and imagined her curled naked around him as he pretended to sleep.

"She wants what everybody wants. She wants to be loved."

"Precisely. She is hungry for love, for home, family, acceptance."

"Do you blame her, after the way you've treated her all these years?"

Dewland lowered his eyes and let out a little breath. "That was hardly an accident, you realize."

"What?"

"The emperor chose to isolate her. It was the hardest thing he had ever done, to treat her so coldly."

"You did that on purpose?"

"To our shame, yes. We could think of no other way."

Brophy snarled and grabbed the little man by the front of his cloak. "Other way to do what?"

Dewland put his wrinkled old hands on top of Brophy's.

"Please, Brophy, this anger is not your own."

"A lot of it is!"

For the first time, Brophy saw a flicker of fear in Dewland's eyes. It sent a cool thrill through him.

"You must understand what we are up against," Dewland said.

"No one knows better than me what we are up against," Brophy hissed. "I was trapped in that dark hell for eighteen years!"

"And Arefaine was in there for three hundred. She committed her first murder at three years old. She killed Father Lewlem because he wouldn't let her eat poisonous berries."

"She was a child!"

"Yes. A child who could destroy the world." Dewland looked pointedly at Brophy and he relaxed his grip on the old man's cloak. "How would you parent such a creature?" Dewland asked. "How would you bring a soul who had spent lifetimes in the darkness back into the light?"

"With compassion," Brophy said. "With love and tenderness. Not with manipulation and neglect."

"You would have shown her love?"

"Yes."

"But you haven't, have you?"

Brophy picked the priest up and slammed him against the trunk of Lewlem's tree.

Dewland swallowed and chose his next words very carefully. "I'm not condemning you. Arefaine is not very easy to love."

"That has nothing to do with her."

"You are in love with the Zelani?"

"Yes."

"And not in love with Arefaine?"

Brophy paused, took a deep breath. "We are becoming closer."

"But you are not in love with her?"

"No. I'm not."

Dewland slowly nodded. "That is unfortunate, but, in the end, you don't have to love her. She has to love you. That is all that matters."

"Enough!" Brophy roared, pounding him against the tree again. "Enough of your riddles. Tell me what I need to know."

Dewland placed his hands gently on Brophy's shoulders. "I will tell you everything I can, but you must promise me you will go to the cave first. Find a way past the gate. Go there and listen for the Voice of Oh. It is the only thing that can convince you to see the wisdom in what you will surely call madness."

Brophy shook him. "Just tell me."

Dewland paused for a moment. His brows drew together, but then he sighed. "Arefaine must complete what Oh started. She must bring all of the black emmeria to Efften and—"

"You want her to kill herself! You want her to sacrifice her own life to contain the emmeria forever."

Dewland nodded. "Yes. That is the only path—"

Brophy threw Dewland away in disgust. The old man flew into the bushes and rolled across the ground. "You disgust me."

"Brophy, she must—"

"She must? She must! What about you? What must you do?" Brophy pounded his fists together to keep them away from the old man's neck. "There's a dragon out there, a dragon that needs to be killed. Yet you're perfectly happy to feed your children to the beast rather than go face it yourself."

"Brophy, I would face that beast if I could, but I don't have that kind of power. None of us have that kind of power. None except her."

"She's the only one. The only person who can kill the man from my dreams?"

"She is. But slaying him would be pointless. If she killed him, who would be left to kill her? Ani is the problem. The sacred fire burns all that it touches. It must be contained forever. She must finish what Oh started."

Brophy's lip curled in disgust. "Arefaine will never throw away her life for the likes of you. And I wouldn't let her even if she wanted to."

The old priest sat up with a wince, cradling his arm against his chest. "She might," he said softly. "To save your life. She might do it for love."

Chapter 6

Ossamyr paused at the rail of the little bridge shrouded in mist. A series of waterfalls spilled over moss-covered rocks in front of her, so close she could almost touch them. Behind her, over the other rail, the mountainside dropped away to nothing, the water falling a hundred feet before plunging into a narrow pool.

She couldn't hear any birds or forest creatures. The light drizzle camouflaged all other sounds except the distant roar of the waterfall far below. She was so high on the mountainside that she was practically lost in the clouds. She couldn't even see the city anymore, and the palace was a dark blur lost in the haze. She tracked the course of the river as it snaked down the narrow valley over a series of cascades and disappeared into underground tunnels beneath the Opal Palace. Ossamyr had used those tunnels to slip past the palace into this narrow valley. She hadn't even gotten wet doing it. Like everything in the Opal Empire, the Ohohhim storm sewers were clean and well made, with broad pathways on either side of the river course. She hadn't seen a single lock or sentry anywhere in the palace. Any Ohohhim with the courage to step out of line would find herself in a thief's paradise.

But it did not feel like an assassin's paradise.

Ossamyr looked at the narrow dirt path that continued up the mountain from the bridge. Two days from now, the emperor's body would be interred in the Cave of Oh at the end of that path, and Arefaine would be there, alone. After spending almost a day in the palace cloaked in a glamour, Ossamyr had finally uncovered that piece of crucial information while hiding in plain sight among the contingent of servants who were discussing the funeral preparations. Arefaine was to spend the night in the cave with the body, listening for Oh's wisdom to guide her forward. She would be there alone, without protection, without her Carriers to distract her from the god's voice.

She'd lost track of Brophy in her search for information about Arefaine, but she'd just have to let him wait until her mission was done.

Ossamyr left the bridge and hiked up the path. She kept her magic wrapped tightly around her, more out of habit than necessity. The glamour only encouraged people to see what they expected to see. The farther she left civilization behind, the less useful such a spell became.

The exquisite mosaic path that Ossamyr had followed earlier ended about halfway up the mountain. Its final images showed the Nightmare Battle in Ohndarien and Brophy lying on his bier atop the Hall of Windows. There was still plenty of room for the story to continue, and Ossamyr had no idea how it would end. Murder? Or disaster? Would there be anyone left to lay out the final scenes?

She continued up the steep trail, careful to keep her steps silent and sure. The hardpacked earth was slick with rain. A single misstep would send her tumbling down the nearly vertical mountainside. Her clothes were soaked from the rain and from constantly brushing against the ferns that overgrew the trail. A relentless chill seeped into her desert-born bones.

As she rose, step after step, she thought about her mission. Reef had assured her that the rainbow-colored crystal she had swallowed would shield her from Arefaine's magic, but she did not share the Islander's confidence.

"The witch relies more on her magic than her senses," Reef had told her. "She can sense everyone for a hundred feet in every direction, even with her eyes closed, but she won't see you. Same as old Efften. They had supreme arrogance in their magical sight, and we unloaded a hundred ships on their shores before they even knew they were under attack. That's the way it will work. And once you get her alone, it's just you against one unarmed girl. She'll throw magic at you first, of course. They always do. And by the time she realizes she can't hurt you, you drive the dagger home. That's the way they all died on Efften."

It had sounded like a good plan weeks ago on his ship, but now that she was here, she could think of a hundred ways it could go wrong. She'd seen what Shara could do to herself physically with the Floani form. Arefaine might not be able to use magic on Ossamyr, but she could use it on herself.

Reef was absolutely dedicated to his mission, but Ossamyr knew that he didn't know everything about magic. Shara had explored depths that Ossamyr couldn't fathom, and Arefaine had the blood of the Morgeons in her veins. No one knew what she was capable of, perhaps not even the girl herself.

For the thousandth time, Ossamyr reached down to her thigh and touched the dagger he had given her. She imagined the sticky gray poison on the blade. Reef had offered to show her how quickly it worked, but she declined. She believed him. If the blade broke the skin, Arefaine would die.

Ossamyr reached the end of the path and waited a moment, slowing her breathing. The cave was not what she expected. It was nothing more than a jagged pit in the sloped ground, circled by crude, moss-covered stones and overgrown with ferns.

She took another step forward, forced herself to crouch next to the opening and peer inside. The rain seemed quieter here. The world seemed smaller. She felt a pull in her gut, something tugging her toward that opening. She swallowed down a dry throat. There was something in there. A light emanated from deep within. Was it some priest? A daily homage? Did they leave a lit torch inside?

She paused, unsure if she wanted to go in. Her glamour wouldn't protect her in there.

Bracing herself, she clambered over the slick rocks into the hole. It descended steeply for a few feet, leading toward a narrow underground opening. She crawled through the cave's entrance on hands and knees, careful to keep her movements quiet. After a few feet, the cave widened into a natural tunnel almost tall enough for her to stand in. Crouching, she placed one foot carefully in front of the other and proceeded forward.

The air was heavy, thick, as if the mountain all around her were desperately trying to crush this unwanted breach. A presence exuded from the very walls, and the tunnel itself seemed to glow. She couldn't tell if her eyes were playing tricks on her, or if the glow was residual light from a source farther ahead.

The light flickered and moved.

She crouched, pressing herself against the rock wall, and stared intensely ahead. Her breath came faster, as if someone were squeezing her rib cage. The light moved again, but did not come closer.

Her body screamed at her to leave, but she rose slowly from her crouch and continued on, following the curve. She stopped, her heart beating madly as she reached a jumbled pile of stones that cut off the tunnel. She crept along the small maze of destruction, peering into the near darkness for a way to get through. Had the angry mountain succeeded? Had Oh's cave collapsed? She worked her way around the pile of stones, wincing as one of them shifted, making a tiny scraping noise. Crouching down, she crawled underneath one boulder and between two others. Little passageways disappeared in the darkness on either side of her, and she felt as if there were eyes in those spaces, watching her quietly as she trespassed on holy ground.

This is madness, she thought. *Get out of here before you're trapped forever.*

She ignored the invisible eyes, ignored her thoughts. Sometimes crouching, sometimes crawling, she squeezed through to the other side. Beyond the cave-in, the tunnel widened into a larger chamber.

Her breath caught in her throat, and she pushed herself against the cold rock.

Brophy stood on the far side of the cavern, looking down at the shattered remains of a great stone tomb. His hands rested on the jagged edge, and his head was bowed. Such a boy. So strong, vital, intense. She closed her eyes, trying to shut out the memory of his laughter, the memory of his earnest look when he'd asked her to run away with him. It had been eighteen years ago, but it rose in her mind as if it was yesterday.

She stared at him like a jumping rat frozen in a cobra's gaze. Why was he here? Why now? This meeting couldn't happen now. Not . . . Not until this was done.

But she couldn't make herself leave. If she tried to kill Arefaine and failed, everything she wanted to say would be left unspoken. This could be her only chance to talk to him, to finally apologize.

Ossamyr retreated into the shadows, fighting to control her breath. What would he think if he found her here? Would he kill her? Expose her mission? Could she make him see anything more than a traitorous queen trying another assassination?

Biting her lip, she peered around the corner, looking at the side of his face. She closed her eyes, barely able to breathe. If this was the only moment she was to be given, then that's the way it was. He had to know. She had to try. She had to make him see.

Footsteps behind her!

She whirled around, listened closely. Someone was coming.

Quiet as a whisper, she retreated into a dark alcove, between two boulders. Sending a surge of ani to her glamour, she leaned her back against the rock wall and pulled her black cowl over her face. The chill of the rock seeped through her sodden clothes.

The footsteps neared, light and lithe. Someone trained or someone young. Perhaps both.

"Brophy?" The voice came from the far side of the rubble.

Ossamyr's hand slipped under her dress and unsheathed the dagger. She could end it now, when Arefaine passed beside her in the darkness. She could cross the distance in a heartbeat. The young sorceress would never know until the dagger was buried to the hilt in her back.

"Yes. It's me," Brophy called back.

Ossamyr winced, her heart aching. She hadn't heard his voice in so long.

He crawled into the jumble of stones not five feet from her. She could almost reach out and touch him.

"Through here," he said.

Ossamyr heard Arefaine crawl forward. In a few moments she would pass right by Ossamyr's hiding place.

Brophy would try to stop her, if she attacked. He'd always seen the world in black and white, and he would have no doubt upon which side of that line Ossamyr stood. Like Baelandra said, Ossamyr's betrayal was like yesterday to the boy.

But *could* he actually stop her if she attacked Arefaine? She knew how fast he was. With surprise, she might be faster, but she might not.

And then what would he do? Would he hate her, loathe her, kill her before she had a chance to explain? Why would he believe the lying, scheming Queen of Physendria over his new lover? The boy had always been gullible. When he fell, he fell hard. She, of all people, knew how true that was. He'd been willing to die, and to kill, for her before. He would certainly be willing to kill for the beautiful goddess of the Ohohhim.

Arefaine reached him. He took her hand and helped her through the narrow opening.

Ossamyr clenched her teeth. Her hand trembled, and she wanted more than ever to stick a knife into the young woman.

But she didn't. She couldn't. Not now.

Instead, she slowed her breathing, calmed her heart. And she listened.

Chapter 7

rophy helped Arefaine to her feet, and they looked at each other for a long moment in the faint torchlight. Her smile was irreverent and wild. She wore a black cloak with an opal clasp over a black gown. There was a little streak of powder just above her ear, but the rest had been wiped from her face. He knew she'd washed it off for him. And he knew why. He sensed her desire like a dark current pulling him away from the shore.

She had lain hidden in the rocks for quite some time, watching him from the darkness while he stood before the broken tomb that once held Oh's coffin. He wondered why she had hesitated, why she had remained hidden. Was she afraid to talk to him? Or was it Oh's presence she feared?

"How did you know I would be here?" he asked.

She winked at him. "Magic."

He frowned, and the carefree glimmer faded from her eyes.

"I heard that you spoke with that priest," she said. "Where else would he send you?"

Brophy nodded, letting go of her hand and walking back to the shattered crypt. Brophy had expected Oh's resting place to be the height of opulence, the crown jewel of a city crafted to perfection, but it was just a dusty little hole in the ground with a broken tomb.

Arefaine stopped next to him, put a hand on the cracked lid. She did that a lot, mimicked his actions.

"Have you heard 'the voice' yet?" she finally asked, the sardonic half smile returning to her face.

"What do you think?" he asked.

She chuckled. "I came up here many times when I was a child. I never heard a thing."

"Then why did you lock the gate?"

She paused, tapping the lid with one fingernail. "To keep everyone else away." She gave him a lingering look out of the corner of her eye. "But I knew a simple lock wouldn't stop you."

Brophy turned and focused on the tomb before him. Arefaine had changed since arriving in the Opal Empire. She was devouring the attention she received from the hundreds of servants and advisors. She felt like she was slipping further and further away from him.

"So what do you think of this great empty cave the priests are so in love with?" Arefaine asked.

"Why do you say it is empty?"

She watched him for a moment. "Because the ghost who is supposed to haunt it died a long time ago." Her playful tone vanished. "The first emperor wasn't a god. He was a mage just like me—powerful but mortal."

"That's not what the emperor believed. He swore he was following the Voice of Oh."

Arefaine's brows came together in consternation. "There is no Oh! There hasn't been for a thousand years."

"How can you be that sure?"

She frowned, staring hard at him. "If you're waiting for a god to appear, you will be here until this mountain crumbles to dust. Oh was nothing more than a weakling driven by fear. He stole the world's greatest treasure and expected everyone to wait meekly in line while he locked it away."

"Maybe," Brophy said. "But there is something here. I can feel it."

"A thousand-year-old bloodstain." She shook her head. "Nothing more."

"Perhaps, but that bloodstain has become the map of your life."

Arefaine turned away from him and took a minute to calm herself. "We're fighting again?"

Brophy said nothing.

"I thought we had agreed to seek answers together," she said. She came back and took his hand. "Are you angry with me?"

He let out a breath. "Not with you."

"I'm not sure I believe you."

He paused, then said, "Let's leave this place. Let's go to Efften. Alone. Tonight."

Her eyes narrowed. "Not during the twelve days of mourning. I've been very careful about maintaining all the customs to ease the transition—"

He put his fingertips against her lips. "You like being regent too much. It frightens me."

She studied his face carefully before replying. "What did that priest tell you?"

"The emperor said you had a decision to make when you arrived on Efften."

"Yes."

"Dewland told me what that decision would be and what choice they want you to make."

Arefaine took a deep breath. Lewlem's soul light flew out of her sleeve and began to circle her head. "What did he say?"

"He and the emperor want you to take all the black emmeria to Efften and seal it within one of the silver towers. They want you to kill yourself, to reenact Oh's sacrifice."

She tried to keep the emotions from her face, but Brophy could see the war going on behind her eyes.

"They don't believe you would ever make that choice on your own, so they wanted to make sure you fell in love with me. They hoped that you would sacrifice yourself to save my life."

She nodded, her jaw muscles flexing.

"That's why the emperor isolated you, ignored you. He wanted you lonely. He thought that would somehow force you into this decision."

She turned away, her breath coming in ragged gasps. Lewlem zipped around her head, and she snatched him out of the air, clenching him in her fist.

"They . . ." The words stuck in her throat. "They raised me for the slaughter?"

"It's not going to happen, Arefaine," he said. "I won't let it."

Arefaine pressed her fist to her lips and stared at Oh's tomb. "There have been enough sacrifices," Brophy said. He stepped around her and grabbed her hands. She tried to pull away, but he wouldn't let her. "There have been enough lives lost to the black emmeria. Oh couldn't resist its power, so he assumed no one could. But I've done it. You've done it. Together we can destroy it."

Arefaine twisted out of his grasp. "Is this part of the lie? Is all of this just to get me to fall in love with you?"

Brophy looked into her red-rimmed eyes. "I hate what they did to you, and I won't be any part of their plan."

She looked back at him, trying to see the truth in his words.

"Come with me," he said. "We'll leave for Efften tonight. Let's go see what's locked in those silver towers and decide for ourselves what to do about it."

Arefaine scoffed. "You want me to just walk away, abandon everything I've achieved here?"

"Yes."

Her lips came together in a firm line, and he waited as she struggled to answer.

"You think I like the power too much," she said in a voice barely above a whisper.

He nodded.

"Perhaps I do. I want them to bow to me. Every last one of them." She drew a breath through her teeth. "They owe me."

"Yes. They owe you," Brophy said. "And you now have the power to collect that debt ten times over. But is that what you really want? Do you want to punish the Ohohhim? Fling them against the Silver Islanders until they are all dead? Will that make you happy? Will that make up for everything you have lost?"

Arefaine clenched her fist, looking at the shadowy ground. Her proud shoulders slumped, and she let out a breath as though she'd let go of all the weight in the world.

"You'll really go there with me, just the two of us?" she asked, looking up at him. "You'll help me find my father?"

"I don't think you'll find your father, but I do think you'll find what you're looking for."

"All right," she said softly, her chin lifted. In the yellow torchlight, he saw the tears standing in her eyes. "I'll go with you. I'll go tonight."

Relief flooded through him, for a moment pushing back the howling voices in his mind that constantly threatened to overwhelm him. "Good," he said.

She finally got her breath back under control and nodded. "There's something I need to know before we go," she said with a little sniffle. "I think I always knew what the Ohohhim wanted from me. And I never cared. Not what Oh wants, or what the emperor wants. They're dead. But I need to know . . ." She closed her eyes and swallowed. "I need to know what you want from me?"

He nodded, knowing what she was asking.

She opened her eyes, looking at him, desperate as a child. "Do you . . ." She winced. "Who do you love, Brophy? Who do you want?"

Brophy sighed and looked up at the ceiling. It took him a long time to answer. When he did, he spoke softly. "I remember love," he said with a bitter half smile. "I remember loving Shara. My aunt. Ohndarien. I even remember loving the feel of the sun on my face." He shook his head. "But that's all gone now. I don't feel anything anymore, just anger, bitterness, rage. I think that part of me is gone, ripped away. And I don't know if I'll ever get it back." The words seared in his chest as he spoke them. It seemed like he should be crying, but there was nothing, not even tears.

"What if we could get that part of you back?" she said, touching the sides of his face.

He cocked his head to the side. "What do you mean?"

"Do you even remember why you agreed to come to Ohohhom in the first place?"

So much had happened since they'd left the Cinder. Since they'd left Ohndarien. He struggled to remember all the things they'd talked about.

"You came here to be free of the voices in your head. You wanted to learn how to shut them out. I think I can do that for you now."

"How?" he asked, suddenly feeling his heart beating faster.

"Let me show you."

Arefaine took a deep breath and her fingertips on the side of his face started growing warmer. He felt a steady surge of her ani flowing between them, into him. He flinched, but forced himself to stand his ground. The energy warped the air around him. Arefaine's face pinched in concentration.

Slowly, the howling voices in Brophy's head faded away. The seething hate that ate at his mind vanished. He gasped, sucking a breath into lungs that suddenly seemed twice as large.

The dark cave, so like the confining prison of his hellish mind, was suddenly bright with dancing torchlight. Each bead of dew on the rough-hewn walls was a sparkling diamond. The slight breeze in the cave tickled the hairs on his forearms. The air felt deliciously cool and wet.

"By the Seasons!" He laughed, looking at his hands as if they belonged to someone else. "What did you do to me?"

He turned his gaze on Arefaine.

She watched him with a small smile on her face. "I've never heard you laugh."

"How did you do it?"

"Something I discovered recently," she said, the words tight. He noticed that she still clenched one of her fists. He could see the strain of what she was doing around her eyes.

"Arefaine?"

"I don't know how long I can keep it up, but at least for now, you're free."

"Oh, Arefaine!" He crossed to her and took her in his arms. "Thank you," he said, kissing her. "Thank you." He'd forgotten what joy felt like, bubbling up inside him like a gulp of Siren's Blood.

Arefaine's sudden, deep breath caused her breasts to press against his ribs. His hands slid down the curve of her back. Their mouths opened, tongues touched.

A surge of warmth shot through him and the kiss turned ardent, desperate lips pressing against each other. Arefaine leaned into his arms and brought her leg up, wrapping it around the back of his thigh.

He lowered her to the sandy floor. She pulled his shirt over his head, and his hand slid between the folds of her dress, touching skin. Her back arched and her cloak slipped open, revealing the curves of her small breasts.

Brophy knelt between her thighs. She lay back and stared at him, torchlight flickering along her pale legs. With a flick of her fingers, she unhooked the opal clasp of her cloak, letting it pool on the floor.

He leaned forward and kissed her, shocked by the sudden rush of desire as their bare skin met. He crushed her to him, his mouth on hers, his fingers pushing into her hair as his weight pressed down on her. Her breasts slid firm and warm across his chest.

Arefaine pushed his pants down past his hips and he slipped inside of her. She gasped, breaking the kiss, pressing her forehead against his, clutching him with all her might as she trembled, thin and fragile like a little bird.

Brophy didn't move. He held the moment, reeling with the raw power of being inside her. When her breath slowed, he drew back, searching her face. Ice-blue eyes found his, and her breathing came fast. She pulled at him, hands clutching desperately.

He leaned over to kiss her, and the feather hanging from his neck swung forward and hit her in the chin.

She blinked, brushing it aside, and kissed him. Her teeth brushed against his lips, nearly biting. He moved against her, inside her. The heat rose between them, making his skin tingle in the chilly air of the cave. His breath came faster as her fingers raked down his back.

One of Arefaine's nails caught on the leather thong, pulling it tight against his throat. Her body tensed. She reached up to his neck and lifted the necklace over his curls. Brophy stopped moving as she set the feather in the sand next to them. Something twisted inside his belly.

"Brophy?" she whispered, wrapping her legs tighter around him.

He stared at the feather.

"Brophy?" she repeated, pushing his gaze back to her.

"Arefaine . . ." he began, slowly reaching for the feather.

"No," she murmured, grabbing his wrist. "Look at me."

Brophy shook his head, reaching for the feather again.

"No," she said, spinning on top of him, rolling them off the cloak and onto the sand. "Brophy," she whispered urgently, grabbing his face, trying to force it back toward hers. "Look at me."

"Wait," he panted, feeling the joy dying inside him. He tried to get up. "We have to wait. I have to think a minute." He gazed at the leather necklace in his hand.

With a snarl, she squeezed the sides of his face. He gasped as a flood of power rushed into him, striking him in the chest, filling him with fire. He grew hard in an instant, painfully hard. The roaring voices of the black emmeria slammed back into his mind, louder than ever. He wanted to bite her, lash out at her with his fists.

"Not this time," she breathed, pushing him to the ground, straddling him.

"Arefaine," he cried, twisting away. But she swelled with power, and she pinned him to the floor. Her lips pulled back in a snarl.

"Stop it!" he shouted, spinning his wrist and chopping out of her grip. She clawed at his face, and they rolled across the cold sand. "Enough!" he screamed, shoving her away from him.

She spun around, her dark hair in disarray. Her fingers dug into the soft sand.

"I could have had you anytime I wanted!" she screamed at him. "Anytime!"

He stood up and backed away, hands in front of him.

"I can make you love me," she said, rising to her feet. "I can do it."

"That's not love," he said, desperate to keep his temper. "That's hate."

Her face contorted, and she lashed out at him. Brophy blocked the blow and shoved her backward. She crashed into the tomb, knocking her head against the stone. His hands curled into claws and he took a step toward her. With a feral cry, he spun away and slammed his fist into the cave wall.

"No!" he growled, spinning back around to look at her.

She stared at him for a moment, a line of blood trickling down her chin. Slowly she brought her arms close to her body, covering her naked breasts. Her lip started to tremble, and she bit down on it.

"Brophy," she whispered, but he turned away from her, unable to meet her gaze. A sob caught in her throat and she fled, snatching her gown off the ground and scrambling through the gap in the boulders.

Brophy sank to his knees, nearly throwing up. He crawled to the feather lying in the sand and squeezed it in his fist. He knelt there, fighting the vengeful voices that threatened to overwhelm him. His beautiful moment of freedom was gone, and the brutal crush of their presence was that much harder to bear. He wanted to kill Arefaine for giving him such a gift and then snatching it away. He wanted to rend her limb from bloody limb.

He curled into a ball and hid his face in his hands. *Help!* he shouted in his mind. *That's not me. It is not me!*

The howling voices receded as another voice appeared in his mind. The same one he'd heard when he first arrived here.

Bide, my son, bide, Oh said, surrounding him like a warm and gentle mist. *Her heart is growing. It will blossom in time.*

"Enough," he growled. "I've heard enough of your *wisdom*. I won't lead her to the slaughter. I won't help you kill her."

As you say, but your heart will blossom as well. In time.

Chapter 8

Ossamyr sprinted down the path, nearly slipping on the mud and tumbling over the edge. She leapt several steps, ducked a sopping tree branch, and shivered as a cascade of water drenched the back of her neck.

The Physendrian queen had fled from the cave when Brophy and Arefaine started kissing. She couldn't watch that, even if it meant her death. She'd crept silently through the jumble of boulders, unable to force the sight of their embrace from her mind. She didn't want Brophy anywhere near that girl, scheming her way into his heart with artful tears over a tragic past. Arefaine was poised to destroy the world, and Brophy refused to see it.

She had planned to flee the scene, catch the girl alone later, but she paused at the sound of angry voices behind her. Arefaine had turned on Brophy, assaulting him with her power.

What had happened? Had Brophy spurned her? Ossamyr couldn't tell, but Morgeon's daughter had run blindly from the cave, sobbing and hugging her clothing to her chest. It was all Ossamyr could do to keep ahead of her on the narrow path, sprinting for all she was worth.

She couldn't get the image of the two of them out of her head. The way Brophy had touched her hand, the way he seemed so invested in her, speaking words she refused to hear. Ossamyr's heart ached when he said he felt nothing anymore. That had been partly her doing. She had plunged the first dagger into his heart.

Ossamyr split her concentration between maintaining her glamour and her footing. She leapt another short flight of steps, slipped on the wet ground. She winged her arms and almost fell, skirting the edge of the steep drop-off, only half in control. She didn't catch her balance until she reached the narrow bridge over the waterfall.

As she ran, she realized this might be her only chance to catch the sorceress alone. There was a huge May Dragon tree just down the trail from the bridge. It was the perfect place for an ambush, if she could only reach it in time.

Her feet thumped across the bridge. The noise of the waterfall roared around her and fell away behind, quickly consumed by the patter of falling rain. The path grew steeper as she raced down the twisting mountainside. She turned a corner and saw the May Dragon tree, its broad trunk nearly blocking the path. Arefaine would run right past it and never see a thing until Ossamyr's dagger was buried in her chest.

Charging into the thick overgrowth, Ossamyr whipped around the tree—

—right into the arms of a dark man. He jerked, plunging his sword into her belly.

"Die, traitor," the Carrier of the Opal Fire growled in her ear, twisting the blade. She looked up into his eyes; saw the two other Carriers behind him.

"The children of Oh will never follow—" The Carrier's eyes flew wide as he saw her face.

She gaped, twitching. Her legs buckled, but she didn't fall. She hung impaled on the man's blade. She breathed a small whimper, unable to summon the breath for a scream.

"That's not her, that's not the child!" the Carrier behind him exclaimed.

Ossamyr's mind reeled, rolling in an ocean of pain. They thought she was Arefaine. They'd come to kill their regent, and Ossamyr's glamour had showed them what they expected to see.

"Here she comes!" the third man hissed, looking up the path.

The assassin threw Ossamyr down, his blade sliding out of her body. She hit the ground hard, sucked in a deep breath, and tried to hold her guts in.

The three Carriers rushed around the tree. Arefaine ran naked down the path, clinging to her dress. Her eyes went wide, and she tried to stop suddenly. She slipped, sprawling on the muddy path.

The first two Carriers came at her from opposite directions, swords arcing down.

"Kill!" Arefaine shouted, and Ossamyr felt the powerful surge of magic. The first man's blade missed Arefaine by inches. He spun with the momentum and buried his blade in his friend's shoulder.

The second Carrier screamed as he was borne sideways. His sword flew from numb fingers, missing the girl. The two Carriers tumbled into the bushes.

The third assassin charged Arefaine. The girl threw her hands in front of her and screamed. Absolute blackness flew from her hands. It slammed into the Carrier, knocking him off the trail and down the mountainside. The liquid blackness engulfed the great May Dragon tree and slithered up its trunk. A bitter howl filled the world, drowning out the roar of the waterfall and the falling rain.

Ossamyr cringed, holding her belly together as she threw all of her magic into a protective bubble, fending off the black emmeria that swirled all around her. The May Dragon tree twisted and snapped. Its trunk undulated like a muscle flexing until it ripped itself apart. The rending wood shrieked as the tree shattered and plunged over the edge.

Ossamyr shut her eyes and forced the blackness away from her. The pressure seemed unbearable. Howling voices whipped through her hair. The foliage blackened and wilted all around her as the plants twisted in agony. Some melted like wax. Others disintegrated.

Arefaine lay where she had fallen. Dark streaks extended outward from her like rays from a black sun. She stared at her hands in horror. A little ball of golden light spun frantically around her head.

Two hunched, blackened beasts slowly rose from the surrounding forest. They slunk toward her. One reached up, ripping the shark-fin helmet from its head. Part of its scalp tore loose from its misshapen head. It howled its rage at Arefaine as it swelled, its bones twisting and snapping.

Arefaine scrambled to her feet and sprinted back up the path. Blood-thirsty shrieks erupted from the corrupted beasts, and they launched after her in close pursuit.

"Get her," Ossamyr whispered, her bloody hands shaking where they pressed at her abdomen. "Rip her black heart out."

Chapter 9

Arefaine clutched her dress to her naked chest as she fled back up the hill. Screaming voices swirled around her, through her, flooding her from all directions at once. She couldn't stop them. She couldn't get away.

She glanced over her shoulder. Her Carriers followed, their claws churning the earth as they ran on all fours. Their eyes burned like coals. Lewlem flew into one of the things' scaly face, and it stumbled, slipping in the mud. The other one leapt over it without breaking stride, drawing closer with every jump.

She raced across the bridge, her bare feet slapping the wet wood.

They were too fast! She had to think. Had to—

She looked back again just as one of the creatures leapt on her, sinking its teeth into her shoulder. Bones snapped and flesh tore. Arefaine screamed as she fell, her fists bouncing off it like she was striking stone.

A white hand suddenly grabbed the beast's neck. Brophy leapt over Arefaine, hauling the creature away from her. He spun and threw her attacker down the steep slope. It skidded to a stop as the second one leapt over it and charged him.

The two Carriers leapt upon Brophy and dragged him to the ground. He fought back, taking and landing thunderous blows. The three combatants became a blur of black hide and white skin.

Agony seared Arefaine's shoulder as she rolled to her knees. Her palm slid across the sharp edge of a bone protruding through the flesh. A surge of energy flooded her and she let it come, filling her like a screaming wind.

Brophy kicked one of the creatures away from him. It broke through the railing and nearly fell, but its claws stuck fast in the wood at the last moment. It dangled over the abyss, fighting for a better grip. Arefaine reached out for its mind, tried to grab hold of it, but her thoughts floundered in an ocean of pain. She couldn't concentrate, couldn't control her breath.

Brophy wrestled with the other corrupted Carrier. It pinned him to the bridge and tried to punch him, but he slipped sideways. The creature's fist splintered the wooden planking. Brophy spun to his feet and slammed both fists into the side of its head, knocking the creature halfway through the hole.

The second beast scrambled over the railing. Brophy lunged forward and grabbed it before it could regain its feet. He spun around behind it and snapped its neck. The thing's head flopped limply to its chest, but it continued to fight, its arms and legs frantically clawing at thin air. Brophy threw the monster at its fellow. The two beasts mindlessly lashed out at each other for a moment, claws ripping through each other and tearing chunks out of the bridge.

Borne aloft by the screaming wind, Arefaine focused on her wound. Closing her eyes, she grabbed her mangled shoulder under the armpit and pushed on it until the splintered bone slid back within her body. With a roar of triumph, she felt the wound bubble, twist, and close.

Brophy ripped away a piece of splintered railing and leapt back into the fray. Black blood flew as he stabbed the abomination in the neck with the length of splintered railing.

Arefaine rose to her full height. She took three huge breaths through clenched teeth and spun her pain, her rage, and all the screaming voices into a single black ball in the center of her body. The blazing sphere burned away all pain, all fear, and a glorious sensation flooded her.

With a smile, she took one last great breath and threw her power at the Carriers. It roared out of her in a screaming black wave. The ani struck them like midnight surf crashing into black rocks. Brophy was thrown backward as the ani devoured everything it touched. The Carriers disintegrated, splattering the mountainside with black chunks of bubbling flesh. The wooden bridge inflated, twisted, and then burst like cracking bones.

The bridge collapsed, and Brophy fell with the shattered remains. He spun, flailing to save himself. He grabbed a broken crossbeam with one bloody hand and jerked to a stop, dangling over the valley below. Black tendrils swept across his face as he stared at Arefaine from the far side of the chasm. His black eyes began to glow red.

Arefaine drew tortured breaths, watching him. The heartstone in his chest flared a blinding crimson that hurt her eyes. Above it dangled the black feather that Shara had given to him.

"Arefaine," he cried, his red eyes boring into her. His teeth grew longer, sharper.

Lewlem spun around her head like an angry insect. She ignored him and grabbed her shoulder, pinching the sides of the ragged wound together. The skin knit and became smooth. She looked for further damage down the length of her naked body and saw the streak of blood on her inner thigh. A wound that couldn't be mended.

"You've got to fight it," Brophy yelled, "Take this!" He reached into his pocket and threw something. A shimmering shard of crystal arced across the gap between them and landed at her feet. She kicked it to the side.

"Fight them," Brophy growled, his wet fingers slipping on the wood. "Push them out of your head. I can help you."

She sneered, gathering her power, gathering her control. "You had your chance," she shouted over the roar of the waterfall.

Reaching out with her mind, she gave him a little shove. His body jerked, and his fingers slipped. He fell, tumbling end over end until he was swallowed up by the mist.

Lewlem flew after Brophy, leaving her all alone on the blackened mountainside.

Chapter 10

ewland's hands were shaking as he held the lantern in front of him, trying to peer into the shadows. Father Lewlem's soul light hovered in front of him, urging him into the dank passageway, but Dewland found it nearly impossible to follow.

He had lived with acute anxiety his entire life. Ever since he first heard the voice of Oh as a young man, he knew the world hovered precariously on the brink of oblivion. He had learned to live with that fear, but it was a vague and distant fear. Now the menace had come home to Ohohhom. It was as real as Brophy's fist around his throat when the Ohndarien had slammed him against the tree. Dewland had never before faced any immediate physical dangers, and he was beginning to fear he wasn't up to the task.

His old friend, Lewlem, returned to him and began circling his head. A veil of calm seemed to cover him, and Dewland was able to take a deep, cleansing breath.

"Thank you, my old friend," he told the little glowing ball. "But remember, you have little to fear. You are already dead."

The priest's hand still shook, rattling the lantern, but he was able to take a few steps forward. He hadn't been in this staircase since he was a young man. It was darker, steeper, and narrower than he recalled. Memorizing the passageways was part of his training as a young priest assigned to serve the emperor. He knew every hidden door and secret passage into the palace, but he had not used them in thirty years. At the time he thought it was a grand adventure to be shown the dark underbelly of the Opal Palace. But the childish excitement of creeping through old tunnels vanished when an actual corrupted creature was waiting for him somewhere in the darkness.

Dewland continued, one careful step at a time, until he reached an empty wall sconce. He was very careful to avoid the center of the stairs and only walk on the little lip of stone on the far left side of the passageway. The steps under the sconce were nothing more than a thin covering of sand and resin hiding a long dark pit. When Oh designed the Opal Palace so many years ago, he knew locks and bars would deter only the most incompetent of thieves and assassins. So the first emperor placed no locks anywhere in his palace. But the forbidden areas, the ones a criminal would be attracted to, were full of traps. Many desperate men lost their lives in these tunnels before the divine queue stabilized and the twelve tribes accepted Oh's wisdom into their hearts. No one had tried to rob the palace in generations, but the traps still remained.

Dewland heard an anguished howl in the distance that made his bowels seize. Lewlem flew away from him, disappearing down the dark passage.

The priest had heard all the stories of those scorched by the sacred fire. When Lewlem was still alive they had discussed the horrors of the Nightmare Battle in detail. Dewland had found the ghastly stories fascinating, but only because the black tales of a distant land were retold in the warm safety of a green garden. He never imagined that he would have to look such an abomination in the eyes.

The howl came again, and the sound of pitiful anguish mixed with raw fury made Dewland cringe. He knew there was a solid stone door between him and those tormented cries, but that didn't make the final steps any easier.

The stairway ended in a hidden doorway near the underground river, but he avoided the door and took a smaller passageway to the right. The side tunnel led him to an arrow slit hidden in the shadows. The narrow opening offered a clear view of the river and causeway below.

A dark figure splashed through the water, swatting at Lewlem's soul light as it dodged around the creature's head. The remains of several bodies were trapped against a metal grate that the river flowed through. Dewland couldn't see the bodies very well, but he could tell that they were pitch-black. And torn into pieces. The black figure continued to slash desperately at the air, trying to catch Lewlem's soul light.

"Brophy," Dewland tried to say, but it came out as a hoarse whisper.

"Brophy!" he called again. This time his voice rang true, and the dark figure spun around, glaring at him. All Dewland could see were three red dots in the darkness. Two of them were his eyes. The third one, much brighter, was the shard of red diamond glowing in his chest.

Brophy roared at him, charging upstream, looking for the sound of his voice.

"Child of my heart," Dewland said, his voice shaking. "You are not alone, you are among friends."

Brophy roared again and spotted Dewland's lantern through the arrow slit high above him. He launched himself at the light, trying to scramble up the slick wall.

Dewland gasped as Brophy made it fifteen feet up the wall, his black claws hooking around the edge of the arrow slit. The priest leaped backward as Brophy reached one arm through the narrow gap, trying to kill him.

"Brophy," Dewland cried, scrambling away. "Come back to us, you can fight it, you can push it back."

The boy howled and tried to force his body through the narrow gap. His face was still recognizable even though his eyes were glowing red and his skin was pitch-black, cracked and oozing. He wasn't completely gone. There was still a human in there, and Dewland had to reach him. Everything depended upon it.

Oh, give me strength, he prayed. *Give me courage.*

"Brophy, I know you can hear me. You are lost in the darkness right now, but come back to me, follow the sound of my voice."

The boy stopped struggling for a moment, panting through needle sharp teeth. He clung to the thin arrow slit with one clawed hand, suspended above the river. Lewlem circled his head.

"That's right," Dewland said, leaning closer. "Hear my voice. Follow the sound of my voice."

Brophy's red eyes closed, and his head twitched from side to side.

"This is not who you are," Dewland continued. "You are the Sleeping

Warden who sacrificed everything for those you love. Your friends. Your family. You must return to them."

He reached out to touch Brophy's hand.

With a roar, Brophy lashed out, nearly raking his claws across Dewland's arm. The old priest screamed, tearing cloth as he yanked his arm free.

Brophy went berserk. Clinging to the arrow slit, he put his feet up on the wall and yanked a chunk of masonry out of its moorings. He flew backward, falling into the river. He leapt back moments later, scrambling up the wall and forcing one shoulder through the enlarged gap.

Dewland stared in horror as the boy stripped his own flesh to the bone to force himself through the jagged opening.

A sudden white light struck Dewland between the eyes. The impact of Lewlem's soul light snapped him back to his senses. The priest scrambled to his feet, stumbled over his lantern, and fled up the stairs.

He tripped in the darkness, sprawling onto the cold stone steps. Fighting the pain, he heard another chunk of masonry snap free and land in the river. He surged forward, practically running on hands and knees. Lewlem reappeared, lighting his way up the narrow stairs. He heard a roar and then a thud as Brophy slipped through the broken arrow slit and hit the floor.

Dewland clutched a hand to his chest and kept running. Lewlem shot ahead and began to spin around a distant wall sconce.

The priest looked back; he could see the three red dots gaining on him. "Oh preserve us," he whispered, taking the steps three at a time. "Save us all."

The guttural pants and claws scraping on stone drew closer and closer, and Dewland lunged forward just before the wall sconce. His jump fell short, and he broke through the false steps. His thighs slammed into the stairs on the far side and his face cracked against the solid stone. He started to slide backward into the pit until his fingers latched onto a jagged piece of stone.

Brophy stumbled into the pit and bounced off the wall below Dewland, screaming in rage until he crashed to the bottom forty feet below.

With all the strength left in his fat, old body, Dewland hauled himself out of the trap and rolled onto the steps. He struggled to rise and threw up on his own hands, retching over and over again. "Thank you, Father, thank you," he mumbled as the bile dripped from his lips.

When he finally caught his breath, Dewland rolled onto his back.

Lewlem flew over to him and he clutched the light to his chest. He could hear Brophy howling below, scrambling up the side of the pit and falling back down.

Slowly Dewland regained his composure. This had to be the Awakened Child's doing. She was the only one who could have done this to him. If she was capable of this, then the world was already tipping toward the darkness. Only Brophy could guide her back. He had to be restored.

Dewland knew the corrupted could be healed—the emperor himself had been rescued from the darkness—but they would need a very powerful mage. They needed Brophy's paramour, the legendary Shara-lani. He opened his hands and looked at the little ball of light that had once been his best friend.

"Go, my brother. Find the woman who loves him; bring her back before it is too late."

Lewlem's spirit became a golden blur. It streaked down the dark stairs and disappeared.

The priest leaned over the edge of the pit and stared into the blackness. He couldn't see Brophy, but he could hear him down there, flinging himself up the walls and falling back down.

"Be strong, child of my heart," he said. "Hang on. All depends upon this."

Chapter 11

Shara sat alone in the dark galley picking at her dinner. It was the same thing she'd eaten the last three nights, dried fruit and brick bread dipped in wine to soften it. Not the best of dinners, but she couldn't risk lighting a fire to cook something better.

Tonight was her sixth on the Farad messenger ship. The little craft wasn't the fastest she'd ever sailed, but it had easily overtaken Vinghelt's fleet. The Summermen's ships were designed for island hopping in the calm Summer Seas, not for long blue-water voyages. They were forced to travel at the speed of their slowest ships, which bobbed like driftwood in the heavy seas, constantly taking on water as the waves swamped their low decks. Many of them would probably be lost in a heavy storm, but the weather held good, and the weeping ones kept them on course.

The few days Shara had spent passing the Summer Fleet had been terrifying. Scores of weeping ones packed the deck of every ship. She maintained a powerful glamour at all times, but she kept expecting them to suddenly come to life and surround her like they did in Ohndarien. But the poor, soulless creatures remained inert unless a course needed to be adjusted or sails needed attention. A weeping one would move to the task, but after each of these tasks was completed, the black-eyed sailors would stop where they stood and simply wait, staring blankly ahead.

Those few days of terror slowly transformed into endless hours of tedium as she left the Summermen behind. She had never been so long in a place where she had nothing to do and no one to talk to. One bleak day flowed into another, rising and falling on the swells.

She spent most of her time trying to unravel the mystery of the voice in the black emmeria that seemed to be controlling the weeping ones. She could feel its presence all around them and slowly learned to detect the shift in the ani when it grabbed hold of an ani slave to manipulate it. The man— she assumed it was a man—said he wanted all those of illuminated blood to return to Efften, where he would create a garden for them to live in. That goal was too similar to Arefaine's for the two to be unrelated. Was that voice talking to the young sorceress? Had she fallen for his lies? It terrified Shara to think that Arefaine was only a cat's-paw to something larger, and she was beginning to feel like a child in a rowboat hunting whales.

Was she on a fool's errand? Did she really expect to stop Arefaine or was she just fleeing to Brophy's side, hoping against reason that he would accept her with open arms this time?

Stop it, she told herself. *Just wait. Wait for the moment to act.*

She emptied her mind, sweeping her worries into her glamour. She had to save her strength. There was no point in exhausting herself in a battle against shadows.

She picked at her food a little longer before packing it away and went up on deck. The night was clear and warm and the stars were already out. The faint wind smelled like the sea, not the fishy smell of a port, but the clean, salty air of the open ocean. The shadowy shoreline of Vizar was barely visible in the starlight off the starboard bow. There was an undeniable beauty to a ship under full sail. It offered the ultimate freedom. It could take you anywhere. The wind was free; the sea belonged to no one.

As she watched the waves, the tendrils of a great hatred began to build in Shara's chest. The black emmeria was at the heart of this misery. All of it. The fall of Ohndarien, Brophy's madness, Baelandra's death, all were caused by the legacy of Efften. Those mages couldn't live without their soaring towers and the slaves to build them. They'd paid for their greed with their lives, but their misdeeds lived on. How many people would have to suffer for a few men's insatiable appetites? Had humanity doomed itself three centuries ago and just didn't know it yet?

Stop it, she told herself again. *Wait for the moment to act.*

Over and over she thought she should have used her magic to search the fleet for Issefyn and that damned containment stone. She had wrested control of Baedellin from Issefyn once before, she could probably do it again. All she had to do was take command of the weeping ones aboard. It would be easy. All it would cost her was another dance with the black emmeria. She shook her head. Part of her was convinced that she could control the magic this time. She could use it without losing herself. But she was terrified by that arrogant, power-hungry side of herself. Even twenty years later, she wasn't that different from that enraged young woman who tortured her Zelani master before she killed him. She had enjoyed doing that. Enjoyed it too much. And that part of her wasn't going away anytime soon.

It was much smarter to beat the fleet to Ohohhom and confront Arefaine directly, but Shara hated doing nothing. She was just starting to realize how frustrating fighting another mage could be.

Giving up her dreams of easy victories, she planted herself by the rail and waited for the long night to pass. Her thoughts, as always, turned to Brophy. She imagined herself sneaking into the Opal Palace, creeping through the dark and twisty passageways to the door of Arefaine's bedchambers. She peered inside to find Brophy in her bed, the two of them lying naked side by side. Brophy rolled over to look at her. His eyes were black as tar, and twin rivers of blackness poured down his cheeks.

Breathing through the fear, she added it to the swirling aura of ani surrounding her, bolstering her resolve.

She imagined Brophy's soul light, blazing in the darkness ahead of her. She clung to the image, a ball of golden ani rushing toward her. She would find that light. She would return to Brophy and together they would end this madness.

Chapter 12

Breathe, Ossamyr thought. *It begins with the breath. It will end with the breath.*

She kept her eyes closed, concentrating. She imagined her wound like a black slash through the center of her body, and her ani was a golden thread woven through the rift, squeezing it closed, keeping her alive.

She'd managed to stop the bleeding, but it took almost all of her concentration to simply hold the wound closed. Even with her magic, it would take days for the wound to heal. But she didn't have days. She had to stay on her feet, had to keep moving.

Gathering her strength, she opened her eyes and peered into the darkness ahead. The roar of moving water muted her footsteps as she entered the tunnel. The underground river beneath the Opal Palace had a vaulted ceiling and narrow walkways on either side of the rushing water. The chilly upstream breeze seemed unnaturally cold on her feverish skin. She shivered, and the sudden movement sent lances of pain up her spine. Ossamyr paused, waiting for the spasm to pass.

I will not die here, she promised herself. *I will not die alone.*

She took a few more steps forward before spotting a golden light in the distance. It flew toward her, growing larger and brighter until a little glowing ball hovered about ten feet in front of her, waiting for her to continue.

"I'm coming," she said to the little light. "Don't rush me."

If it hadn't been for that little golden ball, Ossamyr would probably have died on that mountain. She'd deliriously risen to her feet moments after Arefaine had fled with the corrupted Carriers in pursuit. She'd followed them in a daze, feeling no pain. Her mind was fixated on saving Brophy and killing Arefaine, but she only got a hundred paces before collapsing in the mud, unable to think, unable to move. She didn't know how long she lay there in the rain, but she awoke when the little golden light touched her lips.

Its touch seemed to draw her out of the fog. She examined her wound for the first time. It went all the way through her body, entering just to the left of her navel and exiting alongside her spine. Her lower body was soaked with blood, and she instantly thought of that night in Physendria when Brophy held her through her miscarriage.

It was a fatal wound, she knew it the moment she saw it, but she couldn't leave Brophy up there with that demon child and her corrupted henchmen. Her task still wasn't finished. She had to see the job through. The golden light seemed to sense her conviction and lent her strength. She gathered her ani and sent it to bind her wound. The chip of light emmeria throbbed within her belly, aiding her efforts, lending her reserves of strength she never would have had.

After a few minutes she was strong enough to stand and continue up the mountain. She hadn't gone far before pausing at a curve in the trail. The roar of the waterfall was ahead. She peered through some ferns and saw the destroyed bridge. The wooden planks were warped and splintered and the near side of the mountain was blighted. The vegetation for fifty feet in every direction had been disintegrated. The rocks and earth had been scorched and little mud slides of black ooze had pooled on the trail.

The mountain was still green on the far side of the bridge, and Ossamyr nearly overlooked the naked figure huddled beneath the ferns. Arefaine lay in the mud with her arms clutching a filthy dress to her chest. Her shoulder was a bloody mess. For a brief moment, Ossamyr thought the girl was dead, but peering closer, she realized the girl was crying. Silent sobs rippled through her body.

Ossamyr drew her dagger from its blood-stained sheath and looked for a way to get around the destroyed bridge. The sides of the rain-soaked slope were nearly vertical. Even at her best, she probably couldn't make that climb, and she certainly couldn't do it with stealth. She briefly considered charging the shattered bridge and jumping across the gap. But she didn't have the strength.

She looked again at Arefaine Morgeon huddled in the rain. Had the girl finally looked in a mirror and seen her true self? Had she actually been surprised when that fountain of black emmeria came flooding out of her? And where was Brophy? Where were her guards? Had she killed them when she destroyed the bridge? Were they waiting for her at the bottom of the waterfall?

Ossamyr set aside her questions when she felt a trickle of fresh blood warm on her hip. She'd let her concentration waver. Wincing, she refocused on her wound, squeezing it together.

With a sigh, she let go of hope. Any chance of killing the sorcerer was lost. Ossamyr had lost the element of surprise. Her prey was beyond her, in distance and in power, and Ossamyr would soon die on this rain-soaked mountain without sanctuary or mourning. Her mission had failed. Morgeon's daughter would have to be stopped by another's hand.

Ossamyr imagined the sea battle that would follow. How many thousands would lose their lives to stop that one woman? She looked back at the gap in the bridge. It was more than twenty feet across. She squeezed her dagger and took a deep breath. She would have to try.

The moment she made her decision, the golden soul light began to spin around her head. She could feel its feathery touch upon her mind, trying to dissuade her. She pushed it away in annoyance and continued to gather her power. A sudden series of images came to her mind: Brophy fighting the corrupted. Brophy clinging to the broken bridge, his skin turning black. Brophy falling, disappearing into the mists.

She shook the images from her mind, fighting the emotions that swept through her. Was it a trick? Was the light in league with Arefaine? Could that black-hearted creature have created anything of such tenderness and beauty?

She looked at the light, hovering before her. It had saved her life earlier, she was sure. Another image came to mind. This one showed her in a boat, cradling Brophy's head in her lap.

"Do you know where he is?" she asked the little light.

It spun in a little circle, and she felt the warm glow of affirmation.

"You want me to help him?"

The same glow.

She looked at Arefaine one last time. The girl would have to wait.

Ossamyr opened her eyes, returning to the present. Her thoughts of the past had nearly lulled her to sleep. She had to keep moving or she would never make it.

She followed the light farther into the tunnel, one cautious step at a time.

She was nearly to the other side when a voice called from out of the shadows. "Who's there?"

She froze, concentrating on her breathing, ensuring that her glamour was still in place before she said, "It's all right. It's me."

"Who is me?" the voice asked, calm and unbending. It was a man's voice with an Ohohhim accent, and it seemed to be coming from above her.

Ossamyr drew her knife. Was her glamour slipping? She couldn't tell. Reaching out with her awareness, she tried to probe the darkness, but all she could see was a vague fog.

"The light brought me," she admitted.

"Shara-lani?"

A chill ran up her spine. "No. Ossamyr-lani."

"Who?"

She shuffled closer, wincing with every step, and peered into the darkness above her. The light zipped away from her and hovered before a jagged opening in the wall, illuminating a middle-aged man with a powdered face and rough-spun robes.

"Who are you?" Ossamyr asked.

"Just a moment," the man said, and disappeared.

A few seconds later, stone scraped on stone and a door swung inward a few feet from her. Flickering torchlight filled the dim tunnel, and the man from the broken window emerged. He was small, several inches shorter than Ossamyr, and she sensed nothing threatening from him. His silhouette showed no weapons at his waist, and he seemed relieved to see her.

"Who are you?" she asked again.

"I am Father Dewland, a humble priest of Oh. I sent the soul light looking for help. I didn't expect it to return so quickly, and I didn't expect it to bring you."

"You expected Shara? Where is she?"

The priest came closer, and the light followed him, hovering above his shoulder. He looked at her carefully. "You love him. That is why it brought you."

"I love who?"

"Come," he said. "I will show you."

Turning, he led her through the concealed doorway. Hesitating a moment, she followed, scanning the darkness with her eyes as well as her magic. No guards leapt out to grab her, but her heart pounded in her chest, waiting for a trap.

Dewland ascended a series of narrow, musty stairs. She struggled after him, one painful step at a time. She kept one hand on her belly and one on the wall to steady herself. The climb seemed interminable, and she envisioned the stairway opening into the grand ballroom of the palace. She would appear covered with blood and slime to find Arefaine on a high throne smiling her wicked smile. She would point a finger at Ossamyr, and black fire would erupt from her finger, searing her, as the laughter reverberated through the—

"Are you ill?" the priest asked, placing his hand on her shoulder.

Ossamyr shook her head. She'd slumped against the wall, nearly falling asleep.

"I'm injured," she said.

The soul light flew closer to her belly, and Dewland saw her shiny, blood-soaked skirt.

"Oh, dear," he said. "I didn't see . . . How bad is it?"

"It should have been fatal. It still might be."

"What happened?"

She brushed aside his question with her hand. "Is Brophy up there? I can't make these steps if he's not."

"He is up there, but—"

"She infected him?"

He paused before nodding. "She is the only one who could."

Ossamyr clenched her fists. "She did the same thing to her guardsmen. I was there."

Dewland was silent.

"Her own men tried to kill her," she said. "They failed."

Dewland let out a breath. "Do you know if she harmed them intentionally?"

"Does it matter?"

"Of course it matters. Very much."

Ossamyr's mouth set in a line. "Just bring me to Brophy."

He bowed to her and offered his arm to help her up the steps, but she didn't accept it.

After a short time they reached a gaping hole in the middle of the staircase. A pulley hung from an iron loop embedded in the ceiling and a length of rope lay coiled at the edge of the pit. Ossamyr heard a rumbling hiss from below.

"Is he in there?"

"He is."

She peered over the edge but saw only darkness.

"Is he dead?"

"No, he is dreaming."

"Dreaming?"

"I believe so. When I first found him, he was completely corrupted, a mindless beast. He flew into a frenzy when he first fell in the pit, but after time, he seemed to calm himself and fell asleep. I believe he returned to the dreams that held him for so many years. He knows how to fight the corruption there. That is where he knows how to survive. I cannot imagine the act of will it took for him to do that."

"Can I see him?"

Dewland touched his torch to an unlit brand sitting in the wall sconce. When it caught fire, he dropped his torch into the pit. It flickered on the way down, nearly going out, but it surged back to life after hitting the sand at the bottom of the pit.

Brophy lay sleeping on his side, curled up like a child. His clothes were in tatters. As she watched, a black stripe slithered across his cheek to the edge of his mouth and disappeared. Another spot darkened on his shoulder, then faded.

"What do you want me to do?" Ossamyr asked.

"I want you help him, get him to someplace safe and draw the emmeria out of him."

Ossamyr nodded. Her strength was almost at an end. She couldn't even heal herself, let alone draw this darkness out of Brophy. Shara was the one with the knowledge and strength for this task. But Shara was an ocean away and there was no one else.

"I can help him," she said, hoping it was true. "But not here. I have friends waiting for me offshore." She imagined Reef finding her with Brophy's head in her lap and forced the thought from her mind. "They can help him."

"No," Dewland said. "You have to help him here. He must not leave the city."

"I can't help him here."

Dewland paused. Finally he spoke in a quiet voice. "I remember now who you are. I have heard your name before. You are the Physendrian queen who became a Zelani."

Ossamyr said nothing.

"The sea witch, they call you. The mother of storms. You have been seeking a way around the Silver Islanders, trying to reach Efften."

She nodded.

"What did you seek there?"

"Containment stones to pull the black emmeria out of Brophy and end his slumber."

"That is all you sought?"

"Yes. I have no interest in horrors buried in Efften."

"Yet you came here to kill the Awakened Child."

"I thought you wanted me to help Brophy."

"I do. But you cannot take him from us. He must guide Arefaine through these difficult moments. She is our salvation."

Ossamyr shook her head. "I know what evil whispers into that woman's ears. I have looked into its eyes and seen what it wants. I came here to prevent another Nightmare Battle. To prevent one a hundred times worse."

"But Arefaine is the key—"

"She is the key that will unlock that silver tower!" she exclaimed, wincing at the pain in her belly.

"True. She could release the traitor. But she is also the only one who could cage him forever."

She laughed, short and sharp. "And what are the chances of that? Your 'salvation' nearly killed Brophy," she said, pointing into the pit. "A man she was trying to make love to ten minutes before."

Dewland sighed. "She is impulsive."

"She's not impulsive, she is evil."

"She is the only chance we have," he said solemnly.

She looked away and her bedraggled hair fell across her cheek in tangled ropes. "Will you help me get him to my friends or not?" she said in a low voice. "The only other person who can help him is your precious empress, and she will kill him."

Ossamyr thought of Arefaine crying in the rain somewhere up on the mountain. How long would it take her to recover? How long until she found them?

Dewland bowed his head. At first, she thought he was struggling with his temper, but then she realized he was praying. When he looked up at her, his gaze was serene. "Oh has foreseen the parts that Arefaine and Brophy must play," he said softly. "He knows they must face this test together." He gave her a sad smile. "And yet he has also led the two of us to this time, this place, this decision. We cannot abandon the divine path simply because we cannot see where it leads."

They stared at each other. The only sound to be heard was the distant hiss of Brophy's labored breathing.

"Wait here," Dewland said. "I will arrange for a boat."

The golden soul light circled Ossamyr's head twice and then disappeared down the dark stairs.

Chapter 13

*A*refaine slowly stopped crying and started shivering.

The rain spattered the bare skin of her shoulders and back, and she curled into a tighter ball, rocking herself back and forth. A creeping numbness seeped into her bones and she welcomed it. She liked feeling nothing, she longed for it.

Keeping her eyes closed, she concentrated on the slow steady swaying of her body. She could smell the rain, the damp earth, and the saltiness of her own tears in the back of her throat. As a child, she had rocked like this on many long nights while listening to the rain. She would take a blanket from her bed and curl up on the bench beneath her open window. She was always alone at night. Her attendants would bathe her and dress her for bed before leaving without a word. She'd learned to stop sleeping while very young and spent the long dark hours rocking herself and listening to the rain, dreaming of a place she'd never been.

Her earliest memories were of being alone in the darkness. Anguished voices swirled all around her, and she'd curled up tight to get away from them. Three hundred years she'd spent alone in the endless night, longing for a touch of warmth, a familiar voice.

And what did the Ohohhim do when she was finally released? They left her alone. Always alone. In the dark. In the rain. With screaming voices all around.

She felt a slight warmth on her cheek and opened her eyes. Lewlem's golden soul light hovered in front of her, pushing at her with his false hopes. He had come back to her. After leaving her alone for hours, he had finally come back to her.

A pain seeped into her belly to match the crushing ache in her chest, and the insistent throbbing of her shoulder. Reaching up, she cupped the little light in her palm. It trembled in her hand and she squeezed, imaging her fist turning black, blotting out the glow within. The pain in her stomach grew, creeping up her body, filling her chest, her arms, her head.

Lewlem fluttered in her hand, trying to escape. She wrapped the darkness around him. She hated him. He was part of *their* plan, the conspiracy to crush her with solitude, to make her into a gaping, needy child, starved for a kind word or tender touch.

They had nearly done it. They had nearly destroyed her with white powder, black robes, and golden curls.

The dark fire surged within her, and she sat up, clutching the treacherous light in both fists. She gritted her teeth and stoked the flames, hurling blackness against the light. The soul within fought frantically, desperate to escape her grip.

"You did this to me," she whispered. The golden glow grew weaker, slowly fading to nothing. She took a shuddering breath and looked at her palms. A faint gray vapor rose from her skin. It mixed with the swirling rain and disappeared.

She felt a sudden loss as if a steady pressure had been removed from her shoulders. She would never again be manipulated by that meddling spirit. Lewlem was gone.

"Well done, my daughter. The last of your chains are breaking."

Arefaine turned toward the calm and reassuring voice. A man crouched next to her in a green sarong that whipped in the wind. His chest was bare, and the rain fell through him. A trim goatee came to a point just below his chin.

"Father? Is that you?" She reached out, and her hand passed through the image.

"Not yet, child," her father said with a sad smile. "You see nothing more than a phantom, an empty shade. But this is the closest we have ever been. Our time is near."

"But why now? Why did you wait so long?"

He gestured toward her hands. "Your companion stood between us. He kept me at bay all these years; otherwise I would have been with you every moment."

"Lewlem? Why would they keep us apart?"

Her father brushed his insubstantial hand across her face. The slight warmth made her realize how cold she was. "You know their plans for you. They wish to douse the sacred flames. They want us and our kind gone forever."

Arefaine nodded, remembering Brophy's words.

A sob caught in her throat at the thought of him in the cave, standing naked before her, his face contorted with rage.

She had tried not to think of him, tried not to feel the weight of his betrayal. She told herself she didn't care whether he lived or died, but she had to know. One way or the other, she had to know.

Taking a deep breath, she gathered her power.

"Hush," her father told her. "Rest. The Ohndarien boy is dead. He died in the fall."

Arefaine's chest seized, and she leaned forward, biting her knee until she tasted blood.

Her father shifted, sitting next to her in the mud, and wrapped a ghostly arm around her. She could barely feel it on her rain-spattered back. "I know," he whispered. "I know how much it hurts. I, too, have felt the sting of betrayal, the shock at a senseless attack from someone I loved."

"I never loved him," she spat, tasting the blood on her lips.

"Of course you loved him."

"They made me! They tricked me into his arms."

"No, child, no. No one has that kind of power over your heart."

Arefaine squinted her eyes shut and tried to take a breath. She couldn't.

"You loved Brophy because you saw the greatness within him," her father continued. "He is a child of Efften. The illuminated blood calls to its own.

He was nearly a man worthy of you. That's why it hurts so much."

"Then why? Why did he turn his back on me? Why did he say no?"

Her father sighed, seeming to draw her closer as she shivered out of control.

"He could not see past the lies that were fed to him in the cradle. He could not believe that the monsters from his bedtime stories could actually be his family. His friends. He was a good man, but stubborn to a fault. He didn't have the wisdom to see what a treasure he held in his hands."

Arefaine bit her trembling lip. "No," she said, her jaw aching. "It wasn't that. He loved Shara. He loved her, not me. And I killed him for it." She stood up on shaky legs. "He saved me from . . . From those men, and I killed him."

She staggered to the ragged edge of the bridge. Gripping the broken railing, she peered over the edge. The billowing mist had turned gray in the gloomy dusk. She reached out for Brophy with her magic, looking for the body.

"Please," her father said, placing a feathery hand on her back. "Step back from there. You are frightening me."

"I have to—"

"He is gone. He made his choice. He stood against us, against the City of Dreams. Many others will make the same misguided choice. And they will meet the same fate."

She whirled on her father. "But he was part of that dream!"

"I know," he whispered. He wrapped his arms around her, and it almost felt like he was there. Almost. "I would love to have called him my son. I would have rejoiced at the sight of him by your side. But the dream goes on. The City of Sorcerers will flourish again. And this time no one will take her from us."

Arefaine hung her head. Wet hair fell into her eye as she looked down at the ground and saw the red crystal shard Brophy had thrown to her. Kneeling down, she picked it up, rolling the rough edges between her fingers.

Looking up at her father, she said, "But Brophy was right all along. I am corrupted, aren't I?"

Her father smiled, kind and warm. "Oh, my daughter. You have so much yet to learn."

"But I corrupted those Carriers. The black ani came from me. It's inside me, an endless ocean of it."

"The emmeria is not inside you. You are not its victim nor its slave. You are its master."

"I don't want to be its master!"

"No one does," he whispered. "No one aspires to murder, but many have taken a life to protect those they love. I'm glad you called the emmeria to your aid. You would be dead if you had not."

"I'd rather be dead."

"Don't say that. Never say that. Being powerful is not wrong, is not unnatural. The sacred fire is part of the world. We are part of it, and it is part of us. All sorcerers have access to many kinds of power. The black emmeria is simply one of them, the one that responds to fear, anger, and betrayal. When pain bubbles up within you, of course the black emmeria will be near. That is where it comes from. If you could have stopped those traitors with a kind word, you would have done so. But today you needed more than kind words, and you did what you had to. No more. No less."

"It didn't feel that way. I liked it. I liked it too much."

Her father shook his head. "Raw, blunt power is very seductive. But also very limited. You will probably never need to do that again. You are a very powerful sorceress, but you have been raised in isolation, away from your own kind. There are gaps in your knowledge. Together we can teach you control, grace, and dignity with your magic. Everything you do will be beautiful once we get to Efften. And all of this stumbling about in the dark will become a distant memory."

She turned away, running a hand across her wet hair. "I just—"

"Shush," her father said, placing a ghostly finger on her lips. "It is time to forgive yourself. You were the one attacked. You were the one betrayed. What happened today was not your fault. And once we are reunited in Efften, it will never happen again. Come, my daughter. Return to me. I have waited so long to see your face."

"But the Ohohhim will never—"

"Yes they will. Show a firm hand, and they will follow you. Do you think they want to stay locked in their endless rows. Do you think they want to live in a world beyond the warmth of the sacred fire?"

"But they tried to kill me. Not one of them threw a flower at my feet."

"I know. Change takes time. Remain firm and all will be well. I'll be by your side the entire time."

"You will?"

"I promise."

"Thank you," she whispered. "I don't want to be alone anymore."

"You never will be."

She longed to hug him, cling to him until all this was over. But she would have to wait. Soon enough, she would unlock the towers of Efften, and he would emerge into the light of day after all this time. That day would make all of this worth it. The empty years would fade away, and she would finally be home.

"Hurry," her father said. "Your men are approaching."

She ran over and grabbed her ruined dress. Fumbling with numb fingers, she stepped into it and slipped the wet material over her hips. Wincing, she slipped her injured arm into a clammy sleeve and tucked the red crystal shard into her pocket.

Taking a deep breath, she spun a glamour around herself. They would never see the mud or her wound. They would never see her shiver. They would see a goddess before them, fearless and undeniable in her beauty. And they would follow her anywhere.

Chapter 14

top helping me, woman," Reef growled.

Reluctantly, Ossamyr drew her ani back into herself. Reef's mind was like a fortress; he could instantly sense any intrusion, no matter how benevolent.

"I'm trying to get you to breathe," she said. "It's easier when you breathe."

He gave her a lethal glance, and she kept her mouth shut.

The Islanders' ship creaked and groaned as they fled south under full sail, pounding through the choppy swells. The no-nonsense simplicity of Reef's quarters seemed harsh and unrefined after her weeks in Ohohhom. She'd been so comfortable here on the voyage north, but now Reef's world seemed as distant and unwelcoming as the Opal Empire.

Ossamyr winced as she watched Reef make an incision in Brophy's chest next to his heartstone. He performed the ritual like a giant threading a needle. He was trying too hard, forcing the ani when he should be coaxing it. She desperately wanted to reach out to him, bolster his strength, but she held back and turned her attention from Reef's furrowed brows to Brophy.

The Ohndarien prince still had a child's face, smooth and lineless. His yellow curls were as soft as down. He still looked like the naive teenager she had seduced so many years ago, but he didn't feel like that anymore. He no longer glowed, overflowing with innocence and optimism. She remembered scoffing at his gullibility, assuming he wouldn't last a month in Physendria. But Nine Squares had not broken him. He had broken it. He had broken her, too, changed her forever.

But that boy was gone, the youthful glow stripped from him. The beatific face of a young prince had been replaced by the haunted visage of a desperate man.

He was still unconscious, struggling with his nightmares as he had done for the last eighteen years. Every now and then he would struggle feebly against his bonds. Reef's crew had bound him to the bed hand and foot. His eyes hadn't stopped twitching beneath their lids since she and Dewland had hoisted him out of that pit under the Opal Palace.

The priest had been true to his word. He had rowed her to the little cove south of the city and waited while she used a lantern to signal Reef's ship hidden offshore. The old man had been gracious and polite, but she sensed his trepidation every step of the way. And he was right to worry. He was committing treason against his empress. She didn't envy his return to Ohohhom.

She didn't envy her own return to the Islanders either. She had committed her own form of treason.

The whole time Ossamyr had been away, she had longed to return to Reef's arms. But the moment she saw his rowboat appear out of the darkness, she felt only fear. She hid Brophy behind some rocks and went to meet Reef at the edge of the rocky beach. The massive Islander leapt from the boat with a grin on his face and swept her into his arms, spinning her around. She cried out in pain and nearly collapsed. His smile evaporated as his hands went to her wound.

"What happened?" he cried. "Is the sorceress dead?"

Ossamyr sank to the ground and shook her head. "I . . . I was so close."

He closed his eyes and nodded.

"I could have tried again," she said. "But I had to save him."

"Him?"

He followed her eyes to the rocks where Brophy was hidden. Reef's lips pulled back into a snarl as he yanked the dagger from his belt and strode up the beach.

"No!" Ossamyr screamed. "You'll release the emmeria." She levered herself to her feet and stumbled toward Reef as he grabbed Brophy by the shirt and raised his dagger for the killing blow. "Please!" she cried. "If you ever loved me, don't hurt him!"

The strain had been too much for her. She remembered collapsing, coughing up blood on the wet stones, but nothing after that. Even now, she didn't know if it was love for her or fear of the emmeria that stayed Reef's hand. But he brought them both aboard. She woke up four days later in the same bed with Brophy. She had clean clothes and fresh bandages. He was bound hand and foot.

The next morning they caught their first sight of Efften in the distance. Reef made it very clear that he wouldn't bring Brophy to the forbidden isle. He wanted the boy cured or he wanted him dead.

Ossamyr looked back at Brophy. Blood welled up from the incision Reef had made. It was red at first, but slowly darkened to thick, black ooze. Reef withdrew a shard of clear crystal about the size of his thumbnail from a small pouch on the bed. He placed it lightly against the wound. She felt the malicious ichor eating at Reef's fingertips, trying to dominate him. The Islander was no sorcerer, but his willpower astonished her. Gritting his teeth, he wrestled with the black emmeria, forcing it into the crystal shard.

Unable to do nothing, she sent her magic into him again, refining his clumsy efforts until the black emmeria flowed steadily into the crystal.

He growled at her, pulling the crystal away from the wound and putting it into a burlap sack filled with salt. "Am I going to have to paddle you, witch? You have a suppurating belly wound. Save your damned strength!"

Reluctantly, she withdrew her magical aid, sending it once again to the throbbing burn in her stomach. Reef was right, though. The puncture was infected deep inside, where the contents of her intestines had soured the wound. The Silver Islanders knew how to dress battle wounds, but there was only so much they could do. Reef had stitched her back together himself, but even with the steady stream of ani she was sending to help mend the wound, it was not healing properly. Even if Ossamyr had been in the heart of Ohndarien, treated by a score of Zelani, a wound like this could easily lead to a slow, painful death.

Stop it, she thought. *The body follows the will. Once you believe you* are dying, the body will make it so. She had too much to live for, too much unfinished business, to let a simple fever claim her.

Slowly, methodically, Reef filled another crystal and placed it into the sack of salt. Ossamyr had no idea how the Islander created the little ani crystals. She'd asked Reef once and he'd firmly changed the subject.

Reef continued drawing the corruption from Brophy's wound. He withdrew another shard from his little pouch and placed it against the black wound. The Islander was already showing the strain of his efforts. He needed to relax and let the ani flow freely, but he kept himself stiff as a board, not wanting to appear as if he was breathing too hard.

She nearly snapped at him, but it was no use trying to change the man's nature. She smirked, remembering her fantasy of having both Brophy and Reef in the same bed. She winced at the pain of the chuckle, and her smile faded. This certainly wasn't what she had envisioned.

Reef continued to fill crystals and push them gently into the burlap bag. Finally, the wound seeped true, red blood.

Ossamyr sent her awareness into Brophy's body. He no longer battled the black emmeria, and she could feel his consciousness drifting toward the surface.

"He's about to wake up," she said.

Reef grunted, holding the final crystal against the wound, waiting patiently for the last of the corruption to seep out. With his other hand, he snapped his fingers, pointed at the wooden shelves at the head of the bed. "Give it to me."

She let out a little breath, picking up the vial of thick, greenish liquid. "You don't have to use this," she said. "Brophy is fighting the same fight we are."

"Yes, he is," Reef said tersely, pushing the last half-filled crystal into the salt. "It's too bad he's on the other side."

"You don't know that," she said.

Reef drew his dagger. "This isn't a discussion, Ossamyr. I will not have this man awake on my ship. Now hand me that bottle or I will end this the way I wanted the moment I saw him."

She handed him the vial, and he poured the contents into Brophy's mouth. Brophy choked, swallowed, then coughed. After a moment's lethargic struggle, he relaxed and fell back into sleep.

"That should keep him docile, at least," Reef said. "We'll have to give him more in a few hours."

"Reef, the black emmeria is gone. He's not going to—"

The Islander turned a fierce gaze on her. "I'm not convinced of that."

"But you saw it yourself. His blood ran red."

He grunted and reached for a barrel full of rock salt. He scooped handfuls of salt into the burlap sack, filling it almost to the brim. Crossing the room, he opened a drawer built under the opposite bunk and withdrew a small chest bound in gold. Ossamyr knew what was in that chest. Reef kept it close to himself constantly. He opened the lid, filling the room with rainbow colored light. The ever-shifting colors slid across his tattooed face and his golden eyes started to glow. Reef withdrew one of the precious crystal shards. There were hundreds of them, the product of his people's grueling sacrifice. She wondered what kind of man Reef would have been if he had not poured all his joy and his hope into those crystals. Would he be so serious? So stern all the time? She tried to imagine Reef carefree and playful, and she could not see it.

"This is the one you saw us create that night in the mountains," he said, holding up one of the crystals.

"You know them each by sight?"

"Would you know your friends by sight? Your children?"

He returned to the bed and pushed the shards of light emmeria into the burlap sack one after the other.

"Every one of these shards contains the gift of ani from over a hundred souls. The best people I know gave over a month's worth of their life force to fill these shards. We have thousands of them. Tens of thousands. And we're nowhere close to matching the supply of raw hate created by the wizards of Efften."

Slowly and carefully, he cinched the sack closed, tying it so tight the salt could not shift. His motions were slow and methodical, as if the tiniest mistake would be disastrous.

With a weary sigh, he stood and offered his hand.

"Are you ready?"

She nodded, giving one last look at Brophy, who slept peacefully. As she turned away, she noticed something, and spun back.

"Look!"

The cut Reef had made on Brophy's chest was all but healed.

Reef shook his head. "It is as I feared," he growled. "The black emmeria is healing him."

"But I thought you removed it all. You put it into the crystals."

He snorted. "There is more than one way to be enslaved by the black emmeria."

"What are you talking about?" Her stomach tightened, and she winced. "Shara has withdrawn the corruption from herself dozens of times. I have been corrupted twice and completely healed."

He grunted. "Are you truly healed?"

"Well . . ." She paused. "At least physically."

He shook his head. "Most who come in contact with the black emmeria are overwhelmed by it. It physically invades their bodies and breaks their will. It transforms them into a physical representation of hate and rage."

She listened, remembering when Phandir's bones snapped under her hands, remembering her claws cutting into his flesh.

"But if your will is strong enough, or if you have a profound mastery over the ani, you can bend it to your will. You can feel as if you control it. But that control is an illusion. The mages of Efften thought themselves masters of the black emmeria, but the vile magic built up over time in the organs of their bodies. It became part of them. They were never transformed into mindless beasts, but it eventually destroyed their souls."

She nodded. "I saw all of that when I drank the Siren's Blood."

"Yes, you did."

"But Brophy is not a mage. He doesn't want to master the black emmeria."

"True, but he has been immersed in it for too long. He never drowned in that ocean, but over the years he drank too much of the water."

"But he is a good man."

"Maybe he was. Maybe part of him still wants to be. But he's been married to the black emmeria for eighteen years. It's as much a part of him as every other part of his body. You think he can just release it like that?" Reef snapped his fingers. "No. The ani is all around us. It's everywhere. Every living thing is interconnected by it. Most of it is pure and clear, but the darkness is out there like black smoke that has dissipated into the sky. Everywhere he goes, he is connected to it."

"But he wants to fight it."

"It doesn't matter anymore what he wants! The black emmeria is drawn to itself. And once it has infected you, it will always come back for more. He is already locked in this symbiotic relationship. When he needs power, it is there for him. The darkness feeds him and he feeds the darkness. His body becomes ever more powerful as the mind and soul are slowly given over to hate, malice, and fear. That is what happened to the mages of Efften. That is what happened to Morgeon's daughter in her three hundred years of exile. He and the black emmeria are one now. It has made him powerful. In return, he does its bidding, probably without even realizing it. He will never be free of it."

Ossamyr watched Brophy's smooth, young face as he slept. "I can't believe that."

"I noticed," Reef growled, glaring at her.

"There must be some way to help him. How do we purge the infection?"

"With a knife. Swift and sure across his throat."

"No!" she said, louder than she meant.

He shook his head sadly and shrugged. "If there is another way, I don't know it. We can't help him any more than we can pull the wine out of a drunkard's blood."

"Anything that can be done can be undone."

"Really?" Reef scoffed. "Who told you that foolishness?"

"Shara did."

"Then ask her to fix the boy. I'll bet she'll tell you the same thing I did."

"Even if she did, I still wouldn't give up on him," she cried. "I will not take the easier path a second time."

"And I will not risk my ship, my men, my people, or this world to soothe your precious guilt!"

Ossamyr's breath caught in her throat. She looked at the man whose fingertips she had once kissed while he slept. Had he become an enemy to her? Would he disappear forever behind his golden eyes and tattoos? She couldn't imagine how much it hurt Reef to see her at Brophy's side.

"I never should have brought him here," she said. "I'm sorry."

"Don't be a fool. You'd be dead if you weren't here. And he would be back in the hands of the sorceress."

Ossamyr nodded. "Still, he is not your burden to bear."

Reef waved his hand as if shoving the argument away. "Don't worry. I'm not going to hurt the boy. Yet. We'll keep him quiet until after the battle. You can talk to him once the witch is dead. Then you can see if there is anything left of the boy you once loved." He clenched his jaw. "Then you'll see. Whatever is left of him must be destroyed. Just as this must be destroyed." He hefted the sack of packed salt and crystals.

She nodded. He had put the ultimate decision in her hands. She couldn't ask for anything more.

Reef left the room and climbed the ladder onto the deck. Ossamyr followed, closing her eyes at the pain in her belly. Her magic was the only thing keeping her standing.

The crew stopped working when the two of them emerged. Within moments, all attention was focused on the bag. The only sound was the occasional ripple of a sail.

"It's time," Reef said.

The grim, tattooed sailors came forward to gather around their captain. The helmsman even tied off the wheel and joined them. Ossamyr looked around at their familiar faces. They knew their duty. They had been waiting their entire lives to perform it. Their long-awaited battle had arrived, and they were anxious to greet it.

Reef held up the bag.

"Anyone want to make a speech?"

Not a single murmur ran through the crowd. Many shook their heads no.

"Throw it," the helmsman, a stocky man with deep-set blue eyes, said.

"Throw it far," another sailor said.

Reef nodded and walked to the back of the ship. The island of Efften lay a few miles off their portside rail. They couldn't see the silver towers yet, but they were close.

"Won't it be dangerous to just throw it away?" Ossamyr asked.

"I'm not throwing it away. I'm throwing it away from us," Reef snarled.

Holding the bag carefully at arm's length, he spun around and around.

On the third spin, he roared and flung the sack into the ocean. It sailed high, arcing far above the deep, blue water.

The bag finally hit, splashing down so far away that the ruffle blended in with the swells of the sea.

"That's it?" she asked.

"Not quite. Once the salt dissolves, you'll see what happens when darkness meets light."

She watched, trying to keep in view the place where the bag hit. But with the ship moving and the swells rolling by, she wasn't sure.

A huge explosion burst from the ocean, sending a cascade of seawater hundreds of feet into the air. The tremendous *boom* hit Ossamyr like a blow to the chest, and she stumbled back. Reef's crew whooped for joy, stomping their feet and clapping their hands. Many of them whistled and spun around in circles. The spray poured down on the ship like a summer rain.

"By the Nine . . ." she murmured.

A swell the height of a man rushed toward them from the spot of the explosion. It slammed into the stern, and the ship rocked alarmingly. Ossamyr stumbled, but Reef was there, supporting her with a strong arm while the helmsman whooped again, crashing into the wheel and taking hold of it.

She glanced up for a moment and saw a maniacal glee in Reef's eyes. This was what he lived for. There were many things that were important to Reef, but this was the closest to his heart. He was a whole person in that moment, perfectly aligned with his destiny.

The same thrill lit the grinning faces of his crew. They danced in the brief rain until there was no more.

"Sir!" the helmsmen suddenly yelled, pointing.

Ossamyr spun around, and Reef stepped in front of her. She could feel his surprise as it mingled with her own.

Brophy stood halfway out of the hatch that led belowdecks. He leaned against the handrail with one hand, as if he had drunk too much wine. She flicked a glance at his wrists. Angry red marks and blood showed his successful struggle against the ropes that had bound him.

"We should have killed him," Reef hissed.

Steel rang on steel as his crew drew their weapons and closed in behind their leader.

Chapter 15

Someone called Brophy's name, a woman.

He tried to pick her out of the crowd before him, but everything was blurry. If he wasn't clinging to the rail, he would have fallen on his face.

The sailors spread out, surrounding him. There must have been twenty of them, highly trained. He could barely see them.

"Wait!" the woman cried again. "Let me talk to him! Brophy, let me explain."

His eyes narrowed. The voice was familiar. He couldn't place it, but it made him suddenly sick to his stomach. He concentrated on the sound of her voice, willing his eyes to focus. She was the only one in white, the only one without tattoos. Silver Islanders. Gritting his teeth, he stared at her until her features became clear.

"You?" Brophy growled, squeezing the railing until it snapped. "What are *you* doing here?"

He rose to his full height, his anger burning away the fog. The tattooed sailors drew closer, curved swords lowering as they neared. Brophy retreated to the edge of the ship, stumbling once as he fought the fleeting numbness in his limbs. He kept his back to the rail, making certain that he couldn't be surrounded.

Brophy's whole body was shaking, and he had to latch onto the ship's railing to keep from throwing himself at the pirates. He hadn't been this angry since he left Ohndarien, and he ached for the killing to start. "Stay back," he warned. "I don't want to hurt you."

Several of the sailors laughed.

"Back off, you fools!" the largest of the sailors shouted. He was a monster of a man, not very tall, but thick as an ox. He had to be the most powerfully built human Brophy had ever seen, but he had fought far worse than mere humans.

Some of the crew hesitated at the big man's orders, but others kept moving forward. "Back off, I said!" the tattooed ox roared. "The first fool who attacks him will get his own sword in the eye. And then he'll have a weapon. Now back off."

A rumbling whisper went through the crew, but they did as they were told, backing off and holding their ground, weapons ready.

"What am I doing here?" Brophy rasped through clenched teeth.

"Father Dewland asked me to look after you," the woman said.

Brophy looked at her again. The Physendrian queen looked exactly the same. Bronze skin. Short black hair and those dark eyes.

"Shouldn't you be backstabbing little boys somewhere in Physendria?"

She winced at his words. "I'm a Zelani now. I've spent the last eighteen years in Ohndarien. Shara took me in so I could help you."

"Did she," he said, his tone flat. "I remember the last time you helped me."

He scanned the men facing him. One of the sailors was old and hesitant. His hands were gnarled with age, and he kept adjusting his grip on his sword. He would be the first to go down.

Brophy flicked a glance back at Ossamyr. She held herself stiffly, one hand on her belly as if in pain. There was a fresh bloodstain on her simple white dress. The hairy ox stood slightly in front of her, protecting her with his massive body.

"I see you have a new husband. What happened to the last one?"

Ossamyr swallowed. "I killed him."

"Congratulations," he said. "I'm sure he didn't see it coming."

A small sob escaped her. "Please, Brophy, by the Nine . . ." She paused. "The Islanders can destroy the black emmeria. We can help you." She reached a hand out to him, though they were separated by twenty feet of deck.

Brophy sneered, not believing her act for a second. He turned from her to the ox. "You are captain here?"

"I am," he rumbled.

"Good. Turn this boat around and take me back to Ohohhom, or I'll take it from you and do it myself."

"That is simply not going to happen," the Islander said. "You can't sail this ship alone. You know that and I know that."

"Please, Brophy," Ossamyr said, wiping the false tears from her face. "Let me explain. There is so much I have to—"

"There is nothing to explain."

He looked at the captain, vibrating with rage. "Turn. The ship. Around."

"No," the huge man said.

Brophy gripped the rail, and the wood creaked as his fist tightened. He had to get back to Arefaine before it was too late. She needed him now more than ever.

"I don't know how I got here, or where I am," Brophy said, fighting to remain stationary. "But your people are about to be crushed between the two largest fleets in the world."

A few of the soldiers flicked worried glances at their captain.

"The Summer Fleet will be joining the Ohohhim shortly," he said, hoping it was a lie, hoping Astor had stopped them at the Sunrise Gate. "You people have no hope of standing against their combined might."

Again the sailors looked to their captain. "Hold steady," he growled.

"The only person who can stop them is me," Brophy said. "And I need to get back to the Opal Palace to do it."

The captain leaned over and whispered to the man next to him. The sailor sprinted to the hatch and disappeared belowdecks. Brophy stepped forward, ready to cut through the line of soldiers and stab the running man in the back, but he held himself in check. Once the killing started, it would never stop.

The massive Islander turned back to Brophy. "Our ships have blockaded

Efften for fifteen generations, and we'll cage her for fifteen more if that's what it takes. We will hold true until every last drop of shadow is burned clean by the light."

"Reef, please—" Ossamyr started.

The massive captain waved his hand for silence. "You," he said, pointing at Brophy, "are part of that shadow. And you will not take this ship as long as we draw breath."

Brophy looked into the Islander's golden eyes and knew he wasn't lying. Nodding, he threw himself to the side. The sailor with the gnarled hands barely had time to bring his sword up. Brophy slipped inside the man's guard, twisted his wrist, and wrenched the sword from his hand. In the same motion, he hooked the Islander's elbow and spun. The stunned sailor shouted as he flew overboard.

His deck mates surged forward, but Reef shouted at them to stop. Sword in hand, Brophy faced them all, and they backed off with obvious reluctance.

Brophy turned to the captain, Reef. "Turn this boat around and pick up your man."

"My man can swim. This boat holds steady."

"Don't test me," Brophy growled. "I spent two decades fighting corrupted. Every day. Every night. Without cease. I can kill every last one of you if I have to. That's not a boast. It's a fact."

The sailors held their ground, but he could see their confidence beginning to crumble.

"This is your last chance," Brophy snarled, pointing the sword at the runabout tied to the deck. "Lower your boat and jump overboard."

Reef shook his head.

"Turn the ship around!" Brophy screamed, hacking through the railing with his sword.

"We'll die first," Reef said.

The sailor returned from belowdecks clutching a small chest with golden banding. Reef signaled his helmsman. Brophy looked at the stern in time to see two sailors heave a wooden keg over the rail. It crashed onto the main deck, and oil splattered across the wood.

"What are you—" Brophy began to shout, but Reef grabbed an oil lantern hanging against the cabin wall and hurled it at the oil. Brophy threw himself to the side.

The lantern smashed apart. Flames raced across the deck. Air whooshed over him, blisteringly hot. A wall of flame soared upward, reaching for the sails.

Snarling, Brophy leapt upon the nearest man. The sailor cried out, swinging his sword at Brophy's head, but the strike went wide. Brophy shoved him, and the sailor toppled over the rail.

More of them rushed the little runabout, but a few swings of Brophy's sword sent them scurrying backward. Flames engulfed the rigging, sending a plume of smoke soaring into the sky. Two quick slashes cut the ropes holding the rowboat, and it dropped into the water. Brophy jumped next, escaping the searing heat.

When he surfaced, the water was full of sailors who had done the same. None seemed interested in contesting him for the rowboat. Clenching his teeth, Brophy threw his stolen sword into the boat and flung himself aboard. He unshipped the oars and pushed them into the locks. With a few mighty pulls, he drew away from the inferno of the Islanders' ship.

Brophy watched Reef's crew quickly gather around some floating wreckage that had been tossed overboard. He spotted the captain, his arm around a wet and bedraggled Ossamyr.

His mind filled with visions of rowing over and cutting down every last one of them, but he knew where his thirst for blood came from. He breathed through his teeth until the voices receded into the back of his mind. He would not become a slave to that rage. Not again. Not if he could help it.

Breathing deeply, he mastered his emotions and looked back at Ossamyr. Reef lifted her out of the water, placing her on a floating hatch cover. She cried out, clutching her abdomen. She had to be wounded, badly wounded. She clung to the little raft, obviously fighting the pain, but her gaze was on him.

He looked away, his own hatred mixing with the worst of the emmeria. He took hold of the oars and began pulling.

Hours later, he was still rowing. His rage fueled every stroke, and he never grew tired, never felt hot or thirsty as the sun beat down on him. He thrived on the hard work, and the voices in his head became as docile as a perfect beast of burden.

Night had fallen, and he started marking his course by the stars rather than the setting sun. He knew the Three-Fingered Hand was to the south and kept his stern pointed directly at the familiar constellation. If the large island he had seen to the east earlier in the day was Efften, then he had a long row in front of him.

He must have slept on the Islander ship for days. The last thing he remembered clearly was running down the hill toward the corrupted who were attacking Arefaine. He had vague memories of a fight, a fall, swimming, chasing someone . . . They all mixed with his memories of fighting the corrupted in Ohndarien, chasing the Fiend once again.

He felt like he'd lost all the progress he'd made in getting away from the voices. He was right back where he'd been in the rocks above Ohndarien, teetering on the brink of madness.

Arefaine had done this to him, he was sure of it. But at this point, his return might make the situation even worse. She'd lost herself, succumbing to the allure of the emmeria, but was that Brophy's fault? Had his rejection been enough to push her over the edge? And who were the corrupted that were attacking her? Had she lashed out in anger and corrupted her own men?

He couldn't help wondering if he'd made the worst mistake in his life by pushing Arefaine away. But he couldn't just rip open old wounds and let her climb inside because she wanted to keep warm. If something was to happen between then, he wanted it to be honest. He wanted it to be true.

He tried to quiet his mind and listen for the Voice of Oh. He hoped the ancient spirit could tell him what had become of Arefaine, but the Ohohhim god seemed impossibly far away.

When Brophy wasn't running circles in his mind with Arefaine, he was thinking of Ossamyr and the way she stared at him as he rowed away. Once the rage of the emmeria had left him, he was amazed how little feeling he still had for the woman. That day in the Nine Squares arena was so long ago it hardly seemed real anymore. It was like she had betrayed a stranger, a little boy that Brophy barely knew.

How had she fallen in with the Islanders? And how had she kidnapped him from Ohohhom? Could they really destroy the black emmeria like she said? Nothing made sense anymore. The only thing he knew was that Arefaine couldn't go to Efften alone. The voice she was following—the one she thought was her father—was the Fiend. If it wanted her to do something, Brophy had to stop her.

He continued rowing through the night, sweat rolling down his face and arms. He kept trying to imagine what he would say to Arefaine when he finally found her.

Hours later, something touched Brophy's mind, as light as a feather brushing his cheek.

He stopped rowing and spun about. It was a cloudy night with no moon. The iron sky met the water with an almost indistinguishable line, but he squinted, scanning the horizon.

"Arefaine?" he spoke. Had the girl sent ships to look for him? Brophy wished he could remember more about their parting. He could barely see anything, but as he looked closer, a black shadow appeared along the horizon.

It was a ship, moving toward him.

He secured the oars and grabbed the Islander's sword from the bottom of the boat. The salt-crusted handle felt good in his hand, and the howling voices grew louder in his mind, strengthening him, sharpening his senses. If the Islanders had sent a ship to finish him, they would find it steep work indeed. If it was Arefaine . . .

He might need the sword anyway.

As the ship drew closer he realized how small it was. It only had one mast and a single sail. This was no oceangoing vessel. It was barely larger than an Ohndarien water bug.

The ship drew closer and the only person aboard rushed to the rail. All he could see was her white shirt and long black hair billowing across one shoulder.

"Brophy!" she cried, her voice pulling the breath from him.

He dropped the sword and dove into the water.

Three quick strokes and he was halfway to her boat. She jumped in after him and within seconds she was in his arms, her lips against his, her legs wrapping around his waist. He couldn't think, couldn't swim. He clutched her to him and they sank beneath the dark surface, lost in the joy of finding each other once again.

Chapter 16

Shara watched Brophy's broad shoulders rise and fall in the water as he swam up to the drifting day-sailer. He reached it, gripped the gunwale, and vaulted over in one smooth motion.

"Come on," he called, reaching over the edge and pulling her aboard as if she weighed nothing. "Leave the rowboat. We don't need it."

They stood side by side on the deck for a long moment. Shara smiled so hard her jaw hurt. Her lips were still tingling after their endless underwater kiss. She couldn't believe she had found him. She finally reached out to touch his sunburned face and make sure he was real.

"I must be dreaming," he finally said, looking into her eyes with wonder.

"No more dreams," she murmured. "We've had enough dreams. It's time for something more."

He nodded. His smile had changed. It wasn't the childlike smile she loved so well. It was more cautious, tinged with sadness, but she didn't care. It was Brophy. In her arms. In the flesh. His eyes took in everything, the small ship, the drawn sail. His gaze finally came back to her, lingering on her face. She waited for that look she'd seen atop the Hall of Windows before he made his sacrifice. But he wouldn't meet her eyes, wouldn't really look at her.

Go slow, she reminded herself. *He needs you more than you need him.*

"How did you find me?" he finally asked. "I don't even know where I am."

"I looked," she said. "I never stopped searching for you. I didn't expect to find you before reaching Ohohhom, but you stand out like a signal fire. I caught the light of your heartstone half a day ago."

"With your magic?"

She nodded, remembering how she had started when she felt the barely contained rage swirling through him.

He nodded, falling silent. He vibrated as if desperate to run away but held himself by sheer force of will. She wanted to reach out and touch him again, wanted to throw herself into his arms, but she couldn't. She wouldn't make the same mistake she had in Ohndarien.

He met her gaze, struggling to maintain contact. "I'm so sorry," he breathed. "I never meant what I said in Ohndarien. I never meant to hit you."

"I know," she said, her own body starting to tremble. She longed to touch that crease between his brows, smooth it out and tell him it was all right. "I know you didn't."

His jaw clenched and the scant space between them was charged with lightning. "I had to get away," he said. "I couldn't stay there, not with all that blackness churning inside of me."

"I don't care about that. I don't care about then. All I care about is right now. I never stopped loving you. Never."

Brophy clenched his eyes shut and nodded. He reached under his shirt and pulled out the black feather on the cord around his neck.

Shara started to cry. "Me, too," she said softly, drawing the golden feather out of her blouse.

Brophy caught it as it spun in the air and pressed it to his lips. He kept his eyes clenched shut, his entire face a knotted mask of agony.

"It's all right," she whispered. "It's all right." She grabbed hold of his trembling hands and pressed her lips against them. "We're back. We're back together and that's all that matters."

He tried to reply, but the words didn't come out.

"What?" She felt dizzy. She couldn't feel the rocking of the boat anymore.

"I've wanted . . . To touch you. To—"

"By the Seasons, Brophy. Touch me," she said, a sob catching in her throat. "Love me. Ravage me. It's all I've wanted for—"

He stepped forward, and she met him halfway. His strong arms caught her, lifting her from the ground as if she were a child. She gasped as they kissed, her fingers grappling with his shirt.

"Oh, Brophy," she whispered. "It's been so long."

His eyes glazed with desire and a slither of black crossed his left eye, then was gone.

"Brophy—"

He dropped to his knees, slamming her against the deck of the little day-sailer. His teeth showed as he leaned back and grabbed her blouse. With a fierce twist, he ripped it from her body. She cried out, and then he was on her again, driving her into the wooden decking.

"Wait," she gasped. His mouth clamped on her nipple, sucking, biting, as the rough boards dug painfully into her back. She twisted away, trying to protect herself with her hands. Brophy tore at his breeches with trembling hands, snapping the laces. They came free, and he withdrew, his chest heaving. Shara grabbed both sides of his face, searching his eyes, trying to find him.

The snarl returned to his lips, and he lunged forward. He flipped her around and slammed her against the deck, crushing her cheek, her breasts. He grabbed her breeches and yanked them down. She cried out as they raked over her hips, baring her ass to him. "Brophy, please—" she whispered, trying to reach him.

But he was on her again, heavy as a mountain and hard as stone. She grunted as he shoved himself inside her. Her hands scrambled for a hold as he thrust into her. She squeezed her eyes shut.

"Brophy," she gasped, trying to move with him, trying to make it their dance. But his hands kept her hips harshly against the deck, and he rammed into her again and again.

He cried out in his release, a guttural howl that pierced her heart. He shook against her, then slumped against the railing.

Trembling, she turned around. She winced as she touched her left breast. A line of blood trickled slowly down her palm. Her belly was covered with scrapes. Angry red abrasions striped her hips and thighs all the way down to her half-removed pants.

Brophy looked at her as if he was just waking up. She wanted to cry, but she didn't. She couldn't.

"Shara—" he began, then his eyes went wide as he stared at her. "I didn't—"

"It's all right," she said.

"All right?!" he roared. His fist clenched, and for one crazy moment, she thought he would strike her.

She flinched away and hated herself for it.

He spun about, stalked across the ship. He stopped at the prow of the little boat and fell to his knees. Balling his fist, he punched the deck, and the wood cracked.

Slowly, Shara unbuttoned her pants and gingerly pulled them over her hips before fastening them again. She walked to him, put her hands on his back.

They were silent for a long time.

"I should leave," he said, panting like one of the weeping ones. "I'm dangerous."

Shara took a deep breath, cycling the pain in her breasts, her belly, her hips, into herself and turning it into energy.

"If you left, I would follow you," she said.

"Are you mad? Can't you see what I did to you?"

"What couples don't have their problems?" she said, trying to smile.

He spun around and glared at her. "You make light of it," he cried. "Don't make light of it. Not after what I did!"

"I must," she said, her voice breaking. "Or I will cry."

Brophy put his hands to his face. "This is why I left. This is why I ran away!"

She knelt next to him, grabbing his shoulders. "It's not you. It's—"

"Yes, it is. It is me. I loved it. Everything I did to you, I loved it when it was happening. I wanted to do more. Even now, I want to do more."

She pulled back, her mouth set in a straight line, but she refused to turn away. "I know what you've been through. It's the emmeria, not you. We can fight this together."

He stood up, shaking his head. "You can't fight him! He's in my head! Screaming at me! All the time!"

"He?"

"The voice! The voice in my head! I have to kill him! Rip him out of my skull!"

"All right, we'll kill him. I can help you."

"No." Brophy shook his head violently. "No! I don't want you anywhere near me."

She reached for him, and he pushed her back. He leapt from the little boat and started swimming back toward his rowboat several hundred yards away.

She let him go. She had to. It was part of the promise she had made to herself. She took a deep breath and held back the tears. She knew this was how it could be, and she wasn't leaving. She would never leave him again.

"I'm right behind you, Brophy," she whispered, letting the ache in her heart slowly cycle back into her body. "Wherever you go. Whatever it takes. Run, and I will follow. Fall, and I will pick you up. Die, and I will die with you."

Closing her fist over her feather necklace, she watched him swim away.

Chapter 17

Father Dewland stood next to the shattered bridge with his head bowed and his hands tucked into the sleeves of his robe. It was a rare sunny day, and rainbows shimmered among the swirling mists that hovered along the waterfall.

The priest tried to enjoy the beauty of the moment, tried to cherish the simple gift of life, the joy of drawing one breath after another, but Dewland was long past such things. He had been waiting in this spot for the past three days. He was brought food and water and instructed to relieve himself twice a day. Other than that, he was ignored. His old bones ached with the strain, and he was sweating profusely beneath his heavy black robes.

At the end of the twelve days of mourning, the emperor's body was laid to rest and the Mother Regent had gone to her vigil in Oh's cave. As high priest, Dewland had accompanied her to bless her journey. Just before entering the cave, she had asked him to return to the bridge and wait for her return. That had been three days ago and still he waited.

The nervous apprentice who brought his meals fed Dewland news of what was happening in his absence. One hundred and forty-four new recruits had been fitted with armor and weapons and were waiting to take their vows as Arefaine's new Carriers of the Opal Fire. One hundred forty-four. Twelve times the sacred number. A particularly pious blasphemy.

The Imperial Navy had been mustered and every seaworthy vessel in the empire had been refitted for war. Catapults were being strapped to their decks and their holds packed with pots of incendiaries. Volunteers had been called to man the ships. Soldiers and sailors had shown up by the thousands, arriving in unruly packs rather than orderly rows. A strange disease seemed to have infected the Ohohhim people. They no longer spoke of Oh's wisdom. Their mouths were too full of praise for the beautiful young Arefaine Morgeon.

Dewland had been secretly terrified for his own life ever since aiding Brophy and the Zelani's escape, but that terror had been overshadowed. He now feared for the soul of the empire. He feared for the entire world. The Awakened Child spoke and reality followed. The divine queue was splintering. The horrors of the past were upon them.

Dewland was roused from his worries by a subtle change in the air. He looked up and saw the Mother Regent walking down the path. The craftsmen who were repairing the bridge all dropped to their knees. Dewland did the same.

The mud beneath his knees was still tainted by the explosion of black emmeria. He could feel it through the cloth of his robes, profane and insistent. The First Carrier, Halman, knelt next to him. The young man had a new maniacal light in his eyes that fed Dewland's growing dread. Halman was the last surviving member of the emperor's twelve Carriers. His three fellows had turned assassin, but this man remained loyal. Arefaine had rewarded him by naming him Opal Advisor. He had handpicked the hundred and forty-four. He handled the details of mustering the fleet while Arefaine hid in Oh's cave. He was truly the voice of a new god.

The priest kept his face to the ground, but he could hear Arefaine's approaching footsteps crunch lightly on the earthen path. Wood creaked as she crossed the makeshift bridge with feathery steps, and she stopped in front of him.

"Rise, Father," the child said. "We have much to discuss."

Dewland rose. "Mother Regent, I await your wisdom." He acknowledged her with a slight bow.

"My old teacher, let us speak discreetly."

She touched his shoulder with her fingertips, and a subtle warmth spread through his body. His back muscles relaxed, and he took a deep breath. He remembered Arefaine as a child and how much he'd loved her then.

A wave of revulsion rose within him, and Dewland gritted his teeth against the unnatural intrusion, fighting to keep his thoughts straight, to keep his emotions his own.

Arefaine turned and led him back across the temporary bridge. It was perilously narrow, no more than five thin saplings lashed together. Dewland glanced at the thundering waterfall rushing past him and the rainbow mists far below.

"Come," Arefaine insisted. "It is perfectly safe."

Dewland's fear receded, and he was filled with a sudden hope for their conversation. Hating the child's power over him, he nonetheless found the courage to cross the flexing beams. He reached solid ground as quickly as he could and took Arefaine's sleeve.

Halman followed, trailing the two of them at a discreet distance.

"You seem to have several things on your mind," Arefaine said. "Please speak freely."

Dewland had an overwhelming urge to fall on his knees and confess. But he held back and took the more graceful path.

"I am pleased to see you returned, Mother Regent. You spent quite some time in Oh's presence. Did he have any wisdom to share with you?"

"No."

Dewland swallowed. "I am sorry to hear that."

"Don't be. I stayed in the cave so long purely for political reasons. It is amazing how much more people accomplish when they aren't constantly waiting in line for me to give them instructions."

"I understand. That is very wise of you."

"What did you expect me to hear?" Arefaine asked.

"I would never guess at the mind of Oh."

"Really? You seem to have spent your entire life doing just that."

Dewland felt the anger behind the word like a blow to the stomach. "I followed the emperor's sleeve as best I could."

Arefaine snorted. "Come now, don't hide behind a dead man. You made choices. You helped plot the course of my life. Your whispers in the emperor's ear led me to this glorious shore."

Dewland felt the lash of raw emotion behind her carefully modulated voice. He thought it best to remain silent.

"Is that guilt I hear?" she asked him.

Again Dewland kept his tongue.

"Surely you expected Oh to have told me something in all that time. Surely he should have whispered something in my ear." She leaned close to Dewland and spoke in a ghostly voice. "'Welcome, child. The world's fate rests in your hands.'"

Dewland bit his lip, fearing to run from the venom she whispered into his ear. "'The first thing you must do is suffer for years in silence and solitude. Then you must throw yourself at the first man we give you, abandon all hope and reason and fall helpless in his arms.

"'You must travel with him to Efften,'" she continued, mocking the divine. "'You must liberate your homeland, resurrect the glory of your people. And then, my beloved child, you must lock them away in a towering silver box. You must slit your own wrists, climb into that box, and haunt it forever.

"'You must do this to make our lives easier. Because we are tiny people terrified to leave our perfect little rows.'" She kissed him on the ear and pulled back. "Is that what you expected him to say?"

Dewland began to tremble.

"Did you honestly expect that a little boy with broad shoulders and golden curls could make me swallow your lies? Did you honestly think the touch of his sacred cock would make me that stupid?"

Dewland fell to his knees. A crushing weight squeezed his chest. He couldn't think, couldn't breathe.

Arefaine knelt next to him. "I believe you have a confession to make about that assassin from Physendria and the *man of my dreams*."

Dewland nodded, unable to stop himself. "I . . . I helped them escape. I got them a boat."

"So you admit to treason?"

"Yes." He bobbed his head like a puppet on a string.

"Why?"

"Because he was lost to the shadow. She was my only way to get him to safety."

"But I thought he was your *only hope*, your only way to keep me in line."

"He . . ." Dewland's vision started to fade, but he couldn't stop talking. "He is . . . He lives . . . Where there is love, there is hope."

Arefaine pushed him over, and he sprawled against the wet slope. The crushing grip was released, and he took a desperate breath.

"Get him out of my sight," she spat, and walked away.

Dewland heard Halman rush up to him. Strong hands grabbed him under the armpits and yanked him to his feet. He doubled over in a coughing fit, and the newly appointed Opal Advisor dragged him back to the bridge.

Dewland tried to regain his feet and suddenly found they were hanging over the abyss. Halman dangled him over the shattered end of the bridge, glaring at him with pure hatred. "The lady will never look upon such filth again," he said, his eyes shining.

"Please, my child," Dewland said as the Carrier shoved him backward.

He screamed as the bottom of the bridge rushed away from him. He fell, tumbling end over end through the glowing rainbows. The swirling mists were cool on his face just before he hit the rocks.

Chapter 18

Reef shook her gently, and Ossamyr nodded. She'd seen it coming.

The crewmen cheered as they saw the silver prow of a warship cut through the swells toward them. It had taken them only half a day for someone to investigate the column of black smoke that rose from the burning ship.

Ossamyr clung to the little raft Reef and his men had made for her. Her belly didn't hurt anymore, but the wine probably had something to do with that. They hadn't recovered any water from the ship before it sank, so they had to do with a keg or two of wine.

The only thing that made the ordeal bearable was that the Islanders all seemed to know every drinking song ever created, and they weren't shy about singing them over and over again. If she hadn't been half mad with fever, she almost would have enjoyed herself.

As the ship drew closer, the helmsmen yelled at the crew to quiet down. "Sober up, boys. Shore leave is over. We've got a battle to win."

The waterlogged sailors gave halfhearted protests and complaints about a rather soggy shore leave, but she could tell they were eager for the fighting to start. Most of the Islanders were nothing like Reef. They were grim and threatening around strangers, but among friends they had an irrepressible "drink tonight for tomorrow we die" attitude.

She couldn't help cringing at their enthusiasm. If she had completed her mission, none of them would be dying tomorrow.

The ship pulled up alongside, and the sailors tossed lines down to them. The men clambered aboard one at a time. Reef waited until last, and then helped her roll off the raft and into the water.

"Hold on to my neck," he said gruffly.

"I can do it myself," she said.

"Hell you can," he said. "Just do as I say."

Reef hadn't said a kind word to her since the moment he set his own ship ablaze. He couldn't, not in front of his men. But his actions told a different story. He'd spent the entire time by her side, keeping the raft steady, getting her wine, and making sure her skin was covered under the blazing sun. Neither of them had mentioned Brophy or what it had cost Reef to bring the boy aboard.

Ossamyr relented and wrapped her arms around his neck. He swam over to a rope, grabbed it with both hands, and walked hand over hand up the side of the ship with ease. The two ships' crews were laughing together. They seemed to know one another well. Most of the newcomers were teasing Reef's crew about picking a bad time to take a swim.

The ship was packed. Dozens of tattooed soldiers, both men and women, crowded the deck. Most of them appeared to be making arrows.

The ship's captain walked over and greeted Reef. He was a particularly hairy man with a silver-and-black crescent tattooed on his broad chest. He was shadowed by a fierce-looking woman whose arms were painted with spirals of dark silver all the way to her shoulders. She instantly recognized them as two of the three Islanders who had attacked her on Efften. Reef embraced each of them in turn.

"Thank you, my friends. I owe you once again."

"What happened to your ship?" the woman with the spiral tattoos asked, eyeing Ossamyr. Her distrust was palpable.

"Someone tried to take her," Reef replied. "I had to stop him."

"That sounds like a tale that would take a whole bottle to tell," the captain said.

"That will have to wait," Reef said. "Our assassination attempt failed. We go to war."

The captain nodded once, tersely, and Ossamyr felt the sting of shame in the back of her throat. "In that case, the fleet is yours, Reef. We have nearly five thousand swords on a hundred ships waiting for you just around the cape."

"Good," Reef said. "What news of the enemy?"

"The Summer Fleet has come through Ohndarien and has been sailing steadily west. They have already passed to the north of us and will join forces with the Ohohhim within a few days."

Reef was about to ask another question when Ossamyr interrupted.

"What about Ohndarien?" she asked. "What news?"

"We have few details, I'm afraid. The city has fallen. Either they were bested in combat, or they have joined the enemy."

"No . . ." Ossamyr whispered.

"This is no more than we expected," Reef said tersely. "We proceed as planned. We'll wait in the Narrows between Efften and her northern atoll and brace them in the open ocean. I don't want them landing any men on the accursed isle."

The captain nodded. "I'm glad to hear it. My blood's been waiting for this fight since it flowed through my grandfather's veins."

"Why is everyone fletching?" Reef asked. Ossamyr turned her gaze upon the working men. Light caught the tips of the arrows, casting rainbow reflections on the deck.

"A scout ship caught one of the Summermen's vessels. She'd been left behind with a broken rudder. Our kinsmen boarded and were almost killed to a man," the captain said. The muscles in his jaw stood out as he put down his anger. "The crew had been indentured. Every last one of them bleeds the dark tears."

Reef's lips pressed together tightly. Slowly, he nodded, then flicked a glance at the soldiers working quickly on their arrows. "That will be difficult to face. It may be our undoing. But then, it might be theirs. You've done well."

"Thank you, Reef," the captain said.

"What does he mean, indentured?" Ossamyr asked.

"You saw them in the Siren's Blood," Reef replied. "The black eyes, the black tears."

Ossamyr remembered the visions hidden in the ani wine. The lights had shown her images from Efften, sweeping her up in a living nightmare of a vast ocean of naked bodies lost in darkness and rage.

"But how could the Summermen have been enslaved?"

Reef shrugged his massive shoulders. "They passed through Ohndarien. There was enough black emmeria in that city to enslave half the world."

"But only the mages of Efften knew how to rip a soul from its body."

"True, but one of them is still alive," Reef said. "And his influence appears to be spreading."

Ossamyr swallowed, remembering the pale face she'd seen within the Siren's Blood. One of the archmages had survived. She'd heard his voice once on the quarry floor below Ohndarien's walls when she'd nearly killed Shara at his urging.

"You think he did that to the Summermen?" Ossamyr asked. "The man locked within the silver tower?"

The Islander with the spiral tattoos shook her head. "It couldn't be the Black One. The spell prevents his escape."

"Apparently he has found a way," Reef replied. "But he would have needed help from the outside, probably one of Arefaine's minions, the crone from Physendria, or the Kherish albino. Even Shara could have done it."

"No, not Shara."

"Anyone can be seduced," Reef said. "And she loves power more than most."

Ossamyr was about to protest, but he brushed the subject away with a wave of his hand.

"Never mind the past; we only need to think of the next few days. The indentured are impervious to normal weapons, like the corrupted. But they're highly vulnerable to the light emmeria, and that could give us an edge."

"The force arrayed against us is much larger than we expected," the captain said. "Do we intend to draw them in and flank—?"

"No, we'll take them head-on."

"Head-on?" the woman asked.

"So it will seem. We'll send most of our forces straight at them, but that is only a diversion. The fleet is not our true target."

"What is?" Ossamyr asked.

"Arefaine. She's the only one that matters. The Ohohhim will keep her in the rear, and we'll send two ships around either side to attack her directly. She will undoubtedly use her magic against us, and that will be her undoing."

"How?"

"You remember that explosion yesterday?"

"Of course."

"Imagine one much, much larger."

Ossamyr suddenly understood. They had light emmeria. Arefaine had black emmeria. The two did not mix. "How much larger?"

Reef spat over the rail. "I put ten crystal shards in that bag of salt. We have tens of thousands of shards."

Ossamyr looked at the faces of the captain with the crescent tattoo and the woman by his side. They were not surprised by Reef's words. They knew they were going to die. They had expected it all along.

"All depends upon the witch," Reef continued. "If she stays true to form, we won't have to do anything. She'll destroy herself and every ship in her armada."

And ours, Ossamyr thought to herself.

The captain nodded. "A good plan. A desperate one."

"This is our hour of desperation," Reef said. "Continue your preparations."

The captain nodded sharply. "I will do so at once," he said, then moved off to relay his orders.

Reef turned to Ossamyr and inspected the wound in her belly. "And you," he said, "will be returning to Slaver's Bay."

She paused, feeling the breeze on her face, faintly wet with sea spray. "You don't expect to survive," she said quietly. "None of us."

"Not true," he said. "I expect you to survive. That's why I'm sending you back."

"I'm not leaving."

His nostrils flared at her defiance. "You don't—"

"Shut up," she said. "You gave me the Siren's Blood. You took me to your bed. You gave me your heart . . ." She took a deep breath, wincing as she did.

"Ossamyr—"

"No. I've earned my place in your crew," she said. She shook her head, keeping his gaze. "I'm already in this fight. I won't be turned aside."

He stared at her for a long time before finally nodding. Reaching out, he took her shoulders in his big hands and drew her close.

"All right," he said, his deep voice rumbling in his chest. "To the end, then. For both of us."

Chapter 19

hara winced as she awoke. The predawn chill had crept into her bones as she slept on the deck of her little Farad messenger ship, and she pulled the extra sail tighter around herself.

Last night had been rough. But at least the worst of it was past. She rolled over and looked at Brophy leaning against the back of her boat. She could see little more than his silhouette in the half-light, but she knew he was listening to her every move. She felt the anguish under his calm exterior. His entire body was knotted up, desperate to restrain the emotions that had come bursting out of him in their first few moments together. He looked like he was trying to hold a lightning bolt clenched in his fist. It frightened her, and it made her love him more than ever.

She still couldn't believe she had found him. She had nearly reached Ohohhom when she sensed Brophy's heartstone far to the south, blazing like a ruby in her mind. Her magic took her right to him, and rushing into his arms had been everything she imagined.

But those few moments of joy had shriveled and twisted, as yet another chasm yawned between them. Brophy had been awoken, but he was still lost in the black emmeria. Shara could touch him, but could not reach him, and she had to stay strong. She had to hold firm like a mountain in the shifting black ocean in which he was lost.

Brophy frowned and looked over at her, somehow sensing that she had awoken. She knew that if she smiled gently at him, like she wanted to, he'd only look away in pain. So she sat up and looked away first, easing that choice for him.

Taking a deep breath of the chill air, she focused on the pain in her body, cycled healing energy through herself. The bruises, scrapes, and cuts he had left on her were nothing. Jesheks had put her body through far worse, and she had come through stronger on the far side. But she couldn't help remembering Brophy pinning her to the deck, forcing himself inside her. As much as she had hated it, it never felt like rape. It had felt like she was trying to restrain a delirious person dying of fever. Brophy had wounded himself much more deeply by losing control.

After their fight, Brophy had swum back to his rowboat and Shara followed him for hours as he headed north. He rowed like a man beating his head against a wall, yanking back on the oars with single-minded brutality. His exertions finally bled off his rage, and he shipped the oars with a sigh.

"Shall we try this again?" she had asked, pulling up alongside him.

"Would it matter if I said no?"

"If you continued rowing, I would continue following."

He had looked up at her, those green eyes framed by wrinkles of regret and fear. For a moment she was afraid he was going to run away again, but he stood up and jumped onto the deck of her day-sailer.

Shara had ached to rush into his arms but she'd restrained herself, standing there in painful silence as his rowboat drifted away from them.

He finally gave her a grim nod and slipped past her to man the rudder and set the straightest course for Ohohhom. Within a few minutes they'd left the rowboat far behind them.

Shara had paced the tiny deck for a long time, giving Brophy his space, and the sun had dropped low in the sky by the time he began speaking.

His voice came out in a monotone, as though he didn't want to talk to her, but couldn't keep himself quiet any longer. He told her about the years he'd spent in his dreams and the voice he fought there. His voice grew husky and strained when he spoke of killing his aunt, and she ached to reach out and give him a little nudge with her magic.

She could have helped him cry, helped him crack open and bleed his wounds clean. But she held herself back. He wasn't fighting something that a single storm could wash away. She wanted to save him, but he was already busy saving himself. All she could do was love him, quiet and steady.

He told her everything, from his trip to the Cinder to the desperate battle on the bridge with Arefaine and the corrupted.

She didn't push him for more details about the sorceress, though her heart ached to hear how close the two had become. When he spoke of her, he held something back. That much, Shara could tell. But he still wore her feather. That was enough. She kept telling herself that was enough.

The tale grew stranger after his corruption and awakening on the Silver Islanders' warship. Shara was overjoyed and then puzzled by Ossamyr's arrival in his tale. She'd put her friend out of her mind, hoping for the best by refusing to consider the worst. An alliance with the Silver Islanders seemed the least probable outcome. Ossamyr hated the Islanders, and even more hated being told what to do. Yet Ossamyr's companion, Reef, sounded like the same mysterious Islander who had given her the Siren's Blood. It was yet another mystery that had to be unraveled.

When his tale came to a close, Shara told hers, describing the physical and emotional odyssey she'd embarked upon since diving off Ohndarien's wall and sailing to the Summer Cities. She mentioned little of Mikal, of Jesheks. She hadn't told anyone about what really happened between her and the albino. She wasn't sure if she ever would. She hardly understood it herself.

She ended her tale with a tragic retelling of Astor and Ohndarien's fate. Brophy took the news with a grim nod.

It was well past midnight when their stories were finished, and Brophy had come no closer to her. He'd insisted that she get some rest and she'd agreed, knowing he needed some time alone with his dark thoughts. As tired as she was, sleep had not come easily. She'd lain curled in her blanket for a long time, listening to the boom swing over as the little boat tacked. She could easily sense Brophy nearby, adjusting the trim of the sail. It reminded her of their time together on the Kherish trader sailing toward the Cinder before the Nightmare Battle. The sounds and smells of the ocean were irrevocably woven through her memories of those few golden days they'd shared. Somehow it seemed fitting that she find him once again in the middle of the ocean. The rolling of the little ship and the nearness of his body almost made her feel like she was home again. And after a long time she finally slept. Shara remained silent after she awoke, but it only took a few moments before Brophy noticed her and frowned. "Go back to sleep," he said in a quiet voice. "You may not have another chance."

"I know," she said, swallowing down her fears at what the next few days might bring. She turned toward him, holding the sail around her like a cape. "But I've slept long enough. I can—"

"I know you can manage. But you need sleep. I don't. Not anymore." He rubbed his chin, massaging his clenched jaw. "I don't need to eat or drink, or even breathe. I'm like the corrupted, continually fed by some unseen source."

"Brophy—"

"Please, get some more rest," he said.

"Soon," she promised him. "It's too cold to sleep now."

He grunted and looked back at the gray horizon.

"Do you know where we are?" she asked.

"Not really. Somewhere west of Efften. I think the prevailing current flows south here. We probably haven't made much headway against it."

"That's all right. If we don't make Ohohhom, Arefaine will come to us."

He opened his mouth, then shut it without saying anything.

"What?" she asked, pushing the canvas aside and standing up.

He rubbed his eyes and ran his fingers thought his blond curls. "I wanted to thank you," he said coarsely.

"For?"

"For finding me. For coming to me." Again she thought he was going to say more, but he frowned and looked away.

She longed to reach out and pull the words from the tip of his tongue, but she held herself back. They'd gone too fast earlier when Brophy had made love to her like a prisoner attacking the bars of his cage. She wouldn't make that mistake again.

"You're welcome," Shara said. "There is no place I'd rather be."

"I'm glad we got to talk," he said, shifting in his seat. "It's difficult, trying to be normal again, with you." She walked softly to him and knelt at his feet. "Me, too. It's been a long time."

"It has."

She watched him, perched on the edge of the boat. It pained her to look at him. Without that feral snarl on his face, he was the boy she'd known eighteen years ago, the boy who let Trent boss him around, who blushed when she discussed her Zelani training. Not a single hair was different. But the moment he looked at her, the moment his green gaze caught hers, that boy vanished, and he was foreign to her.

He was six inches away, but she couldn't touch him, couldn't get past the shadows between them.

For eighteen years, he had lived in her thoughts and dreams, a simple, glorious idol to be worshipped. He was always smiling, always beautiful, always in the mood, always focused entirely on her. She'd grown used to loving the idol and had forgotten how complicated the real Brophy could be.

"So what happens now?" she asked.

Brophy shrugged. "According to Oh, Arefaine and I must reach Efften together at all costs."

"Together?"

"Yes."

"Do you believe the voice you heard is actually a god?"

"He's no god. He's just a man, a mage who turned himself into something very much like the Heartstone."

"But you agree with him, you want her to go to Efften."

He shook his head. "Yes and no. Oh wants her to go there so she can take her own life, turning herself into a vast containment stone like her sister did with the Heartstone. He thinks that's the only thing that can stop the black emmeria."

"That doesn't sound like something she would ever do."

"Of course she won't do it," he said, raising his voice. "And even if she tried, I wouldn't let her."

"All right." She looked into his face, wondering what had set him off.

"I'm sorry," he said, lowering his eyes. "I'm mad at Oh, not you."

"Why are you angry with him?"

"Because of the way he has treated her. Because of the way the Ohohhim have neglected and manipulated her all these years."

"What did they do?"

"They conspired to keep her desperately lonely for her entire life."

"To what end?" she asked. It was difficult to imagine such a powerful sorceress as an abused and neglected child.

"They wanted to drive her into my arms, to make her fall in love with me, and then sacrifice herself to save my life."

She swallowed. "Is she in love with you?"

"She might have been. But I pushed her away."

Shara nodded, desperate for more details, but unwilling to press.

"I wanted to tell you," Brophy continued. "I had sex with Arefaine."

"I guessed," she replied, nodding. Hearing the words somehow made her feel better, made him seem less distant. "It doesn't matter. I haven't exactly been virginal lately either."

"I just wanted you to know."

"Thank you for telling me."

He nodded and then turned toward the sunrise.

"What do you want Arefaine to do on Efften?" Shara asked.

"I want her to see the truth. I want her to see clearly and make her own decision. It's more than her just being tangled up in the emmeria. I think the Fiend is whispering in her ear."

"The Fiend?"

"The man from my dreams."

"The same voice I heard in the emmeria?

"Probably. She thinks the voice in the black emmeria is her father. But once she sees the man face-to-face, I think she will recognize him for what he really is."

Shara nodded. "And then what?"

"And then we kill him."

"Do you know how to do that?"

"No, but I know he fears me. And I know he fears Arefaine. He wouldn't be so bent on controlling her if he didn't." He drew a deep breath. "It is amazing what she can do," he murmured, and Shara felt a pang of jealousy. "She . . ." He trailed off, looking at Shara, then shook his head. "If the emmeria can be created, it can be destroyed. The Silver Islanders found out how to destroy it. I've seen them do it. That man, Reef, told you they just need more time."

"A hundred years more time," Shara said, trying not to fear the admiration she'd heard in Brophy's voice when he talked of Arefaine.

"If that's what it takes, that's what it takes," he said. "We contain the Fiend if we can't kill him. Or if Arefaine can do it, then so much the better."

"I agree."

He paused, looking at her, then smiled. His hand shifted on his thigh, as though he was going to reach for her, but he didn't. "I'm glad you . . . see it the way I do."

She wanted to seize the moment, wanted to bridge the gap between them, but she waited. She was not a patient person. She would rather carve her own flesh than sit there and smile, doing nothing.

"Do you trust Arefaine?" she asked. "Is she an ally or an enemy?"

"I have to make her an ally. I have to make her see. There isn't any other option. Oh says she is the only one who can destroy the Fiend."

"Could this voice you heard be lying to you for some reason?"

"No. I don't agree with Oh's conclusions, but I trust his facts."

"But Arefaine's the one who brought this battle upon us. Ohndarien is destroyed because of her ambitions. Wouldn't it be better for all of us if she died? If the Silver Islanders have kept the Fiend contained for this long, why not let them continue? Why bring it to a head now?"

She expected him to get angry. She expected him to rush to the defense of this woman he, perhaps, loved.

"Would it be better if I died?" he asked calmly.

"You are not her."

"But I am," he said. "I am exactly like her. She brought all of this upon us like . . ." He paused, breathing hard. "Like I raped you."

"You didn't—"

"Stop it!" he said. "Don't lie to me and don't lie to yourself! I know what I did! The emmeria is a part of me, the rage, the hatred. And if Arefaine can't be saved, then neither can I, neither can any of us."

Shara nodded, remembering how he pulled her out of the darkness in the Wet Cells. "All right, then we save her."

He took a deep breath, trying to calm himself. "The first thing we need to do is turn her away from that voice pretending to be her father, luring her to Efften."

"What does he want?"

"Freedom. He wants her to release him from his tower. He's locked in there somehow, and she's the blade that can cut him free. But I believe she's also the blade that can kill him. The Fiend knows it, and he takes a risk bringing her to him."

"So you have to convince her to listen to you, not him."

"Yes. I have to convince her to destroy the only love she had ever known in exchange for—"

"Your love?"

"In exchange for my friendship."

Shara's chest tightened. "So you don't love her?"

"I care for her. And I love her after a fashion, but . . . Not like you mean. I love *you*, Shara. Always you. Only you."

She bit her lip, and her hands started to shake.

He watched her with those haunted eyes, and she saw him make a decision. He stood up and took her into his arms. For a moment she saw the boy she'd seen atop the Hall of Windows in those last minutes. Just for an instant. But it was enough to fill her with hope.

"Should we try this again?" she asked.

He slowly, purposefully, rested his head on her shoulder, but his body was as taut as a bowstring. "I can't," he whispered hoarsely. "Not until this is over. Not until he is dead—"

"Shhh . . ." she whispered. He lifted his head, and she let him go. "I know what it must feel like. Remember that night in the Wet Cells?"

"This is not the same thing—"

"How is it different?"

He clenched his fists. "He's in my head! He's . . . everywhere!"

"I know," she said, calming herself with her ani. "But that is exactly how I felt in the Wet Cells. I had become my enemy. I became Victeris. I nearly made you crawl." She paused, letting the memories come, letting them go. "I went to rescue you because I remembered being in love with you, but it wasn't love that drove me. It was hate, a sense of crazy vengeance against Victeris."

"Shara, Victeris was dead. The Fiend is very much alive."

"So are you, Brophy. He is not stronger than you! You said it yourself. He's afraid of you."

He stared at her, breathing through his teeth.

"The rage you feel is his. That is his fear talking. He doesn't want us together. He knows—"

"I don't want us together either!" he yelled. "I can't get anywhere near you!"

Her heart clenched. She was pushing him too far, too fast, but she couldn't make herself stop. "Think about it, Brophy," she begged. "He's a creature of hatred and fear. What would be the one thing he couldn't abide?"

He looked at her, his green eyes narrowing.

"Yes," she encouraged.

"Love," he breathed.

"That was how you reached me in the Wet Cells. That was what banished the darkness. He's part of that same darkness. We can banish him the same way."

He spun away from her, grabbing fistfuls of hair on either side of his head. "I don't want to hurt you again!" he screamed up at the sky.

"You can't hurt me," she said softly, her hand hovering near his back, but still she didn't touch him. "No matter what happens, I'm strong enough to take it. We're strong enough to take it."

He shook his head.

"Do whatever you need to let that hate out. Give it to me if you have to. I know how to let it go. Give me your pain, I know how to use it now."

He turned back to her, his eyes red-rimmed and desperate. "I feel like I'm about to do something horrible to you," he said, his chin quivering.

"No. You're about to stop doing something horrible to me."

She bridged the distance between them, placed her hands on his chest, and stood on tiptoes to kiss him. He closed his eyes.

"What do you want?" she whispered. "What do you want most, right at this moment? Let it out."

"I want to bite you, hurt you."

"Then bite me. Hurt me. I will be all right."

She reached up, cupped the back of his head, and drew his face down to her neck.

She felt Brophy's breath warm on her skin. His lips parted and his teeth slid across her neck.

"Lose yourself and I will find you," she murmured, thinking of the blazing fire hot on her skin and the albino's voice as he stood behind her, a red-hot iron rod in his hand. If she could do that for Jesheks, she could do this for Brophy. "Do it," she whispered. "Just let go and do it."

His jaws clamped down. The pain shot through her, flooding her body with a golden glow. He pulled back, but she clutched him tighter as she felt the blood trickle over her collarbone and down between her breasts.

"Let go," she breathed. "Let him go."

Brophy bit harder, crushing her to him. Her back arched, and she felt her skin tear. He picked her up and threw her to the ground, landing with his full weight on top of her. Her head smacked against the deck, and she cycled the pain into herself.

"Brophy," she murmured, clutching his back, digging her nails into his skin.

His strained breaths roared in her ear as he bit her higher on the neck. She cried out and forced her hands between them, pushing her pants past her hips. He did the same, tearing at his clothing.

She spread her legs, and he slammed into her, knocking her breath from her lungs. She pushed her hips against him, guiding him inside her, pulling him closer.

"Yes," she whispered as he threw himself at her over and over, screaming in her ear like an animal. "I'm all right. Let it go. I'm all right."

His anguished voice filled her head, chasing away the golden glow. His keen of agony was joined by others. A howling cascade of mindless rage poured over her, into her, through her. And for a brief moment Shara was sure that she would die.

Chapter 20

Issefyn hid under the bed, chewing on a blanket. The taste of wet wool stung the back of her throat, but without the cloth between her teeth, she would scream. She had pulled out the drawers under the seamen's bunk and crawled inside to escape the light. She couldn't stand the light. It burned her.

She tossed back and forth beneath her tiny prison. Her hands shook uncontrollably, and her bowels had seized. Her chest and stomach ached from curling herself into a tight little ball.

She bit the blanket harder, kicking the hull over and over. The pain in her foot was only a mild distraction, nothing more. It didn't help, not really. She needed her stone. Speevor should have been here hours ago. The day was nearly over, and he wasn't here yet.

She flipped over, scraping her back on the underside of the bed. She punched the floor, pulled her own hair, beat her head against the hull. Nothing helped. Nothing!

Where was her stone!?

She would have to take it back, rip the stone from his hands. She could break the door down if she wanted. Could breathe into the Floani form and shatter it with a kick. That idiot Speevor with his sightless black eyes stood just beyond. She could break him, could snap his neck. But the fool wouldn't die. He wouldn't even let go of her stone. She'd have to tear it from his grasp, but a dozen more would take his place. She could control them, command them. But *HE* would be there to stop her. *HE! HE! HE! HE* had brought her to this. *HE* would pay.

And it was so bright out there. The light burned her. It was better under here. Pure hell, but better than out there.

Where was her stone? It had been hours. Hours!

Her teeth squeaked as she bit the blanket harder and harder, clenching and unclenching her body. They would bring it before she died. They would have to bring it before she died.

Issefyn heard distant footsteps and scrambled out from under the bed. The lock clicked and turned, and she rushed to the door. Her blouse was open and she held it shut, struggling to stand up straight despite the cramping in her abdomen.

The door swung open, and Speevor stepped into the room. He paused right in front of her, standing stock-still, staring at nothing. His tunic was almost completely black from the emmeria that dripped down his cheeks. In his left hand, he gripped the containment stone. Issefyn's heart beat frantically in her chest, and she grabbed it with both hands.

A wave of blessed darkness washed over her, and she gasped. The stone fed her like cool, sweet water flowing through her body. The crushing weight on her skull disappeared. She was able to draw a full breath as her chest expanded and her cramped stomach relaxed. Power surged into her arms, filling her with lightning.

Speevor pulled the stone away, and Issefyn jolted at the separation.

"Not too much now, Mother," said a familiar voice from across the room. "There's no need to be greedy."

Issefyn sneered.

Victeris was lying on her stripped mattress. He smiled at her, and she longed to kill him.

Speevor tucked her containment stone under one arm and stared at nothing. It was in sight and out of reach. Another one of *his* petty torments. The stone was almost spent. Only the faintest flicker of black floated within it like a snake. *HE* was a fool, wasting all the precious emmeria on maintaining these shambling simpletons, trying to sail this Summer Fleet to its useless doom!

Victeris chuckled. "Oh, Mother, you seem to have ransacked your room again. Were you in some sort of distress?"

Her lips pulled back against her teeth. "Of course I was! You're the one who made me wait all day!"

"All day, it's barely two hours past dawn."

She spun toward the window. He was right; the sun was still low in the eastern sky. She stared at the horizon, amazed at how easily time had gotten away from her. The light sill pained her, but it was bearable after she'd been with the stone.

She turned to the image of her dead son. "I warn you, shade. Don't push me any further. I will repay every kindness you have shown me."

"What?" Victeris chuckled. "What will you do? Make me crawl? Really, Mother. You're acting like a little girl. Stop fighting me and everything you want will be yours." He nodded at Speevor, who held the stone out to her.

Issefyn forced her hand—which was already curled to snatch the stone away—to relax. Breathing rapidly, she turned away from it.

"Well done, Mother. See how strong you are becoming?"

Issefyn clenched her teeth.

"Now that you have had your breakfast, would you like to see what is going on in the world? Or would you rather return to your little nest?" He patted the bed.

She said nothing.

"Come," he said. "The fresh air will do you good."

Suspicious, she followed the ghost out the door and up the steps. The sunlight was painfully bright, and she could feel a hint of her headache return. She squinted and looked forward. Her eyes finally adjusted, and she realized that the fleet was stopped. They had all dropped sails and were drifting in the slight breeze. A second, smaller fleet bobbed on the swells a few hundred yards from them. The black ships bore three pointed stars on their triangular sails, the symbol of the Ohohhim navy.

Issefyn sneered, scanning the ships until she spotted Arefaine standing on the deck of the foremost ship. The upstart wore a black gown and a powdered face and was surrounded by a horde of swordsmen in those preposterous finned helmets, but Issefyn could see little else at this distance.

So the arrogant girl had betrayed the emperor and brought his minions to heel. Let her bask in her glory for now. When the time was ripe, Issefyn would peel that perfect white mask from her face strip by bloody strip.

A lone figure rowed toward the preening brat, crossing the distance between the two fleets. Issefyn brushed him with her magic and sneered.

Vinghelt was struggling to row by himself, fighting the swells with no attendants to do the hard work for him. She frowned and looked at the shade's mocking visage, clothed in the features of her dead son. "Why does he row alone?" she asked.

He merely smiled and said nothing. Issefyn turned back to the scene. Vinghelt caught a line tossed from Arefaine's ship and climbed aboard.

The moronic Summer Prince made a great show of greeting Arefaine as if she were a long-lost friend. He kissed her hand, lingering in a grandiose bow like a groveling peacock with an erection.

For some reason the man seemed to fancy his cock trapped in a block of Ohohhim ice. Issefyn wondered why he even tried. Rutting with that man would be the blandest two minutes of any woman's life. Surely even Arefaine could see that.

"Look at her," Issefyn scoffed. "Treating that worm like a long-lost brother. Has she even asked about me? Has she forgotten who brought her this little fleet wrapped up with a bow?"

"The young Mother Regent has many things on her mind right now."

"Loyalty and gratitude obviously aren't among them."

Arefaine and Vinghelt continued to talk. Issefyn couldn't hear what they said, but as she looked closer, she saw a shadow hovering beside Arefaine. Careful not to draw attention to herself, Issefyn extended her ani, trying to bring the shadow into focus.

When she did, she began to laugh, then turned to face Victeris.

"I see you haunt the girl just as you haunt me."

"A father likes to be near his children."

The shade of a slender man in a green sarong stood at Arefaine's right elbow. It leaned over and whispered something in her ear.

"So that is her father's face you wear. Do you think the real Darius Morgeon would approve?"

"I am more a father to her than that man could ever be. He betrayed everything she loves—"

"—when he locked you away," she finished for him.

Victeris seemed unperturbed. He shrugged. "She sees what she needs to see. For now."

"And when she sees your true nature, how do you think she will feel?"

"A fine teacher moves slowly, only sharing the truth when his students are ready to accept it. As she matures, she will understand."

"I see," Issefyn said, watching Arefaine. The girl looked calm and confident, securely in control. She was not the manipulative hypocrite who hid behind the emperor's skirts as she maneuvered the knife toward his back. Nor was she the brazen girl who threw her power around in Ohndarien like a harlot on parade.

Arefaine seemed to grow bored as Vinghelt droned on and on. She reached out with her mind to inspect the Summer Fleet. Issefyn hastily bolstered her glamour, but she needn't have bothered. As soon as Arefaine's power coalesced, the shade at her side said something, distracting her. She never made an inspection of the ships.

"You're leading her by the nose," Issefyn said, wondering if the shade had overpowered her, or was simply playing a clever game of lies.

"I am nurturing her."

"I'm sure you are."

Issefyn inspected the girl more carefully, wondering what else she had missed. She was surprised to find yet another shadow, this one at Vinghelt's side. The Summer Prince was accompanied by a naked woman with green skin and hair that flowed to her feet like a waterfall.

She laughed. "Are you *nurturing* the buffoon also? Am I the only one who knows your true face?"

"For now."

She sneered. "Why do you bother with these others? You and I are the only ones truly worthy of Efften's legacy."

"Perhaps," Victeris said. "But a father loves all of his children equally. Even Vinghelt contains an ember of the sacred fire. Who knows where its light could lead him?"

No doubt to the same place a flame leads a moth, Issefyn thought.

Once more, Arefaine began to send her magic across the water to inspect the Summer Fleet, and once again, she was distracted by the shade at her side. Issefyn narrowed her eyes.

"You don't want her to see what kind of crew Vinghelt is using, do you?"

Victeris maintained his calm smile, but said nothing.

"Are you afraid your little baby girl would disapprove of your methods?" she pressed.

Victeris shrugged. "There are some things you just don't tell the children," he said.

"She will learn soon enough," Issefyn warned.

"Of course she will," Victeris said softly. "They all do."

Chapter 21

rophy pushed the bulky needle through the threadbare cloth. The needle was supposed to be used for repairing sails, not trousers. His pants would look like Reef's face when he was finished, but at least he wouldn't be hanging out of them.

He looked over at Shara where she sat at the back of the boat, wearing nothing but her oversized shirt, her hand resting on the tiller.

She was smiling.

It nearly broke his heart.

His whole body clenched when he thought back to what he'd done earlier that morning. He'd thrown her on the deck, ripped his own pants off to get at her. It reminded him of that black moment in the Nine Squares arena when he lost all composure and deliberately cut through Phee's eye. That had been the first time in his life that he enjoyed hurting someone. That image of his fighting claw slicing through the other boy's eye had haunted him ever since, but that moment of uncontrollable rage had only lasted a few seconds. What he'd done with Shara that morning had gone on and on.

He remembered striking her, biting her, slamming her against the deck, attacking her like she was everything he ever hated in the world. The rage exploded out of him, his whole body was screaming louder and louder. He was sure he was going to die, that the whole world would rip itself apart if he ever truly let go.

But he did let go, he completely let go, and Shara held him together.

He winced at the memory of his fists pounding against her face. But she survived every blow, somehow healing the wounds with a magic he had never seen before. She accepted everything he threw at her, and his hatred disappeared into her depthless ocean. His searing rage washed over her, through her, and vanished. He flooded her with pure evil, his evil, Efften's evil, all the evil in the world, and she took it all. Took it all and repaid him with love.

He hung his head, suddenly dizzy. He felt so ashamed in the face of her courage and determination, so unworthy. How could anyone love that much? What could he possibly have done to deserve that?

"You keep crying over there, you'll never get those pants sewed," she called out to him.

He looked up, wiping the moisture from his eyes. "You calling me a baby?"

"Yup. Big baby." She laughed, her whole face glowing. Her dark hair fluttered in the wind, and he could see the golden feather beneath her shirt, nestled between her breasts. Her tanned skin was completely unmarked even thought he'd hit her hard enough to break steel.

He turned away and tried to add another stitch with trembling hands.

"Never mind the pants," she said. "I like you better without them."

He shook his head and pushed the needle through the cloth. "That's easy for you to say. When's the last time you ran into battle with your little man hanging out?"

She smiled and gave the tiller a sudden jerk. The boat lurched, and Brophy had to grab the gunnels to keep from being tossed overboard.

"Put that down and come over here," she insisted.

He rose, his heart beating faster, his empty stomach squirming. The Fiend was still there. Brophy could feel him hovering like a storm in the distance. But for the first time since he made his sacrifice, he felt whole again. His heart was his own.

He walked over and knelt in front of her. She leaned forward and kissed him. "This time, let's go slow," she whispered. He wrapped his arms around her and the two of them sank to the deck. Her bare legs slid around his.

The boat suddenly jibbed as she let go of the tiller. The boom swung around and they rolled across the deck, slamming into the side of the boat.

"I said slow," she whispered, laughing in his ear.

"All right," he said, pulling back a little so he could look at her. "Slow."

Carefully shifting his weight, he slipped inside as gently as he could. Her mouth opened, and she took little gasps of breath.

"Now who's the big baby?" he asked, brushing a tear from her cheek.

She smiled, and she suddenly looked fragile, like the slightest pressure would crush her.

"I spent a lifetime waiting for this moment," she said. "This one moment right here."

He nodded, never believing he could feel this way again. She'd had to do the believing for both of them.

She reached out and touched his face, her skin warm despite the chill of the steady breeze. "All those years," she said, her brows drawing together. "I kept telling myself that what we felt was real. Those few days on the way to the Cinder, those last moments atop the Hall of Windows. I kept telling myself that was love and love is real."

He looked into her eyes and felt her magic swirling through them. It felt like every part of them was touching at once.

"A part of me never believed it," she continued. "A part of me always hated myself for playing the fool." Her hand slid across his cheek. "But right now . . ." She smiled as a sob burst from her throat. "Right now I'm very happy that I did."

Brophy felt a tear roll off the tip of his nose. It splashed on her cheek.

He leaned down and kissed her. "We're going to win this one," he whispered, his lips never leaving hers. "I can feel it."

Chapter 22

The sky far to the east was beginning to glow when Brophy spotted what he was looking for.

"There," he said, pointing at the dark silhouettes that dotted the northern horizon. Shara squinted into the darkness.

"By the Seasons, Brophy," she gasped, shaking her head. "That's a lot of ships." She adjusted the tiller and turned their boat directly toward them.

"The most powerful fleets in the world," he murmured, in grudging admiration of what Arefaine had accomplished. She had united two of the largest fleets in the world and was ready to challenge the third.

The sun rose higher as they sailed closer to the vast armada and he could soon make out the black, triangular sails of the Ohohhim ships amid the many-colored banners of the Summer Fleet. He did a quick count. There had to be nearly a hundred Ohohhim ships, and twice as many in the Summer Fleet. The bulky hulls and brightly colored sails of the Summermen's pleasure barges surrounded the austere Ohohhim warships like a gaudy ruffle.

"Have you thought any more about how you are going to approach Arefaine?"

"I've barely thought about anything else for the past three days," he said. "It hinges on the Fiend. This Efflum. He's convinced her that he's her father. I have to find some way to prove he's lying, and break his hold on her."

Shara nodded. "Are you sure you want her to survive this battle?" she asked, looking at Brophy with a frown. "If Ossamyr tried to assassinate Arefaine, she must have had a good reason. I can't help agreeing with her a little bit. The coming bloodbath is Arefaine's doing, and for what? I keep wondering if maybe a hundred years is not so long a time to wait for the Silver Islanders to finish the job they started. Why not let them finish the Fiend? Why do we need Arefaine?"

"We've been through this before, Shara. The Fiend is growing stronger. He's working his way free. Ohndarien has already been overrun by weeping ones. How long until the rest of the world is just like her?"

Her lips pressed together in a line, and she watched him.

"Arefaine is the only one who can stop him."

"All right," she said. "I trust your judgment. We'll do it your way."

"Thank you. The first thing we have to do is stop this battle while we still can. But how do I convince her to turn against the only person she's ever loved?"

"By making her a better offer."

He looked at her, frowning. "No. I won't step back into the role the emperor wrote for me. I won't try to seduce her."

"Who said anything about seducing?"

"I'm not going to try to manipulate her either. I don't even think I could. She's too smart for that."

"So don't lie. Don't say anything. Just be there. Just love her."

He shook his head. "I don't love her. I love you."

She took his hand, squeezed it. "I know," she murmured. "I know that to the center of my bones. But isn't there room in the human heart for more than just one person?"

He watched her, but didn't say anything.

"You may not love her the same way you love me, but you still love her. I can hear it in your voice when you talk about her. The rest of us assume the worst in her. But you've always seen things differently. Just like when you cast the music box off the Hall of Windows. I thought you were insane, but you were right. Your intuition was strong, Brophy, and I trust it. You want Arefaine to be treated decently. You want to protect her, help her find the home she's always looked for. Isn't that love?" She shrugged. "I think it's the best part of love."

Brophy looked at the ships in the distance, frowning in concentration. "You might be right," he said quietly.

"I know I am. If she's going to listen to anyone, she'll listen to you. She loves you."

Brophy shook his head. "Perhaps she did once, but not anymore."

"Love is love, Brophy. It doesn't go away that easily."

He closed his eyes and took a deep breath.

"You need to go to her, and go alone."

"No."

"Yes," she said, squeezing his hand. "The last thing Arefaine wants to see is your other lover by your side."

"But, Shara—"

She cut him off with a look. "I'll be right behind you, just out of sight. But she's never going to hear you with me there."

He frowned. "You're starting to sound like the emperor," he said.

She smiled. "I always liked the emperor. I would have slept with him if I wasn't so busy pining over your bier."

Brophy started to protest again, but his eyes narrowed as he spotted something in the distance. "Look," he said, pointing farther east.

Shara narrowed her eyes. There was a large atoll just north of Efften. The narrow strait between the two islands was full of Islander warships, their steel prows glinting in the morning sun.

"Dammit," Brophy said. "I wanted to get to Arefaine first."

Shara looked back and forth between the two fleets heading straight for each other. "We drifted too far west during the night. I don't think we'll make it."

He took the tiller from Shara, and she stood up, her gaze fixed on the ships in the distance. "It looks like the Silver Islanders are outnumbered two- or three-to-one," she said.

"That doesn't mean much," Brophy assured her. "Ship for ship, no one can match the Silver Islanders on the open seas."

Brophy remembered the grim resolution on Reef's face when he set his own ship ablaze to keep it out of Brophy's hands. That kind of fanaticism had allowed them to rule the Great Ocean for centuries.

"If anyone could win this battle, it is the Silver Islanders."

"Not against Arefaine and that many weeping ones. They're sailing to their deaths and they're taking Ossamyr with them."

"I know. I still can't believe the two of you became friends."

"She changed, Brophy. And she never forgave herself for what she did to you."

"That makes two of us."

Shara shook her head. "She's done no worse to you than Arefaine. How can you forgive the one and not the other?"

Brophy sighed. "None of that matters now. Can you find Arefaine with your magic? Do you know where she is?"

Shara turned to face the Ohohhim fleet. Her black hair fluttered behind her in the stiff breeze. Her straight nose, her full lips, were painted bright against that dark backdrop. Brophy followed her gaze, searching the distant ships for any sign of the young woman who had nearly been his lover and his executioner.

The Ohohhim ships were in the center of the formation. Plumes of black smoke rose from the incendiaries smoldering on their decks, leaving a black haze in their wake.

"There she is." Shara pointed. "In the crow's nest of that largest ship, there in the center."

"Can you talk to her, reach her with your magic?"

"Perhaps, if she lets me. What do you want me to say to her?"

"Tell her that I'm still alive and I need to talk to her. Tell her that the Silver Islanders have a way of destroying the black emmeria."

"Do you really believe that will make her pull out at this point?"

He shook his head. "No. But we have to try."

She turned to face the fleet. They were close enough now to make out the sailors running along the decks of the distant ships. "Yes," she said, closing her eyes and concentrating. Brophy felt her magic swirl around him. "We have to try."

Arefaine stood in the crow's nest of the imperial flagship overlooking the Ohohhim fleet. It spread before her like a shifting forest of billowing white trees, the triangular sails of sleek warships shifting back and forth as they rode the swells. Beyond them, square sails and the bright blue, orange, red, purple, and green pennants of the Summer ships made her fleet the largest the Great Ocean had ever seen.

In the distance, the gleaming metal prows of the Silver Islanders sailed to meet them like a wall of swords. Their force was less than half the size, but there was no guarantee that this battle would be easily won. Her naval commanders had been very insistent about the effectiveness of the barbarians' initial charge. Their only hope was to overwhelm them with numbers, deny them room to maneuver, and build up the speed to use their deadly prows. The steel rams of the Silver Islander ships could cut a ship in half and keep right on sailing. Their navy had kept all comers away from Efften for three hundred years. But it was time for the wheel to turn. Today, history would be shattered. Age-old crimes would be avenged and a new world would emerge from the floating wreckage and blood soaked seas.

Arefaine slipped her hand into her pocket and touched the crystal shard hidden within. She couldn't help thinking that Brophy might still be alive somewhere, hidden among the enemy. She could picture him standing above one of their gleaming silver prows, sword in hand, blond hair shifting in the breeze. She shook the thought from her head. He'd made his choice. Alive or dead. Against her or not. He didn't matter anymore.

Arefaine shrugged under the weight of the satchel across her shoulders. Her father had insisted that she carry the Heartstone and the containment stones she'd taken from Ohndarien with her at all times. It was a damnable nuisance. Their weight was constantly pulling her off balance as the ship swayed back and forth, and the constant howling of the hungry emmeria made it hard to concentrate. But her father had insisted that they were too precious to be relegated to any servant. It would be catastrophic if they fell into the wrong hands.

Ignoring the weight against her hip, she looked out over her men. She tasted their emotions. They were tense, but determined. The only thing that seemed to be bothering them was the stench of the pitch smoke from the incendiaries that billowed from the deck-top cauldrons in endless plumes, stinging the nose and eyes.

They were good men, each one a volunteer responding to Arefaine's silent call to release the sleeve in front of them and escape the divine queue. Prior to departure she'd ordered a final inspection. They all lined up on the dock and she had taken the time to look into the heart of every man and woman in the fleet. She'd touched each one of them on the hand, leaving her mark on their souls. They would not fail her. Not while they still drew breath.

A feathery touch brushed across her mind, and she turned, looking to the east. What was—

"Arefaine, my child," her father said, suddenly appearing next to her in the crow's nest. He placed his ghostly hand on hers, the wind ruffling his green sarong. "It is time to move your ship to the back of the formation," her father quietly insisted. She frowned at him briefly, then turned back to the east, trying to feel for the source of the magical touch.

"Arefaine," he insisted again. "You cannot remain at the head of the fleet."

"I felt something," she said. "Like someone is trying to contact me."

"Magical?" he asked.

She looked at him. "Yes. Did you feel it, too?"

"Of course, my child. It must be the Ohndarien witch who tried to kill you. The barbarians are ascertaining your whereabouts. They will come directly for you if they can find you. You must protect yourself."

She turned a narrowed gaze upon the Silver Islander fleet. "I thought they hated any use of magic."

"Of course they do, but they can finally see justice staring them in the face. They are desperate enough to try anything. Even hiring the services of a wayward sorceress. You must hide yourself from her. We have waited a long time for this glorious day," her father said.

She looked at him, the wind ruffling his long goatee.

"And I want to see it," she said. They had been arguing about this since they left Ohohhom. She longed to be at the front of the fleet when they ripped into those tattooed murderers. She wanted to be right in the middle of it, standing beside her men to meet the Islanders' legendary charge. She wanted to see the expressions on their faces when the children of Efften returned to avenge their parents' murder.

"I know how badly you want to fight. And I know how bravely you would do it. But we cannot risk a stray arrow shattering our dreams."

"Father, no stray arrow could ever—"

"You can't know that. Believe me. I have seen my share of battles. I know how confusing they can be. The Silver Islanders didn't come here to defeat your fleet. They came here to kill you. Nothing else matters to them. They want to annihilate our kind. You are the strongest and they will sacrifice anything to get to you, if you let them. This is the battle for our future. Will magicians be allowed to survive in our world?"

"We will survive, Father. I promise you."

"Then remain at the back. Let your servants do the fighting for you. That is why the Summer Fleet is here. Let them take the brunt of the first charge. The battle will come to you soon enough, I assure you. All the odds are in our favor, but do not give them a chance to steal our victory."

She sighed. "I will remain here, Father. But only because you ask it."

"A wise choice, my child. A half hour of prudence is certainly worth a lifetime of desire."

Arefaine nodded, but she still longed to be in the middle of it. She had prepared for this day her entire life. This was her moment of glory, and she wanted to revel in it.

Taking a deep breath, she let go of her desires and focused on the larger goal. "I'll contact Admiral Wembu," she said. "He'll know what to do."

"Good, my child. Good."

With a thought, she brushed the admiral's mind. In moments orders were being shouted from ship to ship. Her flagship luffed its sails and began to fall behind.

The rest of her fleet did the same and Summermen on either side of her began to drift toward the center, filling the gap. Her allies' ships were ill suited to this sort of battle. Their losses would be heavy. She should have walked among them, looked them in the eye, and bolstered their spirits. But there hadn't been the time. She reached out with her mind to gauge their morale, but she stopped when she heard her father chuckling.

"Don't worry about them, my child. Any sacrifices they make will be handsomely rewarded. After this battle, they will control Ohndarien,

Physendria, and the Silver Islands. Prince Vinghelt's dominion will extend across two oceans. And we will have one of our own guarding our shores. Don't weep at the price of greatness."

Arefaine nodded, shifting the bag of containment stones farther back off her hip. The first wave of the Silver Islanders was nearly within range of her vanguard. The barbarians were packed on their decks, weapons in hand. She found herself searching the crowds for a shock of blond hair and scowled.

"Now," she murmured, and her admiral did not fail her.

A horn rang out and the Ohohhim catapults loosed. Flaming pots filled with pitch-soaked gravel arced into the air. The deadly comet shower rose, and then fell among the white sails of the Silver Islanders, shattering on the decks below, flinging flaming debris everywhere.

Silver Islander ships went up like torches. Even at this distance, she could hear the screams as the murderers leapt overboard.

Taking a deep breath, Arefaine smiled.

Reef stepped in front of Ossamyr as the flaming pots descended all around them. One splashed into the water in front of his ship, sending flecks of dying flame against the hull.

The ship to starboard was not so lucky. Two pots smashed across her deck, spreading fire like rain, lighting everything it touched. A sailor caught in the main spray screamed, running blindly for the edge of the ship. He slammed into the rail and toppled overboard, leaving a tiny splash as the hulls of the Silver Islander ships raced past him.

"Can you find her?" Reef asked, his stony face facing forward, watching the quickly approaching enemy fleet.

The pain in Ossamyr's belly had become almost unbearable. She felt the sneaky tendrils of delirium creeping into her thoughts. The wound was just. She'd had her chance to kill Arefaine and she let it slip by.

The Nine pay their debts in the same coin with which they were loaned, she heard Phandir saying in her mind. *They reward great deeds with glory. They reward failure with shame.*

Phandir's not here, she thought. *Concentrate. You don't have much time.*

"I can," she answered Reef, rallying her strength and sending her attention out again, searching the first ship that hurtled toward them.

"They're not people," she gasped. "I can sense something, very faint, but not like—"

"It's the indentured," Reef said in a rumbling voice. "Don't worry about them. She won't be on one of those ships. Search the Ohohhim fleet." He pointed. "The ship at the back. The largest one. The flagship. Check there."

She threw her energy beyond the bright Summer ships toward the triangular sails of the Ohohhim, stretching. Trying. But they were too far away, and her attention faltered.

Ossamyr drew herself back, breathing hard. She brushed her hand across her stomach, thinking she would find her entrails hanging out. They weren't, but the wound felt dark and ugly. Every time she shifted, she felt as if she would split in half.

Reef looked at her with worry.

If she had been back in Ohndarien, with Shara helping, Ossamyr knew she could fight this infection. But Shara was lost to her, like the rest of Ohndarien. Ever since she leapt into the salt water, fleeing Reef's burning ship, the pain had intensified with every passing hour.

How could it have ended so wrong? Why wouldn't Brophy listen to her?

Because you betrayed him, Phandir laughed in her mind. *You showed him what a perfect queen you are.*

"Shut up," she murmured, then shook her head. She looked up and saw Reef's concerned stare.

"Enough," he said. "The strain is too—"

"No, I can find her."

Once again, Ossamyr sent her awareness out, panting with exertion. The effort increased her pain. If felt as if someone had sewn a red-hot coal into her belly. With every effort she made, the coal burned brighter and brighter, trying to sear its way out.

"There," she gasped, pointing feebly. "You were right. In the crow's nest."

He turned and shouted at his helmsman. "Luff the sails! Hold back. We skirt the fleet and then cut for the center. We aim for the flagship!"

The helmsman nodded and shouted the orders in relay. The crew leapt to the task, and the ship slowed. The sailor in their crow's nest signaled to the ship behind them that Reef had specially prepared. It slowed in response. The rest of the fleet flowed past them at full speed.

Ossamyr glanced at the dinghy resting on blocks next to her. It was packed with wooden chests, each one of them holding a thousand shards of light emmeria. The ship behind them had the same. They were the spears meant to pierce Arefaine's heart.

She turned back to the enemy in front of them. She could see the catapult crews rushing thought the haze, desperate to reload their weapons. They would be here in seconds.

"Will we have time to reach her if we go around?"

"We might," Reef growled. "I certainly don't want to get caught in the snarl. We have no chance of fighting our way straight through the middle."

She touched the poisoned dagger still strapped to her thigh. If only the blade had tasted its prize.

Her fingers moved from the dagger to the shards of light emmeria sewn into her clothing. Ossamyr felt like she was walking into a burning house wearing oil-soaked clothes. Reef's tunic was the same, and everyone else on board the ship. If Arefaine used her magic on any one of them, she would win the battle for them. One explosion would spread to the others until the chests in the dinghy exploded, taking Arefaine and everyone else with it.

Ossamyr winced as her belly tightened, trying to ignore her pain. She glanced back at the men and women who packed the deck behind her. They'd been handpicked by Reef, the finest archers and swordsmen in the Islands. They stood shoulder to shoulder in grim determination, their tattoos blending into a chaotic mass of shapes and colors. Not one of them expected to see the sun set that day.

"Incoming," someone shouted, and she spun back around to see a second volley of flaming balls arcing toward the Ohohhim fleet. Their vanguard took the brunt of the attack. More Silver Islander ships went up like torches, but they didn't falter. Their brave captains continued sailing as long as they could, trying to hold on and run their burning ships into their enemies.

"That's the last shot they'll get off before we ram them," Reef growled.

Ossamyr reached out, fumbling with his forearm and then gripping his enormous hand. He looked at her, and it sent a surge of pride through her. Such a great man. And she'd had so little time with him. It was her curse. She'd spent most of her life with a man she despised, and only a few short days with the ones who really loved her. That was the Nine's punishment, truly. She had denied her love and it had been denied to her.

"I want you in the dinghy with the light emmeria in case the ship is sunk," Reef rumbled. "If we go down, you can get away with it."

She started to laugh, then winced, putting a hand to her belly. "And I want to live forever on that island you took me to. Neither is going to happen."

"You can barely stand," Reef said. "You've done your part. Save your strength."

"If I had done my part, this battle would never have happened."

Reef held her tight, her stalwart oak of a man keeping her on her feet. He looked down at her. "I'm not sure I could still love you if you ever let go of all that guilt you adore so much," he said wryly, then kissed the top of her head. "But I would certainly try."

Their ship veered west, skirting the battle, as Silver Islander ships sliced into their enemy's formation. Wood crackled like a hundred simultaneous thunderclaps as the Islander fleet sliced through the Summermen.

Ossamyr hugged Reef and looked ahead, keeping her eyes locked on Arefaine's flagship.

"You fool, you've killed us all!" Issefyn cried, watching an Islander ship slice right through a pleasure barge, cracking the ship in half.

"Calm yourself, Mother," Victeris said, watching the slaughter before them.

Issefyn clutched the railing, and tried to see out of her itching eyes and concentrate past the relentless pounding in her head. She'd thought her ship was tucked safely in the back of the formation, but the Islanders had ripped right through their first line of defense and engaged the second. The ship she'd watched cut through a fat wallowing tub had already rammed the next ship it came to, burying its sharpened prow into the side of a triple-decked party boat. All across the line it was the same story. The Silver Islanders had weathered the burning rain of the Ohohhim catapults and rushed their flaming ships headlong into the Summer Fleet. The crack and groan of splintering wood rose from all over the battle. Scores of weeping ones were flung into the water to drown. Still more slid down canting decks and were also claimed by the ocean.

"You didn't expect us to come through this battle unscathed, did you?" Victeris asked.

"It's a slaughter," she cried. "You've sent poets to fight barbarians," she said. "Mute poets who bleed black from the eyes. A cunning strategy. What will you throw at the enemy next? Little girls?"

Victeris merely smiled. "The worst of it is already over," he said. "Or didn't you know?"

"I know that your side is losing. I know that much."

He chuckled. "Keep watching."

The Silver Islanders' initial onslaught was devastating, but once they lost their momentum, they had no room to maneuver. Their small sleek boats bogged down in the wreckage of the larger vessels. The one right in front of her had gotten its prow lodged in the ship it had rammed. Its stern was already rising out of the water as it started going down with the larger vessel.

The second and third rows of Summer ships were entering the battle, pinning the Islander ships between them. Before long it would turn to hand-to-hand combat.

"And now, Mother, I must take my leave. My attention is needed elsewhere."

To control your mindless army, she thought. *How many can you manage at once? I wonder.*

But she said nothing to him, and he vanished. She continued watching the battle, resisting the urge to turn around and look at Speevor, who stood several paces behind her clutching the containment stone.

The weeping ones began fighting now, leaping over to the Silver Islander ships as the Islanders rushed to brace them. As soon as they did, Issefyn turned.

And smiled.

Speevor stood inert, limp arms hanging at his sides, with only his fist tight around the containment stone.

One shaking step at a time, Issefyn approached, but the mindless hulk didn't respond to her presence. Swallowing, she reached out, slowly, and touched the containment stone in his hand.

The glorious power flowed into her, filling her like golden water. Her eyes stopped itching, and her headache vanished.

"Yes," she moaned, took a deep breath, and looked at Speevor. He still swayed limply with the motion of the ship.

With her newfound strength, she grabbed the stone and tried to wrestle it from his unyielding grasp. She threw her magic into the effort, screaming as she put a foot on his stomach and yanked with all her might. But the stone wouldn't budge, not an inch. With a shriek of rage, her fingers slipped from the stone and she fell to the deck.

Speevor slowly turned to her, his black eyes locking on hers. "Now, Mother," he said with Victeris's voice. "Let's not squabble at a time like this. Be a good girl, and sit quietly until the battle is over. You'll get what you want in time, I promise you."

Issefyn hissed through her teeth and stalked away.

I will find you, shade, she promised herself. *I will find you. I will steal your power and I will return these petty torments upon you a thousand times. You will crawl for me. I swear you will crawl.*

Shara crouched at Brophy's side as he flipped the tiller and tacked. The boom swung around, and they both ducked. It settled on the other side, and the sails filled, grabbing the wind and pushing the sleek little vessel forward. They leapt across the water, skirting the sinking hulk of a smoking Silver Islander ship. Their ship lurched as they bounced off a pile of floating debris, chunks of wood tangled with rope and waterlogged sails. Bare-chested Islanders leapt from ship to ship, attacking Summermen in their brightly colored linens. Swirling smoke hung in a haze over the water. The mighty ships looked like wounded fish bound to one another as the two sides fought viciously for every inch of deck.

"We need to get through all this!" Brophy shouted over the shouts of sailors and the groans of cracking wood. "Is Arefaine's flagship still on the far side?"

Shara closed her eyes, sending her awareness forward. She touched people briefly, seeking that bright fire that would be Arefaine. She found her almost immediately, still atop the crow's nest on a huge, black Ohohhim ship near the northern edge of the convoluted battle.

"She's there." Shara pointed. "All the way in the back. Once we get close enough, I'll hang back and you go talk to her alone."

"I still don't like that idea," he shouted back at her.

"Neither do I, but it has the best chance of working. Don't worry about me. Just stay with Arefaine as long as necessary. If we get separated somehow, I'll meet you on Efften."

Brophy turned to her to protest, but she snapped her fingers, pointing to a burning ship floundering to their left. He flipped the tiller, swerving so close to the flames that Shara could feel the heat on her face. All around them the Islanders' battle cries mixed with the screams of the dying and what sounded like thunder cracks. Brophy ignored it all, stared into the swirling mists as he maneuvered the little boat through the chaos.

"There is a gap to port," Brophy said, skillfully skimming between two ships. "We can make for—"

"Brophy, look out!" Shara screamed.

A ball of fire flew toward them through the swirling smoke as they cleared the shadow of the Ohohhim ship. Brophy wheeled around, grabbing her shirt as he leapt backward. Yanked off her feet, she followed him into the water as flames exploded all around.

Prince Vinghelt stood at the prow of his ship watching the glorious hand of his goddess at work. Fessa had recently left to attend to the battle. He desperately missed her soul-stirring presence at his side, but the victory she had promised was nearly at hand.

The Islanders' initial charge had been momentarily terrifying. But destroying ships had gained them nothing. Vinghelt's men tumbled into the ocean by the thousands, but they had been chosen by the goddess and could not die. As soon as the enemy's charge had been broken, his Fessa-blessed countrymen swarmed their ships and attacked, immune to any blade or bow.

The nearest Islander ship was foundering less than a bowshot away. Her sails had caught fire and her crew was scrambling to cut them loose and slip emergency oars into place. They were helpless, a cup of glory he could not leave untasted.

Vinghelt reached out with the wondrous power Fessa had rewarded him with and touched the mind of his helmsmen. *Take us closer,* he thought. He'd barely mouthed the words, but his entire crew sprang to life, adjusting the sails to catch the wind and turn toward the enemy's burning ship.

Get ready to board, he thought to his men, his holy warriors. Forty sailors, each with the black streaks of piety down their faces, rushed from the rigging to the starboard rail. Grappling hooks were raised and made ready to throw.

One of the Islanders, a woman holding a bloody cloth to a burn on the side of her tattooed face, spotted them approaching and shouted a warning. Three archers rushed to the rail and nocked their arrows.

He smiled at the fools as he stepped behind the nearest crewmember for cover. Their weapons were useless against the wrath of the goddess and the Summer Wind that blew before her.

They let loose their arrows, their tips sparkling in the sun. Explosions rocked the ship. Vinghelt was thrown backward. There was a dull crack and pain lanced through his back where he'd struck the opposite railing.

He instantly curled into a ball, trying to fight through the pain and the ringing in his ears. What had happened? Surely there had been a mistake. He rolled to his knees, looking for cover. More explosions rocked the ship. Black light and rainbow colors filled the air and then disappeared in tiny sparkles. With a yelp, he crawled behind the foremast and closed his eyes.

A third series of explosions rocked the ship and Vinghelt hid his head in his hands. *How could she have abandoned him?*

The goddess had told him to keep his vessel on the perimeter. Vinghelt's magic blood was too valuable to risk in battle. The goddess needed her champion. She'd promised he would be safe. He was destined to rebuild the City of Sorcerers and rule that blessed city with his kin.

"Fessa!" he cried. "What's happening?"

He tried to reach out with his magic, tried to shout at the mindless idiots all around him to change course and sail away. But there was nobody there, no empty minds for him to reach.

Barely able to breathe, he opened his eyes. His hands came away from his face, covered with black blood. He desperately wiped them on his shirt, but the blackness wouldn't come off, it looked like it was seeping into his skin. He furiously rubbed his palms on his thighs, but it didn't help, the blood wouldn't come off. Panting like one of Fessa's blessed soldiers, Vinghelt peered around the mast to see what had happened.

The rail where his men had been standing was shattered. The wood hung in splintered fragments over the edge of the ship. His entire crew had been slaughtered. They lay scattered in bloody black chunks across the ichor-slicked deck. The few who survived were crawling across the deck on severed limbs, dragging their blackened entrails behind them.

Vinghelt turned away, retching, but nothing came up. His heart was beating so fast, he was sure he was going to die. More explosions flashed all around him, like a chorus of thunderclaps across the entire fleet.

Vinghelt curled up and hid his head in his hands. *How could she have abandoned them?*

Turbulent waters closed over Shara's head. Something struck her shoulder and spun her around. She fought to gain her bearings, looking for Brophy.

Above her, the black hulls of ships contrasted with the orange glow of fire and sudden flashes of swirling colors. She swam upward and broke the surface, sucking in a lungful of smoky air and coughing it back out. A ship slid past her, rolling her about, and she kicked away from it, trying to escape its wake.

"Shara!" Brophy's voice seemed to swirl around her. A hand emerged from the smoke, and his body followed as if he were flying. He clung to a tattered rope, his feet braced alongside the ship's hull. She reached out, and he caught her wrist, dragging her along behind him.

"On my back," he said, pulling her up to his shoulders. She wrapped her arms around his neck, coughing up smoke and seawater as he climbed up the rope hand over hand. The flames of their destroyed ship were hot on her back. She took the pain and used it, giving herself energy as Brophy climbed.

He swung a leg over the rail and levered them both onto the deck. She landed next to him, finally regaining her breath and calling on the Floani form. A dozen little battles raged before them on the ship. Bare-chested Silver Islanders with swords and axes were fighting Summermen weeping ones wearing brightly colored blouses and thin dueling swords.

One of the corrupted duelists spotted them and charged. His eyes were black as night and his thin blond beard was stained black along the sides of his mouth. Brophy leapt toward him, ducking the blade and bringing his head up, crunching into the man's chin. The Summerman's blade sliced thin air behind Brophy, who followed with a right cross that would have felled a horse. The man spun a half cartwheel and slammed into the deck, but his black eyes never closed, and a moment after he struck the deck, he was starting to get up again.

"Run!" Brophy said, drawing his sword.

She grabbed his hand, and he led her through the melee. Another weeping one jumped at them, stabbing. Brophy parried the blade, riposted, and stabbed the man in the chest. The corrupted sailor staggered back as though Brophy had thrust a blunt stick at him and charged again. Brophy caught his wrist, spun around, and threw him overboard.

Three nearby weeping ones gang-tackled the only remaining Islander on board. The burly man's battle roar was abruptly cut off as one of them snapped his neck. They all turned their black eyes on Brophy and Shara.

"Can you keep up with me?" he asked, breathing hard.

"I will go wherever you do," she promised.

He grinned at her, as if some part of him had been freed amid this death and chaos and finally felt at ease. With a nod, he ran across the deck and leapt to the rail. He cleared the distance between their ship and the next, skidding to a stop.

Shara charged her legs with energy and leapt after him. He took her arm as she landed, steadying her as she stepped quickly to absorb the shock.

Two more weeping ones charged them. Brophy rushed at one and Shara at the other. With a snarl, Brophy blocked the man's strike and smashed his sword against the thing's face. The weeping one fell to his knees and immediately started to rise.

"No!" Shara shouted, spinning inside the swing of the next attacker. The power behind her voice stunned him for a moment. He dropped his sword and, careening off balance, hit the rail. She kicked him high in the back. He tumbled overboard without a sound.

A dozen weeping ones at the fore of the ship turned, looking in their direction. One of them exploded in a shower of multicolored sparkles, blowing the tight cluster apart and scattering them across the deck.

Shara jerked her head up, peering into the rigging. A Silver Islander was balanced precariously on a yardarm, taking aim with his bow. He let the arrow fly and another weeping one exploded. She staggered away, shielding her eyes.

"There!" Brophy shouted.

She spun around, thinking he had shouted at her. But he was already running away across the deck. She looked beyond him and saw the Ohohhim flagship. It was less than a hundred feet away, with nothing but open water between them.

"Brophy!" she shouted, but he didn't hear her. Leaping to the rail, he sheathed his sword and dove into the debris-strewn water. She started after him—

A blinding pain struck her in the back of the thigh, and she cried out, stumbling to the deck.

Flipping around, Shara gasped as she pulled the arrow out of her leg. It had gone into her flesh only half an inch, and it was tipped with a blunt crystal, swirling with colors like a bottle of Siren's Blood.

Looking up, she spotted the archer up in the rigging as he nocked another arrow and aimed at her.

Issefyn stared out at the battle and seethed at the shade's stupidity. The indentured should have swung the battle to their favor by now. She could feel the shade's influence all around her, directing their actions. But the ani slaves on her ship were completely dormant, the shade was either unwilling or unable to commit them to battle. She glared at Speevor, standing like a stone, clutching all her power in his wretched grasp.

Efflum had been a fool not to trust her. If the battle was going badly, she could aid in the effort. She meant to kill him later, but she certainly wouldn't do anything foolish until their victory was complete.

With a growl of frustration, she turned back to the battle. A sudden gust of wind cleared her view and she spotted a familiar figure through the swirling smoke and haze. A broad smile spread across her face. Shara was lying wounded on the deck of the Summer ship in front of her. She hissed in frustration as yet another prize lay just beyond her reach.

Take cover, my child, a sudden voice spoke into her head. She spun around and saw the gleaming prow of an Islander ship charging them from the opposite side. Its deck was lined with archers, carefully taking aim.

Issefyn ran toward Speevor. An arrow glanced off the railing right next to him, but he stood there oblivious to everything around him.

"Get down, you idiot!" she screamed, but he didn't even flinch.

A second arrow struck him in the shoulder and his entire body disappeared in a flash of swirling lights.

Issefyn threw herself to the ground as more explosions rocked the ship. Something struck her in the back and the bloody stump of a severed arm pinwheeled across the deck next to her.

She was on her feet in an instant looking for her stone. She rushed around looking for it until a sudden fear gripped her heart. She stopped and looked up in time to see the steel prow of the Islander ship slice through the railing, parting the wood like water.

The ship rocked, and she fell, tumbling across the deck. Twisting around, she saw the towering silver ram of a warship halfway through the port side.

More arrows rained down on her crew, and they exploded. Silver Islanders leapt from their ship and charged onto the deck. One ran in her direction, swinging a sword overhead. The pommel swirled with rainbow colors, and Issefyn saw her death in that blade.

Throwing herself to the side, she barely evaded the swing. The sword bounced off the deck right next to her, and she scrambled away on all fours. But the brute's left hand held a dagger, and he brought it down on her.

Sharp steel plunged into her back, and she screamed, falling forward onto her belly. Everything seemed to slow down as he drew it out to stab again, but one of the ani slaves tackled him, knocking him to the side.

The noise of the battle faded until all she could hear was the beating of her own heart. She reached behind her to feel the gaping wound next to her spine. A voice seemed to call out to her and she looked up to see the containment stone resting against the aft splash wall.

Her fingers scraped on the wood as she tried to pull herself forward. More explosions rocked the deck, but she could barely hear them. An Islander rushed over to the containment stone. He knelt next to it, reached out, but didn't touch it.

"It's mine!" She screamed the words, suddenly wet in her throat. She leapt to her feet and charged across the deck. The Islander shielded the stone with his body and brought his sword up, but Issefyn dove right at his blade, knocking it aside, and fell on the stone.

Her fingers touched the warm black facets. Power flooded her, and this time it didn't stop. It came and came. She felt the Silver Islander's sword slash into her body, felt the explosion, but it was nothing compared with the ecstasy of the black emmeria.

Gathering the stone to her chest, she rose to her feet, her fingers elongated, curling around the crystal. Her back arched as her spine cracked, twisting as it stretched. Her flesh boiled, ripping itself apart as it grew and knitted itself back together.

An Islander plunged his blade into her side. She swatted him across the deck, feeling his ribs snap against the back of her hand. She screamed from the pure joy of it, the orgasmic rush of power.

Another Islander charged and swung at her, and a distant pain fired into her leg. She looked down at him. He seemed so much smaller than he should be. Reaching out one long-fingered hand, she grabbed his head.

It popped like a grape, and the man collapsed.

Issefyn threw back her head and howled at the smoky sky.

Shara dove to the side as the second arrow flew toward her. It skipped off the deck by her back, and she rolled to her knees. She reached out with her ani toward the man, but couldn't find him. Like Reef, he was invisible to her magic.

He reached into his quiver and withdrew another arrow. Shara was about to charge him when she saw a monstrous arm slam over the rail on the far side of the ship. The dripping black thing was as tall as a tree. Multijointed fingers tipped with claws as large as scythes thudded into the deck, digging deep. The rail snapped under the weight as the creature hauled itself up.

"By the Seasons . . ." Shara whispered, feeling all the strength drain from her body.

Long, slimy hair hung down like tentacles on either side of the tall, thin features. The creature's eyes were long, as if they had melted, dripping down its face. Its mouth was the same. One giant tooth jutted upward and one jutted downward in a mouth that could not close. Its drooping lower lip touched the deck. Wood snapped as it lurched aboard.

The archer turned, yelling as the thing stood up. It was half as tall as the mast, and the ship groaned under its weight, the deck tilting toward it.

The archer barely clung to his perch as he loaded and shot another arrow. It hit the creature and exploded, blowing a chunk of its arm away. The creature howled, reeling, but it did not die. Black ichor ran from its wound, wiggling and transforming into worms. The worms interlaced across the ragged hole, forming a net. The net melted into smooth skin.

Shara gaped.

The creature reached up into the rigging and grabbed the archer. It flung him away like a doll. The man screamed until he smashed into the hull of the next ship over, then fell limp into the water.

Then it turned and looked at Shara.

"Issefyn?" she gasped.

Arefaine stood high in the crow's nest, watching the carnage all around her. Below, on deck, Carriers of the Opal Fire stood mute, awaiting the destruction that slowly came their way.

So far, all her Ohohhim troops had been held back in reserve. Her allies were facing the full brunt of the attack. She watched the colorfully dressed Summermen fight in the distance, saw the Silver Islanders use some kind of fire arrows on them. Great, colorful explosions of raw ani sparkled across every deck.

It made no sense for the Islanders to use weapons imbued with ani. It went against every barbaric thing they stood for. She cautiously reached out with her magic. Of course she couldn't find any of the Islanders, but she noticed something odd about the first Summerman her mind touched. It was disturbing. His life light was very low, like he was somehow less than a person. A songbird had more fire in its center than the strange westerner, and yet he fought with the same utter fearlessness as the Silver Islanders. She tried to find out what was wrong with them, but he suddenly disappeared and she cried out, flinching away from a light that burned her mind's eye.

"Father," she whispered, wishing he could explain what was happening, but she hadn't seen him since the fighting started. She still longed to be in the middle of the battle, dealing out death to the merciless barbarians who had killed her family, but her father had beseeched her to stay here. He'd assured her that his spirit could not die, and his powers would be enough to defeat the enemy.

She let out an impatient breath. The longer she stayed here, the fewer reasons she found for sitting this out. The Silver Islanders fought like maniacs with their strange and deadly weapons. They had done much more damage than Arefaine would have thought possible, and still they came. The savages had given everything to this mad rush, caring nothing for their own lives. Their rage was almost spent, and they would never be able to regroup. The tide was about to turn.

Her hands gripped the edge of the crow's nest, searching through the swirling smoke and colorful explosions. She noticed a single Islander ship skirting around the battle to the east. It had nearly flanked the entire fleet and was turning toward her. A pair of Ohohhim ships were maneuvering to intercept, but the wind was against them and it didn't look like they would make it in time.

Arefaine watched the enemy ship, and a smile spread across her face. *No more waiting.*

She sent her magic out to grab hold of the man at the helm, but found nothing. Just like that damned Silver Islander in Ohndarien, he was invisible to her magical sight. Less than a wisp of air, less than a ghost.

Stories from the past flooded her. This was how they'd destroyed her home. Screaming savages, killing the innocent. Flames all around. Destruction. Houses pulled down with mothers and children inside. Blood on the cobblestones.

Her Carriers shouted something to her, but Arefaine couldn't hear them. Her ears rang, obscuring the shouting, the crashing, the crackling flames. If she could not attack the men, she could still sink that ship. Her emmeria could tear apart the wooden planking just as she had destroyed the bridge back in Ohohhim.

Arefaine pointed and let loose all of her hate. A thin flood of black emmeria shot across the distance, but it dissipated along the way. It rippled, warped, losing most of its potency before touching the prow of the warship. Arefaine needed more power. Slipping a hand inside the satchel around her neck, she touched one of the containment stones. A gush of rage and howling voices flowed through her. She allowed it to spiral through her body, collecting in her chest before she thrust it at the tip of the warship.

In her magical sight, the black emmeria spun through the air like a blind serpent.

Her father suddenly appeared next to her, shouting.

"Arefaine! No! Draw it back!"

"What?"

She reached out frantically, trying to pull the magic back to her, but the emmeria had a mind of its own. It hungered for those living souls on that ship. As soon as it touched the silver ram, it soaked in. Steel bubbled and wood splintered as the ship crumpled in upon itself. The ooze raced along the sides. Silver Islanders ran like madmen, diving overboard.

"No, my child, no," her father whispered.

Her magic reached the center of the boat, and suddenly exploded. A blinding flash of multicolored light outshone the sun.

Arefaine ducked, hiding her face in her hands. Her knees had barely hit the base of the crow's nest when the shock wave struck the ship. She heard a sudden crack followed by a deafening boom. The mast snapped and started falling. She was thrown against the rail and tumbled over the edge. She barely had time to suck in a breath and scream in denial before she hit the deck.

Chapter 23

The explosion engulfed the entire horizon, and the Silver Islander ship disappeared in the conflagration. Blinding light of all colors burned into Brophy's eyes, and he shielded them with his arm. "Arefaine!" he screamed.

A massive wave spread outward from the blast, engulfing all the ships and bearing them forward like foam in the surf. Brophy dove. He churned hard with his arms, diving deeper, deeper. Something hard and sharp raked across his back, spun him around.

And then the wave caught him, spinning him around and around in its powerful embrace. He rode it, turning, holding the scant breath of air he'd taken before diving. Then the wave was passed, and its wake pushed him forcefully the other way.

Brophy lashed out, his shoulders burning as he forced his cupped hands to move through the angry water. He broke the surface and gasped. Seawater showered down from above as if the entire heavens had opened up with a ferocious storm. He could barely see ten feet in any direction.

But the cascade of seawater from the explosion soon became a light rainfall, then a misty drizzle. Through the haze, Brophy gaped at the devastation. Half the ships in the battle had been destroyed. Some had broken into pieces; others were tossed on their sides and slowly sinking.

Casting about, he finally spotted Arefaine's ship. It was foundering from the explosion, tipped on its side and caught up in a massive jumble of ships thrust together like driftwood washed up on a shore.

A few Islander ships had been swept back by the blast, but they were regaining their bearings and heading toward Arefaine.

Looking behind him, Brophy searched quickly for Shara, but he couldn't find her in the chaos. Torn, he looked back at Arefaine's wounded ship, set upon by all the forces the Silver Islanders could muster. They would get to her, and then they would make the biggest mistake in the history of the world.

Shara's alive, he thought to himself. *She's a Zelani and she can take care of herself.*

He told himself that. Tried to force himself to believe it. He gave a quick glance to Arefaine's crippled ship, then snapped back and dove into the water, swimming toward the last place he'd seen Shara.

Ossamyr knelt on the deck, coughing up seawater and fighting the ringing in her ears. She'd known what would happen when she saw Arefaine throw the surge of tainted ani toward the ship packed with shards of light emmeria. She'd seen what a few crystals could do and that ship had been holding thousands.

She'd braced herself, grabbing the rail, but she couldn't believe what actually happened. The explosion had rocked the entire ocean, throwing up a twenty-foot wall of water. All three fleets were scattered or destroyed.

Reef and his crew had been prepared; they turned into the wave, hitting it at full speed. The wave swept over the deck, engulfing the entire ship. She would have been swept away if Reef hadn't grabbed her arm at the last moment. Her wrist still ached where he had clung to her as her body flapped helpless in the surge like a leaf in the wind.

Their ship cut through the wave intact, but several men were swept overboard. A tangle of ropes and rigging wrapped around the foremast, making her list to one side.

"Are you injured?" Reef shouted at her. His voice sounded warped and distant as her ears still rang from the sound of the explosion. "Are you hurt?" he shouted again.

"No more . . ." she gasped. "Than I was . . . ten minutes ago."

She looked up in his face; his golden eyes shown like a madman's.

"Is she dead?" Ossamyr asked.

"Her ship is intact; we have to finish the job."

"Then go! Go! I'm fine."

Reef nodded and rushed to his remaining men. "Cut it!" he shouted, running across the deck that was canted steeply to the side. He snatched an axe from the side of the cabin even as two other sailors ran toward the tangle. One of them lost his footing and slid along the slanted deck until he hit the rail with a cry of pain.

Reef and his crew went to work on the tangled ropes with axe, knife, and sword, chopping frantically as water sloshed over them. The ship groaned, and Ossamyr heard cracking noises as the lines snapped free, catching one of the sailors and dragging him overboard, screaming. Reef and the other sailors threw themselves backward as the ship righted itself, rocking back and forth so violently that Ossamyr almost lost her grip on the rail.

Staggering to his feet, Reef lumbered back to Ossamyr, shouting as he went.

"She's there!" he roared, pointing. "That ship there!" Ossamyr had never seen the man so intense. He was as tight as a bowstring, a permanent snarl on his lips as he gazed unblinkingly at Arefaine's ship.

Seawater burned the back of Shara's throat as she climbed up the wet rope. She reached the top and peered over the splash wall. The deck was empty, so she hooked a heel over the edge and hauled herself over, flopping in a heap as she tried to gather her wits.

The ani explosion had been one of the most terrifying things she had ever seen. Her body was still shaking from the flood of raw power. She didn't know what the Silver Islanders had done, but it had nearly killed them all.

She was concentrating on taking long breaths, trying to slow her heart, when a spine-chilling roar made her limbs freeze.

Spinning around, she peered over the rail. The monstrously corrupted Issefyn she'd seen just before the explosion was crawling out of the water onto the Islander ship next to hers.

"By the Seasons, what have you done?" Shara whispered.

The Islanders charged Issefyn before she could climb aboard. She screamed at them, and Shara flinched, covering her ears. Black ichor flew from Issefyn's gaping mouth, flecking the Silver Islanders. Some screamed as they exploded. Those who didn't explode twitched and shouted as if they'd caught fire.

And then they transformed.

Limbs contorted. Skin blackened. Howling, they turned on their uncorrupted comrades. A few of the Silver Islanders jumped into the ocean. The rest fought bravely, pitting their ani weapons against vicious claws and teeth. Small explosions rocked the ship as the corrupted were struck with rainbow crystals.

Issefyn shrieked in horrific triumph, turning her face to the sky.

Shara summoned her magic.

Issefyn spun around. Her glowing red eyes locked on Shara's. *You!* A thunderous voice roared through her head, forcing its way into her mind.

Shara focused her ani into a tremendous Lowani shriek and directed it at her friend's mind. If she could find the woman trapped within the monster—

Issefyn howled and swatted her efforts aside. *Not this time, pig butcher's daughter.*

Shara stumbled back under the onslaught, fighting for her life.

Issefyn howled again, swiping her claw and knocking sailors and corrupted into the ocean like toys. She leapt onto Shara's ship. Her black claws sank into the deck. Shara stumbled up the steps toward the prow, fighting the ferocious pressure on her mind.

I've always been more powerful than you, Issefyn's voice rushed through Shara like a thousand tortured souls.

Shara backpedaled, fear creeping over her heart like frost. How could she defeat this creature? A torrent of black emmeria bubbled through Issefyn's body, fulfilling her every desire.

Shara vaulted onto the forecastle and grabbed the mast. Wood cracked under her feet and the ship shook.

Shara flicked a glance backward toward the bow. Issefyn rushed forward, swinging at her. Leaping back, Shara sprinted for the bowsprit—

Issefyn's long hand snaked out, tripping Shara, and she skidded face-first into the railing.

Shara flipped about, scrabbling backward, but Issefyn grabbed her calf, lifted her like a slab of beef, and threw her across the ship.

Shara screamed as she slammed into the maindeck. Her head smacked against the wood and her vision swam.

Issefyn leapt from the forecastle, landing on all fours above her. Shara tried to twist away, but Issefyn pinned her to the deck, knocking the wind from Shara's lungs. She tried to rally, tried to form her thoughts into a spell that would protect her. She tried one last desperate ploy. She used Jesheks's magic, Necani, sending as much unbearable, searing pain into Issefyn as she could, driving one terrible spike into the corrupted woman's mind.

Issefyn's sepulchral voice laughed in her head as she absorbed the flood of tortured ani, reveling in it. Her distorted features seemed to smile as she loomed over Shara, blurry in her swimming vision.

It's time you learned what true power is, Issefyn hissed in Shara's mind. She raised her darkened hand over Shara's head. Her taloned fingers curled into a fist.

A sudden blinding red light flared behind the monster. Issefyn's hulking form cut a stark silhouette against the angry crimson. A long blade sliced through the center of her chest.

Black blood sprayed across Shara, gouting onto the deck. Issefyn screamed, sharp and wailing, ending in a wet gurgle. The top half of her body toppled away, crushing the rail to Shara's right and falling overboard.

A lean man swathed in dingy white cloth stood where Issefyn had been, a powerful ani blade in his hand. The monster's legs frantically kicked the deck like those of a child having a tantrum. The man kicked them through the hole in the rail into the ocean.

Shara squinted at the figure. Intense red eyes stared at her from beneath his hood. "Jesheks!"

He knelt next to her, put a hand on her forehead.

"Sleep," he said. His powerful ani flowed into her, crushing her hasty defenses.

Shara slept.

War raged around Jesheks, but he stood in the eye of the storm. The boat upon which he'd found Shara was empty now, and hemmed in by distant sounds of clashing swords, shouting men and women.

He knelt next to Shara where she lay sleeping on the deck.

The fear suffused him again. It had dogged him from the burning of the Floating Palace all the way across the Physendrian deserts to Ohndarien. It followed him across the Great Ocean to this naval battle at the end of the world. The fear had brought him to her.

His heart hammered, reverberating throughout his entire body, but he kept himself still.

The scent of her filled him, her sweat, her fear, the feminine scent that haunted his dreams. He had never cared about such things before. The details of the flesh had always seemed like vile by-products of mortality. But now every nuance and sensation was a treasure.

Her brief, clinging tunic was worn, tattered. He could see her soft flesh beneath, the curve of her breast rising and falling as she slept.

He gently stroked her forehead.

Oh Shara, he thought. *How we will dance together, minds, bodies, and ani spiraling into the unknown.*

Her eyes fluttered as she tried to surface, tried to escape the magic in which he'd enclosed her. He channeled more strength into his spell, and she slumped.

She was magnificent. Even asleep, she battled. But he was fresh, and she was not. She could not hope to win.

Gathering her into his strong arms, he stood. His body reacted when they touched, and he wanted more than anything to push her down again and spread her legs right here. Right now.

With a gasping breath, he threw his head back and cycled the feeling through his body. Such crazy, wild power. He must learn to master it, and then he would unleash it upon her, as she would unleash herself upon him.

He looked down at Shara draped across his muscled arms, her black hair cascading past his ragged wrappings. For the first time he felt right touching her. He had made himself worthy of her beauty as his grace and strength had grown to match her own.

The journey from Ohndarien to Efften had been long and trying, but his transformation was now complete. Jesheks had conquered the secrets of aging long ago. It had been six decades since he'd slain his first master, and Jesheks had never looked his seventy-four years. Time had not touched him, but he had never reveled in his youth. He'd always hated the body he'd been born into and treated it like an enemy, abusing and neglecting it.

But that night with Shara had changed what he saw when he looked in the mirror. He'd found a new vision of himself, a vision worth pursuing, and his mind bent to a new task. Using his magic over the last few weeks, he had sculpted his body into a new form, shrinking his great girth, converting his fat into muscle. He sought the physical exertions he had always avoided before. He must have climbed to the crow's nest a hundred times a day, paced the perimeter of his ship endlessly during his travels, channeling his ani to accelerate the transformation.

And now he had become the vision Shara had seen in their shared dream. He was the man she desired, in every detail. His long white hair fell across his broad shoulders to his slender waist. His pale skin was stretched tight across his muscled chest and flat stomach. He could be everything she wanted now, a man equal to her in mind, body, and blood.

Shara lay warm and soft against his belly, so light to him now. Her legs dangled limp over one arm, her head over the other. Her long black hair almost touched the ground. He leaned forward and brushed his cheek against hers. That simple touch sent a storm of longing through his chest, and his penis, re-created with his strongest magic and an iron will, pressed against the front of his pants, growing rigid in response to her nearness. He drew a quiet breath, cycling the new sensation through his new body.

And that also, he thought. *We will dance that dance, as well.*

He looked up when he heard a splash and the thump of boots against the hull.

He threw a casual glamour around Shara and himself. He didn't want anything to ruin this perfect moment.

Brophy surged over the edge of the rail, spraying seawater.

Ah yes, Jesheks thought. The young gallant, searching for his love. Gathering Shara closer to his chest, he intensified the glamour.

"Shara!" Brophy shouted, looking about the deck.

Jesheks held himself perfectly still. Brophy was not a mage, but he was the Brother of Autumn. Jesheks wasn't sure what abilities the young man possessed, and he couldn't leave anything to chance. Jesheks could smell his fear, his urgency.

He watched as Brophy cast around, looking for his beloved. Frustration and fury twisted his face. He ran to the broken rail where Issefyn had toppled, looking to see if Shara had fallen after, then ran along the side, searching. The young Ohndarien moved within a foot of Jesheks and never saw him.

"Shara!" Brophy called in desperation. Clenching his fists, he cast another futile glance across the water to the next nearest ship. He glanced back the way he had come, toward the Ohohhim flagship, which had become the center of the battle. A fellow Ohohhim ship had gone to her aid, but two Silver Islander ships had converged upon it. The battle would soon be joined.

Which young woman will it be, daring boy? Jesheks thought silently. *It is time for you to make your choice.*

Every strand of muscle stood out on Brophy's tense arms, and he hovered there for a long moment. With a frustrated growl, he turned and dove into the water, began swimming toward Arefaine's flagship.

Happy hunting, Jesheks thought. *I wish you well on your hopeless task. You have a young magician to catch.*

And I, well . . .

He inhaled Shara's fragrance, bringing his lips down to her brow.

I have a ship to catch.

Ossamyr concentrated on her breathing as Reef prepared his crew for the attack. She gathered what power she could, half lost in a delirious haze. She'd thought she would die in the explosion, but now she had hope, just a glimmer of hope. But as quick as the hope came, the searing fire in her abdomen stole it from her.

The helmsman guided the vessel right up to Arefaine's ship. The Ohohhim flagship was caught up in a tangle of other vessels and foundering from damage in her starboard side. She was slowly sinking, aft end first, as her tattered sails flapped wildly in the steady wind. Silver Islanders and Ohohhim soldiers fought all along the sinking wrecks. The legendary Carriers of the Opal Fire surrounded their fallen empress, their blades blurring as they kept Reef's countrymen at bay. There were dozens of Carriers left, and they fought as one with perfect form and discipline.

She carefully reached out with her magic and found that Arefaine was unconscious, but still alive.

Reef's ship maneuvered with aching slowness. Ossamyr watched three men die by the blade while they edged ever closer. When the gap between the ships was still dangerously wide, Reef leapt to his ship's rail and launched himself across the distance. He barely made it, grabbing the other ship's rigging as he slammed against the hull. Swinging out, he kicked against the side and flipped over the rail.

He ran at the closest Carrier, slashing. The Carrier deflected the first strike. Reef feinted, drew the man out, then chopped his arm off and followed with a strike that took his head. He spun past the next Carrier's strike, and it missed him by an inch. Reef continued his spin and struck the Carrier in the temple with his elbow. The man's knees buckled and Reef headed for the next Ohohhim.

Ossamyr's eyes swept the ship, trying to gauge the enemy's numbers and their chance of success. Her gaze was drawn to the back of the boat as someone clambered over the almost submerged rail. Seawater dripped from his arms and his face, from his curly blond hair.

"Brophy!" she shouted.

He didn't hear her, or he ignored her. Like a demon, he sprinted up the deck to the cluster of Ohohhim who protected their empress.

Reef noticed Brophy's arrival, too. He flicked a glance at the boy, perhaps hearing Ossamyr's shout, perhaps chilled with the same feeling she'd had, like the rush of wind before a storm. But Brophy was still a deck length away, and Reef had a job to do.

Another Carrier ducked to avoid Reef's sword, leaving a gap in their protective circle. Reef rushed through the opening, charging toward Arefaine.
There was nothing standing between the two of them now.

Ossamyr held her breath as she saw Brophy move with inhuman speed
across the deck. Reef raised his sword to land the killing blow on Arefaine's
unconscious body. As he swung, Brophy threw his sword. Reef dodged to the
side, sending his strike wide. His blade sank into the deck above Arefaine's
limp shoulder and nicked her cheek. Brophy barreled into him, carrying him
away. The two warriors crashed into the deck beyond Morgeon's granddaughter, grappling for control of Reef's sword.

Reef's ship bumped against the sinking flagship. His remaining crew
charged onto the deck, brandishing their weapons as they rushed forward.
They crashed into the diminishing imperial force.

Ossamyr gritted her teeth as she stepped over the rails, and she hobbled
toward the melee, her gaze locked on Brophy and Reef's death struggle. Reef
was one of the fiercest fighters she had ever seen, and the man was stronger
than an ox. But Brophy had won the Nine Squares, and he had done it before
his imprisonment in an eighteen-year battle.

The Brother of Autumn kicked Reef away from him and snatched up a
discarded sword. He leapt to his feet and kept after Reef like a lion, hacking
at legs, at arms, slashing though every parry Reef could muster. Reef's only
salvation lay in constant retreat and complete defense. Brophy's sword was
everywhere, at his head, at his chest, slip to the side, and hack at the arm.
Reef blocked each stroke while stepping backward.

But he was running out of deck.

"Brophy, stop!" she shouted, whimpering at the pain in her belly.

Please, she thought. *Not this choice.* She'd made this choice once and it had
destroyed her.

Swords clashed. Men screamed and died against the starboard rail as
she hobbled toward the bow. Reef threw a dagger at Brophy's eyes. His
sword whipped up, caught the blade, and sent it spinning, but it gave Reef
a precious second. The Silver Islander stepped cleverly up the steps to the
forecastle, and almost lost his leg as Brophy followed.

"Brophy, please stop," she whispered, but he couldn't hear her.

He pressed Reef hard, forcing him across the deck. When Reef had no more space to retreat, he would die. Sweat streamed down his face, and his thick arms shivered with each monstrous stroke Brophy dealt.

Ossamyr thought of Phandir. She saw Brophy's innocent face, saw his stunned expression as she poured fake blood across Phandir's fake wound. She saw the hope in his eyes disappear like a tiny candle snuffed out forever.

I had no choice, she had said to him. *I'm sorry,* she had said.

Forgive me.

Closing her eyes, she sent all of her magic into Reef.

The ship was sinking, and Brophy wanted to be done with this fight. If he could have turned his back on Reef and let the man go, he would have. But Reef was cunning and quick, and easily the strongest man Brophy had ever fought. And only one thing mattered to him. Left alive, he would give anything to kill Arefaine. His last stroke had almost done the job, and his victory would have doomed them all.

Brophy struck hard, felt the flagging muscles in Reef's mighty arm. The Islander jumped back, barely avoiding Brophy's follow-up. Reef was a powerful man, but he was only mortal. He would tire. He could not keep up this pace.

"Jump," Brophy said as their swords clashed. "Save your life. I don't want to kill you." He stepped forward, pushing the huge man back and almost slicing Reef's sword arm, but Reef stepped sideways, changing angles and sword hands. Brophy stepped back at the sudden swing, and Reef bought himself an extra foot of deck, an extra moment of life. He breathed through flared nostrils like a lathered horse, but he didn't say anything.

Suddenly Brophy's neck hairs prickled. Magic flowed past him, all around him. He tensed, drawing back, giving Reef a precious second to regroup. But the magic was not aimed at Brophy. He flicked a glance toward the back of the ship, seeking the magician.

Ossamyr stood to port of the ferocious melee, her head bowed, her body bent. One arm extended toward them, fist clenched and shaking.

One second was all Brophy could spare. He knew what was happening. He'd seen Shara do it before.

Brophy's sword whipped up as Reef's came crashing down. Reef seemed to swell. His clenched teeth glowed, and the power behind the blow was monstrous. It drove Brophy back a step. He snarled, came back at Reef with a quick slice, but the Islander's block was there. His arms no longer trembled. His golden eyes glowed with an inner light.

With a grim smile, Reef pressed Brophy back a step, using his superior weight to push them. Brophy bent, came back, slashed at Reef's head. The Islander ducked and nearly chopped off Brophy's leg.

Brophy danced away, and Reef took the opportunity. He took two quick strides to the edge of the forecastle and leapt over the edge toward Arefaine, sword extended.

Brophy rammed into Reef in midair, knocking him off course. They landed on top of a wounded Carrier who was holding his gaping wounds with both hands. The man screamed as he was driven to his knees. Brophy and Reef rolled into the other combatants. Brophy came to his feet, and a Silver Islander lunged at him. Brophy sliced into the sailor's chest. Reef came to his feet, shoving the wounded Carrier out of his way.

The huge man's eyes narrowed as he saw something in the distance. Brophy quickly danced back, buying himself a moment to glance over his shoulder. A crowd of Ohohhim soldiers was swimming toward the ship. She'd sunk so far that her aft gunnels were already underwater. The Carriers would be able to swim right onto the deck and join the fight.

Reef charged the remaining Carriers, and Brophy blocked him once more—

—but the move was a feint. Reef spun right, drawing Brophy off balance, and came around with a lightning-quick swing. Brophy's block was hasty, and the monstrous power in Reef's magically enhanced arms shattered his blade.

He ducked, and Reef's blade whistled over his head. Brophy came up inside his guard and slammed a fist into Reef's jaw. The Islander reeled backward. Brophy dropped to a crouch, stealing a dead man's sword.

He brought it up between them as Reef looked at him with grim determination, his bloody fist clenching his weapon.

The swimming Carriers reached the ship and scrambled up the slanting deck, weapons in hand.

"Get Arefaine out of here!" Brophy roared to the approaching Ohohhim. "Get her to another ship."

Arefaine's men charged into the fray. The Islanders were now outnumbered and quickly began losing ground. One of the Carriers picked Arefaine up as his countrymen gathered around her.

"Come." Brophy beckoned to Reef with his free hand. "Let's finish this."

Ossamyr hid behind a mast as a group of Ohohhim warriors killed the last of Reef's crew and carried Arefaine onto Reef's vessel. They had to be stopped before they could escape. Perhaps she could use a glamour to slip into their group. She still had her poisoned dagger strapped to her thigh. It would only take one scratch. The unconscious girl would never be able to save herself. But first things first. She had to get Reef away from Brophy.

The two men still fought like demons. She flooded Reef with her life force and he glowed with power. But Brophy was indefatigable. He bent under Reef's onslaught like a willow tree, giving ground, but then suddenly whipping forward and leaving a slash on Reef's arm or his leg.

She panted, trying to control her breath, to send more energy. But her strength was flagging, and she suddenly realized she had fallen to her knees. How long had she been there?

It didn't matter. Nothing else mattered. She fed Reef, throwing every ounce of her will into the task.

The Ohohhim began chopping at the lines that held Reef's ship to their sinking flagship. Ossamyr felt like she should try to stop them before it was too late. But they were forty feet away. It might as well have been a mile. She didn't know if she could even get to her feet.

Ossamyr struggled upright. Her belly felt like it was slowly ripping in half. She moaned and looked down. Her stitches had come open.

Steel clanged on steel as Reef and Brophy continued their fight. Dazed, Ossamyr realized she had stopped sending magic to Reef. She looked up, trying to send more, but she was spent. Stumbling toward them, she stretched out a hand, trying to stop the inevitable just by reaching.

But Brophy sensed the weakness in his opponent. Reef lunged, making a desperate cut at Brophy's midsection. His sword ripped through Brophy's tunic, but didn't find flesh. Brophy spun and ducked in one motion, bringing all of his strength into one swing.

His blade severed Reef's thick leg, and the giant man toppled. His sword clattered to the deck, and blood gushed onto the wood.

"No!" Ossamyr screamed. She stumbled across the slanting deck.

Reef clutched at the wound with one hand and grabbed his sword with the other. Using the blade as a crutch, he tried to rise again as his blood poured out of him. He managed one lurching hop toward Arefaine before crashing back to the deck.

Ossamyr rushed to his side and collapsed next to him.

Brophy stood over them, bloody sword dripping, but he didn't attack. Ossamir held Reef's head in her arms. "Oh Reef, no . . ."

He looked at her, dazed, gave a brief glance at his leg. His eyelids drooped. "I couldn't beat him," he murmured. "I couldn't do it . . ."

His eyelids slid shut, and his huge body went limp.

Vinghelt stayed huddled in a ball, not daring to move. The Silver Islanders who had come screaming aboard his vessel had run past him, thinking him dead, but they had all been washed overboard in the explosion. The goddess had proved her power once again. He never should have doubted her.

The enemy had abandoned *Fessa's Blade*, but for a long time he could still hear the clash of steel, smaller explosions, and the screams of the dying. The Silver Islander ship that had rammed them had somehow miraculously managed to stay stuck to *Fessa's Blade* during that immense wave that rocked them. To a man, the Islanders had all clambered west, climbing from ship to ship toward some unknown objective.

Vinghelt thought about sneaking across the deck and trying to make off with the Silver Islander vessel, but it was too dangerous. What if there was a contingent waiting belowdecks?

Unsure what to do, Vinghelt continued to play dead, wondering when Fessa would return to him with news of their victory. The long minutes passed and the sound of fighting slowly faded into the distance. Eventually all was quiet except for the creaking of the rigging and the lap of waves against the sides of the ship.

Slowly he opened his eyes and looked around. Seeing nothing, he crawled to the side of the ship and peered over the splash wall.

The ocean looked like a razed city. Everywhere he could see smoldering ships were slowly sinking under the water. Thousands of dead bodies bobbed in the waves alongside broken masts and splintered chunks of wood. The tattooed men's corpses were strewn across the decks of every ship he could see. There were two dead weeping ones for every Islander, but the crazy pirates had been overwhelmed by sheer numbers.

The noble remnants of his Fessa-blessed countrymen gathered in small groups on the decks of the remaining ships. A few of them scoured the wreckage or the water for enemy survivors, but most of them stood stockstill in mute victory.

Vinghelt turned his gaze upon the other side of the battle. A single Islander vessel fled to the north in full retreat, but otherwise the sea was theirs. They had won.

Even the Ohohhim ships had been destroyed, further evidence that Fessa smiled upon her children. Vinghelt's grin widened. *Yes*, he thought. *The fools should never have thought to thwart the goddess.*

Vinghelt stood up and brushed a hand down his sleeve to straighten it, and his hand came away sticky with blood. He frowned, rubbed it on his pants. The price of victory didn't matter. All that mattered was the glory of the goddess. The Great Ocean was his now, all his. His victory was complete, and he was the lord of everything he could see, from here to Ohndarien to the Summer Deserts and all the way back to Vingheld. And when he continued onward to Efften, the secrets of the isle of sorcerers would be his as well. After he had absorbed them, after he became the most powerful man in the world, perhaps then he would travel north to the empire of his fleeing comrades and conquer their lands for Fessa as well.

Fessa's love would soon spread across the entire world, from the Summer Seas to the coasts of Kherif, from the Southwyldes to the Vastness. With a Fessa-blessed army at his back, nothing could stop him from bringing his Eternal Summer to the entire world.

"Well done, my love," a beautiful voice said behind him. Vinghelt whirled, and then let out a breath of relief.

Fessa stood there in all her radiant glory. Her gown flowed down her body like the water of the ocean, and her regal bearing mesmerized him.

"Our victory is complete. It is time to move on. Our faithful servants will gather our forces and repair our ships. Then they will spilt up, traveling to the far corners of the world to seek out those of illuminated blood and bring them home," she said, her voice filling him with a joy he could barely contain. "And you shall return to Ohndarien and solidify our influence there. I promised I would make you king, didn't I?"

Vinghelt smiled, feeling the power of the goddess all around him.

"East, my love," Fessa said, brushing his cheek with her hand. "We go east."

Brophy stared at the screaming woman as she clutched the dead Islander's head to her chest. For a moment, he didn't know where he was. The roaring voices inside his head drowned out all other sound except that heartrending scream.

He looked down the length of his blade and saw it covered with pure red blood, the same blood that pooled below the dead man's severed thigh. It slowly ran down the slanted deck as the ship continued sinking.

The woman frantically hugged the Islander. Her blouse and breeches were stained red from her stomach all the way to her knees. The roaring voices in his mind told him to slash her, to finish her and anyone else who came close. With an effort, he pushed the compulsion away and slowly realized who she was.

It was Ossamyr. Of course it was Ossamyr. Brophy shook his head and looked for Arefaine. There was no one else left alive on the ship. The Ohohhim had freed the Silver Islander vessel and already had the sails up. She was safe, at least for now.

Brophy dropped his sword. It slid down the deck and sank into the water. He fell to his knees and stared at Ossamyr as she grieved.

"Why?" the Physendrian queen sobbed. "Why did you stop him?"

Brophy kept panting, feeling empty and alone now that his battle rage had left him.

"Why did you let her live?" she cried.

"You were making a terrible mistake," he said.

"Do you have any idea what she's going to do on Efften? She's going to set that thing free!"

"I know why she's going, and I know who awaits her. But she won't set him free. She will kill him."

"Is that what you think?" she said quietly. The way she held the Silver Islander bothered Brophy. This was not the queen who would barely bat an eyelash at a servant who had died doing her bidding. He remembered what Shara had said about Ossamyr and her endeavors to free him.

"Are you still so naive, Brophy?" Ossamyr asked. "Arefaine's not going to kill him. She's going to join him."

"That is possible. But we're going to have to trust her."

"Trust her? Like you trusted me?"

Brophy clenched his teeth. His hands itched for a sword, but instead he said, "You're right. I did trust you. I trusted you with my heart and my life. You took my hope on that day, Ossamyr, every last bit of it. Why?"

She bowed over Reef, cradling his head in her lap. "I was afraid, Brophy. Just afraid. When Phandir discovered my plans, I didn't know what to do. All I could see was your death, my death. I didn't see anything beyond."

"You planned everything from the beginning."

"No," she cried. "Never. I felt more with you than I could handle. It terrified me," the queen said, looking up at him like a lost child. "By the Nine, Brophy, I was so in love with you."

Brophy lowered his head and stared at the deck. The rising water lapped against his feet. Flashes of his days in Physendria ran through his mind. Laughing with Ossamyr. Tickling her. Making love to her in a round bed hanging from the ceiling.

"I was weak, Brophy, at the time when I most needed to be strong. I didn't set out to hurt you. I just failed you."

Brophy pressed his hands against his face. "Then I wasn't crazy," he murmured. "You did love me. I wasn't wrong to trust you."

"Of course I loved you," she interrupted. "I love you still. But you should never have trusted me. And you can't trust Arefaine either. You have to kill her," Ossamyr begged. "Kill her, before we're all her slaves."

"You don't know her like I do. I can change her mind."

"Brophy, I've seen where those people's souls go. I've heard their screams. Don't let her do that to anyone else. Don't let her release what is locked in those silver towers."

"She's not the monster you think she is. All she wants is to be loved."

"Sometimes love isn't enough," Ossamyr said weakly.

"I know," he said, looking after the Silver Islander ship that had been commandeered by the Ohohhim. It was almost out of sight. "But sometimes it is."

The waves had covered Brophy legs and were lapping against Ossamyr's knees. He grabbed her to keep her from sliding. She held tight to Reef.

"You're bleeding," Brophy said.

"It doesn't matter anymore," she said softly, not seeming to hear him. "Not for us. Not for me. I can't stop her now." She turned her gaze on Brophy. "You chose your path with Arefaine. Do what you must. If you think she is our salvation, then follow your heart. The Nine know that you were always better at that than I was. But before—" She coughed, doubling over, and wiped her hand across her mouth. It came away smeared with red. "But before you go, you need to know something. There hasn't been a single moment in the last eighteen years when I wouldn't have given my life to take back that day in Physendria and follow my heart instead of my fears. Not a single moment."

A wave washed over them, covering Reef to the waist. He began to slip from her grasp. Brophy reached out and grabbed his tunic.

"No," she said. "Just let him go."

"Did you love him?" Brophy asked.

"I hope so. I really hope so."

He hesitated another moment, and then let the mighty Silver Islander sink beneath the water.

"I'm sorry, Brophy," she murmured. "I'm so sorry. After all these years, that's all I wanted to say."

Another wave washed over them, and Brophy began to swim. He kept Ossamyr's head above water, leaned over, and kissed her on the cheek. The roaring voices seemed very quiet at that moment.

"It's all right. It was a long time ago," he said. "It doesn't matter anymore. It just doesn't matter."

Ossamyr smiled weakly before closing her eyes.

"Let me go, Brophy," Ossamyr whispered. "Go find Shara; she's been waiting for you for a very, very long time."

Brophy looked down at Ossamyr's copper skin as it turned a deathly pale. A single gasp escaped her lips as a wave washed over her face.

"May the Seasons protect you," he murmured. "May you feast with the Nine and return to this world stronger and wiser than before."

Brophy let the Physendrian queen sink beneath the surface.

PART III

Children of Magic and Lies

Prologue

arius Morgeon.

Darius winced at the sound of Oh's voice drifting into his mind.

"Don't you ever talk to me again," he whispered. "Never again."

The archmage's tears fell unchecked upon his sleeping daughter. He touched the curve of Arefaine's cheek. Her eyes darted back and forth beneath her tiny lids. He could only imagine what she might be dreaming.

Live, he thought, pulling the infant child to his chest. *Live long enough for me to make this right.*

Her little body hung limp in his arms. She was warm, too warm, but her breathing was calm and steady. He wrapped his ani around her like a cocoon, making sure she stayed asleep. He wanted to do more, but there wasn't time. He had to hurry.

Darius rose amid the shards of shattered crystals. The entire floor was covered ankle-deep with shimmering fragments. Far above him, the alcoves lining the walls of the Great Tower sat empty, testament to the madness that had almost consumed them all. Only moments ago, a devastating storm of black emmeria had swept through this chamber, nearly escaping into the world.

Darius's arms trembled as he looked at the founder of Efften, battered and bloody against the far wall. Once again he was bound with the delicate silver chains that had caged him for nearly a year, but they would not hold him for long. A long shaft of daylight from the entranceway lit the battered archmage in sharp relief. A bubble of blood grew larger and smaller at the corner of his mouth as he breathed. Darius longed to wrap his hands around Efflum's neck and squeeze. But it wouldn't work. Nothing had worked.

He wrenched his mind away from his former teacher and staggered to the tower doors. The city was in flames. The port was packed with the gleaming prows of Silver Islander ships. Screaming tattooed men with axes in both hands rushed through the streets, cutting down everyone in their path. The slaves had returned to repay their masters. A reckoning had come at last.

"Father!" a lone figure shouted, running across the courtyard and up the tower's steps. Darius opened the filigreed doors and Jazryth rushed through.

"The Islanders! They've—" She cut herself short as she slipped on the broken crystals and nearly fell. Her eyes found Efflum's battered form, and she put her hand to her heart.

"How did he—"

"Those fools set him free."

Jazryth closed her eyes and swayed. The muscles in her jaw tightened, and she opened her eyes. "Who?"

"Lyss and his friends. They cut his chains, freed him to help fight against the Islanders."

"Where is he? Where is Lyss?"

"I'm sorry," he said. "He didn't make it." Jazryth's lips twisted as she fought the tears. She put a trembling hand over her face.

Darius shook his head, seething in anger toward his daughter's desperate, but well-meaning husband. The young man had died in the ani storm his father had released along with all of his friends. His rash attempt to release his father had nearly destroyed the world. And now it had cost his daughter's heart as well.

Jazryth tore her hand away from her face, keeping it in a fist at her side. Her eyes were red. She looked at the shards beneath her feet, and immediately looked upward at the walls. Her eyes widened as she understood. "The emmeria," she mouthed, scanning the debris. "Where . . .?"

"Efflum shattered one of the stones to draw power from it. It set off a chain reaction. They all shattered." Darius couldn't keep the venom from his voice as he nodded at Efflum. "That madman would have killed us all if I hadn't arrived."

"But where is it?" she said quietly, still looking. "Where did the emmeria go?"

Darius looked down at Arefaine, sleeping in his arms.

Jazryth stared at her sister for a moment and then gasped. "Father!"

"She's safe," Darius insisted. "As long as she's asleep, we're all safe." He held Arefaine out to Jazryth, but she took a step back.

"What did you do to her?!"

"I did what I had to do!"

"What you had to?"

"I had no choice!" he cried, his voice cracking. "It was too much power, I couldn't contain it. The black emmeria would have destroyed us all—" Darius clutched the infant to his chest. His voice dropped to a whisper. "He said she was our only hope."

She followed his gaze to Oh's coffin. "You did this because of him? Because of a ghost? In a box?"

"Please." He stepped toward her, again offering the baby. "Please, you have to take her. Efflum could wake at any moment."

Jazryth backed up, shaking her head. "I can't," she murmured.

"You have to keep her asleep," he insisted. "And then you have to get her out of here. If the Islanders find her, they will kill her and destroy us all."

"It's too late," she moaned. "The city is overrun."

"Jazryth!" he snapped. "Efften doesn't matter anymore! You have to take Arefaine. Take her as far away as you can. Find a place to hide her, then come back for me."

"Come back?"

"I can't do this alone!" he implored her.

Jazryth stood, tense, a deer ready to run. "What about Mother. Why can't Mother—"

Darius took a deep breath, but he saw the recognition in his daughter's eyes as she realized the truth. Slowly the cracks in her strength began to mend, and he saw his daughter return.

"All right," she whispered, coming toward him. He handed Arefaine to her. Jazryth took her sister from him, but held her at arm's length. "I'll get her off the island," she said. "I promise."

"And then return."

She looked at him, a long crease between her brows.

He motioned toward Efflum. "I can't kill him. I already tried. He has magic I'll never understand. But I'll keep him in the tower as long as I can."

"But the Islanders—"

"They'll never get in here, but I can't hold that man forever. You must come back with help," he said, seeing the uncertainty in her eyes. "You must come back."

"I will," she said. "I promise."

He embraced her quickly, holding her one last time. "My strong, beautiful daughter," he murmured in her ear before he released her. "Go now. As fast as you can."

She paused, ready to run. "I love you, Daddy."

"I love you, Jazryth. Now fly."

Her ani flared as she took a deep breath, and she ran from the tower, Floani energy rushing through her body.

Darius watched her for a moment and then turned to Oh's coffin. With a brutal swipe, he brushed the crystal debris from the top, cutting his hands. He slammed his palms on the tarnished silver lid and clenched his teeth.

"There," he seethed, "it's done. I fixed your mistake. Your failed pupil will never again draw upon his wretched emmeria."

Efflum moaned, shifting in his sleep.

Darius sneered, pointing a finger at the silver doors of the tower. They slammed shut with a booming finality.

Drawing another deep breath, he turned back to the coffin. "You got what you wanted, old man. I've sacrificed my children upon your altar. But know this. I will always hate you. By all that is good in this world, I will hate you and everything you ever did to us."

Efflum shook his head. His eyelids fluttered. Crushed crystals scraped on the floor as he tried to push himself upright.

Darius felt a singular calm descend over him, and he prepared himself for the battle to come.

Hurry, Jazryth, he thought. *Hurry back to me.*

Chapter 1

 refaine," her father said, his voice soft and distant.

Arefaine winced, struggling to push the throbbing pain from her head. She fought to open her eyes, but she couldn't make them focus.

"You have slept too long, my dear. Bring yourself back to us. Efften awaits."

"What?" Arefaine mumbled, hugging the canvas bag to her chest. She could feel the warmth of the containment stones within. "Where am I?"

"Aboard a Silver Islander warship."

"What?" She jerked upright, the sudden jolt of fear burning away the haze. It was true. Rough wooden beams and planking surrounded her. Strong and utilitarian. No black-lacquered walls. No tall ceiling. No Ohohhim. "Have I been captured?" she asked, throwing aside the blankets and standing.

The room rocked, and she reached out, steadying herself against the damp wall covered with condensation. Her hand went to her aching head and found a bandage tied around it. She pulled the white cloth away and threw it across the room.

"Gently, my daughter. Gently. I nearly lost you several times today." Her father's ghost placed an insubstantial hand on her arm.

"What happened? How could the Islanders have won?"

Her father chuckled, the skin crinkling around his pale blue eyes. "Oh no. Our enemies have not won. They have been obliterated, slain and cast into the sea. The betrayal of Efften has finally been avenged."

Arefaine's chest expanded as if a thousand cords around her heart had suddenly been cut. "The barbarians are dead?" she whispered, and sank back to the bed, unsure if she should jump up and scream or curl into a ball and cry.

Her father nodded. "Every one of them."

She pressed her palms against her face, and the pounding in her head receded a little as she took a deep breath. She tried to remember the battle, but the details were jumbled.

"What happened? How did we win?"

"The battle was never in doubt. Our numbers assured us victory, but the Islanders attacked you directly."

Arefaine nodded as the images came back to her. She could see the silver prows of the barbarian ships heading toward her. "I remember that. I tried to use my magic against them."

Her father nodded. "We nearly fell into their trap. They used the same tactics today that they used to destroy Efften hundreds of years ago."

"What tactics?"

"They have learned to create a substance that is anathema to true magic. It destroys the sacred fire and any who use it."

She fought to collect her memories. She had a vague recollection of a loud noise and a blinding flash followed by a sickening drop. "Is that what caused the explosion?"

"Yes, they were able to pervert your power and use it against you, creating a blast that destroyed half our forces."

"Half our forces!"

"Shhh, calm yourself. All is well." He bowed his head until the tip of his goatee nearly touched his slender chest. "Victory often comes at a cost."

"What cost?"

"I am afraid the entire Ohohhim fleet was destroyed."

She gasped, trying to remember the faces of the men who had sailed with her. She couldn't recall a single one. All she could see was the blinding flash. "You tried to stop me, didn't you?"

"I did, but I was too late. You were thrown from the crow's nest and knocked unconscious. For a moment I feared the worst."

Despite the pain of her loss, Arefaine's heart swelled to hear the emotion behind her father's words. She reached out to take his hand. There was no flesh to touch, but she could feel the man within and the love he bore her.

Her father collected himself and continued. "Your flagship was damaged in the explosion and the barbarians boarded the sinking ship. Fortunately, I was able to protect you and convince your men to commandeer an enemy vessel. The battle was fierce, but we prevailed."

Arefaine nodded, feeling both relieved and cheated somehow that she hadn't been able to witness it. "How long until we reach Efften?" she asked.

Her father sighed. "I am afraid we would already be there if not for certain complications."

"What complications?"

"Your captains made a decision in your absence that you may not agree with."

She frowned. "What decision?"

"They tried to return to Ohohhom."

"What?" She tried to stand up, but nearly fell and had to cling to the edge of the bed.

"Slowly, please." His feathery touch on her arm urged her to sit back on the bed. "The Ohohhim fled the battle after you fell unconscious and tried to return to the Opal Empire. I was able to stop them. And we are headed south once again."

"Why would they flee?" she asked. "And how did you stop them?"

"They fled because they are a cowardly race. You deserve better servants."

"What do you mean?"

"Come and I will show you. I have a gift for you."

With a little help from his ghostly hands, she rose to her feet and staggered to the door. Her balance was off, but it was getting better. Bracing herself against the wall, she pulled the heavy door open and walked down the hall to a ladder leading topside.

She climbed the ladder and found the deck of the ship full of Summermen, perhaps a hundred of them. They all stood facing forward, their backs to her. Their loose, garishly colored shirts fluttered in the breeze.

"What is this? Where is Halman?" she asked, feeling dizzy again. There was something horribly wrong with the sailors from the Summer Seas. In her magical sight, they were empty, hollow shells with no life light shining within them. Vague memories of the battle drifted back into her mind. The entire Summer Fleet had been like this.

"Go see for yourself," her father told her. "You need never fear treachery again."

Arefaine crossed to the nearest sailor. He turned to look at her, and she drew back with a wince. His eyes were as black as the Heartstone, and dark streaks ran down his face like tiny rivers.

"What did you do to them?" she whispered, trying to make sense of the chilling sight. She had read about the ani slaves and the black tears they shed, but that practice had been forbidden long ago. Her father had led the crusade against them.

"I have indentured them for you."

"You control these things?" she asked. "You created them?"

"Yes, I did."

She felt dizzy and her father stepped over to place a calming hand on her shoulder. "How?"

"I will show you sometime, if you wish to learn."

She shook her head, unable to look away. "How many are there?"

"Thousands."

"Why didn't you tell me? Why did you hide this from me?"

Her father lowered his eyes, the pain clearly written on his face. "I wasn't sure how you would react. Conscripting lesser beings into a greater cause is always an unpleasant matter, something I wanted to protect you from. I can't help thinking of you as a child that needs to be sheltered."

Arefaine stared at the depthless black eyes of the man in front of her. It was the same blackness that rushed to her aid in her time of need, the same blackness that consumed Brophy as he clung to the bridge. It made her sick to her stomach, but she remembered her Carriers' betrayal and swallowed down her feelings.

"I am no longer a child. I have done whatever is necessary to return to Efften, and I will continue to do so."

"Of course. I know you will. But there are still things I wish you never had to see."

"That is very sweet, but what you have done to them is no worse than my sending men to die in battle," she insisted. "You are right. Such servants will not betray me, and we will need manpower to rebuild Efften."

"Yes we will. I am so glad you can understand."

Arefaine wandered through the black-eyed Summermen, her head spinning. She'd had no idea her father was this powerful. Even from his prison he could create and direct such an army. What would she be capable of someday?

"Can you show me how to control them?" she asked.

"Certainly," he said with a smile. "Watch what I do."

She felt the ani coalesce around the nearest Summerman. He was young, less than twenty. His purple shirt had been ripped open, exposing his muscular chest. She saw the way her father reached into his body and coaxed his limbs to life. The handsome young man dropped to one knee and drew his sword with a flourish. "May I have this dance, my lady," he said in a monotone.

Arefaine grinned and reached into the man next to him. There was no resistance as her mind slipped into his body like a hand into a glove. She wanted him to step forward, and he did so immediately. It was as if he were connected directly to her thoughts, her very desires.

"Step back," she made him say. "The lady is with me!"

"Do you dare to back those words with steel?" the first one said, spinning his blade around. She looked at her father's shade, and his eyes glinted in amusement.

"Certainly," Arefaine made her man say. "But I warn you, I have friends!"

Arefaine slipped her mind into four others and made them draw their swords in unison.

"I have friends as well," her father's puppet replied, and half the men on the ship drew their swords.

Arefaine laughed with delight as her men raced to brace her father's. The whole ship exploded into battle as she sent her toy soldiers against her father's. Summermen leapt around the deck, swinging their swords in exaggerated arcs.

It wasn't fair. She'd only grabbed a few, and her father had taken the rest.

What happens if I do . . . this? she thought, reaching out to try to take one of her father's Summermen from him.

This time, there was resistance, but with a playful push she knocked her father's influence out of the man, grinning at his shade as she did so.

He seemed surprised, but his men leapt upon the sailor she had taken from him, continuing the mock battle. The swords rang and blows were landed, but the weapons had no effect on the indentured.

At first, her men were pushed steadily back, but she soon grabbed another Summerman from her father's control, and then another. Giddy at the use of her power, she took them all one by one until the entire crew was hers. All save the first one her father had taken.

After a token resistance he backed off, but the practice was good. It came so naturally.

Her father watched her strangely, a wrinkle in his brow, but when she turned to look at him, her face glowing, he merely smiled tolerantly.

That handsome young man who first came to life walked forward and bowed at her feet. "My lady, forgive this unseemly display, but I could not abide the thought of you with another man. My heart, my life, and my sword are yours if you would have them."

Arefaine reached down and took his hand, pulling him to his feet. Leaning forward, she brushed her cheek against his and whispered in his ear, "Perhaps tomorrow." She shoved him away and caused the rest of the crew to circle her father's shade and draw their swords in salute. She laughed and felt like she did the moment she'd stood up to dance with Astor. Like chains were falling off her, like anything would soon be possible.

"It is such a joy to see you laugh," her father said, walking up to her. He cupped her cheek with his ghostly hand. "I haven't played like that in a very long time."

"I've never played like that."

"You will soon," he promised. "Every day."

She nodded, looking into her father's startling blue eyes, longing for his embrace. This was what it was like to have someone who truly understood her, who could do what she did, who wasn't afraid of her power. She wanted to dance with him. She wanted to run and swim, learn and debate, create and build with their magic. She wanted to live, truly live. And for the first time she felt like that wish was coming true.

"Come," her father said. "There is one more task you must perform before we are rid of the Islanders forever."

He motioned her forward and she caused the black-eyed Summermen to make a path for them as they walked to the front of the boat. But Arefaine didn't look them in the eye. The sight of their black orbs still made her uneasy.

Her father led her to a canvas-covered rowboat near the bow. As she drew closer, Arefaine felt a strange sensation, as if she were being pulled toward the little boat.

"What is in there?" she asked.

"Pull the canvas back and see for yourself."

Reluctantly she pulled back the stiff cloth and peered inside. Dozens of chests packed the bottom of the little craft. She flipped open the lid of the nearest, then stepped away.

"Do not touch it, my child," her father advised. "It would be death to you."

Arefaine stared at the chest full of little crystals, swirling with rainbow colors.

"This is what the Islanders attacked me with," she said.

"Yes. It is the same perversion of the sacred fire the barbarians use to create the Siren's Blood."

"Is that why I cannot see them with my magical sight?"

"Yes, they swallow these crystals to hide from our illuminated sight."

"Just looking at it hurts."

He nodded. "If any form of magic touches those crystals, they explode. That is how they defeated us so long ago. And it nearly worked a second time."

"What should I do with it?"

"We could take it to Efften with us, study it, if you wish."

"No," she said, shaking her head. "I don't want to be anywhere near it. Throw all this overboard," she said to the Summerman next to her. "Dump it into the sea."

Four of her ani slaves stepped forward, hoisted the little rowboat over the rail, and overturned it. Chest after chest fell. One of the lids cracked open, creating a shower of rainbow-colored crystals. One after the other, they hit the water and sank below the surface.

Chapter 2

Shara turned and kissed the warm, rough fingers caressing her cheek. "Brophy?" she murmured.

Then she caught his smell.

She leapt out of bed and smacked her head against the wall, pulling the linen from the mattress as she tried to scramble backward.

"You? How?" she gasped, fighting to regain her bearings.

Jesheks rose from the edge of the bed, staring at her with his red eyes. But this was not the man she knew. The Kherish Necani now had a swath of long white hair, broad shoulders, and thick muscles under white skin smooth as ivory. She tried to push through his glamour to see the obese man underneath, but she couldn't break his spell. Or there was no spell.

"What are you doing here?" she asked, finally rising above her panic.

"I came to save your life."

She was in a modest ship's cabin. The small bed and even smaller table and chairs were the only furniture. The walls were covered with carvings of the nine Physendrian gods. The ship was heeled over slightly, obviously sailing under a gentle breeze.

Shara tried to trace back how she had gotten here. What had happened? How long had it been?

"You put me to sleep," she said, remembering his hand on her forehead. "And you . . ." She paused. "You saved me from Issefyn."

He nodded. "I did." His new body was profoundly unsettling, like he was an impostor in the realm of beauty. Even his red eyes were different. They had lost their superior glint and had become darker, haunted.

Shara took a long breath and smoothed the front of her dress. Someone had garbed her in a light shift with short sleeves. She couldn't help imagining his white fingers sliding over her skin as he undressed her sleeping body.

"Why have you done this?"

"Because you would not have come with me if I asked."

Shara took a deep breath, leery of the raw emotion she saw in the Necani mage's eyes. His complete transformation set her off guard. Had he stolen her away from Brophy for this? For some petty seduction? Or had he actually fallen in love with her?

"Where are you taking me?" she cautiously asked.

"Away from here. These waters are not safe for you—or anyone—right now."

Shara nodded. "I appreciate what you did for me during the battle, but I need to get to Efften. You had no right to bring me here against my will."

"I don't think that would be wise."

"Wise or not, I have to go." She stepped off the bed and headed for the door. Jesheks stepped into her path, blocking the narrow doorway with his body. Shara felt a sudden surge of fear as the albino mage loomed over her. Had he grown taller?

"I need to find Brophy," she said in a low voice, gathering her power for a fight.

Jesheks gathered his own power. He wasn't drawing the energy from pain. He was drawing it from . . .

She took a step back, glancing at the front of his simple sailor's trousers where the fabric was stretched tight by his erection.

He followed her eyes and grimaced. "You are overwrought. I understand."

She shook her head, shielding herself from the crude Zelani energy swirling around him. His desire, and fears, pulled at her. Had he done all this—had he re-created himself—for her?

"I have to find Brophy," she said again, steadying herself with that mantra. She sent her ani outward, doing a quick search of the ship to see if there were others she had to worry about. The deck was lined with weeping ones.

"Shara, please, I don't doubt your strength or conviction. But I don't think you understand what you are facing. The man Brophy and Arefaine rush to meet is beyond their power to contain. The weapons at their command will be useless against him. If you follow Brophy to Efften, you will die with him, and we will lose our only chance of—"

"Jesheks," she said, fighting to keep her temper. "You presume too much. There is no *we*. We were nearly friends once, but that is all. You saved my life, and I am grateful. But I'm not running away with you to continue your Zelani training. I need to find Brophy immediately. If you want to help me, I would love that. But we will both regret it if you try to stop me."

Jesheks stared at her, the jaw muscles standing out against his pale skin. He had to swallow before speaking. "Neither of us wants to live in the world the man in that tower plans to create. If you come with me and 'continue my training,' as you say, then we might have a chance of defeating him."

Shara looked into his eyes, trying to spot a lie, but she couldn't see one. "What do you know about the man in that tower?"

"I know everything. I have drunk the Siren's Blood. I can't imagine many who could have journeyed deeper into that agonizing darkness than I did."

"You know how to defeat him?"

"I have a theory, but I need your help and time to put it into practice. Time we will not have unless we get away from here."

"So the only way to stop him is for you and me to run away and become lovers. How very convenient for you."

He winced at her words. "Unkind, Shara. Have I ever lied to you?"

"No, but you seem perfectly willing to abduct me."

"Your safety is paramount."

"As is your personal agenda," she said, fearing she was pushing him too hard. The man was clearly obsessed with her. The transformation he had wrought upon himself was nothing short of amazing. If she had more time, she could have been gentler with him. But she might already be too late.

Jesheks closed his eyes and held up a hand to pacify her. "My apologies. You are right. I want . . ." He struggled for the words. "Some of my motivations are selfish, but I never intended to hold you against your will. If I intended to imprison you, I would have kept you asleep."

"Why didn't you?"

"I was taking a chance that I might see a certain look in your eyes when you woke."

Shara frowned, refusing to let go of her anger. "You didn't find what you were looking for."

"No, I did not." The albino kept his features rigidly in check, but she could feel his emotions writhing beneath the surface. She didn't know whether to fear him or feel sorry for him.

With a sigh, Jesheks stood aside. "This was obviously a mistake. I'll take you to Efften immediately if that is what you wish."

"Thank you," Shara said, brushing past him and heading for the ladder.

She climbed the rungs quickly, suddenly eager to get as far from the Necani mage as possible. She emerged onto the deck amid a small crew of the weeping ones. In the distance, she saw the isle of Efften, just a bare speck on the waves to their rear.

Jesheks followed her. She felt the ani swirl between him and the weeping one manning the helm. He spun the wheel and the Physendrian ship slowly tacked back toward the wind. The ship leaned as its course altered and several weeping ones moved to adjust the sails.

Shara was about to thank him, but Jesheks turned away and raised his hood, shielding his sensitive eyes from the bright sun. And Shara's gaze.

"If this wind holds steady," he said, "we should dock on Efften well before sunset."

"Thank you," she said.

Jesheks nodded, still not looking at her. His burning gaze was fixed on Efften.

Chapter 3

Arefaine leaned over the prow of the Islander ship, trying to catch a glimpse of the harbor around the trees. The five mage towers had risen above the horizon hours ago, like silver beams of light. She watched the morning sun glinting off them as they grew ever larger and more beautiful. The wave of euphoria that had passed through her when she first saw them still hadn't left. Her whole body vibrated with anticipation. She and her father had finally done it. They had returned home to Efften. There were no Silver Islanders to stop them now, and the City of Dreams belonged to the illuminated scions once again.

Even at a distance she could tell Efften had been completely overrun by the jungle. She had expected the city to be in ruins, and was surprised so much had survived the centuries of weather and neglect. The towers rose as the sentinels of the city, the guardians of the mages' secrets. They still stood proud and strong, an eternal testament to the power of beauty and imagination. She could scarcely imagine the wonders that had been wrought within them. If the towers were still here, all else could be rebuilt.

The city covered the entire southern tip of the island. She would have to take the city back from the wild, but she would do that slowly, a little bit here and there. Not all the trees would have to go. She felt a need to foster a kinship with the green and growing things, and her new city would embrace and nourish all life.

Idea after idea rushed through her. There were so many places she could begin. After her father was released, they would explore the city together, finding all the treasures left behind. When her kinsmen arrived they would choose strategic buildings to reconstruct. There would be thriving marketplaces, schools for children, and symposia for her citizens to share their wisdom. There would be festivals, games, public art, and gardens. The streets would teem with mages and the light of magic would shine into the dark places of the world.

"Your smile is contagious," her father said, appearing behind her. "Seeing your joy makes me feel young again."

Her father had remained at her side during the entire voyage, ever since she'd awoken. She couldn't always see him, but she felt his presence hovering around her like the sun, warm on her shoulders.

Arefaine turned back to the island and studied the towers. The canvas bag containing the three stones swung against her hip. She could feel Efften's legacy humming inside.

The Silver Wharf grew larger as they neared, and Arefaine sent her awareness out, exploring. The dock was empty, and she searched farther into the city. It was filled with life. Animals, birds, insects. But she didn't find a life light bright enough to be a human.

"My child?"

"Yes, Father."

"Are you looking for the Ohndarien?"

Arefaine pressed her lips together.

She almost said that she was merely checking for any remaining Silver Islanders, but she didn't want to lie to him. Deception came as naturally to her as breathing, but that time was past. She didn't have to lie anymore, not about what she wanted or about who she was. She could declare her dreams for all the world to hear. The chains of Ohohhom were disappearing, and the closer she came to Efften, the more of those bindings fell away.

"Yes," she finally admitted. "I was looking for Brophy. I keep hoping that you were wrong, that he is not dead."

She felt a deep pang of regret for that moment at the bridge. She had replayed it in her mind a dozen times. She had lost her temper, behaved like a child. She closed her eyes and the bitter taste of sunberries filled her mouth.

"I had a dream that he was in the battle," she admitted. "He saved me from the Silver Islanders after I had been knocked out. He was suffused with the sacred fire when he fell. It could have saved him."

Her father nodded. "I sincerely doubt that anyone could have survived that fall, but it is possible that I was mistaken. I certainly wouldn't underestimate him or the power that drives him. We were delayed by sailing north; if he survived, he may well have made it to Efften by now."

"Do you think so?" she asked. Mixed emotions stirred inside her. The first was fear that if Brophy lived he might yet find a way to shatter her dream. But she also felt a strange and tremulous hope that he had come to help her. Could he possibly have forgiven her? If she could convince Brophy to forget her past, she could convince others to focus on their collective future. New ideas were always opposed until people saw the benefit. She didn't want the world against her. Everything she was building was, in the end, for them.

Arefaine kept her eyes locked on the city of her birth as the indentured brought the Silver Islander ship expertly into the harbor. Twelve docks made of white marble radiated out from a vast market space overrun by vines and bushes.

Dozens of boats were still tied to the marble pier. Most of them had rotted out below the waterline. But a few still clung to life, refusing to succumb to the ravages of time. Their elegantly carved wood had once been painted silver, but most of that paint had flaked away over the years, leaving speckled guardians of the Illuminateds' will. Most of the city was worn and broken, decaying, but the soul of Efften, just like the few remaining ships, still endured.

Her heart soared as her servants brought the ship alongside one of the stone quays at the famous Silver Wharf. Several indentured leapt over the rails and secured the mooring line. She couldn't wait for her servants to run out the gangplank, and jumped directly to the shore. Her feet tingled as she landed, and she felt a sudden lump in her throat.

"I'm home," she murmured, crouching to touch the dock. She pressed her palms against the smooth white stone that had been created by magic rather than dug from the earth and turned her face toward the sun overhead. She had imagined this moment since she was a child. And now that she was here, in her new kingdom, she couldn't wait to get started rebuilding.

A dozen men jogged down the gangplank and formed a protective circle around her. She glanced up at Halman, the only Carrier who had been loyal to her throughout. He panted laboriously, waiting for his next command, and she could smell his musky breath. Arefaine frowned as he stood there, seeming to stare at her with unfocused eyes.

Annoyed, she turned back to touch the dock again, but the power of the moment was gone. The euphoria she'd felt had fled.

"How does it feel to be home at last?" her father asked, walking down the plank to stand next to her.

She forced a smile. Halman's black tears preyed on her mind. "It's glorious, Father. The city is everything I dreamed of. But—" She looked at the Carrier again. He seemed in pain, one shoulder hunched slightly forward as his chest convulsed with that ceaseless, hurried breath.

"What is it, my child?"

She considered hiding her thoughts again, but no. She was no longer the emperor's shadow, a gilded wraith bound in silence. "This is no place for the indentured, Father."

He didn't answer for a moment, then said, "They brought us victory, my child."

Regret heated Arefaine's face. "Yes," she said. "I know. But we don't need them anymore. And I don't want to live in a home—" She took a deep breath, suddenly wishing she hadn't spoken, but she forced the rest of the words out. "I don't want to live in a home built by slaves."

Her father considered her carefully, his eyebrows furrowed. Then he smiled. "Of course, my child. Don't think on it anymore. These creatures were a necessary evil, a regrettable choice forced on us by our enemies. Once our kinsmen have joined us, we will release them from their service and send them back to their homes."

"You can do that?"

"Of course. I'll show you how and we'll do it together as soon as we can."

She nodded. "Thank you, Father."

"Arefaine," he said, smiling at her. "Remember, you are no longer among strangers. You don't have to be afraid to speak your mind."

She nodded, instantly feeling better.

"Look around you," he said, indicating the jungle, the city, and the ocean with his hand. "It is all ours. You have come home; revel in it."

She smiled. "Of course, Father. I'm sorry. Please, show me our city."

He offered his ghostly arm, and she took it. Together, they walked up the dock onto the cobblestone shore. The market was overgrown with short bushes that bore clusters of small yellow fruit. Generations of pits littered the broken cobblestones, and the tangy smell of fermenting fruit mixed with the salty scent of the sea. Beyond the open market, the crumbling ruins of an enclosed plaza showed through the undergrowth. Charred roof timbers still protruded from many walls that had been too sturdy to be torn down by the barbarians. She tried to imagine what it had looked like before.

"Come, my child," her father said, beckoning her forward. "I cannot wait to see you with my own eyes."

They wended their way through the jumbled cobblestones toward his tower in the distance. Her father sent half of the indentured ahead to make sure the way was safe. The rest stayed with them, encircling them protectively.

As they walked, her father pointed at one of the mighty silver towers.

"That spire was built by Hestorn the Blind," he said, indicating the northwestern tower. It rose like a spear, with a fluted conical top. Its tall, thin windows nestled between the flutes. "He was rarely at home, constantly traveling about. They joked that Hestorn was the only blind man to see all the corners of the world. He was in the Southwyldes when the barbarians attacked, but he never returned home." Arefaine thought she saw a hint of anger or disappointment cross her father's face, but then he smiled. "Perhaps he was devoured by those half-naked cannibals he was determined to befriend. He probably never saw it coming."

Arefaine returned her father's smile. She had never known him to make a joke before. The shadow of his long imprisonment must be lifting from his heart.

"That one there," her father said, pointing at the closest tower to the south, "was built by Rellana. She was a true archmage, strong in all forms of magic, but she favored Zelani and Necani above all and loved mixing the two. She was a very popular teacher, especially with young men." He raised a knowing eyebrow. "In her later years, she developed an obsession with storms and lightning. See that spike?" Rellana's tower rose elegantly, twisting like the spiral of a horn. At the top, it flared out in a small, round platform. Arefaine looked closer, and she could barely see a thin spike that shot up even farther.

"I see it," she said.

"She would stand up there during storms, calling the lightning to herself. The woman was convinced she could harness its power."

"Could she?"

"Who can say? All we know is that one night she went up there during a hurricane and never came back down." He waved a hand. "Perhaps she became one with the lightning. Perhaps that was her aim all along."

"And that one?" She pointed to the tower on the northeastern side of the city. It was square, while the rest were round. They could not see its base, but the middle of the tower tapered gradually as it rose out of the jungle. It was smooth, brilliantly silver, with many windows to the world.

"Yes, of course you would know that tower, it was the first to be built. That was designed by your ancient ancestor Alc. He was one of Oh's original disciples and the first master of the Alcani form. When he first arrived on Efften, he made a break with his past, changing his name to Morgeon, which means—"

"Unchained," Arefaine murmured.

"Exactly," her father said. "He declared himself a free man, free from the bonds of Ohohhim subservience and fear. His tower is now yours."

She looked at him sharply. "No, Father. It is still yours. It will always be yours."

He gave her a gentle smile and put a hand on her arm. "You are very generous, Arefaine, but it is yours by rights. The future is for the young, and the tower must pass to you. You have earned it."

She stared at the tower in the distance, and tears came to her eyes. The tower of her ancestors would be her new home. "It will be our tower. And all will be welcome in it."

"As you say, my child."

"Tell me about the tower in the center." She pointed at the tallest tower of all. It rose, round and smooth, with no windows, and flared near the top, spreading outward to form a vast silver bowl. She could just make out the tops of the trees growing within. "I've seen drawings of it in books, but not much more. Have the gardens atop it survived all this time?"

"That one," he said slowly. "That is where I have been held prisoner all these years."

"It's beautiful."

He shook his head sadly. "I haven't thought of it that way for a long time. But you are right, it is beautiful, and I will see it that way again." He sighed. "It was the last to be built on Efften, and it was designed to connect and enhance the other four. It is the soul of the city, the center from which all else radiates."

And the site of his terrible imprisonment. Her step quickened at the thought of her father caged for so long. "How did they do it? How did those ignorant savages keep you here?"

"Ah," he said, fluidly matching her increased pace. "It wasn't the Silver Islanders who caged me. I was betrayed before they even breached the city. I was imprisoned by one of my own."

Arefaine stopped, staring at him. "But I thought that the Islanders were holding you all this time."

"Yes, and no. The barbarians have patrolled the walls outside of my prison for centuries, preventing anyone from rescuing me, but they are not the ones who put me there."

"Then who? And why didn't you tell me this before?"

"I thought you knew," he said. "I forget you have been raised on the fairy tales the Ohohhim pass on to their children to keep them in line. The truth of the matter is much different."

"Then tell me," she said. Her hunger for her people's true history had been with her for as long as she could remember.

"Have you heard of a mage by the name of Efflum?"

"Of course. He was Oh's disciple. He and his followers founded Efften."

Her father nodded. "Yes. Efflum was the most powerful and respected mage in Efften. His magic allowed him to live for nearly a thousand years."

Arefaine nodded, wondering if she would live so long. Why not?

"In the city's final days," her father continued, "there was great division among the mages, with Efflum at the heart of the disagreement."

"I have read of this. They fought over the use of the indentured."

"That was part of it, but not all. It was an ethical disagreement. A question of how one's power should be used, if and when we should place limitations upon ourselves."

"I'm not sure what you mean."

He waved his hand. "The details are not important. The only thing that matters is that the disagreement grew violent. A civil war nearly broke out, and Efflum was imprisoned to prevent further bloodshed."

"You sound like you don't think he deserved that."

Her father shrugged. "Deserve it or not, he was imprisoned and remained there for several years."

"What happened to him?"

"The barbarians invaded. During the attack, Efflum's followers freed him to help fight. He went to the vault where all the raw emmeria in the city was stored and began gathering the power to destroy their enemies. But one of the misguided men who had imprisoned him tried to stop him. Brother fought brother as Efften was destroyed around them.

"Tragically, a number of containment stones were shattered in that battle. At any other time, this would not have been such a disaster. If we were not at each other's throats, if the city was not in flames, we would simply have put the energy back into storage. But there was no time for that. The only solution was to place the emmeria in your dreams. At first I thought it would not work, but even as an infant the illuminated blood shone in you like no other. And that light saved us all. And we will soon get our chance to repay that great debt to you."

"But, if the Silver Islanders aren't holding you anymore—"

"They never held me, my child. They merely guarded my prison."

"Then who is?"

"I am held by our most ancient and most powerful enemy."

"Who?"

"The father of us all."

"Efflum? He is still alive?" She paused. "Father, I can't fight him."

"Have no fear, child. You are far more powerful than you imagine. Believe me, this is well within your abilities."

"But . . ." she breathed.

He gave her a reassuring smile. "Trust me, my child, you will not fight alone. I have been locked in a struggle with our enemy for three hundred years, just a whisper away from being able to escape. Against the two of us, even he cannot prevail."

"I will try," she said, feeling the warmth of his confidence in her. "You know I will try."

"Ah, I cannot tell you how good it is to have you here," he said, brushing her cheek with his ethereal fingers. "I have dreamed of freedom for so long I can barely remember what it is like."

"I've never known what it felt like," she said, smiling at his joy. "Until today."

She took a deep breath and looked toward the tower shining in the distance. "Come. Enough talk, let's finish what we started."

They continued through the overgrown streets as the indentured cleared a path with their swords. They left the plaza and passed what looked like a collapsed bathhouse. The old pools were full of stagnant green water covered with floating white flowers. The walls had once been covered with mosaics, but they had all been vandalized beyond recognition decades ago.

Beyond the bathhouse was a canal crossed by elegant walking bridges at regular intervals. Arefaine paused, sensing and seeing something at the same time, just ahead of them across a canal. It looked like the corpse of some kind of animal. The courtyard where it had fallen was bereft of plant life of any kind. "What is that?" she asked, moving closer.

He followed her gaze and sighed. "One of my failures," he said. She looked at him hesitantly. "Go ahead. Go see for yourself."

She jogged lightly up the street to the nearest bridge, crossed over, and approached the corpse carefully. The creature was huge. Even flat on its side, the thing's meaty shoulder came up to her waist. Long, twisted horns curved out on either side of its head. Black matted hair stuck up all over, and she could detect no signs of decay. Black marks streaked out from the corpse as if it had exploded, and some of its bones were strewn as far as a dozen feet away. There were other creatures beyond it, perhaps twenty of them spread across the courtyard as if an entire herd of the creatures had come to this place and died here, blown apart.

"They were corrupted," she said.

"Yes, they were," her father said, catching up with her.

She walked among the shattered remains, and the indentured followed silently, keeping their protective circle around her. "And they fought with the Silver Islanders," she said, stopping over a body that had definitely been human, though it had decayed almost to bones. A broken horn was lodged deep between two bent ribs.

"How long ago did this battle take place?" she asked. None of the corrupted had decayed. Bugs would not touch them, but this person had been human.

"Many years, my child. This is no place for us to linger in our moment of triumph. Come. Let us see other parts of the city. This is a memory of violence that, I hope, we need never visit again."

But Arefaine did not follow him. A glimmer of color caught her eye, and she leaned closer. On the ground where the Silver Islander's belly had once been, there lay a shard of multicolored crystal. She frowned.

"What is all this?" she asked, rising and looking at the herd of grisly bodies.

"A failed escape attempt, my child," he said.

"You called these creatures to rescue you?"

"I did." He nodded. "Many years ago when you were still a child. But the Islanders stopped them. I made many such attempts. They all failed. If you walk through the city, you will find many battlefields like this, especially on the beaches. This herd made it much further than most."

"But . . ." Arefaine stared at the foul remains, so tainted that nature would not touch them. She had read everything there was to know about the corrupted, but until she had unleashed her own black ani upon her traitorous Carriers, she had never felt what it was truly like to be in their presence. The horror of that moment came rushing back to her. Her corrupted Carriers had been feral, single-minded. She couldn't imagine controlling them, becoming one with them such that they would do her bidding. Bending them to her will.

She looked at her father. He stood there, watching her with concern, and a chill ran up her spine. She glanced quickly at the circle of defenders, and for a moment she thought the corrupted and the indentured weren't very different at all. She shoved the thought down.

"You used these creatures?"

"I had to."

"Yes, but you were the one who led the crusade against the creation of the indentured. You were the strongest critic of Efften's reliance on the black . . . on the emmeria."

"Where would you get such an idea?"

"From the emperor," Arefaine said.

Her father raised an eyebrow at her.

"I also read it. All the books say the same thing."

"Books written by?"

"Ohohhim," she admitted.

"Exactly."

Arefaine swallowed down her anger. When would the lies end? She shook her head. The emperor was dead. Dewland was dead. Oh was dead. Nothing they had said mattered anymore.

"Remember, you were raised by our enemies. They went to great lengths to infect you with their fears, to vilify all power in any of its forms. But ani is not inherently evil, any more than a net or a plow is inherently evil, no matter what the fish or the forest think. Ani is a tool, a very powerful tool, as are the stones you carry. The indentured are also a powerful tool. Are they dangerous? Of course. Should they be used in all things? Of course not. Like a knife, you must use them with caution, and only when necessary. But should all knives be thrown into the ocean for fear of being cut by one of them?"

"But surely you feel the way I do around them. They're . . ." Arefaine put a hand to her abdomen. "They make me sick to my stomach."

"I understand, my child. I would have preferred to employ different methods, but I had little choice. My only other option was to place you in danger, which I would not bring myself to do. So I tried to free myself any way I could."

"But these creatures are so foul," she said, looking down at the corrupted beast.

"Foul enough to stop the evil Islanders, or so I hoped. I took up the sword that I had to hand, my child, as any man would in defense of his family."

She searched for the right words to explain to him why this wasn't right, but she couldn't find them. Couldn't he feel it in his bones?

"I'm sorry, Arefaine," he said quietly. "This is not the reunion I dreamed of, not this fierce battle with the Silver Islanders, this tainted homecoming. I dreamed of freeing myself, and then rescuing you from the Opal Empire. I wish I could have brought you to a beautiful garden without dragging you through the thorns, but I failed." He paused, watching her. "And now you have to rescue me instead."

Arefaine looked into her father's weary features, wanting to embrace him and wanting to run away at the same time.

A sudden explosion shattered the silence and a flock of screaming birds fled from a nearby tree. "What was that?" she gasped, turning and jogging in the direction of the noise. It had come from her tower.

"Arefaine, wait!"

But she didn't listen to him. She raced up the street, over another bridge, and between two tall buildings toward the center of the city. More explosions echoed off the buildings ahead of her, one right after the other. She turned a corner and found herself in a huge clearing. The largest spire in Efften loomed over her, the top of it lost in the glare of the sun. A formidable barricade had been constructed around the silver tower's base. Stones and debris from the ruined buildings had been stacked into circular battlements nearly ten feet high. The wall was sturdy and well built, but still a feeble defense against the swarm of indentured clambering over it like crazed ants.

A lone Silver Islander woman stood at the top of the barricade, shooting arrow after arrow into the horde. The attackers exploded as they came. The first lost his arm, spun away, and tumbled down the rocks. The woman shot again at the next, who was almost upon her. His head exploded, and he fell over backward, crashing into two more behind him.

But there were too many. The woman reloaded and turned as a third indentured reached the top of the wall. She shot. His stomach exploded, and he twisted sideways. She nocked another arrow, but two more had come up behind her. She turned as the nearest grabbed her wrist and snapped it. The woman cried out, struggling as they pulled her down the back side of the wall, out of sight. She screamed, her ragged cry sharp and desperate, and then all was quiet. Arefaine turned her head away.

Her father appeared next to her.

The three indentured who had dragged the woman out of sight reappeared again, picking their way nimbly over the stones. Their hands were bloody to the wrists.

Arefaine said nothing, only stared at the silent wall. The indentured all slowed to a stop and stood panting at the base of it. She wondered why her heart raced and bile rose in her throat. The woman was a Silver Islander. She deserved to die. She deserved worse than death.

Then why did Arefaine feel this way?

"Our enemies left a few of their fellows behind to guard my prison," her father said. "But that is the last of them. The Silver Islanders are no more."

Hesitating, Arefaine finally nodded. She swallowed and said, "Yes," in a voice that sounded dead to her ears. "Yes, that's good." She looked at the clearing. The cobblestones had a black sheen, like the bottom of a copper kettle baked in a fire. Like the site of the herd of corrupted corpses, nothing grew in this place. The jungle that had overtaken the rest of the city refused to come here.

The indentured who had been blown in half by the Islander woman's last arrow was crawling toward her. He had a mane of curly black hair, and his bright blue shirt slowly turned black as it soaked up his blood. As soon as she looked at him, he stopped, laid his head on the ground, and continued that grotesque panting breath. She stared at the black-eyed man, fixated, and she didn't know what to feel.

I am not a child, she thought. *And this is part of war.*

"I regret this unpleasant business, daughter. But I assure you it is all over now. We will be together in moments." He pointed at the top of the tower where the monolithic dish blotted out the sun high overhead. "I'm up there, in the garden," he said softly. "It is almost over."

Her father's prison was made of the same strange, silver stone as the other towers. It must have been almost a hundred feet around at the base and several hundred feet tall. Birds flew near the middle, and the trees beyond it seemed like flowered twigs in comparison. A curtain of vines climbed the sides of the tower for nearly a third of its length. Beyond them, it tapered as it rose, sharply at first, and then more gradually as it approached the top, smooth and perfect. Then, at the last, it bloomed into a huge atrium around the edges of which she could see a fringe of green lit by a corona of sunlight.

Arefaine stared up at it as she walked mutely to the ring of stones and began climbing. She passed the last Silver Islander guard. Her arms, legs, and head had been ripped from her body. Her dark blood blended with the black stones beneath her. Arefaine turned her gaze away to the tower.

She had to focus on what must be done. All this could be cleaned, wiped away as if it had never been. They would start anew, and when she rebuilt Efften there would be no indentured, no corrupted, no shadows anywhere in her city of light.

Once beyond the makeshift wall, she looked for the tower's entrance. Broad silver steps led twenty feet up to a pair of filigreed double doors twice the height of a man. Thick, gnarled roots grew through the gaps in the doors, spilling down the stairs and rising up the sides. She tried to imagine what kind of tree could have roots that large and how it could be growing inside the windowless tower. The roots were so entwined through the doors she wasn't even sure they could be opened.

Arefaine turned from the tower to the mutilated Silver Islander and the trio of bloody-handed indentured who stood around her, breathing like dying dogs. She swallowed down the sickly feeling in her throat.

"I don't want them here, Father," she said suddenly.

"I know, my child. We will let them go as soon as we can."

"No. I want them gone now!" She looked at him, tears in her eyes. "The dream isn't just to restore Efften. We need to rebuild her better, without repeating the mistakes of the past. Weren't the indentured one of those mistakes?"

Her father held up his hands. "Of course, of course. Do not upset yourself over it. I will send them away directly."

The indentured came to life before he had finished speaking. As one, they turned and ran up a northbound street and disappeared from view. The only one who remained was the one with thick black hair who had been blown in half. His frantic panting slowly tapered off as her father extinguished his meager life light. She turned away.

"There, we are alone now," her father said, gazing up at the tall staircase. "It is time."

Chapter 4

rophy hacked through a cluster of vines, clearing the path for another couple of feet. His sword was thick with sap and dotted with green bits of all the vegetation he'd slain to get to this point. He followed a muddy slope next to a river, working his way ever southward.

He had never seen jungle this thick. The entire island of Efften was covered with the twisted-trunk trees that soared overhead, blotting out the sun.

When Arefaine's ship had sunk beneath him, Brophy had treaded water for hours, waiting for Shara as long as he dared before swimming south toward Efften. He'd pushed through wave after wave all night, trying to reach the City of Sorcerers ahead of Arefaine.

The black emmeria's anger burned within him, and he would have drowned without it driving him forward. He rode that wave of endless rage all the way to the shores where it had been created.

He had spent the first ten minutes slogging through the sand around the beaches, but finally decided to cut inward and brave the jungle. He'd found an abandoned and overgrown road and fought his way along it for most of the day.

Arefaine would already have reached the island, he was sure, and every second was precious.

A few more swings, and he crested the top of the hill and stopped as the jungle dropped away.

Before him stretched the city of Efften. The cliff below Brophy disappeared into mists as dozens of creeks dropped over the edge in a series of gentle cascades. The little waterfalls fed an immense, crescent-shaped lake that bordered the edge of the city.

Five silver towers soared skyward, dominating the ruined landscape laid out at his feet. Songs were written about those towers: "The Spires in the Flames" and "Besha's Flight." "The Day the Mages Came Home," "Crab of the Silver Wharf," and "Alohmena." Every child in the world had heard those stories and songs dozens of times, and each was inspired by this place.

The jungle had moved in on the city, fringing everything in green. Only the tallest buildings and an elegant network of canals could be seen through the trees. The buildings were sculpted by magic, and Brophy could see detailed carvings along the tops of some, stories told in stone. Other buildings told stories in the way they stood, partnering with other buildings across a street or connected by high, thin walkways over sparkling canals. Arching white marble bridges crisscrossed those waterways, creating a spiderweb design that seemed almost symmetrical. The entire city toyed with the imagination of the viewer while at the same time embracing the chaotic clusters of trees, ferns, flowers, and vines. It was as if a deal had been struck between the mages of Efften and the laws of nature. Each bent for the other, sometimes demanding, sometimes accommodating, and in the end creating something wholly unearthly.

Brophy looked over the city, built on the backs of ani slaves. Her beauty had been bought with the darkest of coin and now the hollow palaces sat abandoned, a mute testament to their grandeur and their folly.

He shook his head. What a waste.

Beyond the city, he scanned the shoreline to the west. A flicker of movement caught his eye, and he squinted. An Islander ship lay moored to one of the docks, its furled sails fluttering in the breeze.

It was Arefaine. It had to be.

She arrived some time ago, a quiet voice spoke into his head.

Brophy's lip curled, and he checked the urge to spin around and look for it. The voice was unmistakable, even though he'd heard it only once before. In Oh's cave.

"I was wondering when I would hear from you again," he said, feeling his body tense.

Time is short, Oh said, his ethereal voice almost a whisper. The resignation in his tone set Brophy's teeth on edge. *You must stay by Arefaine's side, no matter the cost. She has already reached the central tower. I have seen that spire fall again and again through the shifting veils of time. If you fail, it will collapse. A hurricane of our own hatred, pain, and greed will spread out from the rubble, rushing across the face of the earth and destroying everything in its path. Only Arefaine can stop it.*

"So you have said."

And she will not stop it unless you are by her side.

"I told you before. I will not help you kill her."

I wish there was another way.

Brophy snorted.

Our world rests on the brink of oblivion, Oh insisted. *Only you can help her make the right decision.*

"Not if that decision is to kill herself."

There is no other way.

Brophy retreated from the edge, turning his back on Efften. "There is always another way," he said.

With a growl, he turned and leapt over the cliff. The wind and mist rushed past him, and he dove into the lake below.

Chapter 5

Arefaine followed her father up the steps to the tower's filigreed gates. She could feel the power inside, throbbing like an unnaturally slow heartbeat. Her father stood next to her, waiting patiently, and the Heartstone, her sister, was tucked warmly in the satchel under her arm. She didn't know why she hesitated. She wanted something that wasn't here, something that eluded her. The archway came to a point twice as tall as she was. Bas-relief carvings of willowy trees formed the outer edges of the gates, and the silver bars were wrought into the shape of intertwining branches. Roots and vines of all sizes pushed through the gaps in the filigreed gate, latching onto anything they touched. The vegetation had pushed the gates open a couple of inches but also held them fast.

"I'm afraid you will have to force your way inside," her father said.

She walked closer, careful not to touch the hungry roots. They felt alive, more like a person than a plant. They were saturated with ani, overflowing with it, but it wasn't corrupted. It was something else. She peered into the gloom inside the tower. Its interior was entirely filled with a mass of twisted roots. Their vast brown coils wrapped over one another like the coils of enormous snakes. A swelling of ani she had never felt before was in the heart of the twisted mass.

"There is something in there," she breathed.

"This building is the center of all power in Efften. The heart of this tower is flooded with ani, like a giant Heartstone. The lifeblood of our empire flows through her walls."

She shook her head slowly.

"The vitality and power of anyone who steps within is multiplied. You will see." He reached out and brushed one of the green serrated leaves sprouting from the vines. "As you near the top, the effect becomes stronger. At the height of Efften's glory, the garden overhead fed the rest of the towers like a mother feeds a child in her womb. But no one has pulled from her reserves for centuries, and the garden's growth has gone unchecked."

"The tower feeds this immense tree?" she asked. "Nothing unmagical could grow so large." Arefaine tested the gate, tugging lightly. The roots shifted as if alive, but would not release their grip. "How do we even get inside?"

"It is not as great a hurdle as you might think. A little emmeria from your sister and these roots will wither away."

"No," Arefaine said suddenly, more forcefully than she meant to. She didn't like her father's casual use of the emmeria or the indentured. It was childish, she knew, but she couldn't get the thought out of her head. Hadn't the time come to use better tools?

"I'll chop them away," she said, drawing her dagger. She called upon the Floani form, filling her body with strength.

"Arefaine, this is wasting precious time—"

"I'm going to chop them," she repeated firmly, and set to work. Her Floani-filled arms hacked through the fibrous roots quickly and efficiently, and a few minutes later, she was able to yank the door a few inches farther open.

Climbing up the doors, she turned sideways and wriggled through the narrow gap. She clambered over the mass of roots into the huge, circular room. The sight took her breath away. The tower was completely hollow, rising above her in one massive chamber as far as she could see. A giant column of dirt-encrusted, flaking roots filled almost the entire space, twisting and intertwining as they rose into the darkness overhead. They looked like horrific serpents frozen in a desperate battle. She gazed upward into the gloomy dark, but could not see the end of it. A silver staircase spiraled along the outer wall, skirting the serpentine cluster of roots. The walls were lined with row after row of empty alcoves rising up into the darkness above.

She could definitely feel what her father had described. This was a place of power. The hairs on the back of her neck prickled, and her magic was close at hand, hovering around her like a dense cloud. Her senses were fantastically acute. The earthy smell of soil permeated the tower, and while she felt she could have heard an ant moving, the tower was utterly silent. Unnaturally silent.

She crawled over the sprawling roots, their rough bark scraping her knees and palms. Her passage was slow, almost reverent. Her foot slipped between the huge roots, and she winced at the inappropriate noise. She felt like a child sneaking into the emperor's silent chambers, craving his welcome even as she feared his wrath.

She reached the stairway and left the shifting roots to stand on solid stone.

Her foot scuffed one of the steps, sending up a gout of dust that revealed a mirror shine underneath. She tapped it with her toe. It sounded and felt like stone, but looked like silver.

"This place is incredible," she murmured.

"Of course," her father said, reappearing beside her. "That was what Efften strove to be, something beyond the normal world."

Arefaine turned to one of the myriad alcoves. They were small, barely large enough to hold a bowl of fruit. She thought they were empty, but each held a small pile of glass shards under a thick layer of dust. She stopped and picked up one of the fragments.

No. Not glass. Crystal.

She rubbed it between her fingers, feeling the sharpness of its edges after all this time. *These are the shattered containment crystals,* she thought to herself. She looked upward at the warren of alcoves. There were thousands of them. Tens of thousands.

Her head swimming in amazement, she continued up the stairs. Clouds of fine dust swirled around her feet with every step as she climbed. Her whole body vibrated with energy. As the light from the doors below began to fade, she noticed that a ghostly light illuminated the tower from within. She looked for the source, but could not find it.

"What is making the light?" she asked.

"Ah," her father said. "I never did fully understand it. Rellana was the engineer. She said something about tiny glass rods carrying sunlight through the blocks of silver. But the tower glows at night as well. So there must be something else to it, yes?"

Arefaine brushed her hand across the luminous silver walls, feeling giddy in this highly charged place. Her eyes followed the pillar of roots. Farther up, they choked off the entire width of the tapering tower, but she thought she saw a light in the distance.

"That is the top?" she asked, squinting.

"Yes, we are almost there and . . ." He trailed off.

She stopped climbing, and looked at him. "What is it?" Her hypersensitive ears heard something. A faint click. She looked around, but all she could see was the convoluted roots and glowing silver walls with their empty alcoves.

"Arefaine, before we reach the top, I must warn you about something."

A cold feeling spread over her scalp. She suddenly felt very exposed and pulled her magic close to herself.

"What?" she asked.

"I know it is nothing more than an old man's vanity, but the years have not been kind to me, my child. I am embarrassed to have you see the state into which I have fallen."

She paused. "What do you mean?"

"I have not eaten in three centuries. I have not had a drink or felt a human touch in all that time. And it is difficult when you are so lovely to know that I have become so foul."

Arefaine's taut muscles relaxed, and she let out a breath. She gave him a reproving smile. "Father, I love you. I don't care what you look like."

He smiled. "Of course you don't. As I said, it is an old man's folly." He kissed her hand with his ghostly lips. "I will leave you now. When next I see you, I want it to be with my own eyes." His apparition disappeared, leaving her alone in the glowing tower.

Tapping the energy all around her, Arefaine suffused herself with power and continued up the stairs, around and around. The tower narrowed, and the dangling roots soon blocked her way. She had to turn sideways, tearing her way past the crusty vegetation until she could see daylight shining through the matted vegetation. Wriggling into the gap, she fought her way upward until she emerged through a muddy little fissure between two enormous gnarled roots. The smell of soil and dust mixed with a heady fragrance of flowers.

"It's so beautiful," she murmured, crawling out of the hole onto a swath of vibrant green grass. Every imaginable flower bloomed in abundance, creating brilliant splashes of color against the ever-present green of the leaves and ferns. Daffodils, roses, tulips, snapdragons, sunflowers, and flowers for which she had no names flourished around her and rose up the silver terraces of the garden set within a giant bowl.

She took a deep breath as she turned, taking in the visual feast, overcome by the abundance of life. There had been many beautiful gardens in Ohohhom, but nothing to compare with this.

Her joy slowly evaporated as her gaze fell upon the gnarled gray tree behind her. It squatted in the middle of the garden, a slash of dark brown against the fanfare of color. It was easily twenty feet in diameter and only half again as tall as it was wide, making it hunch like some angry giant. Its spiny branches grew sideways from the fat trunk, as though trying to protect it with a wall of spears. The sallow leaves only grew from branches on one side of the trunk.

This was the source of that horrible root structure she had climbed through. She shivered, walking slowly around the massive trunk. The ground was bumpy and uneven, as if the tree had suddenly burst through the ground in one massive eruption. Her gaze flicked from the sickly bark to the branches, which reminded her more of the spines of a corrupted beast than the limbs of a tree. She expected them to reach out and grab her, and she cycled her breath through her body, ready to call upon her magic.

"Come around to the other side, my child," a thin, creaky voice said, seeming to descend from the branches. "Let me see you."

She tensed, looking up, but could not find the speaker. Cautiously, she stepped over the thick roots and worked her way around to the dead side of the tree.

"Father?" she called. She kept looking for a cage of some kind. Was it up in the branches? She had always pictured her father trapped in a dark, dank jail.

"This way," the voice creaked.

She continued around the trunk, but there was nothing. Only tufts of withered grass and those brown flaking roots.

"Where are you?" she asked.

"Up here."

She turned, looking up, and gasped. Stepping back, she clenched her fists, and her magic roared inside her.

An emaciated man hung over her, half entombed within the trunk as though man and tree had melted together. His skeletal toes barely protruded from the living wood. His stick-like knees emerged from the bark below his chest, face, and left hand. Where his wretched body could be seen, thin skin hung from his bones like cracked parchment. Yellow ligaments, white bone and dry muscles showed through the cracks. His head was a blind skull, the eyes shriveled up into two sallow yolks nestled in their sockets. His nose had shrunk to a pair of gaping holes that shivered when he breathed. Stretched lips pulled away from yellow teeth webbed with tiny cracks, and wisps of curly black hair clung to his papery scalp.

Only his bony right arm was completely free, as if he had just torn it from the side of the tree that was blackened and rotting. He beckoned to her, but she couldn't make her feet move any closer.

"F-Father?" she stammered.

"Welcome, child. I've waited so long to see you."

Chapter 6

Issefyn screamed and screamed and screamed, never stopping, never drawing breath. The agony poured out of her in an unending torrent, her own voice lost in the mournful peals and howls of rage all around her.

The others were everywhere, under her, over her, crushing her under the weight of their writhing bodies. They were all naked in the dark, shuddering, kicking, lashing out at one another. And screaming. All of them screaming.

Issefyn fought them, fingernails gouging flesh, biting anything that came close to her. She had to get to the top of the pile, she had to get out from underneath them all. She was being crushed, suffocated as she screamed. But there were too many of them. For every one she threw off, a dozen more squirmed back to crush her again.

"Mother." The voice came from her bones, from the inside of her head.

"'Teris!" she cried. "Kill them, 'Teris. Kill them for me."

"Wake up, Mother. Wake up."

Issefyn thrashed around, looking for the voice. Looking for the way out.

"Come back to me, Mother. Come back."

She felt a sudden yank, as if a black hand had reached inside her belly and pulled her up by the spine.

"Please," she screamed. "Please, 'Teris, please!"

The black hand pulled her through the mass of writhing bodies. Those around her clung to her, latching onto her arms and twining their fingers through her hair. They were pulled along with her, sliding through the ocean of limbs slick with sweat and offal. Finally she broke through to the surface, and the black fist lifted her into the storm with sheets of purple lightning racing across the sky. She felt her insides rip and come loose as she was hoisted higher and higher until she was overwhelmed by the lightning, her closed eyes seared by the blinding light.

Issefyn's eyes snapped open. A haze of silt drifted in front of her, and she sucked in a breath. Water rushed into her lungs and she thrashed.

"Mother," 'Teris said, floating lazily next to her. "Calm down."

I'm drowning! she yelled, but there was no sound. A few stray bubbles fled her mouth.

"You're not drowning. Calm yourself, Mother. Really."

Curling into a little ball, her hands clutching her stomach, she found something ragged and stringy. She felt around, clutching at the spongy ropes.

Something was wrong with her legs.

She looked down, forcing her eyes to focus through the murky water. Her body ended at her waist. Ragged entrails stretched a few feet out from the wound, floating like tentacles.

"Come, Mother," Victeris said. "I need you at the tower."

She turned.

You did this to me! she croaked. Again, no sound came out, but Victeris seemed to understand.

"Your beloved containment stone did this to you, Mother."

The stone! Where was her stone? She floundered around in the leaves looking for it. A pale corpse lay on the ocean bed next to her. No. Half a corpse. The severed legs of an old woman, completely naked. Her withered thighs and sagging buttocks shifted with the slight current.

"Calm yourself, Mother. You know where the stone is. You can feel it."

She closed her eyes, throwing her scattered thoughts around her. It was there! Right there! With her all along. She grappled with her bloody waist, tearing at the squirming intestines. Reaching up, past her ribs, her fingers closed on the stone. A rush of joy flooded her, and she lay back, drifting in the water. She pulled the stone out of her chest cavity and pressed the warm stone against her breasts.

"The tower, Mother."

What?

"Your stone is almost empty, Mother. But there is more at the tower. All the power you can use, and more."

Yes, the tower. She flipped over and tried to stand up. But she couldn't move. Couldn't stand. Couldn't swim.

"Come, Mother, follow me. I'll bring you to it."

She reached out toward Victeris's voice, her hand falling on the sand. A gout of silt spumed up. She dug her fingers into the soft mud and pulled herself forward.

"Good, Mother. Hurry, before Morgeon's daughter and her lover take it from you."

Issefyn reached out again, pulling herself forward. The hand that held the stone dug into the ocean floor, and she pulled power from it, moving faster and faster, slithering through the sand and water.

Chapter 7

Arefaine stared at the creature in the tree, unable to speak.

"My daughter," the old voice creaked.

"You're not my father. Where's my father?" she said, her voice frail.

"Arefaine, you—"

"Where's my father!"

The cadaverous face let out a slow, hissing breath. "He is here, child. Right next to you." The thing pointed with his free right arm.

In horror, she looked closer. There, at the base of the tree, nestled between two huge roots, was another skeletal figure, his naked skull grinning at the dirt. The papery flesh upon his chin still held a wisp of a gray goatee and tattered green cloth wrapped around the bones of his hips.

"That is—" She hesitated.

"Your father, yes."

She spun around. "Then who are you?" she demanded, her voice rising.

"I am the man who brought you here," the thing said to her. "The man who stood by your side all these years."

"You're not my father."

"No," the thing said, his teeth moving, forming words as if he had lips. Arefaine felt dizzy. "I'm not. But listen to my voice. You know who I am. It was me all along."

"You've been . . . You're . . ." She struggled as the truth dawned on her.

"Yes," he creaked.

"No."

"Arefaine—"

"If that's my father"—she stabbed a finger at the skeleton on the ground—"and he was the one who fought Efflum, who trapped . . ." The world seemed to slant, and she stumbled sideways. She put a hand to her head.

"My child, listen to me—"

"I'm not your child!" she shouted, backing away from him.

"I may not have been the man who impregnated your mother, but we are still kin. Our blood calls to each other. Your father filled your dreams with hatred and fear, and I was the one who found you in that darkness. I was the one who helped you. Me! I stayed with you all these years, delivered you from those cowering chalk faces. In every way that matters, I have been your father. And in every way that matters, you have been my daughter."

Arefaine's breath came fast and desperate. She tried to control it, but her lungs wouldn't obey. She couldn't get enough air.

She stared down at her real father's corpse, the wispy beard, the sarong. A corpse. Nothing more than a brittle corpse at the base of this evil tree. She felt as if a huge chasm yawned at her feet. Everything she'd ever known was a lie. The isolation of the Ohohhim—the unbearable loneliness—had only been bearable because someday she would find her father, and he would lead her home.

And there he was. Bones and roots and dirt. That was home.

Her fingers reached inside the satchel that held the Heartstone. Jazryth. Her only other relative, warm and filled with dark magic. Strength flowed into her as she touched those rough, chipped facets, and her dizziness faded.

She turned her tear-streaked eyes to look at the thing embedded in the tree.

"You're Efflum, aren't you?" she asked hoarsely.

"Yes, I am."

"It was you. All along."

"Your father has not spoken to you since the day he sent you away."

Her breath came quickly again, and she felt her control slipping. "You lied to me," she said in a low voice.

"Since you were a baby, you assumed I was your father. I let you keep that assumption. I called you my child. But, Arefaine, all of the illuminated scions are my children."

She clenched her teeth. The emperor had played this game for years, saying one thing, doing another. "You're no different than the rest of them!" she hissed.

"No. They wanted to use you to quell their fears. I helped you reach your dreams. *Yours.*"

"You deceived me!"

"It's true that in a small way I allowed you to deceive yourself. I did not break your illusions, but only to protect you. I did it because I love you."

"This is what you call love!"

"Yes, I call this love. I came to aid you when everyone else had abandoned you. You needed a guardian, and I gave you what you needed. You needed hope, a gentle touch, and I nurtured you. Would you have made it out of the darkness without me?"

She sneered. "Did you actually think this scheme of yours would work? You thought you could draw me here, to this place, to free you. Did you actually think I was that stupid?"

"Please, Arefaine, don't be turned away by my appearance. I am the same man you have known all these years—"

"Known all these years? I never knew you! My real father lies here, dead. And you killed him. Did you think I would forget him and put you in his place?"

"Your real father never cared about you. Not the way a father should. He loved his ideals first and you second. He plunged you into an eternal nightmare!"

"Did he?" she spat. "Forgive me if I don't believe you."

"Come now, Arefaine," Efflum said sternly. "This is beneath you. When children are scared, what does their mother tell them? She tells them there are no monsters, that everything will be all right, that Mommy and Daddy will never leave them. She tells them the Snow Queen brings them presents in winter, that Grandmother still loves them after she dies. She promises that if you share with your brother, he will share with you. All lies! Convenient deceptions!"

She clenched her fists. Her magic swirled around her, and she longed to plunge her fist into the tree and destroy this horrific, emaciated creature.

"But children need those lies, Arefaine," Efflum creaked. "They cling to those lies until they are strong enough to see the world as it really is."

"I'm no child," she said.

"You were a child. You needed reassurance, and I gave it to you."

"You actually believe that, don't you? No wonder your children turned against you!"

"Enough!" Efflum shouted, his thin voice cracking like a whip. "You say you are no child. Then it is time to grow up, Arefaine Morgeon. Your father used you to complete a task he was too cowardly to face on his own. Just like the emperor tried to use you. Just like Brophy tried to use you."

"Like you are trying to use me now?" she said, forcibly holding her magic at bay. Was that what he wanted? For her to lose her temper? For her to unleash all of the emmeria upon him, upon the tree?

"Yes," he said. "I am trying to use you. You want truth? Then grow up, and hear the truth. I have been trapped here for three hundred years! You know what that feels like. You know about the madness that threatens to take you when you are trapped, alone in the dark. You escaped from your prison because I was there, because I shielded you. I held your hand through the endless night, through your murderous rages. I am only asking for the same favor in return." He reached out with his free hand, opening it to her. "You have your freedom. Give me mine!"

She watched him through narrowed eyes, studying the blackened part of the tree, the rotting cavity that used to hold his right arm. "You freed that hand. Why not the rest?" she asked.

"Your friend Issefyn helped me break this hand free when she finally let go of that damned containment stone. A containment stone that you left with her. For that, I thank you. But I am only partially free."

Arefaine glanced down at her father's skeleton. "Is that how you killed him, then? With your free hand?"

Efflum's teeth clacked together in frustration. "No," he said. "I didn't kill him. When Brophy smashed the music box, Darius tried to keep me from using the flood of ani suddenly released into the world. He tried to prevent it from reaching me. He wasn't strong enough. The strain killed him."

"Another lie for the child?" She sneered.

"No."

"Again, forgive me if I doubt your word."

"Arefaine, I never claimed to be an innocent. Efften rose because I stole the power to build her. She survived because I spilled the blood to hold her. And she fell because I was imprisoned by weak-willed fools who refused to let me defend her. I've done hideous things to protect those I love, and I will continue to do these things, one after the other, until I die! *That* is what a father does."

"That day may be sooner than you expect," Arefaine said in a dark tone, her finger caressing the Heartstone.

Efflum's teeth came together again, his shriveled eyes and bony face giving no hint of what he was thinking. When he spoke again, the shrill volume of his voice had lowered. "You have every right to be angry," he said. "I understand your pain. I, too, was lied to by a man I trusted. I, too, have been abandoned and betrayed. These are the unfortunate curses that have fallen upon us. But should we lash out at our kin because of them? Who do you have, if not me? And who do I have, if not you? We are alone, Arefaine. Our power forces us to be lonely, for no one else can possibly understand what we feel, what we see, what we can do. No one except for our own kind." He paused, and she watched him. Her hand gripped the Heartstone.

"I am your kin," Efflum said. "No one else. Even among mages, we are unique. The strongest of them all. Whatever else you think of me. Whatever else I have done, you know that to be true. Who else understands you like I do?"

He fell silent, hanging above her, watching her. She could find nothing to say, and in the suddenly bleak landscape of her future, she saw the truth of his words. She had nothing to return to in Ohohhom. Without her dream of Efften, she might as well be dead.

"You are an extraordinary young woman. I wanted to claim you as mine, and I probably clung to that pleasant fiction longer than I should have," Efflum conceded. "But I saw the pain inside you, felt it as my own. I didn't have the heart to hurt you any more. I knew if I could get you to come here, to behold the grandeur of Efften and all that it could be, you would feel the dream within your grasp. With or without your blood father. Your dream of having a family is still possible."

"That's nothing but a false dream you planted in my head."

"I planted it? No. I may have fostered it, but it was your dream. It was an aspiration that couldn't help but blossom in your heart. And now it is here, next to you, all around you. Am I the father who spilled his seed to create your limbs and the color of your hair? No. But I am the father who will sacrifice his life to make your dreams come true. I am the father who will hold the glory of Efften within his heart and mind, until we call the illuminated scions back to her shores. We want the same things, Arefaine. What does it matter if we are not father and daughter?"

"Because you made my whole life a lie."

He paused again, his desiccated face expressionless.

"You say you are not a child, but you are being childish," he finally said. "You are standing here, in the greatest tower of the City of Dreams. And you know it is not a lie. The power you feel here is real. The secrets I have to share with you are real. If you will not listen to me, then listen to your own heart. You have seen Efften's beauty, her greatness. You have seen what she can be, perhaps even clearer than I. She belongs to you, and to me, and to all of the illuminated scions. She deserves your love. She deserves to shine."

Arefaine turned away from the animated corpse and its squat, ugly tree. She looked out over the garden to the top of the magnificent bowl, and at the sky beyond. Reaching up, she wiped her tears away.

"There are a rare few in this world capable of creating something of true beauty," Efflum said. "Don't waste that gift. You are an illuminated scion of Efften. You were born to outshine all others in the world, those petty and jealous beings—lesser beings—who will always try to take our home away from us. I wish I could have told you the truth from the very beginning. I wish I didn't have to kill and corrupt and enslave others to reunite us. But I did it. And I would do it again."

Fear and doubt, hope and hate, spun through Arefaine's chest. She couldn't get a handle on them, didn't know what to feel. Was this the end of her path, a failed and damnable lie that left her gasping for breath, with nowhere to turn? Or, if she listened to Efflum, was it only the beginning?

Could she forgive a deception for the sake of a dream? What, really, had changed?

"What do you want from me?" she asked in a flat voice.

"Oh, child. I want so many things. I want you by my side. I want your advice on how to rebuild our home. I want your help in bringing back the great race and making sure they are never threatened again."

"With the indentured? With corrupted? Using the *black* emmeria?" she said, calling it by the name that the Ohndariens used.

"Using whatever methods we need to succeed," he said.

And that, she knew, was honest.

"I don't know if I can do that," she said. "Not at that price."

He paused. "I make no demands upon you, Arefaine. You are free to go whenever you wish. But ask yourself this, where will you go? What other home will call to you like Efften? There are none. Not in the entire world. And if you live here and make this city what it must be, there will be those who will try to take it from you. What will you do to stop them?"

"I don't know."

"I admire your compassion, but I can't say I share it. Not anymore. It took me many years, many losses, and much pain and betrayal to understand the way the world is."

She looked up at him, his dry, brittle limbs sticking out of that horrible tree.

"Go if you must," he said. "But I beg you, child, let me touch your hand before you leave. It has been so long. So very long. The mind plays tricks. And I would know, for certain, that you have been here before you leave me." He reached out his nearly translucent hand toward her, stretching as though he would break himself.

Pity welled up within her, and she went to him, stopping just beyond his reach.

"Can you forgive me?" he rasped in that unearthly voice.

"I don't know."

"Can you try?"

She hesitated, looking into those shriveled, yolklike eyes. They repulsed her, but his words had hammered their way into her heart. What would she have done in his position? Fought and clawed and tried every way she could to be free, just as he did. What would she have done if her fellows had betrayed her? Corrupted them, sent them over a waterfall to die.

She closed her eyes and bowed her head. She couldn't see the light out of this darkness. What if there was no light? What if life was simply this way? Stumbling blindly through the twilight, swinging at shadows. What if those brief beams of clarity were only in her mind? Fanciful notions of her imagination, lighting up for one brilliant moment and fading. What if there was no real truth?

She opened her eyes and looked back up at him. Reaching out, she touched his fingers. They were dry and oddly warm. "What do I have to do?" she asked quietly.

He remained silent for a moment, then said, "The stones. I need the stones you carry in that bag. They have the power I need to break these bonds and bring my body, my family, and this city back to life."

She reached into the bag that rested against her hip. Her sister's stone was warm against her fingers, and within her swirled an ocean of power, the legacy of Efften, a dream that had been fractured but had not yet died.

"Please, my child," he said, clinging to her hand.

Arefaine felt a sudden presence as someone entered the tower, his fiery life force blazing in the distance.

"Quickly, my child. Our enemy approaches."

Concentrating, she heard something, a distant voice rising from the earth below her. A voice calling her name.

Arefaine took one step away from Efflum, and he grabbed for her. She felt the bones beneath his fingertips as he clutched at her hand, but she twisted free.

"You cannot trust him," Efflum warned, his voice rising. "He fought for our enemies. He tried to kill you, and he is coming to finish the job. Give me the power I need, and we will destroy him together."

She shook her head.

"You are making a mistake!" he called after her as she ran. "Don't let him near you!"

Arefaine slipped between the two massive roots, scraping her legs on their rough bark. She fought through the gnarled vegetation to the tower's interior.

Someone was running up the steps. His fervent steps clanged loudly in her ears.

"Arefaine!" he roared, bursting into view, a filthy sword held tightly in his fist. He skidded to a stop, his fierce gaze falling upon her.

She stood frozen, one hand on the Heartstone. He was only a step outside of sword range, and she knew how quick he was.

They faced each other in silence, and her heart thudded in her chest.

"Arefaine," he said softly.

"You've come to kill me," she said, watching. If he even twitched, she would unleash every ounce of magic she possessed and tear his body to pieces.

But Brophy did twitch. He opened his fist. His sword clattered onto the silver stairs.

Her breath caught in her throat. The fire in his eyes faded, and relief softened his features. He hesitated, then moved slowly toward her. A sob caught in her throat.

"No," he said, opening his arms, "not to kill you. To help you." And all the fight seeped out of her. She slumped into his embrace and began to cry.

Chapter 8

Shara stood at the rail as Jesheks's weeping ones steered the ship back toward Efften. It moved with agonizing slowness under the slight breeze. She considered jumping overboard and swimming, but she knew that wouldn't be any faster.

"Can you feel it?" Jesheks asked, coming up behind her. "Something's happening at the tower."

"It doesn't matter, I'm still going back."

"I know."

She turned and looked at him. All the power and vitality seemed to have gone out of his beautiful new body. She reached over for his hand, but he pulled it away.

"I'm sorry," she said. "I know this is not the reunion you dreamed of."

"No, it is not," he said, his brows hunched over those haunted eyes.

She gave him a soft smile. "Perhaps next time you should avoid kidnapping me."

"Next time I will." No amusement filled his gaze. Each word she spoke was like a needle poking a raw nerve.

"I know how my reaction upon waking must have hurt. I've been there myself."

"Have you forgotten?" he said through tight lips. "I enjoy pain."

"No, you used to enjoy pain."

"And now?"

"Right now you have nothing to replace it." She tried to imagine him going off and building a life for himself someplace. She tried to imagine anyone loving him. She couldn't picture it. "I know you were hoping—"

"What I was hoping doesn't matter," he said. "Beautiful young women belong with beautiful young men. That is a truth I have always known, a truth I should have faced long before now."

She looked into his perfectly sculpted face. "Jesheks, beauty has nothing to do with it. Brophy and I—"

"Don't." His jaw trembled as he shook his head fiercely. "There is no need for pleasant lies between us. We both know where your heart lies; there is nothing else to say."

With a quick nod, he left her at the rail and went below. Shara stood alone for a few moments, staring at the tower. Brophy must be in it. It was not too late. He was still there. She could get there and help him. She had to believe that.

At an unspoken command from Jesheks, the weeping ones snapped to attention as the boat slid up to the dock. They jumped overboard, ropes in hand, and secured it.

Shara leapt after them, ready to run all the way to the tower.

"Wait," Jesheks called out.

She hesitated, turned. He jumped down the dock and threw aside his cloak. "Take this with you." He shrugged and a belt slipped off his shoulder. He held forth the Sword of Autumn, sheathed in its scabbard.

"Where did you get that?" Shara asked, suddenly remembering the moment when he'd saved her from Issefyn. The red flash. She'd thought it was his magic, but it had to have been the sword.

"I stole it."

"I left that with Astor to defend Ohndarien from the weeping ones!"

He shook his head, as if brushing aside a gnat. "They don't matter. You do."

Shara bit back her angry retort, let out a breath. "Thank you," she murmured, taking the sword.

"One more thing," Jesheks said.

Feeling like she would burst from the delays, Shara spared him one last glance.

"You may be able to use this, too," he said.

"What?" she asked, exasperated.

"Knowledge. I wanted to explore it with you, but . . ." He shook his head. "I know how the indentured are created, I saw it in the Siren's Blood."

"Jesheks—" she said. She looked at that far tower, aching to know what was happening.

"I believe the weeping ones can be restored."

"Do you know how?" Shara asked, pushing her impatience aside with an effort of will.

He shook his head. "No. But I am certain that their souls have not been destroyed. They are removed. They are imprisoned within the black emmeria."

Shara brought her mind to the problem at hand, wrenched it away from her worries. "Yes. And?"

"And what can be imprisoned . . ." he let the sentence trail off.

"Can be released," she said, and she understood. It was as if a white light had turned on inside her mind. "How can you be sure?"

"You've seen the swirling lights in the Siren's Blood?"

"Yes."

"Those are the souls of the freed. They are weeping ones who were released from the black emmeria. It is their stories you relive when you drink the wine."

Shara said nothing as she let the information sink in. "That means that someone has done it before."

He nodded. "Someone has already found out a way to release the souls trapped within the black emmeria. And if the black emmeria is made up of those souls, and they are all released . . ."

"No more black emmeria," Shara murmured. "But how? How were they released?"

"That is the most important question of all. If the black emmeria is nothing but a concentration of tortured souls, how did some return to the light?"

"Jesheks, do you know?" she asked. "If you know, you must tell me. It could mean—"

"I do not know." He shook his head. "I only have a theory."

"What is it?"

He looked into her eyes. His gaze was penetrating, resigned. "I assume someone did for them what you did for me."

She remained silent, remembering their night together on the Floating Palace. "I don't see how—"

"Neither do I," he said. "That is why I wanted more time."

"I have to go," she said, feeling she had delayed far too long already.

"I know."

"Are you coming with us?"

He shook his head. "I cannot."

"We could use your help if things go badly."

"If they go badly, my assistance will not matter."

She moved forward to embrace him, but she saw the alarm in his eyes and held back, taking his hand instead.

"We will finish what we started. I pro—"

He snatched his hand from her grasp, held it up in a warding gesture. "No. I don't want any obligations between us. Go. Do what you must and I will do the same."

She searched his eyes for one last moment, then turned and ran up the dock toward the silver tower in the distance.

Chapter 9

"I'm so glad I found you," Brophy said, stroking Arefaine's hair as he held her on the glowing sliver stairs. For the first time she felt right in his arms. "Everything is going to be all right."

"I thought I killed you," she murmured into his shoulder.

"I'm not so easy to kill," he said.

"And after all that . . ." she began to say, but trailed off. She let go of him, but he still held her. "Brophy," she said, her voice calm. "Let me go."

He released her, and she took a half step back. "You came here to stop me, didn't you?" Her blue eyes were filled with confusion and distrust.

"I'm here because—"

"He came here to kill you," a man's voice said.

They both spun around, and Brophy's lip curled in a sneer. The man from his dreams strode toward them down the stairs. His pale white face was framed by chin-length black curls. Thin eyes, black as night, stared down the short nose. Hatred surged in Brophy's chest. His arms and legs tensed, and the fear he had come to know so well in his dreams raced through his veins. He crouched and reached for his sword.

"I didn't come here to kill her," he said, "I came here to kill you."

"Fath—" Arefaine started. "No, Efflum. Stop this. Brophy threw down his sword."

"Well, he's picked it up again, hasn't he?"

Brophy's fingers wrapped around the pommel as he prepared to attack.

"A pathetic gesture, certainly," the Fiend continued. "You could send him to his grave with a flick of your finger."

Brophy's body ached for action, but he knew it wouldn't work. The man was an illusion. His feet made no impressions on the dusty stairs. Brophy couldn't win this battle without Arefaine. She must be made to understand.

With effort, Brophy turned his gaze away from the Fiend. "Arefaine, this thing is not your father."

"I know," she said, her brow furrowed. "My father is dead, but—"

"This is the man I told you about, from my dreams," he continued, biting out the words through clenched teeth. "You cannot believe anything he says."

"Be careful, my child," Efflum said. "Do not be seduced by this boy's promises. He came here with his Zelani. His lover waits outside to celebrate with him when we are dead. Look in his eyes and you will see the truth."

"Yours is the only death I seek, Fiend," Brophy said. "Just you."

"Brophy, please—" Arefaine whispered. "That's enough."

"How will you kill me, boy?" Efflum snapped, showing his teeth. "With your meaty fists and precious curls?"

"I said enough!" Arefaine shouted, throwing her arms outward.

An invisible weight slammed into Brophy, throwing him down the stairs. He grabbed the railing, barely catching his balance before being thrown over.

Arefaine stood alone on the steps, bent over as though exhausted. Her long dark hair hung on either side of her face. Efflum's shade was gone, banished by her magic.

"Arefaine, where is he?" Brophy asked softly, regaining his feet.

She looked down at him, her fist clenched. "Is it true, what he said?" she asked in a calm, deadly voice. "Is Shara here?"

"Where is he!?"

"He's still trapped. Trapped up there in this tree." She pointed at the thick roots.

"He can't get out?"

"Not without my help."

Brophy let out a breath and dropped his sword back on the stairs.

"Is it true, Brophy? Is Shara here?" she asked.

Brophy opened his mouth, but the words didn't come.

"You hesitate," she said, and her eyes narrowed. "She is here." Her tone was dead.

He shook his head. "I lost her. She was with me and now she's gone. But we came together. To find you."

"Find me and do what?"

He paused, letting her watch him. "What do you think I came here to do?"

Her face twisted in anguish. Closing her eyes, she put her fists to her forehead. "I don't know what to believe anymore," she murmured.

"You know what I want. I've told you."

"You want to kill him. You want to keep Efften buried forever in the past," she said, her blue eyes searing his.

"I wanted to come here with you. I wanted to stand by your side when you looked in that thing's eyes for the first time, and decide together what must be done about him."

"And what do you think should be done?" she spat.

"I want him dead."

Her eyes widened, and her nostrils flared. Her fist clenched.

"That's unfortunate, because you can't kill him."

He faced her without flinching. "No. But why would you let something like that live? How could you possibly want him free?"

She faced him, stony and unmoving.

"Arefaine," he said softly. "What can he offer you except power? But you have all the power you need. You can move empires, bring countries to war. Is that who you want to be? Is that the way you want to live your life? Alone with an army of weeping ones at your back?"

Her brows came together, but she remained as tight as a bowstring.

After a long moment he said, "I'm sorry, about what happened in the cave."

She scoffed. "Sorry that you started, or sorry that you stopped?"

He moved toward her, and she watched him coolly.

"I'm sorry I couldn't give you what you needed. If I wasn't with Shara, I would be with you. But I *am* with Shara. I will be with her for the rest of my life. It doesn't mean I don't care for you. It doesn't mean I don't love you, or that I won't fight for you."

"Fight for me?" she said, raising her eyebrow mockingly. "Is that what you're doing? I thought you were trying to seduce me, use me for your own purposes."

"I'm not trying to seduce you."

"Well, you weren't doing a very good job if you were. Mentioning your undying love for another woman is not the best pillow talk."

"Arefaine, I still care—"

"How? How can you still care for me? I tried to kill you, Brophy!" She swallowed, and finally unclenched her fist. "I might still kill you."

"Why?"

"My kindred are coming. From all over the world. Coming to this place to rebuild it. And you are standing in the way of our dreams."

"Then bring them. Let them all come. I want you to rebuild Efften. I want you to be reunited with your kin. I want you to have *your* dream. Not Efflum's."

Arefaine paused, her features softening.

"The beauty of this city is staggering. She deserves to be reborn, but you have to face reality first. You can't make this a paradise until you acknowledge the ruin we're standing in and how it got this way. The black emmeria must be destroyed. We have to clean up the mess we have made."

"Oh yes," she said sardonically, looking down at the Heartstone slung around her waist. She wanted to touch it, but she resisted the urge. "And that will be so simple, I'm sure you know exactly how to go about it."

"No. I don't. But together we will find a way."

"Oh's way? Are you his new disciple, then? Shall I slit my wrists and lock magic away forever, drain the world of what is truly spectacular?"

"No. I disagree with Oh. I disagree with them all."

"All?"

"Ohohhom, Efften, and the Silver Islands. Each was formed, in its own way, by the black emmeria. They all were presented with the same question: What should one do in the face of evil? They all chose the wrong answer. Efften saw evil as a tool. In their arrogance, they thought to tame the black emmeria, bend it to their will. They failed. The Ohohhim saw evil as an undefeatable foe and chose to run from it. They feared the temptation so much that they became something less than human. The Silver Islanders responded to evil with maniacal hatred. But hate is a part of the very thing they would destroy. Rather than find a way to defeat evil, they threw away their lives in suicidal attacks against it. Three great peoples. Three doomed choices. There has to be a fourth way."

"An Ohndarien way?" Arefaine asked.

A surge of longing flowed through Brophy at the mention of his beloved city, already lost in this ceaseless war. "Yes," he said softly. "An Ohndarien way, if you will."

Her fierce gaze faltered, and she looked at the ground. "What is the Ohndarien way?"

"You build a wall around the evil. And you stand shoulder to shoulder with your family and friends and you make sure that evil never gets out. I want to build that wall with you. I want to stand on it with you. I want you to rebuild Efften. But not as a paradise, as a prison. Ohndarien has been destroyed. So it's time to move Ohndarien here."

"So we build our own prison and live within it?"

"No. We build the prison, lock the black emmeria within it, and work together to discover how to destroy it forever."

"No one knows how to do that."

"Maybe not, but the first step is killing that thing up there."

"Killing him won't destroy the emmeria."

"No, but it's a damn good start."

Arefaine sighed. "I don't even know if I can kill him."

"Oh said you could."

"I won't do it his way. I won't kill myself."

"I wouldn't let you."

He closed the scant distance between them and took her hand. Her fingers curled lightly over his. Brophy leaned forward and kissed her very softly on the lips.

"Can you let me love you, even if it's not the way you wanted?" he asked.

She let out a little breath, and slowly nodded. "I can try."

"Then that's a start. Let's go look this thing in the face." He tugged her arm lightly, began walking up the steps. She followed him, then stopped. He pulled up short and looked down at her. Silently, with no expression on her face, she slid her arms around his neck and hugged him softly.

He responded, squeezing her to him.

"I was so in love with you," she whispered breathlessly into his ear. He drew back and kissed her, and she clung to him as though she would draw all of her dreams from his lips. His heart ached that he could give her no more than that.

"How sweet." The Fiend's oily voice drifted down the stairs. "The celibate young lovers are going to kill the vile monster locked in a cage."

Arefaine's eyes flashed as she withdrew from Brophy. "I've had enough of your lies, 'Father.'"

He shook his head, and his ghostly black curls swished across his silk robes. "Pathetic, child. I had such high hopes for you, but it appears the daughter is just like the father. You are of the lesser race after all."

"Arrogant words from a wispy husk of a man imprisoned in a tree," she said. "You are a good liar, but a very bad father. I never should have listened to you. But it's not too late to fix my error."

He chuckled, deep and throaty. "But you are mistaken, my child." He paused, watching her with a smug smile that sent a chill up Brophy's spine. "All I really needed you to do was to destroy those damnable Silver Islanders. The rest" —he nodded, never breaking eye contact— "can be accomplished by other parties."

"Other parties?"

"Of course. You don't think I would rest my entire fate in the hands of a love-starved little girl, did you? My other daughter is knocking at the door as we speak, and you, Daughter of Morgeon, are out of time."

Chapter 10

Issefyn clambered up the marble stairway toward the tower's entrance. She cradled her containment stone in one fist, clutching it to her chest. She crawled forward, one step at a time, on elbows worn raw and bloody. Her agony had become distant and dull as the emmeria poured through her in a dwindling stream, forcing her mind to endure when her heart had long since ceased beating.

She looked back and saw the wet trail she'd left up the steps. Her bowels trailed ten feet behind her, covered in sticks and leaves.

"You are almost there, Mother," Victeris said, taking the steps slowly and gracefully next to her. "All will be well when you get inside."

She clacked her teeth together in anticipation. Soon she would return to her true form. She would tower over her enemies once again. Arefaine would cower before her, begging for mercy. Brophy would writhe in pain as she crushed his chest in her fist. And Shara. She would kill Shara slowly, sending her screaming to the bottom of the ocean, dragged down by the weight of her dead lover. Her son had promised her.

She stopped at the twisted gates clotted shut with roots. One side had been wrenched open, and chunks of severed roots lay scattered across the landing. She peered inside, squinting against the dim interior. A snake pit of monstrous brown roots twisted through the room.

"What is this place?" she rasped, feeling the power warm on her face.

"All the power of Efften, waiting for you to claim it," Victeris said.

"It is at the center of all those roots. I can feel it."

"Yes, it is. Destroy the roots and it shall be yours."

Issefyn hissed. "Those roots are your prison. This is what Darius created to hold you."

"That fool could never hold me. My prison was created by another. Darius was only the turnkey."

Issefyn's wheezing laugh rasped in her raw throat. "And why would I set you free?"

"Because you'll die if you don't," the shade calmly replied as he slowly dissipated.

She reached up, her fingers twining into the filigreed door. There was a gap at the top where the roots had been cut away. She tried to pull herself up with one hand, her severed body dangling below her. It was no use. She was weakening, her life barely sustained by the power of the emmeria. She could not climb without letting go of her stone, and she would not let go of her stone.

The power beneath the roots called to her like a cool oasis in her desert of agony. She needed to get in. She uncurled her arm and pressed her stone against the largest root right in front of her. Breathing out with little more than a feeble grunt, she forced the last of the emmeria out of the stone and into the roots.

They writhed, turning black. The darkness spread outward, consuming the roots like black fire racing up a thread. The entire root structure convulsed, scattering clumps of black ooze as the roots turned to a rancid black mush. The silver doors, no longer held closed, swung inward.

Clutching the empty stone, she crawled forward on her elbows, wading through shards of wood melting into black sludge. She looked up and saw that the roots extended up the glowing tower as far as she could see. The brown roots turned black, the infection rising upwards as the putrefying roots fell apart in ragged clumps.

Issefyn ignored the fetid liquid falling around her like rain and looked to her salvation. In the very center of the tower's floor sat an oblong shape half buried under the filth from the dying roots. She crawled toward it, reaching out, feeling the inferno of ani within. She lurched closer, grappled with the smooth edges, and climbed on top of it. Her bare skin slipped across the black ooze until it touched the warm metal.

This was the source of everything. This was the breast that Efften suckled through its infancy. This was the source of Efften's might through all her glory, the seed from which an empire had sprouted. And that empire would bloom again. Her empire.

Issefyn's ravaged heart shuddered once and started beating again.

Chapter 11

"Your other daughter?" Arefaine asked, feeling a subtle shift in the energy of the tower.

"Yes, the tall queen you took as a disciple."

Brophy looked back and forth between her and her father's shade. "What's happening?" he asked. "What's he talking about?"

"The tree!" Arefaine said, rushing forward, right through the Fiend's apparition. Snatching his sword from the ground, Brophy leapt after her, sprinting up the stairs toward Efflum's prison.

"Come, my children!" the shade called after them. "Come for me!"

Arefaine's magic boiled in the air around her. It was like a living thing, and it longed for her to use it. She and Brophy flew up the stairs. Warm air rushed past them, and the putrid stench hit Arefaine like a physical blow. Her eyes burned, and she gagged on her last breath.

"What's happening?" Brophy shouted. "Is he getting loose?"

"Yes," she screamed back at him.

The cluster of roots started to quiver and then undulate. Shaking the burning tears from her eyes, she looked down and saw the massive column slowly turning black. She threw her magic against it, pushing the vile energy back.

She clenched her teeth in concentration, slowly losing ground as the roots continued to disintegrate. It wasn't just the emmeria she was fighting. Efflum had joined the struggle, throwing his will against hers.

Brophy paused by her side, uncertain what to do.

"We've got to keep going," she whispered, "up toward the light."

He grabbed her hand and led her up the stairs, hacking through the roots barring their way. He practically dragged her through the cluster of dying vegetation as she threw her will against Efflum and his black emmeria.

Within moments, Brophy had pulled her through the gap in the roots into the garden above. Arefaine panted uncontrollably, feeling like her skull would crack. She was losing. He was stronger than she was. That had never happened before.

The tree groaned as streaks of black emerged from the roots below and snaked up the trunk, zigzagging along the contours in the bark. Every place the darkness touched shriveled, created trenches in the wood.

Brophy rushed around the tree, and she struggled to follow him. He skidded to a stop in front of Efflum's desiccated form, half embedded in the trunk. Brophy raised his sword in both hands.

"No!" Arefaine put a hand on his arm. "Your sword is useless—"

Brophy shook her off and struck Efflum full force in the chest.

His weapon shattered, and Brophy pitched forward, his momentum burying the broken blade to the hilt in the dying tree.

Efflum laughed, his papery voice growing stronger. As the tree died around him, Efflum's flesh was restored. Sunken cheeks filled with vitality. Yolklike eyeballs grew and whitened, forming pupils and irises. Skinny limbs swelled, growing muscles.

"You have to go," she whispered to Brophy.

He yanked the broken blade out of the tree and whirled to face her. "What!"

"Go!" she screamed at him.

"I'm not leaving you."

Insufferably stubborn man! Her mind raced, desperate to keep the tree alive.

Efflum's desiccated cheeks were filling out as he smiled. "It seems you have misplaced your loyalties."

Brophy leaped at him again with the broken sword. Efflum's right hand lashed out, knocking him to the side.

Efflum laughed. The corpselike man was gone, transformed into the pale

Ohohhim whose form they had seen on the stairs. His wisps of tattered hair thickened, darkened, and curled along the sides of a round face.

Arefaine longed to throw her power against him, to overwhelm him as she had done with Issefyn and Jesheks, but she hesitated.

"Don't stop now, Daughter of Morgeon," Efflum said, feeling his rejuvenated face with his free hand. "Throw your power against me. Tear me limb from limb." His black eyes twinkled, and his voice dropped to a whisper. "Feed me some more."

With a growl, she threw her power into the tree, bolstering the plant's strength with her own, filling the decay with the life of her magic.

Efflum laughed. "Foolish child," he said. "You have no idea what this fight is about." He pointed a finger at Arefaine, and Brophy leapt in front of her.

"No!" Arefaine screamed, raising a shield around him.

But the attack wasn't aimed at him. Or at her.

The Heartstone exploded, the shards slicing into her side.

A blast of screams knocked her sideways, and a howling hurricane swept through the garden.

"No!" she yelled, seeing too late what Efflum was after. She threw her ani against it, shielding herself and Brophy from the gnawing hatred of the black emmeria. She clutched at the remaining containment stones in her satchel.

The howling wind whipped through the trees in the garden, killing them, melting them like wax. Efflum's prison split down the middle with a thunderous crack. Chunks of wood and bark scattered the ground as he ripped his left arm free.

"Run," she cried, imbuing herself with the Floani form. She grabbed Brophy by the arm. She had to get him out of here.

"Arefaine—"

"RUN!" she shouted, propelling him toward the stairway and sprinting after him.

Brophy leapt into the hole, and she jumped after him. They fell through disintegrating roots and landed in a heap on the silver steps. He yanked her to her feet and practically carried her down the stairs. The howling voices of the black emmeria swirled around them, rushing down the tower.

"Arefaine," Brophy yelled. "We've got to stop him!"

"Run," she said, struggling to stay on her feet. They pounded down, around and around. The howling voices slowly faded as she felt the emmeria being drawn upward. There was enough vile magic to enslave the world, and Efflum was absorbing it all.

They had nearly reached the exit when she glanced over the railing to see if the doors were clear. She saw something at the bottom of the tower. A filthy box. No, a coffin, with something crawling on top of it. The creature had two arms and a long, ragged tail. It scuttled over the lid, trying to pry it open.

Arefaine pulled up short, tugging on Brophy's arm. In horror, she stared at the creature. Lank, greasy gray hair. The wrinkled face and skinny arms. It was human, and . . .

"Issefyn?" she said.

The creature snapped its head around, staring at her with red eyes.

"You," Arefaine said as the woman rolled off the sarcophagus and scrambled toward them, dragging her severed body behind her. "You did this. You set him free."

The abomination howled at them, her face twisted into a mask of pure rage.

Brophy rushed forward, fists clenched, but Arefaine's magic reached Issefyn first, ripping through her like a thousand tiny knives. The old woman screamed for a second before her half body splattered against the wall in a black smear.

Brophy skidded to a stop, staring at the bloody wall.

"Go, just go!" Arefaine shouted, pushing him down the stairs.

He nodded, jumping the last few steps and slipped on the black slime, falling to his side. He winced as his hand was sliced by one of the thousands of crystal shards that covered the bottom of the tower. With the strength of her Floani-enhanced arms, Arefaine hauled Brophy upright and shoved him forward.

Ragged stumps of half-decayed roots protruded from the half a foot of jellied decay that filled the base of the tower. As they worked their way across the floor, another chunk of root fell from above, splattering foul muck across them.

"Out!" she said, shoving him through the open gate onto the landing. He ran down the steps and her heart twisted in her chest. Go, she thought, grabbing the gate. Go find a fourth way. An Ohndarien way.

She pushed the gate shut with a loud clang. Brophy skidded to a halt, spotted her immediately, and charged back up the stairs.

She quickly laced the gate with a simple spell, the illuminated silver instantly reacting to her wishes. She locked it tighter than the roots ever could have, locked it against any mortal who wanted to enter, and against any sorcerer who wanted to leave.

"Arefaine!" Brophy slammed into the gate. He shook them, his muscles standing out in his arms, but the bars didn't budge.

"What are you doing?" he yelled.

Now she could relax. Now she need not rush. Her destiny was already heading down the stairs. All she had to do was wait for it.

She reached out and touched Brophy's fingers where they tried to rip the gate from the wall. "Thank you, Brophy. Thank you for coming here, for helping me make this decision."

"No," he grunted, trying to pry the bars apart with his bare hands. His face turned red as he strained. The silver bit into his hands, and blood seeped from his cut palm. "No!" He let go and slammed his fists against the bars. "Arefaine, open the damned doors!"

"Brophy, please," she said, reaching out through the gate for his hand. "Stop."

"Open the doors!" he screamed.

"Go back to Ohndarien," she said. "Go back to Shara and . . ." She couldn't say it. "This is my battle. Everyone knew it. Everyone in the world except me."

"Let me help you."

Arefaine shook her head. "There is nothing more for you to do."

He finally stopped straining against the magical gates, and took her hand. "Arefaine, don't do this. Oh was wrong. You weren't meant to be a sacrifice. You were meant to live and to love and—" he choked.

"I have lived," she whispered. "And loved, if only for a moment. It is enough. It will have to be enough."

"Arefaine!"

"I could never have done this without you."

"AREFAINE!" He threw himself against the gate.

She turned and walked back into the tower.

Chapter 12

A refaine waded through the ankle-deep sludge of decay toward the stairway. She paused as Efflum came into view. He descended regally, robes as black and smooth as oil covering his body from chin to feet. He walked like a monk, a holy man on a sacred pilgrimage, assured of the righteousness of his cause.

She narrowed her eyes, letting her magic pull away his veils, revealing him for what he really was. His glamour vanished. He was healthy and whole, but his hair was straggly, his face scraped, and his body naked except for the dirt and grime.

That is the first truth I've wrenched from you, she thought.

"The lover screams for his beloved," Efflum taunted as he descended the stairs. "Or should I say, 'The liar screams for his second choice.'" He chuckled.

Arefaine's lips tightened into a line. All her life she'd wondered when and how she should use her power. As a child, she'd had nightmares of losing control, hurting and killing people in fits of rage. She had held herself back ever since, never truly letting go until that day with Brophy on the bridge. Even then she could have done more, could have taken down the whole mountainside if she'd wanted to.

But she was meant for this battle. For the first time in her life, she could unleash everything locked inside her for all these years.

"You can still join me, Arefaine," he commanded. "I am a forgiving parent."

"I have every intention of joining you," she said. "We'll be staying in this tower together for quite some time."

Efflum sneered, stepping between her and Oh's coffin. "Open the gate," he said. She saw his magic flare as he absorbed the raw emmeria swirling all around them, an unending torrent of screaming voices. "Let loose your little spell and let us enter Efften as we were meant to. As mentor and pupil."

"I was meant to finish what my father started three hundred years ago."

His expression soured, and he shook his head. "Your father was a fool. And, apparently, so are you."

With a striking motion, he swatted at her like she was a fly.

Arefaine cried out as the force threw her across the room, slamming her against the wall. Her arm snapped, and she screamed.

He'd smashed through her defenses like they were paper. He was no longer the feeble creature trapped in the tree. He was swimming in an ocean of black emmeria. He had become one with it.

She struggled to her knees, bringing her limp arm around front, trying to force it to work.

"Let the gate go," Efflum said, his eyes cold.

Arefaine shook her head, gathering what power she could. Again, Efflum gestured, and his magic slammed into the locked gates. She gasped as the backlash hit her. Something snapped deep within her chest, and for a moment she was certain she would be ripped in half.

The onslaught went on and on. Efflum clenched his fist and threw all the energy in the room at the gates. The thin silver warped and bowed out toward Brophy as he yelled for her on the other side. The stone near one of the hinges cracked, sending a jagged fracture up the tower like a bolt of lightning. She tried to resist, tried to push back, but didn't know how. Arefaine gritted her teeth, but a whimper escaped her. Her arm was in agony.

Finally Efflum relaxed his clenched fist, the assault ebbed, and he massaged his fingers as if he'd just hurt himself.

"I am impressed," he said with a slight smile. "That attack should have done to you what you did to Issefyn." He indicated the bloody smear on the tower wall. "You would have made an excellent pupil."

"I suppose I should be flattered," she gasped, trying not to show how her entire body was shaking.

"Arefaine!" Brophy shouted from the gate. "By the Seasons, let me in! Let me help you!"

She flicked a quick gaze over her shoulder, but she couldn't look him in the face, not now.

Efflum turned from the gate and threw his might against the cracked wall. The tower groaned with the thunderous blow. Arefaine tried to rise to her feet and slipped in the black sludge.

Do not despair, brave child. All will be well. A voice floated into her mind unbidden. Not her voice and not Brophy's.

There was no one else in the ichor-splattered interior of the tower. Who . . . ?

And then she saw something. The lid of the silver coffin had shifted. A wisp of golden vapor drifted through the gap.

Oh? she asked in her mind.

Yes, child. I am with you now, here at the end.

Efflum continued his assault on the tower, trying to blast his way to freedom.

I can't beat him, she said. *He's too powerful.*

You are not as weak as you fear, and he is not as strong. I have known this man since he was a boy. His mind is fearsome, but his heart is weak. Hold a mirror up to him, and he will shatter.

How?

Watch. Wait for your moment.

The golden vapor over Oh's coffin spun in a circle, coalescing into a pale ghost. The figure was tall, with long robes like Efflum. He smiled gently. It was a sad smile, born of vision, suffering, and a thousand hard choices. She saw the emperor in it. She saw Dewland and Father Lewlem. It was Oh, the first mage, the Father Ohohhom, after all these years.

Efflum noticed Arefaine's glance and turned to see what she was looking at.

"My old friend," Oh said.

Efflum sneered. "So, you have poked your head out of your tomb at last."

"We have lived long enough, you and I," Oh said calmly. "It is time for the two of us and our old hatred to pass from this world."

"Just as you let my wife pass from this world," Efflum spat. "Remember, *Father*, you drove me to these shores. You made my hate."

"No, the hatred you feel is of your own making," Oh said. "You were the first man to defile the sacred fire. You were the first to use it to enslave, to destroy. Your corruption brought this misery to the world."

Efflum scoffed. "You chastise me? You, who wiped out whole armies in the name of peace and wisdom!"

"I did. To my shame. But I repented. I turned away power, and you built an empire upon its abuses."

"You didn't repent, you *ran* away!" Efflum said. "You became so terrified, you couldn't even save a dying friend."

Oh lowered his misty head. "No, I could have saved Zelew, but I knew she wanted to die."

"Liar!" Efflum shouted.

Oh folded his ghostly hands within his ghostly robes. "Didn't you realize how much the power changed you, lessened you? You have mourned your wife's death for a thousand years, but you never noticed that she stopped loving you long before she died."

"You talk to me of love? You've never loved anyone!"

"You remember the first day you called forth the emmeria?" Oh said, ignoring him. "You corrupted the falcon."

"I remember that you exulted in the discovery!"

"I did, but Zelew did not. The two of you fought. You struck her."

"Be careful, old ghost," Efflum said, gathering power for another attack.

"She never looked upon you as she had before, did she? She stayed by your side, but only to placate you, to keep you calm so that you would do no more damage."

Efflum threw his might against the ethereal form. The sarcophagus slid across the floor, sending up a geyser of black ooze before slamming into the far wall. Oh's form faded, flickering in the howling wind. He held up a ghostly hand, but it did nothing against the wave of tainted ani that was washing over him. The lid of his coffin was thrown open and the dust within was scattered by the baleful hurricane. In seconds the golden light faded to nothing, and Arefaine knew that Father Oh was no more.

Once again she was all alone in the howling darkness.

Efflum turned to her, his dark eyes wild with triumph. The wind whipping through the tower died down as his temper faded.

"Do you doubt me now, child," he said, his thin hair fluttering atop his papery scalp. "Enough of this nonsense. You have no hope of stopping me. Open the door. Set me free."

Arefaine took a deep breath and wrapped her arms around her body, holding her ribs where something had ripped deep inside of her. She felt something in the pocket of her robe and reached inside to grasp the shard of red diamond that held Brophy's father's soul.

A flicker of memory came to Arefaine, an image of Brophy's face as he looked at her with pity and horror in Oh's cave.

Swallowing down the taste of blood, she pushed off the wall and rose to her feet. "Oh was right. Zelew stopped loving you the day you discovered the emmeria, didn't she?" Arefaine said. "You crossed a line and she could never forgive you."

"You know nothing of such things," Efflum hissed.

"From that moment on," Arefaine continued, "she looked upon you with nothing but pity. You had become a broken thing she could not fix, a well of hatred that she tried to fill until it bled her dry and she longed for death."

Efflum stared at her, his hands curled into claws.

"You are to blame for your wife's death," Arefaine said. "Aren't you? All these years, you've blamed Oh for the crime, but you are the one who destroyed her—"

"Enough!" Efflum yelled, flinging a gout of black sludge away from himself, splattering the walls.

Arefaine backed up, continuing to press him. "And in your grief over what you'd done, you committed that same crime over and over, destroying lives, shattering souls until someone finally stopped you. Until *my father* stopped you."

Efflum started toward her, his teeth bared.

"Is that why you want a family so badly?" Arefaine shouted over the roar. "Because you polluted the only one you ever had?"

The archmage screamed and a gout of black emmeria burst from his lips. It rushed through the tower like a tornado, picking up rotten roots and broken crystal shards and flinging them into the air.

She threw herself back, trying to shield herself. She could block the biting, chewing presence of the black emmeria, but the hard crystals slashed at her. The entire tower swirled with putrid brown chunks and deadly shards spinning through the air. All the black emmeria in the tower flowed through Efflum, rushing through his hands and cycling back to him in an endless torrent.

Arefaine huddled into a ball, trying to protect her chest, face, and throat. The crystals flayed her skin, pinning her against the side of the tower. She clung to Brydeon's heartstone, desperate to outlast the storm because she finally knew what to do.

She knew how to defeat Efflum.

Shara sprinted up the steps, shouting at Brophy. He stood at the top, gripping the silver gates that barred the tower's entrance, shaking them as he yelled. Beyond the gates, a storm raged inside the tower.

"What's happening?" she shouted above the roar.

He turned, eyes wide. "Shara!" he shouted as she rushed into his arms. "You've got to help Arefaine," he yelled into her ear. "He's killing her."

Shara touched the gate, feeling the immense power raging on the other side.

"What's happening," she shouted again.

"Efflum's escaped! I've got to get in there."

Shara shook her head. "If I open these doors, it will be the Nightmare Battle all over again."

"But we have to help her!"

Shara stared through the gaps in the gate, trying to see past the swirling debris. A filthy, half-naked man stood in the center of the tower channeling an incredible amount of black emmeria. He flung it at Arefaine as she huddled against the wall. The poor girl was barely conscious.

"By the Seasons!" Shara gasped. "How can she survive—" Her words were cut off as the filthy madman turned from Arefaine and flung his fury at the tower's gates.

A tremendous force slammed into the side of the tower, throwing Brophy backward. The silver vines turned black. The lock sagged outward, melting like wax.

"No!" Shara shouted, rushing forward and throwing her shoulder against the gates. They clanged shut again. She threw her ani into the enchanted metal to bolster Arefaine's spell.

Efflum battered the gates again. The blow rebounded into Shara as if she'd been hit in the chest with a hammer. She cried out, sinking to her knees. Brophy caught her, lifting her back to her feet.

"What happened?" he yelled in her ear.

"Arefaine's dying," she yelled back. "She can't hold the gate."

Forcing her clenched eyes open, Shara peered into the whirling storm. A dark silhouette rose up in front of her. Glowing eyes, wisps of black curly hair on a white scalp.

"Let go of the door, child," Efflum said. "Help me, and I will spare you."

Shara said nothing, concentrated on holding him in.

"I'm going to ask you one more time to step aside," Efflum said. "I have no desire to spill illuminated blood, but my patience is at an end."

Shara noticed something out of the corner of her eye, but turned away, forcing herself to meet Efflum's gaze. Brophy shifted behind her, touching her hip. The Sword of Autumn slipped free of its scabbard. Arefaine had risen to her feet and was sneaking up behind Efflum.

"You'll spare our lives if I let you pass?" Shara asked.

Efflum nodded.

"Both of us?"

He nodded again.

Arefaine raised her hand to strike. Something glittered in her hand.

Brophy leaped forward.

He thrust the blade through the bars all the way to the hilt. Efflum leapt back. Right into Arefaine.

She plunged a shard of red crystal into his back. Red and black light exploded in the heart of the tower. Efflum screamed.

Shara turned away, blinded by the light. When she looked back, Efflum was stumbling backward, a gaping hole where his arm and shoulder used to be.

He fell to his knees, clutching the wound. Muck sprayed the walls. Crystals hit the ground, shattering and skidding to a stop.

"I'll kill you all!" he screamed.

As he spoke, the ragged ends of his torn flesh expanded and black emmeria flooded the wound, repairing the damage.

Arefaine reached out two hands toward him. Shara felt a powerful shift in the ani as a faint bubble surrounded Efflum, barely visible. The howling black emmeria still raced inside the tower's confines, but it flowed around Efflum like a river around a stone.

Fighting at the pain in her head, Shara realized what Arefaine had done. There was a perfect sphere around Efflum, a void bereft of black emmeria.

"It won't save you," Efflum cried, his voice thin. He turned, struggled to his feet. His half–re-formed arm hung limp at his side.

Brophy put his hands on the bars. "What is she doing?" he asked.

"Shielding him from the black emmeria," Shara answered. "Starving him."

Brophy nodded. "She did that with me. In Oh's cave. She took the black emmeria away from me."

Arefaine stood rigid in front of Efflum, all of her will bent on keeping him from his power source.

"He can't access the magical forms," Shara said. "Zelani, Floani, Necani, any of them. They're all based on being human, on being alive."

Gaping like a fish, Efflum shuffled toward Arefaine. She had her eyes clamped shut in her struggle. He reached out with his remaining hand and grappled at her throat.

"Arefaine!" Brophy warned.

"Shhhh," Shara said, putting a hand on him. "She knows where he is. She can't let the spell go."

"But he's—"

"Shhh!" Shara said fiercely, all her energy focused on keeping the damaged gates closed.

Efflum lifted Arefaine off the ground and lurched toward the wall, slamming her against it.

Brophy's hands tightened on the bars.

Arefaine tensed, but she didn't fight back. Efflum squeezed as hard as he could, his chalky face contorting with the effort. Arefaine's lacerated face turned red, but she kept her eyes closed. The bubble around her enemy did not waver.

Slowly, she slid down the wall to her feet as Efflum's strength flagged.

"Coward," he croaked as his arm gave out, and he collapsed against her. He fell to the ground as she backed away. "You traitor," he gasped, crawling toward her with one arm. "Betrayed us all . . ." His muscles shrank as his body wasted away to bone, sinew, and papery skin. His eyes retracted into his skull, shriveling to sallow yellow raisins dangling in their sockets. "Illuminated blood grown so thin . . ." He tried to push himself forward, and his left hand crumbled away to powder. He looked at the stump of his arm in horror. Skin flaked off his face. His jaw broke loose on one side and fell away from his neck. He croaked something unintelligible.

Arefaine opened her pale blue eyes. "Die," she whispered.

Efflum exploded in a silent puff of dust, and the bits drifted to the ground.

Arefaine slumped to her knees, holding the bubble around the dust until it settled. Shara felt her release her spell. The dust was immediately swept away in the swirling storm.

"Is he dead?" Brophy asked.

Shara nodded. "He's dead. He's finally dead."

Brophy's heart pounded in his chest as he called out to Arefaine, but she didn't answer. The battered sorceress stayed on her knees, cradling her broken arm and sucking in breath after breath as the black emmeria shrieked around her. Her pale skin was scraped raw by the storm of crystal shards and she could barely hold herself upright.

"Shara," Brophy insisted, shaking the gate lightly. "You have to let us in."

"I can't," she replied. "I don't think I could hold back that much black emmeria, even for a moment."

"She's dying," he insisted. "We have to get her out of there."

Shara looked at him, her lips curled in a little frown.

"We have to try," he said, taking her hand.

Shara took a deep breath, wincing as she did, and then nodded. Brophy could feel the ani shift around him.

Arefaine's head jerked up. She pointed at the gates and the blackened silver began to glow. "No!" she croaked.

"Arefaine—" Shara began.

"No," Arefaine said again, lurching forward. "Not yet."

"What? What is she doing?" Brophy asked.

Shara closed her eyes and yanked on the gates. "She's locked them," she said through gritted teeth.

Arefaine limped toward the silver coffin.

"He's dead," Brophy shouted. "Let us in."

Brophy watched in horror as the lid of the coffin slowly opened of its own accord. Arefaine knelt before it and put her hands on the edge.

The sound of screaming rose to a crescendo and began spinning about the room. Arefaine raised her hands, and the howling began to focus and flow into the coffin. Screaming voices and blinding lights swirled into a little tornado that disappeared into the shadowed interior of the silver box. The voices grew louder and louder as they were concentrated. Brophy covered his ears, feeling like his skull would split. "What are you doing?" he screamed, unable to hear his own voice.

And then the lid slammed shut. The tower was plunged into darkness and utter silence. The only thing Brophy could hear was the ringing in his own ears.

Arefaine staggered forward, collapsing on top of the coffin.

"Arefaine?" Brophy called.

She hesitated for a moment before turning toward him. Her tangled hair hung in her face, but he could see her eyes in the darkness like pinpoints of glowing ice. A small smile crossed her face.

"Brophy," she breathed, as if she'd forgotten he was there.

"You did it," he said, his heart thumping against his chest as he reached through the gate, holding his hand out to her.

"Not—" she said, breathing several times. "Not yet."

"Arefaine—"

"Good-bye, Brophy." She turned away from him and pressed her palms on the lid of the coffin, as though she would hold it shut with her weight. She reached into her sleeve and withdrew a tiny silver dagger.

Brophy's chest seized. "No!" he shouted. "Not this way! There's another way!"

"There is no other way," she murmured, so softly he could barely hear her.

"Shara, do something!" he said.

"I'm trying!" Shara's face was a tight mask of concentration as she held the bars, trying to undo Arefaine's spell.

Arefaine raised her arm, exposing her wrist. She placed the dagger against her skin and slowly drew it down. Blood spilled down her arm from palm to elbow. She switched the dagger to her other hand and grimaced as she sliced open her other wrist.

Her blood poured onto the coffin. It gushed from her, soaking into the caked dirt and spilling onto the floor. Then the crimson splash began to bubble. It sizzled and dried. Flakes floated upward and disintegrated, turning into puffs of red smoke, and then rainbow lights.

Arefaine slumped forward, spreading her body out on the coffin as her limbs shriveled, as if the searing-hot coffin were sucking all the water from her flesh.

"Please, no," Brophy said in a hoarse voice.

Arefaine's body curled in upon itself like burning paper, and then she was still. The rainbow lights swirled around her desiccated body and the coffin like a cocoon, closer and closer, and then joined with the silver surface. Waves of colors ran across the silver, back and forth, as if below the surface. The silver seemed to run molten, obliterating the seam between lid and coffin, making the thing whole.

"Arefaine!" Brophy screamed, slamming himself against the doors. They gave way suddenly, and he stumbled into the room, falling to his knees.

He lunged through the sludge until he reached the coffin. He reached out a trembling hand and touched her blackened, shriveled shoulder. Her entire body crumbled, turning to dust in his hands.

Chapter 13

rophy!" Shara's voice broke the silence. The tower rumbled ominously.

He said nothing, and turned his face away from her, away from the coffin. Images swam through his mind. He remembered when he first saw Arefaine as a baby, cradled in Shara's arms as she turned the handle of the music box. He thought of the first moment Arefaine had kissed him. He remembered the joy in their embrace when he finally found her on the tower stairs.

He clenched his fist, needing to grab something, needing to hit something. "Why?" he shouted. "Why?"

"No living person could hold that storm back forever," Shara said, her hand on his shoulder. "Not even her."

Brophy pressed his palms against his eyes, shaking his head.

A grinding sound, like two stones being rubbed together, echoed through the tower.

"Brophy," Shara said, her voice suddenly sharp. "We've got to get out of here."

He glanced up. The walls of the tower were crisscrossed by a spiderweb of cracks. The structure groaned and a small chunk of stone crashed to the ground next to him.

Shara shook him. Brophy looked at her in a daze.

"The tower is coming down!" she screamed as another plummeting rock shattered on the tower floor. "We have to get her out of here! Now!"

Brophy jumped to his feet and grabbed hold of the coffin. He pushed with all his might, but it didn't budge. He tried again, wondering why he was so weak. He tried to call on the anger, the bottomless well of rage that had fueled him for so long. But it was gone. The black emmeria was gone.

Shara leapt to help him. Taking a deep breath, she grunted and drove her shoulder into the coffin. Together, they yanked it a scant foot through the sludge.

A cracked stone smashed into the coffin. A chunk of wall crashed to the ground just behind him.

"Go," Shara yelled. "RUN!"

Brophy spun and lunged for the door as broken masonry crumbled all around them. A chunk struck Shara on the head, knocking her down.

"Shara!" Brophy ran back. Slipping in the sludge, he grabbed his lover and threw her over his shoulder. The tower ground and popped, sagging to the side, as the entranceway crumbled. Brophy weaved, barely avoiding a stone the size of a horse. Its impact exploded outward, and tiny bits of rock cut into him like knives.

He leapt for the last sliver of daylight, bounced off a rock and spun around—

—and he was out, tumbling onto the landing. Rolling to his feet, he raced down the stairs as the whole tower came down, silver and stone exploding outward, dust shooting upward into the sky.

Shara coughed, lost in a billowing cloud of white dust. She struggled to sit up.

"Are you all right?" Brophy asked.

Shara nodded, reaching out, touching his face. They couldn't see each other through all the billowing dust.

The shocking reality of what had happened filled her.

"The coffin," Brophy said, as though reading her thoughts. "Could it survive—"

A distant howling answered his question, and dread raced through her limbs like ice water. The two of them jumped to their feet.

A stiff breeze blew away the swirling dust, giving Shara a brief glimpse of the collapsed tower. The keening wind grew louder and louder until—

The rubble exploded, throwing silver chunks of stone into the sky. A spire of blue flame shot skyward and bloomed like a flower.

Brophy knocked Shara sideways and threw himself over her body.

Silver chunks of stone and twisted steel flew out of the blast, crashing into buildings, cracking the streets. A tornado of energy whirled upward, blue and black colors mixing, intertwining, fighting. The black grew and grew, and soon the blue was gone.

"Come on!" Brophy shouted, hauling Shara to her feet.

They raced down the street, but the wind caught them, spun them up, and tumbled them to the ground. Shara screamed denial as the shock wave hit her, tearing her from Brophy's grasp. It swept them both along like fallen leaves. She winged out her arms, and her fingers found a crack between cobblestones. Gritting her teeth, she held herself against the storm. She felt the acid bites of the black emmeria on her arms, her face. The howling voices on the wind drowned out all sound. Everything around her turned black: streets, buildings, fountains, walkways. The jungle withered and died. The air darkened as if the black emmeria had stained the very sky.

Through the gray wind, Shara saw Brophy pinned against a wall across the street. His eyes were shut tight, and he held desperately to the Sword of Autumn as his face slowly turned black. The red light of his heartstone faded in the growing darkness.

Shara let go and the wind blew her to him. She braced herself against the stone and grappled for his hand. The corruption was devouring them both, but she clung to the Sword of Autumn and together they fought the infection. With a shout, Shara thrust the black emmeria from Brophy's body and formed a bubble of protection around the two of them, forcing the wind to either side. Arefaine had just given her life to keep this storm at bay, her life's blood turning Oh's coffin into a second Heartstone, but even her magic could not help a simple silver box survive that much falling stone. It was all for nothing, everything they had ever done, all for nothing.

Brophy shouted, snapping Shara out of her daze, but she couldn't hear what he said. He pointed toward the harbor, and she nodded.

Shara didn't know what hope there was, but she turned their sluggish feet toward the ocean, and they ran.

The world had become a horror. Jungle trees twisted and blackened. Grass became writhing worms that bit at their shoes as they ran. Fern fronds became black whips, bent on snaring them.

They skidded to a stop at the dock, and watched the dark storm spreading across the face of the ocean, racing toward the horizon.

"It's everywhere," Shara said. "There's nowhere to go."

Brophy squeezed her hand as they spun around, seeing the same devastation everywhere they looked.

A sudden blinding light threw back the darkness. Shara spun around, looking north. A rainbow-colored dome rose out of the ocean like a bubble and expanded outward filling the horizon.

"What is that?" Brophy yelled.

"That was where the sea battle took place," Shara said.

Brophy nodded. "The Islanders," he whispered.

Shara gasped. "Light emmeria," she said, recalling the Silver Islanders' exploding weapons, remembering what one of those arrows had done to the corrupted Issefyn's arm. "It has to be the light emmeria. Reef said they had a weapon to fight the emmeria, but they didn't have enough."

Brophy stared at the horizon.

A haze of crackling lightning arced around the growing bubble of swirling colors. It raced toward them, eating the black emmeria as it came.

"What do we do?" Brophy asked, holding the Sword of Autumn up and stepping in front of Shara.

She shook her head, her eyes wide. "I don't know."

The rainbow bubble expanded until it reached the clouds, then it faltered. As quickly as it had come, it collapsed, devoured by the howling darkness.

Shara fought to settle her mind and direct her thoughts. Her magic danced around them, but she had no idea what she would do next.

Brophy held the Sword of Autumn in both hands. The howling voices were gone, fled to the far corners of the world. The bright, sizzling light show had passed, but in its wake, sweltering dots remained in his vision.

"Shara?" he murmured.

"I'm here," she said, and her hand gripped his.

His vision slowly returned, revealing a bleak world. The dock was still slick with black ooze. Trees hunched at the edge of the beach, shivering and fighting to get free of the ground. Gnarled limbs quested out, scrabbling at the sand. One of the trees pulled its roots out of the ground, and it crawled toward them like a giant crab.

"You should have listened to me," came a high-pitched voice from farther along the shore. Brophy and Shara both spun around.

"Jesheks?" Shara stared at the figure that walked toward them. The man was almost six feet tall with a long mane of white hair and skin as pale as chalk. He wore a Physendrian robe that had been tattered to rags, and his pink eyes squinted in the gloom.

Brophy moved between Shara and the stranger.

"The emmeria's escaped," Shara said. "All of it."

"I know," the stranger replied.

"We have to stop it," Shara said.

"We will." The albino reached a hand toward her face. Shara screamed, clutching at her chest.

"What are you doing?" Brophy shouted.

"Becoming the man she taught me to be," he said grimly.

Brophy yanked Shara away and leveled his blade at the man's face. Her eyes had turned black, and thick tears welled in the corners.

With an animal roar, Brophy launched himself at the evil mage.

"Jesheks!" Shara screamed, fighting to protect herself, but the albino wasn't there.

She gasped for breath. A writhing mass pressed down on her, crushing her from all sides. Stale breath and human sweat assailed her nostrils. A thousand cries of anguish flooded her ears. An elbow slammed into her eye, and she shouted. A knee slammed into her gut, and she twisted. Scant light illuminated an ocean of squirming bodies. Hot, slick flesh pressed against her from above and below. She was drowning, buried in naked human bodies.

Pale skin. Brown skin. Black skin. All fighting, throttling one another. She squirmed, trying to escape, but there was nowhere to go. A meaty hand grabbed her face, pushed her downward. Her neck bent sideways, and she screamed. Other hands grabbed her shoulders and her arms, twisting and pushing.

No!

She fought. They forced her down, but she had to get up, had to get out, to the air above. She shrieked, grabbing hands, pinching, scratching, whatever she could do to claw her way upward. They fought her, but she twisted fingers and broke them. She drew blood with her nails and reveled in the screams that followed.

Someone poked her eye and tried to gouge it out. She turned her head away, and a fingernail raked her scalp. She grabbed the man's testicles and pulled. He howled, and she climbed past him, higher into the squirming throng of bodies.

She moved toward the top, viciously fighting for every inch. But she never reached it. There was no top. There was no bottom.

"Let me out," she said. "Let me out!" She scraped at a woman near her, who howled at the pain.

"Let me out!" the woman shouted back, grabbing Shara's hair and pulling.

"Let me out!" another voice echoed, and a hundred more after.

Jesheks worked his jaw, testing to see if it was broken. He swirled the pain inside his head and added it to his pool of ani.

In front of him, Brophy stood still, panting as the black tears formed on his cheeks. The young man was faster than he'd expected. Much faster.

And stronger, Jesheks thought, feeding off the pain. It had been a wicked punch. But satisfying.

So satisfying.

Fingernails raked across Shara's forehead, going for her eyes again. She grabbed a wrist, but it slipped free. It was the same tattooed man as before. Baring her teeth, she fought her way toward him. He wanted to blind her! She caught hold of his ankle as he tried to get away. He dragged her through arms, torsos, legs. But she wasn't letting him go. He'd pay for what he'd tried to do.

An arm slid over her breast and hooked under her armpit. It was iron strong, and it yanked her back. She lost her grip on the tattooed man's ankle.

"No!" she screamed as muscular bronze fingers dug into her skin. She grabbed them and scratched, trying to pry the fingers off her breast. He pulled her to him, his hairy, sweat-slicked chest sliding across her back. Shara turned and sank her teeth into his flesh as blood welled up in her mouth.

He let go and she turned to punch the man, but he had begun attacking someone else. Shara twisted, suddenly without an enemy, and realized that she had fought her way to the surface.

The sky above was a bloody purple, and lightning forked back and forth constantly, thunder booming. The sea of writhing bodies went on forever, stretched into darkness in all directions. Vague memories spun through her mind, overwhelmed and fragmented by the screaming voices and distant thunder.

Shara closed her eyes and fought to block everything out.

Breathe, she thought. *Breathe. Regain your wits.*

She pulled the thick, putrid air into her lungs and pushed it out, tried to establish a cycle of breathing. The people below her pinched her, grabbed her hair, pulled her down. But she kept breathing through her fear and rage, turning the pain into power.

Lashing out at those around her, Shara fought to stay on the surface. She looked over the struggling sea of humanity. This should be familiar. She should know where she was.

All around her she saw more bodies falling from the dark sky. A large man hit the pile just a few feet away, clubbing anyone within reach.

The thought brought an image to her mind. Pale skin, red eyes. She held on to the image, swimming toward it in her mind, fighting to understand. And then she knew.

I'm lost in the black emmeria, she thought. *I'm a weeping one.*

She remembered Jesheks reaching for her chest, yanking something out. *He sent me here. To hate. To fear.*

To her left, the large newcomer fought like a lion. The screams of the wounded surrounded him. Shara watched him, trying to pierce this veil, trying to see the truth.

Despair spread through her heart like winter. For a flickering instant she knew what she had to do, and then it was gone. She clenched her teeth. The thought was so hard to hold. "I hate this place," she cried.

"I hate this place!" a woman screamed behind her, clutching her head.

"I hate this place!" a man echoed in the distance.

No, she thought. *Fight it. Use the pain.*

Again she looked at the writhing arms and legs, tried to see true.

The newcomer still maintained his perch atop everyone, clawing and kicking. A mass of people had pushed him up, creating a little mountain. The harder he fought, the more others seemed drawn to him.

And then Shara saw his face.

"Brophy!" she shouted, but he was lost in battle and didn't hear her.

He punched a burly man in the face again and again until his foe toppled unconscious down the squirming hill. Two women grabbed Brophy's arms, and he elbowed the first in the face, twisted free of the next. Another man surfaced and grabbed Brophy's head, pulled him painfully backward. Brophy spun, thrusting both thumbs into the man's eyes, knocking him away.

She stared at him, knowing he would never give up. He had never quit in his entire life.

Love for him flickered inside her.

Brophy snarled, threw another screaming man off his mountain.

All we wanted was our little cottage. Fresh mornings on the sea. Love-making at night. Candles burning next to our bed.

Her tortured mind eased for one scant moment, thinking of that beautiful possibility.

And suddenly Shara realized that no one was hitting her.

Jesheks stood at the edge of the dock watching the horizon, waiting for the end of the world—or its salvation.

Shara lay across his arms. His new arms. The arms he had sculpted for her.

He looked down at her body. Her dress was filthy, covered with black slime. The black emmeria clung to the fabric, plastering it against the curves of her body. Her chest rose and fell rapidly as she panted.

"It's the only way I knew to save you," he told her unblinking black eyes. "The only way for you to save us all."

Jesheks had seen the distant explosion. He'd known what it meant, and what was coming.

The Kherish mage closed his eyes, not wanting to see Shara this way. Slowly, painfully, he let the last vestiges of hope drain from his body and float away.

Ever since he'd drunk the Siren's Blood, he had known the part Shara had to play. For far too long he had lied to himself, pretending that he was the one meant to stand by her side on this darkest of days. But Shara was not meant for him.

The pain of knowing that he was not the one whom she loved burned within him. But it was a sweet pain. The sweetest pain of all. That was all one could ask for.

Jesheks opened his eyes and looked out into the harbor. The water was lowering. It was slow at first, then quicker, as if something were sucking it away. Slimy seaweed clung to the sand as the ocean pulled back. In moments, a vast complex of black, corrupted coral appeared, its twisting structure glistening in the sun. Jesheks flicked a gaze upward, squinting.

Then he saw the wave.

Fear blossomed within him, and he breathed through it, tasting his own death at long last. The Islanders' light emmeria had exploded, and the ocean had responded in the only way it knew.

The wave drew closer, cresting as it rose over the horizon. A gale-force wind rushed before it, sweeping into the harbor and nearly knocking him backward.

The wave, ten times the height of a man, would only be a few minutes behind it.

Setting Shara on her feet, he touched his forehead to hers. Her horrid panting breath was hot on his cheek.

"Good-bye, my love," he said. "You are the best and worst thing that ever happened to me."

Chapter 14

Vinghelt clutched the wheel, limping his vessel eastward. Something had gone horribly wrong. His Fessa-blessed kinsmen had suddenly stopped obeying his commands. They all stood still on the deck and stared at nothing, useless as cordwood.

The goddess had abandoned him. He kept calling her, but she would not answer. He had nearly reached Ohndarien to begin his new life in her service when all of his men suddenly stopped moving. Just an hour ago he'd been ready to reclaim the walled city and then push south to solidify control of the Summer Deserts. And then he would look to the west, return to his native Efften, and continue his reign from the City of Dreams. But then everything had come crashing down.

Fessa had abandoned her children.

A sudden wind slammed into the side of the ship, nearly sweeping him overboard. Vinghelt clung to the wheel as the vessel listed hard to port. Sails were ripped from their moorings and fluttered madly in the breeze. Heart in his throat, he spun the wheel, turning away from the wind before the ship capsized.

When the ship had righted herself, Vinghelt spun around. His jaw dropped. His bladder let loose, and warm urine seeped down his breeches.

"Fessa, no!" he cried.

A tidal wave was growing on the horizon, the crest of it higher than his mast. "I did nothing but serve you!" he cried. "It was all for your glory! All for the love of your children!"

He closed his eyes and the wave engulfed him.

Chapter 15

Shara looked down, astonished to find that she was slowly rising above the mass of writhing bodies. Someone leapt out of the sea of tormented souls and grabbed her foot, but his grip slipped and he fell back with all the others.

She held on to her thoughts of Brophy and their little island, their cabin completed, the door closing slowly as they fell into each other's arms.

She looked around for Brophy and saw him just below her. His arms rose and fell as he laid about him. He fought more furiously than anyone. Such passion. Such strength. Such fire.

"Brophy," she called to him, knowing he couldn't hear her above the wailing, the thunder. She floated toward him, her soul-body obeying the commands of her will.

She reached out to touch him lightly on the shoulder.

He turned and slugged her in the face.

Pain exploded, and she fell back, sucked down into the mass of flesh. Blood streamed down her face.

"No," she whispered, fighting the arms dragging her under. They pulled harder, pushing her underneath them. "No," she said again, fighting the fear bubbling up within her.

This is the realm of spirit, she reminded herself. *What you think becomes real.*

She pushed away her anger. She took their gouges and scrapes. She let the hands and feet, elbows and teeth do what they wanted, and she focused on Brophy.

Again she rose. Out of the human sea, floating alongside him. She came up softly behind him and wrapped her arms around his great chest.

Calm, she thought.

His hands scrabbled behind himself, grabbed her arm, twisted. Pain fired through her, and she took it, using the Necani Jesheks had taught her. The more he tore at her, the stronger she became, holding him tight.

The other lost souls latched onto the two of them, dragging them down.

Remember me, she thought, weaving her magic around them like an embrace. *Remember the wind blowing through our hair. Remember the feathers we caught, high on the mast of that Kherish ship so long ago.*

He head-butted her, grabbed her breast, and twisted viciously. She gasped, held him tighter. Howls and screams filled her ears.

Brophy clubbed her over the head. His fist smashed into her jaw, and stars exploded in her vision. She grabbed the sides of his face, trying to see into his wild, sightless eyes. "Brophy," she whispered, "Brophy, come back to me."

Slowly, his face turned to hers. He blinked twice, and his eyes focused.

"Remember us," she said over and over. "Remember."

"Shara?" he asked.

"Yes," she whispered. "Yes, it's me."

He looked around as if for the first time. The two of them were floating above the sea of filthy bodies.

"What's happening?" he asked. "Are we—"

"No," she said. "It's the black emmeria. We're still alive. We're weeping ones."

He shook his head, and they began to sink. "What do we do?" Someone grabbed his leg and tried to climb him like a tree. He growled, kicked her off.

"No!" Shara said, turning his gaze back to her. "Stay with me. Think of me."

"But they—"

"Don't look at them, Brophy. Look at me. Think of me. Of us."

He clenched his teeth, but he didn't turn back to the fray. They clung to each other.

"Is this how it ends?" he murmured in her ear, pressing himself against her. "I don't want to stay here. I don't want to fight anymore."

"Don't fight. Don't fight."

She looked into his green eyes, and soon she couldn't feel the kicking or the scratching. It was her and Brophy, and she laughed at the joy that bubbled up inside her. She kept her eyes locked on his, smelling the scent of him, feeling his skin on hers.

Baedellin wept bitterly, curled into a little ball. She wanted her mother. She wanted her mother more than anything, but Mother wasn't here.

She covered her head in her hands as they bit her, kicked her, pushed her down into the suffocating depths over and over again.

Someone grabbed her legs, pulled them apart. She kicked him, squirming over wet bodies to get away. She scrambled away as far as she could until she fell exhausted on the wrinkled thighs of an old man who couldn't stop sobbing.

"Look," he said. "Look. It's so beautiful."

Baedellin twisted around to see what he was pointing at. Somewhere above, through the tangle of limbs and hair, calves and feet, a light shone. It was a warm yellow light, like she remembered from some time long ago.

Many of those around her fled from it, burrowing past her, but she pushed toward it. Others, like her, did the same, fighting one another to get to it. Somehow, Baedellin crawled to the surface and saw the most glorious thing.

A man and a woman, wrapped in a tight embrace, floated above her, shining like a small sun. But the light didn't hurt her eyes. She felt like a flower seeing the dawn for the first time. She thought of her mother, her father. She remembered her brother Astor, his broad shoulders, his kind features.

She reached her hand toward them and suddenly she was floating. Below her, a mound of bodies grew out of the teeming ocean. They rose as a pillar, trying to reach that strange sun and the beautiful people within.

Shara! Baedellin thought as she drew close and recognized the Zelani mistress. *And Astor!* Had he come for her? Had someone finally come for her?

No, not Astor. It was Brophy, the Sleeping Warden.

Shara turned as Baedellin neared, and a smile spread across her face.

"Baedellin," she said, holding out her arms to the girl. Baedellin rushed into the embrace. A great empty space in her was suddenly filled.

"Take me home," she whimpered. "I don't want to go back. I never want to go back."

"Shhh, little one. Stay here. Stay with us."

Baedellin cried, clinging to Shara with all her might

Another man floated up to them. Brophy extended a hand to him and the man joined their embrace. He sighed as the light filled him.

Baedellin looked down again, and she saw a skinny woman start to float toward them, then another man, and another.

"They're coming," Baedellin said, fear filling her heart again. "They'll pull us down."

"No, sweet Baedellin," Shara said, stroking her hair. "Let them come. They'll lift us up."

The light around them began to grow.

"It's working," Shara whispered in Brophy's ear as more and more souls rose out of the writhing mass and joined them hovering in the air.

"I can feel the joy pulling at me, wanting to take me home," Brophy replied, grinning at her.

Home, thought Shara, feeling the same.

Brophy's outline began to blur, the tips of his hair shimmering with multicolored energy.

"Come on," he said. "Let's go back."

"Not yet," she said, shaking him to bring him back to the moment. "I have to stay until it's done, until we save all of them."

Brophy glanced at the bodies below them. They were all crawling toward them, swimming over one another toward the light.

"They're lost," Shara insisted. "We have to show them the way home."

"You're right," he said, and her heart soared at his agreement. "This is how we defeat the emmeria. The Ohndarien way."

"I love you," she said, watching his entire body glow with an inner light.

Shara turned to the others. The tattooed man who had tried to gouge out her eyes now held her hand, a bewildered smile on his face. She kept an arm around Baedellin and leaned over to rest her chin on the little girl's head.

The light grew. In moments, they had swelled from a group of ten to a group of twenty, then to a group of a hundred. Glowing, floating souls gathered around Shara, feeding off the love she gave to Brophy, which spread to Baedellin, to the tattooed man, and everyone who touched them.

An elderly man with long black Ohohhim curls faded in a yellow light, smiling as he went. His body shimmered, coalescing into a single golden ball. The brilliant point of light spun around them twice and then disappeared up into the sky.

"Follow him," Shara insisted. "You have to find Jesheks before he takes me away from you."

Brophy started to shake his head, but stopped when she put her fingers on his chest. "I can finish here," she said, "but you have to keep us safe."

Brophy nodded. He leaned over to kiss her, and his lips slowly faded away as his body shrank into a glowing red ball.

It hovered there for a moment and then shot into the sky, disappearing over the dark horizon.

Baedellin watched the people all around her turning into little balls of light and flying away from this horrible place.

"Shara," she said, and the Zelani mistress looked down and smiled.

"Yes, Baedellin."

"I'm not afraid anymore," she said.

Shara nodded. "There's nothing to be afraid of."

The warm golden light that surrounded them made it hard to see. Multicolored orbs were breaking off from the group, scattering in all directions.

"Shara, am I dying?" Baedellin asked, her voice becoming softer as her body became translucent. "It's all right if I am. You can tell me the truth. I'm not afraid anymore."

"Dear Baedellin," Shara said, hugging the girl. "You're not dying. You're . . ."

But Shara's fingers slipped through her grip as Baedellin faded away.

Seawater erupted from Brophy's mouth. He coughed, rolling to his side and tucking into a ball as his lungs spasmed. He coughed again, vomiting onto the wet ground.

His neck ached, and he squirmed to a sitting position, his back against a broken wall.

"Shara!" he whispered, trying to clear his head. His entire body hurt as if he'd fallen down an endless set of stairs.

After a few moments he was able to open his eyes, blinking in the bright sun. Somehow he still held the Sword of Autumn clenched in his cramped, clawlike grip.

"By the Seasons," he gasped. *What had happened?*

The city of Efften was devastated. Twisted, blackened trees had been uprooted and swept into piles against collapsed buildings. The streets lay under half a foot of water, packed with sand, seaweed, and other debris. He stood up and looked around. All five of the towers had fallen.

"Shara!" he shouted, casting about him. Vague memories returned to him. His body flailing in the surge of the ocean, slamming into buildings. The water receding around him, dragging him along like a doll.

Forcing his wooden limbs to move, he ran up one street and then another. She could be anywhere. The Kherish albino had taken her away from him as he watched helplessly with darkened eyes. He ran through the streets, checking every pile of debris for a hint of her white dress.

Finally he saw something, a white lump lying beneath a snarl of tangled tree limbs half submerged in a puddle. He ran toward it, fearing what he might find. Drawing closer, he saw the long white hair tangled in the twigs and branches. The dead albino's skull was caved in, his back and shoulders flayed to the bone. He rolled the man over and found Shara, cradled protectively in his arms.

Brophy pushed the wet hair away from her face. Her skin was ashen, her sightless black eyes unmoving.

"No!" he gasped, pushing on her stomach. Water leaked from her mouth, but she didn't move. He shoved on her stomach again, forcing more water out. He put his mouth to hers and breathed into her lungs, backed up, and pushed on her again.

She coughed. Her body convulsed, arms pulling in toward her chest.

"Shara," he breathed, giving her space. She sputtered, and began breathing.

"Thank the Seasons." He leaned over and hugged her.

He had barely caught his breath when he heard a gravelly purring in the tangle of trees above him. He picked Shara up and backed away.

A sleek black panther with bulging eyes crept to the top of the tangled trees. Its paws were larger than its head, with wicked, hooked claws as long as Brophy's fingers. It purred again, revealing a long, wormlike tongue.

He pointed the tip of his sword at the creature's teeth, waiting for it to spring. Out of the corner of his eye, he saw another corrupted creature, some sort of ape, shuffling toward him. Others drew in all around him. Sea creatures, flightless birds, a lizard the size of a horse.

The panther twitched, then hesitated. It looked up at Brophy, and crouched, then twitched again.

A sparkling light appeared at its shoulder and floated up into the air. The panther thrashed sideways, creeping a few paces away. Behind it, the trees shook, and sparkling lights emerged from the corrupted branches, floating up into the sky.

Dozens of little lights appeared along the panther's skin, then engulfed it in a cloud of light. It transformed. Paws shrank. Bulging eyes receded.

A blaze of sparkling, rainbow lights emerged from within all of the corrupted beasts surrounding Brophy, obscuring them in bright clouds of light.

In seconds, the panther shrank to its normal size. It looked bewildered and slunk away from Brophy. It dodged around the other creatures, loped between the buildings, and disappeared.

Everything became what it had been before the black emmeria had tainted it. Animals ran off into the jungle. Fish flopped on the wet ground, seeking water.

Brophy shielded his eyes from the blinding color of all the lights, laughing at the joy that coursed through him and thinking of his beloved Shara.

Chapter 16

Shara hovered alone in the air as the last of the glowing balls drifted over the horizon. The sea of writhing people had disappeared, revealing a pale blue haze that seemed to stretch on forever. The purple clouds had gone. There was no more red lightning. The screams of the tortured no longer filled the air. It was silent, serene.

They had done it.

She was just about to leave when she saw one last soul, a pure white light, hovering in the distance.

"Jesheks," she breathed, knowing him in an instant.

She floated toward him, seeing his red eyes glowing within the white light that encased his insubstantial body. He was beautiful. His silver hair flowed down behind his white shoulders and muscled torso. For the first time she saw a gentle smile on his face.

"Once again, you surpass my every expectation," he said as she drifted up to him.

"This was your theory," she asked. "This is what you wanted to do all along?"

He lowered his eyes. "Yes, except I wanted it to be me, not Brophy, by your side." He shook his head. "But that was never meant to be."

"You made us weeping ones to send us here."

"It was a gamble," he admitted. "But I am happy to see that you succeeded. Somehow, I knew you would."

"Perhaps you understand love better than the rest of us," she said.

He smiled. "Who would have thought it?"

She took his hands and held them. They were warm, but she could
barely feel them.

"This may have been my idea," he said, "but I could never have done what
you and Brophy did. I knew *what* to do, but only you knew *how* to do it."

She opened her mouth to speak and paused, searching his face for some
sign of anger or regret. She couldn't find it. "Where will you go now?" she
asked.

His smile turned wry, and his eyes narrowed, reminding her of when
she'd first met him. "I don't know," he said.

"You will always have a home in Ohndarien."

He gave her a strange look. "I would have liked that, I think."

She looked at him curiously, then realized what he was saying.

"I am dead, Shara. Drowned. I escaped my body just before the end." He
smiled. "I had to come see if you succeeded. When you leave, I'll be moving
on." He shrugged. "To whatever comes next."

Shara reached out and placed her hand upon his chest. No heart beat
beneath the ivory skin.

He laughed and took her hand, bringing it back down. "Ah, the lovely
maiden cries for me. At last my life is complete."

"Don't mock yourself. Not now, not after what you've done."

He began to fade into a white light.

"Jesheks!" she cried.

"Your pain is so lovely," he murmured. "So very lovely."

She held his hands until she couldn't feel them anymore. The white
light slowly drifted away from her, heading toward the blue haze far above.

"Thank you," she murmured. "You are a beautiful man. So beautiful."

She closed her eyes against her sorrow and thought of Brophy.

Chapter 17

rophy cradled Shara's limp body in his arms, watching the glowing balls spreading outward across the ocean, rushing toward the horizons.

He looked down at his lover. She was sleeping peacefully, cradled against his chest. With a deep sigh, he kissed the top of her head and began walking toward the center of the city.

Trudging through puddles of seawater, he returned to the ruins of the central tower. The silver stones lay in a heap thirty feet high. The shattered remains of the garden lay amid rubble, the only thing still green in this blackened and shattered city.

Brophy pulled Shara closer to his chest and climbed the shifting blocks to the top of the pile. At its center lay a gaping hole like a volcanic caldera where the black emmeria had exploded out of Oh's coffin. Sliding down the steep slope, he found the mangled remains of the silver sarcophagus at the bottom of the pit.

Brophy didn't know what he had expected to find here. He knew that Arefaine was gone. Darius was gone. Jazryth and Oh were gone. But he felt the need to touch the silver, to give his quiet thanks for the sacrifices made in this place.

Moving closer, he rested his palm on the warm silver. It was empty, nothing more than a misshapen metal box.

For a moment he thought of taking it back to Ohndarien, placing it in his old gazebo atop the Hall of Windows. But Arefaine was a child of Efften, not Ohndarien. She deserved to be buried here.

No, not buried. Burned.

She'd once told him she wanted her flames to soar into the sky, and the smoke to carry her up to the heavens.

Brophy pulled a shattered branch from the rubble and tossed it onto the coffin. It was soaked with seawater like all the others, but he would wait here till they dried. He would build a pyre worthy of Arefaine Morgeon, worthy of her father, her sister the Heartstone, worthy of Oh, the first emperor, father of them all. He would light that pyre under the stars, so all the world would know that a queen had died here and saved them all from oblivion.

Brophy headed for another branch, and Shara stirred in his arms. She murmured and her hands grasped the back of his neck, pulling herself closer to him.

"Brophy?" she whispered.

"Yes," he whispered back, kissing the side of her face.

"I feel horrible."

"But you smell good," he said.

She raised her head, looking up at him.

"It's over, isn't it?" he asked.

"Yes, it's over."

He pulled her closer to him, feeling her body for the first time without the howling voices screaming in the back of his head. He had never felt anything so good.

"I'm all right," she said, wiggling her legs. "You can put me down."

Brophy shook his head. "No, I'm never letting you go. Not for the rest of my life."

Chapter 18

Astor stood on the edge of the Windmill Wall, looking into one of the rifts left by the tsunami. The wall had saved most of the city, but it had taken that damage on itself. Giant cracks ran through almost every part of it, and three sections had crumbled away to the waterline. All of the windmills were destroyed, along with the Sunset Gate. It would take hundreds of men dozens of years to put it right.

He breathed in deeply, trying to control his despair. Below him, the splinted and waterlogged timbers floated amid the rubble of Ohndarien's wall. Only the ocean was unchanged, drawing back and pushing forward the same as ever.

A warm hand touched his arm, and he turned to look into Galliana's blue eyes.

"You shouldn't stand so close to the edge," she said. "The stones are no longer stable. How silly would you feel if you fell off and died after all we've been through?"

"Would anyone notice if I did?" he asked.

"I would."

He sighed. "I don't even know what we're doing here anymore. I'm as empty as the weeping ones standing around in the Citadel, staring at the walls. Should we—" He choked on the words, then gritted his teeth. "Should we kill them? Put them out of their misery and move on?"

"Maybe. But not yet. I'm not ready to give up on Shara. Something happened out there, Astor. That wave was not natural."

"Yes, but what caused it? The shattering of the Heartstone? The release of the black emmeria?"

"Or maybe its destruction. Either way, I'd feel better if you weren't so close to this edge."

Astor shook his head and stepped back. A few chips of stone fell away from his feet and tumbled into the ocean. He looked over at Galliana, and suddenly thought about how he used to look at her just a few months ago, back when he was still a child. Not so long ago he would lie awake at night thinking about her, longing to touch her smooth skin, aching to have her by his side alone in the dark.

He looked down at his boots. He'd not thought about such things in a long time. He wondered why he did so now.

"You're very beautiful," he said, turning to look at her.

She raised an eyebrow.

"I just thought I should say it."

"Are you prepared to back that up?"

He smiled.

"Ah. A smile. Well, my work here is done." She took his hand. "Come on, Astor, take a walk with me. Through the city. Into the Citadel. Into—" She stopped, her expression changing. Her eyebrows furrowed, and she stared out to sea. Astor turned.

"Look," she said, pointing.

"What is it?" He didn't see anything.

She shook her head. "I don't know. Something headed this way. A storm?" She paused, watching intently. "Some kind of magic storm."

He saw it now. It seemed like a bright haze. A cloud filled with sunlight, traveling much lower than a cloud, and much faster. He tensed. "It'll be on us in moments."

"Let's get off this wall!" She pulled him away. They were a hundred paces from the stairs, even farther from the Citadel. He ran with her, but they hadn't gone a dozen steps when the shimmering cloud swept over them. A thousand tiny colored lights whipped past them, and Astor felt a rush of joy. The surge of emotion came and went with the sparkling lights, which turned toward the Citadel, sweeping over the walls and into the courtyard in a steady stream.

"I know what they are," Astor said, daring to hope. "I know!"

Astor burst into Baedellin's room. The door slammed against the wall and shuddered as he rushed inside.

His father cradled Baedellin's skinny body, sobbing.

"Dad?" Astor said, sinking to his knees next to the bed.

"Astor?" Baedellin said in a voice rough with disuse. "Is that you?"

"Bae!" He leaned over and hugged them both. Tears ran down his face as he cried with his father.

"I thought I saw you," Baedellin croaked. "In my nightmare. I thought it was you that saved me, but it was the Sleeping Warden. And Shara-lani. She came into that horrible place for us, and she set us free."

Astor nodded, hugging his sister as tightly as he could. The three of them clung together, Baedellin resting in their arms, her head warm against Astor's chest.

They remained that way until a noise at the door made Astor look up. Galliana entered the room and sat on the bed next to them. Her fingers slipped into Astor's hand, and she said, "It's the same, all through the Citadel. They're all waking up."

"The weeping ones?"

"Not weeping anymore," she said. "They have returned."

"We were lost in the dark," Baedellin said. "Shara and Brophy showed us the way home."

Epilogue

It was well after dark when Baedellin rowed Shara up to the little dock Brophy had built on the sandy shore of their island.

Bae held the water bug steady as Shara stepped onto the sturdy planks. Every inch of the dock was meticulously polished blue-white Ohndarien marble. She doubted anyone had ever spent so much loving effort to build a dock, but that was how Brophy had been these last few months. He took gentle care with everything he did, and would not be rushed.

Baedellin turned her water bug about and waved, assuring Shara that she'd be back at first light. Shara thanked her for the ride, turned, and started up the path to their cottage. The path was paved with stones from the far side of their island. Brophy had quarried them all himself.

Shara paused, took off her shoes, and started climbing again. Last week she'd discovered that he had begun inscribing playful little messages to her in some of the stones, and she liked her feet to touch them as she passed.

A silhouette of their house rose against the backdrop of a starry sky, and she stopped at the closed door. She put her palm flat against the wood, sanded fine and painted by Brophy. It had been his very first task when he'd returned, and it bore a simple painting of two feathers hanging from the same cord.

She touched the image gently before entering the dark cottage. She lit a lamp, crossed to the fireplace, and built a fire. In no time, the little house was warm and cozy.

Putting her pack aside, she slipped out of her clothes and into bed under the heavy sheepskin lined with linen. As she laid her head back on the goose-down pillow, the events of the day sifted through her mind as they always did before sleep.

News of King Phanqui's coronation arrived from Physendria today. As a rebel leader and royalty from the time before Phandir's fall, Phanqui had been the front-runner in the grab for the crown once the Summermen left the city. But at least five other rivals still claimed rights to it, half of whom were campaigning to attack the Summer Cities while they were still weak.

Thankfully, Phanqui knew what a mistake that would be. He was a good man and would wrangle the others into shape eventually. His first royal decree had been to start up the Nine Squares again. That would keep his bloodthirsty young rivals distracted for a while.

She'd had dinner with Lawdon and Mikal tonight before she returned to the cottage. They'd fought again, but that was nothing new. The two of them fought constantly. They seemed proud of the number of arguments they could manage to have in the course of one day. Lawdon insisted that Mikal go south to help keep the peace while Phanqui's reign was still in its infancy. Mikal was one of the few remaining Summer Princes, and during his stay in Physendria, he had somehow succeeded in befriending many of the rebel leaders. He had been instrumental in the peaceful withdrawal of the Summermen forces, and had become good friends with Phanqui. And if there was anyone who could turn the vengeful Physendrians into drinking buddies, it was Mikal.

But he refused to travel before Lawdon had the baby, even though she had six months left in her pregnancy.

Shara knew that Lawdon was secretly proud of Mikal's obstinacy. The louder she complained, the more she approved, it seemed, and Mikal knew it. He had winked at Shara while weathering Lawdon's tirade, made every manner of apology, and stubbornly refused to change his mind.

Shara had been pleasantly surprised by the two of them. Months ago Lawdon and Mikal had moved into an abandoned house high on Eastridge. Shara had thought the former water bug would never leave the sea or settle in Ohndarien again, but Lawdon seemed perfectly happy to spend her days herding her younger siblings and arguing with Mikal. The woman even made a fantastic lamb stew these days. Who would have thought?

Shara yawned, and her thoughts slowed. She closed her eyes.

Of course she'd have to visit the King of Faradan very soon. His grain prices this season were exorbitant.

And Galliana was slowly putting the Zelani school back together. Shara should really spend more time with the new students—

She yawned again.

The early days were the most critical. And then there was. . .

Her thoughts slipped away, and Shara fell into a pleasant sleep.

A soft hand on Shara's cheek brought her to the surface of her dreams.

"Hello, beautiful," Brophy whispered, slipping under the comforter.

She rolled over and wrapped her arms around him, keeping her eyes shut. "You're clothed," she murmured, nuzzling his ear. His curly hair tickled her nose.

"Am I?"

"And drunk." She laughed, smelling the wine on his breath.

"Why, yes I am," he said proudly.

She chuckled and finally opened her eyes. "You must have had a busy day," she said, kissing his neck.

"I had a promise to keep. A man should keep his promises." He yawned. "And I am a man of my promises."

"What were you doing?"

"Bottles. Astor and I snagged two bottles of Summer wine. We made a fire in the boulder field on south ridge and drank them both."

"Very impressive."

"Yes. And we drank them both. And we talked about girls."

She laughed. "Really?"

"Absolutely."

"And what do you two know about girls?"

"Practically nothing."

She laughed again.

"But we both decided that we are thoroughly in favor of them," he said.

"Good. I'm glad that's settled."

Brophy kissed her again, on the mouth, on the chin, on her neck. She arched her back as he bit her lightly. She reached down and pulled his shirt over his head. He pushed the covers off her and slid between her legs. The soft leather of his pants was pleasantly cool on her warm, bare skin.

"I love you, Brophy," she said.

"And I love that you are very, very naked right now," he murmured.

She laughed lightly. "I just realized today that it was almost nineteen years ago when we were sailing from Physen to the Cinder and first talked about running away to a little cabin someplace. I can't believe we finally made it."

"We're doing pretty good, aren't we?"

She smiled. "For a hog butcher's daughter and a stupid kid without the sense to dodge a rock, yeah, we're doing pretty good."

He leaned over her, kissing her neck again. "Now, about this nakedness thing," he murmured, his kisses shifting to the base of her throat, then between her breasts, slowly moving lower. He smelled of wood smoke, cheap wine, and the sea. But mostly he smelled like something she'd never known before.

He smelled like home.

Acknowledgments

FROM TODD:

Thanks to my wife, Lara, for being my inspiration, always. And thanks once again to Amy and Tiana, who kept an eye on our children while Lara was working and I was running through the May Dragon trees.

FROM GILES:

Thanks again to Tan for carrying the load while I was the invisible man. And thanks to Todd for sharing yet another adventure with me beginning to end.

FROM THE BOTH OF US:

Thanks to our advance readers Liana Holmberg, Aaron Brown, Elliot Davis, Kristen Maresca, Jessica Meltzer, Megan Foss, and "The Sparkling Hammers" Aaron, Chris, Leslie & Morgen. Thanks once again to Langdon Foss for his outstanding drawings of Ohohhom and Efften. Thanks to our agent, Donald Maass, for his continued passion for this story. Thanks to Diana, our editor, for her input on this book and for being so patient as we blew past too many deadlines. And thanks to Stephen Youll for his outstanding cover art. *No friendships were destroyed in the writing of this book.*